MAIREAD
O'DRISCOLL

Absolute
Beginners

POOLBEG

Published 2007
by Poolbeg Press Ltd
123 Grange Hill, Baldoyle
Dublin 13, Ireland
E-mail: poolbeg@poolbeg.com
www.poolbeg.com

© Mairead O'Driscoll 2007

1 3 5 7 9 10 8 6 4 2

A catalogue record for this book is available from the British Library.

ISBN 978-1-84223-282-8

Typeset by Patricia Hope in Bembo 10.75/14

Printed by
Litographia Rosés, S.A., Spain

Note on the author

Mairead O'Driscoll was born in Co. Offaly and now lives in Midleton, Co. Cork, with her husband Leonard. She works as a Public Health Nurse with the HSE. *Absolute Beginners* is her second novel. Her first, *Pebble Cove*, was published by Poolbeg in December 2006 and she is currently working on her third.

www.maireadodriscoll.com

Acknowledgements

Yet again, I hardly know where to begin. The publication of *Pebble Cove* was everything that I had hoped for and more. For this I must thank, first and foremost, the readers who have made this exciting journey so amazing. I would like to thank most especially all the people who not only read *Pebble Cove* but who took the time to email me with enthusiastic and supportive comments – each and every contact meant so much to me and spurred me on with *Absolute Beginners*.

A big thanks to all at Poolbeg, especially to Paula, Niamh, Lynda and David, for everything.

Thanks also to my editor, Gaye Shortland, who must surely be the calmest soul in Cork!

To my agent, Ger Nichol, who has been wonderful, a big, big 'Thank You' for all the support, advice and guidance.

As always, Mam, Dad, Nonie and all the gang at home have been there for me through thick and thin. I'm pleased to announce that I will now be back in circulation for visits, phone calls and baby-sitting!

To my ever-patient friends – phone calls and walks

will now resume as normal! Sincere thanks to all of you for the 32-county promotion of *Pebble Cove* – I really mean it when I say that I couldn't have done it without you.

To my colleagues at Midleton Health Centre – life is wonderful when it's shared with such special people.

As ever, the support and encouragement of my husband, Lenny, has been unstinting. Thank you, Len, for being beside me in December.

For Lenny,
I love you this much …

⟷

And in the sweetness of friendship let there be
laughter, and sharing of pleasures.

For in the dew of little things the heart finds its
morning and is refreshed.

KHALIL GIBRAN

◄○►

A violet by a mossy stone
Half-hidden from the eye!
Fair as a star, when only one
Is shining in the sky.

WILLIAM WORDSWORTH

Chapter 1

Rosa twisted slightly to get a better view of the back of the skinny jeans that she'd arrived home with earlier. Satisfied that they sat just right, she wriggled out of them and tossed them to one side while she tried on the floaty chiffon dress that she'd picked up in Razzmatazz on Patrick Street.

Swirling like a little girl with the gauzy material floating around her legs, Rosa stared critically at her reflection before kicking off the Jimmy Choos that she'd got on her last trip to London and slipping into a pair of peep-toes.

"That's better," she said out loud, pleased at the effect the shoes had on her slender legs. Wondering if the dress's blue and white check made her look like Dorothy of Yellow Brick Road fame, she pulled it off and picked up her other purchase, a black sheath dress that she'd spotted upstairs in Brown Thomas on one of her coffee breaks earlier in the week.

"Too formal," she announced to herself, glancing back

at the chiffon dress that lay in a pile on the bed. The tiny check was barely visible, certainly not too in-your-face. Trying it on once again she struck a few poses in front of the mirror, wondering if she looked ethereal and interesting or plain childish, like an overgrown ten-year-old at a birthday party.

Perhaps if my hair was up I might look like an adult, she thought, holding her riotous blonde curls back from her face to see if it made any difference.

Before she knew it the doorbell was pealing, a sure sign that her parents had already beeped the horn to let her know they were waiting outside.

As usual, Rosa threw open the upstairs window and held up five fingers to indicate that she'd be ready sometime in the next five minutes. Her parents were well aware by now that this signal generally meant ten. They sat patiently below in their gleaming Mercedes while their only daughter put the finishing touches to her make-up, knowing full well that if they went inside at all they'd be delayed even longer. Many a time they'd had to phone a restaurant to excuse their lateness on account of a crisis with a hair-do or an outfit on Rosa's part.

Inside, Rosa dragged a comb through her curls and scrunched a handful of them together at the nape of her neck with an ornate clip that she'd got from her mother at Christmas. Convincing herself that she didn't look like child, she touched up her make-up and dashed down the stairs, practically stripping the oriental runner from the treads in her haste, acutely aware of her parents waiting outside.

Maurice and Bernadette had bought the house in Bramwell Court the previous year, ostensibly as an investment property, and had offered it to their daughter to caretake until such a time as they decided what to do with it. Rosa suspected that they wanted her to gain her independence in an environment that was under their direct control and had been irritated at their habitual protectiveness until she'd realised that she couldn't afford any of the prices that the estate agents were mentioning, even for a one-bedroom apartment in the middle of nowhere.

A year on, she actually appreciated the fact that she had the spacious, elegantly decorated house to herself. She'd gradually moved all her things from her parents' house in Douglas and felt completely settled in the leafy cul-de-sac. Admittedly, it wasn't the sort of place that generated an exciting social life, with most of the other houses appearing to be occupied by staid couples in their fifties.

Anyway, she promised herself, things were about to change for the better. She only had to persuade her mother to get her onto the introductory course at The Gourmet Rooms and her life would be on track at last. If she discovered she had a flair for cooking, then it would simply be a matter of time before she embarked on a more extensive course that would lead, finally, to her own restaurant.

Rosa had a vision of the kind of discreet, darkened dining-room that would encourage elegantly understated guests to park their expensive cars along the tree-lined street outside her home and partake of the exquisite fare on offer at Number 3.

The house was perfect for such a venture, with its airy

well-proportioned kitchen running the full width of the house at the back. To the front, two large reception rooms opened off the hall, one of which extended into a substantial sun room, almost doubling its size. Rosa envisaged the room to the right of the hall as a reception room where guests could enjoy an aperitif as they perused the menu. Plush upholstered armchairs, intimately grouped, would also encourage the clientele to linger in a relaxed environment at the end of their dining experience. The larger room, to the left of the entrance hall, would make a perfect dining-room, with the conservatory area opened on the weekends to accommodate the larger guest list. If everything came to pass the way she planned she'd break a door through to the dining-room from the kitchen so that food wouldn't have to be transported via the hall.

In the spacious entrance hall, she took a final glance at herself in the ornate gilt-framed mirror that graced the wall above an antique mahogany escritoire her father had inherited from her Great-aunt Hilda – destined to be an unobtrusive reception desk, ideal for taking bookings and processing bills while maintaining a graceful ambience.

First things first, she cautioned herself as she slammed her front door, uncharacteristically suppressing the bubbles of excited anticipation that were forming in her head at the thought of opening the doors of Number 3 to the public. Once she'd succeeded in persuading her mother to exert her not inconsiderable influence on the formidable Mrs Carter, Rosa was certain that one of the coveted places on the heavily booked cookery course at The Gourmet Rooms would be hers.

Bounding down the limestone steps, she was heartened to see her parents smiling indulgently at her through the windscreen. Surely they'd see that this latest idea would herald the beginning of a new life for her? Surely they'd agree to help her?

Chapter 2

As soon as she opened her eyes, Kate Lewis remembered what day it was. He or she, although Kate always believed it would have been a girl, would be thirteen today.

When she'd been a teenager, Kate and her friends had spent endless hours spinning their Claddagh rings around on their necklaces to ascertain whether they'd have boys or girls and how many of each. No matter how many times they did Kate's, the result was always the same – one child, a girl.

In those days, she'd had a very definite plan to call her baby Ellen and somehow the name had stuck. Little Ellen would have been a fully-fledged teenager today, she mused, probably bickering with her parents about going out in clothes that were so small that they couldn't properly be classed as clothes at all. Or hiding at the back of the school so she wouldn't be caught smoking – something that Kate herself had done with enthusiasm but which she most likely wouldn't have tolerated if her daughter was at it.

She lay in the warm cocoon of the duvet for twenty minutes, fantasising about the imagined trials of parenthood until the snooze button activated again and broke in on her thoughts.

Timmy would have been thrilled to have an almost-grown-up daughter.

Don't start again! She steeled herself, pressing her eyes tight to stave off the tears that threatened. The piercing beep-beep-beep of the alarm brought her sharply back to reality. The thought of having to open the shop and put on a face for the regulars seemed like an insurmountable hurdle but Kate knew that there was nothing like a frantic morning in Good For You to chase away the bleak hollow in the pit of her stomach. Temporarily, at least.

She'd spent the previous day under a black cloud that had refused to lift until she fell into a fitful sleep at five in the morning. But the luxury of throwing herself on the sofa and weeping for hours on end was fine on a Sunday. Right now, she'd just have to pull herself together and face the Monday morning routine.

Knowing that she couldn't arrive at work looking like the wreck of the *Hesperus*, Kate riffled through her stock of Bach flower essences to see if there was anything that would lift her spirits. White Chestnut definitely, she decided, plucking the small glass bottle from among its companions. Expertly squeezing the tiny dropper she felt the familiar brandy-like taste on her tongue and tried to visualise the remedy chasing away the never-ending thoughts that had been racing around her mind for the past twenty-four hours.

Standing under the soothing needles of warmth in the shower, Kate did her best to empty her mind and focus instead on the list of orders she had to get out before lunch-time.

Angela Rowan usually arrived before ten so she'd start with getting together the selection of soya milk and yoghurts and whatever lactose-free foods were on the list for her son. Freddie had been diagnosed with galactosaemia shortly after birth and had to adhere to a strict diet. Angela was one of Kate's best customers and was confident that even if something new came on the market that would fit in with Freddie's diet, it would be ordered for her before she'd even mentioned it to the proprietor of the health shop.

Anja Hoening, another of her regulars, would be along to pick up the monthly supply of eco-nappies for her twins. Kate made a mental note to sellotape two sample tubes of a new calendula cream that had just come in onto the packs of nappies for Anja to try out, knowing that the earthy Finn would rather use a natural product on her babies' skin than a mixture of synthetic chemicals.

Mrs Carter would be in at one o'clock on the dot. The detailed list – handwritten in a neat, precise script that could only belong to the neat, precise proprietor of The Gourmet Rooms – was always handed in on a Friday afternoon and the order collected by the lady herself on Mondays.

In the early days, Mrs Carter had checked each item before leaving the shop but after a few months of receiving the quality products exactly as she required, Kate was heartened to notice that one day she just picked up the neat cardboard box and left after a few minutes' general conversation.

Kate always prepared the box for The Gourmet Rooms with care and gave a sizeable discount to acknowledge the substantial amount of business that the cookery school provided. A container of choice porcini mushrooms and authentic tahini paste were on today's order as well as the usual organic grains and fresh yeast for Mrs Carter's famous breads.

Now that her mind was occupied with the morning's business, Kate began to feel normal again. Dressed in white linen trousers and a matching tunic that came down below her hips, she added a string of large turquoise beads that her sister had brought from Thailand the previous summer.

This morning she knew she needed the light foundation and lipstick to make her look presentable, although her eyes didn't look too puffy considering the day and night she'd put in.

She stared at herself in the mirror for a few moments, taking in the neat chestnut bob that swung in around her small heart-shaped face. Her brown eyes looked despondent. Making yet another conscious effort to shake herself up, she abandoned her self-study and made her way downstairs, her resolve strengthening as soon as she entered the oasis of calm below.

Even before pulling up the blinds and letting the morning sun streak across the polished timber floor, Kate could find her way around the little shop. The contents of all its nooks and crannies were as familiar to her as the features of her own face and she rarely changed the position of the items on the shelves. Most of the regulars tended to wander around the shop picking out the products they wanted, happy that Kate was in the background for assistance if they needed it.

The silence of the little shop was comforting to her as she lit a tea light and added a few drops of lemongrass oil to the aromatherapy burner, always the first task of the day. Soon the fresh, vigorous scent would permeate the space around her, hopefully stimulating her sluggish brain into action.

Most of the customers had at some stage commented on the delightful aromas that filled Good For You and Kate always marvelled at the advertising power of the small act of choosing an essential oil to suit her own mood every morning. On several occasions, people had admired a scent and then gone on to buy the particular oil when Kate told them which it was.

The doorbell chimed as she began to reorganise the small selection of books at the back of the shop. Surprisingly, Mrs Carter strode purposefully in. Kate was immediately glad that she'd prepared the box for The Gourmet Rooms on Saturday afternoon, leaving space at the top for the fresh items she was expecting this morning, knowing that Mrs Carter was the type of woman who wouldn't tolerate inefficiency.

"I know I'm a bit early, Kate, but I'm afraid one of the staff is out sick today," Mrs Carter said pleasantly, allaying Kate's immediate fear that last week's order hadn't been up to scratch. "I hope I'm not *too* early?"

Kate prided herself on providing a good quality service

and would be annoyed with herself if something had been unsatisfactory for as solid a customer as Mrs Carter.

"Not at all. The order is almost ready. Except for the buttermilk but Declan should be along any minute with that."

"As I'm here, I wonder if you have any cherry juice – a concentrated one if possible?"

"There's an organic one that's very nice. I'll just get it down for you."

Kate pulled over the little set of steps that she used for getting the least frequently used items from the higher shelves and reached for a bottle of the luscious cherry juice that was so valuable to the many gout sufferers she supplied. The tall slim bottle, just above her reach, wobbled as she touched it and toppled to the floor, its contents spreading in a crimson pool around the feet of her most valued customer.

"Oh, my goodness, I'm so sorry! Your shoes are ruined!" she exclaimed, horrified, as she alighted to inspect the damage. Thank God Mrs Carter was the only customer in the shop!

"They're absolutely fine. Will I move this bag?" Mrs Carter indicated a large hessian bag full of dried beans near the counter, in the path of the advancing pool of cherry juice.

"Thank you, I'll do it," Kate insisted, shifting the bag immediately and darting to the store cupboard for the mop. "Would you like to sit in one of the armchairs while I sort this out? Declan should be here with the buttermilk soon."

Her hands were jittery as she ran the mop over the

floor, praying that Mrs Carter, who was now rolling a leaflet stand to one side for her, wouldn't skid on the wet floor and injure herself.

"You've no idea how many times a week this happens during the cookery classes."

Disarmed by her understanding and still emotional from her thoughts of Timmy and her baby, tears sprang to Kate's eyes. Swiftly she shoved the mop out into the small hallway that housed the stairs to the flat and turned to wash her hands, hoping that Mrs Carter wouldn't notice and think she was a complete wreck.

"Are you all right this morning, Kate?"

Her voice was kinder than Kate would have expected from such a brisk woman and caused two tears to trickle down her cheeks unbidden.

"God, I'm sorry," she sniffed, pressing her fingers to her eyes to stop herself breaking down completely. "Bad night's sleep."

"Are you sure that's all? Would you like me to hold the fort for a few minutes?"

Of all the things that Kate would ever have expected, the idea of Mrs Carter behind the counter in Good For You wouldn't have come to mind.

"Thank you, really – but I'm fine. Better off working to be honest." Then, seeing the look of understanding that passed over the other woman's face, she said quietly, "I had a miscarriage years ago – the baby would have been thirteen today. I'm a bit shaky, that's all."

"It's a loss that most people underestimate. I too lost a baby in the past."

Before Kate could get to say anything in response, Mrs Carter's face became closed as if she had said too much.

"Tell me, do you have any interest in cooking?"

Startled by the question, Kate was about to say that her own dashed-off recipes would hardly be up to Mrs Carter's standards but thought better of it, not wanting to seem like a boor who didn't appreciate the value of good food.

"I've lost interest over the last few years," she admitted instead, starting to feel a bit better now that the conversation had taken a more normal turn. "Cooking for one can be a bit unrewarding."

A woman of few words, Mrs Carter nodded sympathetically before proceeding to the point. "I've been meaning to ask you for a while if you'd like to join in on one of the courses, complimentary of course. I do value the service that you provide us and you've been more than competitive with prices over the years." Then she added gently, "And cooking can be very therapeutic."

"Well, thank you." Praise from Mrs Carter was praise indeed and Kate felt like a schoolgirl getting a medal. Building up a solid client base had been hard work but lately it seemed to be paying dividends at last. "And I'd love to go on one of the courses – I could certainly do with a bit of motivation in the culinary department."

"Good. Would you consider yourself a beginner or would you prefer to try the Intermediate or even the Advanced course?"

"The beginner's course would be marvellous," Kate enthused, interrupted by the doorbell as Declan Gleeson burst in bearing a boxful of organic goat's milk and her supply of buttermilk. "Morning, Declan, just in time," she greeted the florid dairy farmer.

Kate plucked out the cartons of buttermilk that would complete the order for the cookery school and added them to the box.

"That's everything," she confirmed, "and thanks again, Mrs Carter – I'll really look forward to the course."

"Pamela," the older woman insisted with a smile as she left. "I'll let you know what dates are available when I'm in next week."

"Fine-looking woman," Declan commented almost as soon as the door had closed behind Mrs Carter. "And single," he added longingly.

Declan was a bachelor farmer in his mid-fifties who'd made several efforts to get himself married, always to no avail. When he'd first started delivering to Good For You and discovered that Kate was 'available', he'd made a few attempts to strike up a romance but had been headed off time and again. His limited experience with members of the opposite sex had somehow led him to believe that any woman who was currently unattached was available, but Kate thought that Mrs Carter in particular wasn't the available type.

Attractive in a grave sort of way, Kate often wondered what Mrs Carter looked like at night when she unwound the roll of silver hair that was always pinned neatly at the nape of her neck. Her clothes too were somewhat severe, almost a uniform of neutral-coloured dresses with neat collars and toning lightweight cardigans.

"Does she come in here much?" Declan was asking now, his eyes gleaming fanatically.

Kate had nightmarish visions of her most valued customer being wedged ignominiously up against the herbal-remedies counter as Declan enthusiastically tried out a few of his best chat-up lines. She knew this was entirely possible as she'd been that soldier on more than one occasion until Declan had finally taken no for an answer.

"Hardly ever," she lied brazenly. "Usually sends one of her minions."

The sudden drooping of the farmer's jowls indicated that he believed her and Kate silently heaved a sigh of relief. At least she would be spared the sight of Declan pacing the floor every Monday, hankering in vain after the unobtainable Mrs Carter.

After Declan's forlorn departure, a steady trickle of customers kept Kate occupied until lunch-time. Because she was the only member of staff, she had to close the shop then, something she was considering remedying in the near future. Now that the business was established, it was time to get an assistant who'd be able to take over at lunch-times, weekends and holidays, which she'd had to forego for several years.

Maybe that would be her next step – that and the cookery course. Perhaps it was time to think about getting on with her life instead of hiding behind her little shop, she mused as she filled a pitta pocket with chicken and salad. Kate's mother was always reminding her that she was only thirty-eight, young enough to pick up the pieces and start again.

Guilt overcame her suddenly as she thought of Timmy, little unborn Ellen and the poor blameless farmer who'd thought he was on his way home from the mart. What about all the things that they would never get the opportunity to enjoy? And here she was moping about having no life.

Chapter 3

"What do you mean, you're not going? You promised after the last time that you'd go to whatever came up next."

"I know," Lucy lied feebly, "but it's my parents' wedding anniversary. I can't really tell them I won't be there."

"Well, what time is the meal booked for? You could come down to Hegarty's after it."

Cathy Rohan was thrilled with this idea while a cold sweat broke out all over Lucy. She knew what the work nights out were like. The few she'd actually been badgered into going to had been horrendous, with everyone having a ball while she stood like a wallflower wishing the hands of her watch around so she could escape. It wasn't that the crowd from The Friary weren't nice. She got on fine with them at work but she just wasn't good at the social side of things.

Lucy looked at herself, critically as usual, in the full-length mirror in the changing room as soon as she escaped

17

from Cathy and her plans. She knew she should make an effort to get out more and make friends but, taking in her stocky figure and lank brown hair, she knew how out of place she'd feel if she did decide to go to the night out in Hegarty's after all. Cathy had finally let up when Lucy promised to come to the pub after her parents' mythical anniversary meal.

Lucy felt there was something radically wrong with her the way she shied away from anything remotely sociable. It wasn't just that she felt fat and frumpy compared to the others at work. Jessica Harte, one of the job-sharers, was much heavier than herself, yet she seemed to look fresh and elegant in whatever she wore. And the fact that she was overweight never seemed to make her shy and awkward the way it did with Lucy. If anything, Jessica was one of the more vivacious members of staff, always ready for a night out and the chief organiser of many.

Cathy was the same. Lucy doubted if she'd ever in her life felt a sense of dread at the mere mention of a summer barbecue or New Year's Eve party. In fact Cathy actively sought out the next event, something that Lucy could never in a million years see herself doing.

She jumped in alarm when the door of the changing room swung open to admit Una Riordan, the nursing manager.

"Cathy tells me you'll be going to Hegarty's after your parents' anniversary do. We'll be there until all hours according to her and Jessica so you should be in plenty of time."

Lucy just returned her encouraging smile and nodded, cursing Cathy's enthusiasm. Una meanwhile had pulled a large holdall from her locker and was now pulling off her uniform.

"They're finishing school today and the sports day is on – the kids are after entering me in this Yummy Mummy competition!" she told Lucy as she flicked on the shower and hurriedly divested herself of her underwear.

"What's that?" Lucy asked, a pang of disgust hitting her as she noted how tanned and toned Una was, despite being well over forty with three children. Lucy's own underwear looked grey and miserable compared to her boss's lacy knickers and bra, and the thought of casually stripping off in front of someone else horrified her.

"A sort of mad beauty contest, I think!" Una called over the hum of the shower. "They've decided that they'd be discriminating against some of the mothers if they're not able to take part in the sporty things. This is supposed to be an alternative. I was in the sack race last year so I suppose it's an improvement!"

Lucy couldn't imagine anything more discriminatory than being asked to go on show in front of a whole school but Una seemed to be taking it in her stride. She was out of the shower and rubbing on body lotion in less than two minutes, obviously keen to get to the event looking and smelling fabulous.

"Up or down?" she asked now, holding her glossy auburn layers in a knot for Lucy to consider.

"Up's good," Lucy told her, stuffing her navy uniform trousers and tunic into her rucksack.

"Up it is, then." She glanced at the slim gold watch her husband had presented to her for her fortieth birthday. "God, I'd want to buck up if I'm to be there for three."

Lucy felt like a complete frump in her navy fleece and jeans as Una produced a deep pink linen suit from her locker. Next came matching espadrilles and a white top that held together at the front with three satin ribbons.

"These'll have to do," she said, looking critically at the espadrilles. "There's no way I can wear sandals around a football pitch all afternoon."

Lucy admired her confidence, knowing that she herself would probably wear something completely impractical if she were ever in the position of attending a Yummy Mummy competition. Not that it seemed likely.

"I'm off, Una. Enjoy the sports day."

"I'm off the next two days so I won't see you until Friday in Hegarty's," Una reminded her, a vast array of make-up now appearing on the small vanity unit.

"Okay so, see you then," Lucy told her guiltily, knowing that it was unlikely that she'd venture to the pub at all.

Una's presence in the changing-room had upset her. She knew that she really should do something about her weight but the thought that she'd never be as toned and fit-looking as Una depressed her. Cathy too always looked brilliant, her jet-black hair always glossy and neat – even in the regulation work ponytail. Everything about Cathy was glossy, even her obsession with glossy magazines – her 'night duty bibles', as Lucy called them. She read the glamour magazines in detail and always took on board whatever new advice was on the go about trends in make-up or how to wear belts and how many buttons on a shirt to leave open. She'd spend half the night reading out tit-bits to Lucy, oblivious to the fact that she was engrossed in a book and hated to be interrupted. Last week it had been complementary therapies. They'd had their break at the desk and Cathy had spent the whole hour telling Lucy about the wonders of essential oils.

"It's all about the feel-good factor," she'd said, dragging Lucy away from the dashing Vronsky in *Anna Karenina*, a book she'd heard reviewed on a new Book Club programme that had started the previous weekend. "You know – well-being and all that as the first step towards looking good and becoming fit. Lavender helps you to sleep well apparently. And there are sensual oils that you can put in body lotion – I might try that. There's even one for fighting cellulite! Or we could have invigorating oils to keep us alert on night duty."

"Would it not keep all the patients awake too?"

"I suppose. We could find out about it, though."

It was hard to dampen Cathy's enthusiasm, Lucy thought now as she left the leafy sanctuary of The Friary, Cork's most exclusive Aged Care Centre. On a hill over-looking the city, it was set in spectacular rolling lawns, the mature oaks and beeches separating it gracefully from the surrounding roads and dwellings.

As she did on many of the days when her morning shift left her with nothing to do but go back to her house in Bramwell Court to stare at the four walls, Lucy drove into the city, parked her car and made her way to the little bookshop on Cabin Street. She liked Bookends because it was small and a bit cosy, unlike the other bookshops around the city with their open, bright aisles and lack of seating. It was the kind of place that other people called fusty but Lucy liked it because she could browse for a whole afternoon before picking the four or five books that would keep her going until her next trip.

And on a day like today, when her shift ended at two and the whole evening stretched out emptily before her, it was comforting to know that she could settle back in one of the antique armchairs at the back of the shop and lose herself in whatever books took her fancy.

Chapter 4

Agnes Cotter surveyed the final sheet and laid it on top of the sheaf of pages that she'd spent the day typing. As usual, she inserted the bundle carefully into a clear polythene sleeve and tucked it away in the faux-leather briefcase that she'd got in Lidl the last time she'd been in town.

The briefcase made her feel as if she was a legitimate part of the labour force, even if her hours were unconventional and the work sporadic. Having said that, she couldn't really complain. Lately, the jobs had become more regular, with some of The Office Shop's clients actually asking for her by name. Agnes figured that this was because, once she got into the lingo of a particular subject, she was quickly able to decipher the often badly handwritten scripts that she had to type.

Her concentration had not been at its best today, she had to admit. Poor Bea had spent a very restless night. Probably because she spent so much of her day resting, she was a martyr to insomnia. Unfortunately, she required company for the counting of sheep that was a feature of everyday life for her and Agnes was getting worn out from providing the endless cups of Horlicks at ungodly hours.

Beatrice, at eighty, was fifteen years older than Agnes and had been disabled since she was twelve, before Agnes was even born. Although she did have some power in her legs she preferred to use a wheelchair instead of the undignified crutches that she'd been forced to use years ago. The accident, their mother had often told Agnes, had taken away Bea's chance of a proper life and it was up to all of them to make sure that she was properly looked after. Sometimes Agnes wondered guiltily how her own life would have worked out if Bea had decided to climb anything other than the large pile of logs in the backyard that fateful day in 1933.

While Beatrice was able to do a little more for herself than she actually did, their parents had charged Agnes with caring for her sister and she felt that she should do it whole-heartedly and not be quibbling about the few things she had to contend with.

Subsequently, Agnes's life was taken up with the daily tasks of meeting her sister's needs, great and small. Having resigned from her job so many years ago, she relied on the small amount of money that her sister gave her from her pension and the slightly bigger amount that she made from the typing but hadn't yet disclosed to Beatrice for fear she'd make her give it up.

Some day, Agnes was fond of dreaming, I'll get to do something for myself. She'd been dreaming of this since she was twenty-three when their mother had become ill and she'd come home to look after Beatrice. She knew that she was well past marriage and children, even past a career now that she was almost at pension age. But she never gave up thinking about what she'd do if she were free to spread her wings.

Watching the clock so that she wouldn't forget to wake Beatrice from her nap, she flicked on the television to watch a bit of *Afternoon Tea*. She was a great fan of the chat show, especially the celebrity slots. Agnes was always fascinated by famous people, the type who had done the kind of exciting and glamorous things that she herself had never had the opportunity to do. She was never quite sure what exciting escapades she might have been tempted towards if she'd had the chance although nowadays it seemed that you didn't actually have to be famous for doing something in particular anyway. As long as you were loud-mouthed and big-breasted you could be on any amount of television shows.

Today's celebrity was different. Irene Lucas was interviewing Pamela Carter. Mrs Carter had always been well known in Cork social circles but had recently come to the attention of the rest of the country when she'd participated in a documentary series about the changes that the 'Celtic Tiger' had brought to Irish society. The notion of living in a throwaway era had been the theme of the series and one of the sections had looked at the way that traditional skills like cooking had faded into the background in the face of longer working hours, fast food and the availability of takeaways and ready-made meals.

Mrs Carter, however, was going back to basics with the latest addition to her extensive range of cookery courses.

For almost thirty years, she'd run a variety of courses from her handsome Georgian house in Sunday's Well, one of the better areas of the city. Until recently, most of the courses had been geared towards experienced cooks wishing to formalise their skills in order to open restaurants and cafés or to add a dining component to businesses like pubs, galleries, garden centres or shops. Now she'd added a new dimension to her programme at The Gourmet Rooms, catering for the Celtic Cubs who had lost the art of cooking. The ten-week curriculum was geared towards complete beginners and set out to instil a certain standard of culinary expertise into the participants.

After some persuasion, Mrs Carter had allowed the documentary maker to follow the Absolute Beginners course for the ten-week period, with a few well-known faces volunteering for the benefit of the television audience. Irene Lucas, hostess of *Afternoon Tea*, had been one of the volunteers and was now interviewing Pamela Carter in the lead-up to the show being aired.

Agnes was fascinated that, as well as the glamorous Irene, several big names from the world of sport, television and society in general had been assembled in the impressive Georgian house less than ten miles from her own home. If only she'd known, she could have made it her business to be in the area of Sunday's Well at the appropriate times, perhaps getting a glimpse of or even speaking to one of them.

Imagine meeting Irene Lucas – now that'd be one for the books! Or even Paul and Danny O'Sullivan, the rugby heroes who apparently couldn't boil the proverbial egg. It seemed that the Limerick-born twins had been the life and soul of the group for the ten weeks, despite Mrs Carter's reputation as a formidable taskmaster who brooked no nonsense from her clients.

Irene was buoyant as she recounted her ten weeks in the kitchen at The Gourmet Rooms under the tutelage of Mrs Carter. Agnes, engrossed in the show, forgot all about Beatrice as she imagined the excitement of experimenting with the undoubtedly expensive ingredients that would have been used and the thrill of producing a superb soufflé or an exquisite dessert.

She was disgusted when Beatrice rang the little bell that she kept beside her bed to summon her sister. They had just got onto the subject of Lily O'Neill, a former lap-dancer who'd transpired to be a dab hand with a whisk. The documentary was to be aired the following evening at half nine, thankfully after the evening news. If it had been on at the same time, there was no way that she'd have been able to watch it as Beatrice watched the news religiously as part of her rigorous daily routine.

Tearing herself away from *Afternoon Tea*, Agnes headed down the hall to lift Beatrice into her chair, knowing that she'd be cross because she had neglected to wake her at her usual time. She was only fifteen minutes late yet she knew that Beatrice would blame tonight's sleeplessness on her poor timekeeping.

Not to mind, she told herself stoically. *And* she'd thought of *just* the thing to save her wages from The Office Shop for. As soon as Beatrice went for her evening nap, Agnes was going to ring The Gourmet Rooms.

Chapter 5

It was a quarter to six when Lucy finally approached the Bookends counter with her selection. Mr Madigan and his wife – not unlike two bookends themselves – always inspected her choices and commented while they rang up the sale.

"That's his best yet," the elderly man observed as he handed *Star of the Sea* to his wife for wrapping. Lucy loved all of Joseph O'Connor's books and was already excited about getting into this one after reading the first twenty pages in the bookshop.

"This one might take you a while but it's a great story."

This was *Shadow of the Wind*, a book that she'd been meaning to get for the past few weeks. Lucy loved a book that took her a while to read, rather than one that was done with in a few days, particularly during the summer when the evenings were so long and hard to fill.

She noticed the little health shop as she rounded the corner on her way to the carpark. Cathy's diatribe about the essential oils came to mind and she wondered if she dared go in and ask. It was nearly six so at least she could leave if she felt like a spare part in there. In the back of her mind, she knew that she'd have to make more of an effort to look better and get out more. It might be easier to try the health shop first rather than face a gym or worse still, the make-up counters in Brown Thomas.

Thankfully for Kate, the afternoon had flown by in a buzz of customers, old and new. She slipped her feet out of the glitzy Indian sandals and savoured the coolness of the timber floor, glancing hopefully at the clock and willing the hands to reach six so that she could bolt the door before anyone else came through it.

There was a time when she used to spend most of the day looking hopefully towards the door every time a passer-by paused outside in the street, yet now here she was wishing for the stream of customers to dry up so that she could have a breather before putting the place in order for the following day. She was exhausted after the poor night's sleep and was longing to escape to the flat and put her feet up.

She started now as the bell over the door rattled suddenly, announcing the arrival of a mannish-looking girl dressed in jeans and a fleece sweatshirt. Kate smiled her usual welcome, preferring to let customers browse a bit instead of demanding to be of assistance. Many of the people who came into the shop had no idea what they were looking for but would generally explain their needs once they'd looked around for a few minutes.

The girl, however, approached the counter straight away, her forehead crinkled anxiously. Immediately Kate noticed that despite the heavy frown and unkempt appearance, her eyes were quite beautiful – the most startling blue.

"Do you sell essential oils and that sort of thing?"

Her voice was strangely gruff, her tone almost challenging.

"We do indeed. Was there one in particular that you wanted?"

"I don't know really. Something for relaxing or for sleeping, I think."

Sensing that the girl knew little or nothing about the product that she was about to buy, Kate knew that she'd have to educate her to some degree first.

"Well, if you haven't used essential oils before, something like lavender or geranium would be good ones to start with. They're among the least expensive so you can't go too far wrong with them. Would you like to smell those to see if they appeal to you?"

Reluctantly, it seemed, the girl followed her over to the tiered display of essential oils looking as if she were about to be sold a consignment of illegal drugs. Having sniffed the tiny glass bottles a few times, she nodded with what looked like approval before deciding abruptly to take one each of lavender and geranium.

"What exactly do I do with them?"

Kate was startled by this. Most people had an aromatherapy burner in their house, or had at least used essential oils in the bath or mixed as a body lotion. Yet here was someone who came in to buy a product without even knowing what to do with it. Intrigued, she was glad that there were no other customers in the shop, sensing that the gruff girl before her wouldn't have asked if there had been someone else there.

"Well, if you have an aromatherapy burner, you could add a few drops to some water to get the scent around your house. Like this here . . ." She indicated her own burner when she noticed a spark of interest in her customer's eyes.

"Is that what the smell is? I noticed it when I came in. Do you sell the burners as well?"

"There are a few different sizes on the top shelves and the tea lights for them are there as well. But you could start by adding a few drops of oil to the bath, to see if you like the idea first. Or you could try a few drops of lavender on the pillow if you have difficulty sleeping. You could come back for the burner if you find that you like the scents."

"I may as well get one now," the girl mumbled, taking a large ceramic burner – one of the more expensive ones – from the shelf at random.

Kate rarely tried to push a product on a customer, particularly one that was totally new to the idea of natural health products, knowing that being faced with a complicated array of accoutrements was a sure-fire way of putting people off the whole concept. Generally, once a customer had found their feet with the more basic products, they came back again and again, broadening their horizons each time.

Looking somewhat surprised, presumably because Kate hadn't tried to inveigle her into buying anything more than the two essential oils and had practically discouraged her from taking an aromatherapy burner, the girl left with a quiet "Thanks".

Curious about the gruff demeanour and unruly appearance that were strangely at odds with her choice of purchase and the fact that she obviously had plenty of money to spend, Kate crossed to the window to observe her latest customer, rolling down the bamboo blind as she did so.

Somewhat predictably, the girl glanced up and down the street nervously before secreting her packages in the bulky rucksack that was slung over her shoulder. Always prone to conjecture about what drove people's personalities, Kate wondered fleetingly as she secured the latch what had made the girl with the bright blue eyes so suspicious about the world.

Lucy felt like breaking into a run as soon as she left the shop but realised how ridiculous it would look. Instead, she walked along as swiftly as she could without it appearing as if she'd just burgled the place. She hadn't, but it was how she felt. She knew that it wasn't a big deal to go into a shop and pick up a few little bottles, yet somehow she'd felt stupid, as if the shop assistant would wonder what someone like her would want with something so indulgent and luxurious. The lady behind the counter in Good For You hadn't seemed to take much notice however, sitting dreamily on a tall stool exuding an aura of serenity that

Lucy thought might result from the floral scent that permeated the little shop.

Now that she'd actually got up the courage to buy some of the remedies that Cathy had talked about for de-stressing, Lucy was eager to get home and examine them in detail. She'd been too nervous to listen properly to what the little lady in the beaded dress was saying about the 'properties' of the essential oils and was glad that she'd at least had the nerve to buy the burner.

Lucy still wasn't convinced about Cathy's theory that you had to start looking after yourself if you wanted to look good, thinking it was all a bit simplistic. Surely if it were that easy then the concept would be public knowledge and everyone on the planet would be pampering themselves and looking and feeling a million dollars. However, practical if anything, she figured that a relaxing bath would at least ease the multitude of pains and aches that she'd accumulated at work over the past ten years. The Friary was fine, no better or worse as a workplace than most jobs, but many of the elderly residents were completely immobile and the task of getting them up and dressed day after day was strenuous and never-ending. Lately, she'd begun to feel more like a forty-eight-year-old than a twenty-eight-year-old.

As always, the house seemed strange and empty when she opened the front door. Her boots clattered noisily on the timber floor of the hall as she made her way across to the kitchen. As usual she had the urge to tiptoe, feeling that she must surely be disturbing somebody.

The chrome kettle was still full from the morning and

she wondered briefly if she should fill it with fresh water each time instead of just re-boiling the same water. There were loads of bacteria that lived specifically in stagnant water and at the rate she used it, the one fill of water would last days. Deciding that it was unlikely that she'd be killed by a predatory germ in her own kettle Lucy dropped a tea bag into one of the shiny black mugs that had been there when she'd bought the house and reached guiltily for the biscuit tin. Not guiltily enough to stop her picking out a Penguin and a Time Out though, she berated herself as she crossed to the sitting room.

The lady in the health shop had included a few leaflets with the oils and Lucy read through them intently as she sipped her tea. She knew she'd be better off without the two chocolate bars but it was all very fine for people like Cathy who actually had a social life and therefore something to look good for. Much as she adored them, Lucy was aware that the residents in The Friary wouldn't notice if she was a Size 8 or a Size 28 so long as she chopped their dinner up small enough and remembered to turn the television on in time for *Murder, She Wrote*.

Reading on, it seemed that the essential oils were divided into categories. Lucy was a bit perturbed that the two that she'd bought were in the floral range, as opposed to the spicy, woody, citrus or green groups. Her faith in the shop assistant's judgement wavered almost immediately when she read this, knowing that she was an unlikely candidate for anything remotely floral.

Later, as she lay in the bath, the aroma wasn't at all sweet and sickly as she'd expected but more fresh and heady. She wondered if ten drops of each was too much combined with the ever so slight turbulence that the jets created. She'd put it on at the lowest setting having read that the oils should be dropped onto the surface of the water rather than in the flow of the taps.

It was her first time to actually use the bath, preferring the vigorous cleansing of the shower. The bath was a modern version of the old free-standing enamel ones, with the jets built in. Lucy had always considered it to be one of the more intimidating objects in the house, sitting aloft on a sort of raised plinth that was tiled in the same glistening black as the rest of the bathroom. She'd felt slightly ridiculous stepping into it and now felt even more unworthy as she caught sight of her feet as they rested on the footpad.

She plunged them under the water again, telling herself that there was very little point in painting and pampering them when she wore her navy flats at work and her boots or trainers at home. The thought of going into a chemist and picking out a pearly pink nail polish was terrifying enough, never mind having to wear sandals for anyone to see it.

Chapter 6

"Oh, my God, Mum, that's brilliant!"

Rosa could hardly catch her breath, she was so excited. This was the start of it. Ten weeks was nothing and soon she'd be able to move on to a much more ambitious course and get her restaurant started up.

"It's only the Beginners' Course, Rosa," her mother cautioned, used to her daughter's enthusiasm.

"I know that but I'll be well able for it. She'll probably be doing the very basics like Queen Cakes and Victoria Sponges and I did all that in school. It'll be a stepping stone to the Advanced Course – if I like it and everything, that is."

Rosa still hadn't told her mother exactly why it was that she was so eager to do a cookery course, knowing that one or both of her parents would come up with a reason why an upmarket restaurant wasn't such a good idea. It would all end up, she imagined, the same way as her idea for an exclusive beauty salon had when her father started talking about renting a premises and getting insurance and making sure that she had fully qualified therapists.

Rosa had only been interested in the kind of therapies that she might offer and hadn't really thought out whether it would be cost-effective to have a large range of obscure therapies carried out by various practitioners. On this occasion, she planned to be very much in control of the situation before she disclosed her intentions.

"Well, you'll have a good idea after ten weeks whether you'll like it or not," Bernadette said now, hoping that the course wouldn't be too much for her daughter. She'd been on the Ladies' Committee at St Angela's with Pamela Carter for many years and knew exactly how high the lady's expectations could be when something needed to be done.

"How much does it cost? Do I pay every week or what?"

In her excitement, Rosa hadn't even paused to consider the price of the course. She wanted it so badly that she didn't mind what she had to skimp on to pay for it. Her part-time job on the Customer Service desk at Brown Thomas didn't pay much but at least she had the staff discount to make up for it. Although that wouldn't pay for an expensive cookery course, she thought now with a pang of anxiety.

"That's all done and dusted – Dad sent her on a cheque this morning to hold the place for you. It was a late cancellation so you're lucky to get it."

"Thanks a million, Mum. I just know I'll love it. What night is it on?"

"Tuesday – seven until ten. You'll have to make sure to get off work on time though, Rosa. She's very particular."

"Of course, I'll be on time!" Rosa was completely unaware of the dire status of her timekeeping.

"I'll ring you anyway to remind you," Bernadette told her indulgently, knowing full well that Rosa could forget about the cookery course if something more exciting came her way. She just got caught up in things – that was all.

"That's absolutely marvellous," Agnes intoned in what she thought could be described as a well-modulated voice, thrilled to hear that there was a place available on the Absolute Beginners course. It had occurred to her to go for a more advanced course but she'd eventually concluded that it would be better to shine in a beginners' class than look foolish in an Intermediate or Advanced one.

She kept her voice low as she discussed the finer details so there was no chance of Beatrice hearing her if she woke early from her nap. She could tell her about the cookery course later once she'd recovered from her sleep and had her dinner.

"It runs from seven until ten," Mrs Carter informed her crisply. "There's no need to bring anything with you. Everything you need will be provided at the classes."

Agnes listened carefully as Mrs Carter outlined the details of the course, finally coming to the price and the means of payment.

The phrase 'not for the faint-hearted' popped into her mind unbidden at the mention of the fee. Agnes had known that The Gourmet Rooms was an exclusive cookery school but she'd had no idea of the scale on which it operated until now. Fighting back the need to choke on her words, she held her own and said that she'd put a cheque in the post immediately.

As soon as she'd hung up the phone, Agnes headed quietly for the sanctuary of her bedroom, anxious to examine both her Post Office book and her Credit Union book. Her forehead was a little clammy, she noticed, as she crept past her sister's room and opened the door of her own room softly.

Quaking at the thought of clearing out both of her accounts to pay for the cookery course, she tried to calm down and reassure herself that it would be worth it. With all the typing she was getting these days, she'd have her bank balance back to a fairly healthy state in no time.

Just as she closed her small metal safe and stowed it away under the bed, she heard Bea's shrill voice calling out from the next room.

"You'll need to go to the Post Office tomorrow, Agnes. There's a phone bill to pay and the television licence."

"Grand so, Bea!" she called back, righting the valance of the satin bedspread to hide the few things that she kept a secret from her sister. "Will we have the lunch early and I'll take off?"

Agnes was delighted with this excuse to get into Rathcabben to organise her cheque for The Gourmet Rooms. Considering the frugal way that her sister managed every penny of their household expenses, she certainly wasn't going to fill her in on the exact cost of the ten-week course. If the price had shocked Agnes into a near panic attack, she could hardly imagine what it would do to her sister.

"As long as you're not gone all day. I have the cheques ready so all you'll have to do is hand them in."

This was Bea's contribution to the running of the household – that and giving orders to Agnes at every hand's turn. She managed all the bills from the Old Age Pension that Agnes collected for her every Friday with military precision, grudgingly handing Agnes her allowance and the grocery money. The small inheritance that their parents had left was to be kept for a rainy day. Sometimes Agnes was amused at the fact that they'd spent forty years waiting for a rainy day and wondered if one or both of them would actually be dead before such a day came.

"I'll put the kettle on," she called out now, her nervousness at the thought of spending all of her savings on a cookery course failing to abate. Perhaps her madness might warrant the Rainy Day Fund being called into action sooner rather than later.

Chapter 7

"Honest to God, Lucy, surely you can't be going to survive for a twelve-hour shift on beans and waffles? I should have come earlier and put on a proper dinner."

Maura Dalton, as usual, was astounded at the carry-on of her daughter.

"I'll be getting a break during the night. And a morning break before the day shift come on," Lucy retorted obstinately, baffled as to how her mother could raise this stubborn, awkward streak in her every time. It was no wonder she was buying essential oils to relax her when she was listening to this tirade every week.

"And what'll that be? Tea and toast, I suppose. What about vitamins? You'll get no vitamins in potato waffles, I can tell you that for nothing."

Maura was opening and closing all the doors of the pale beech kitchen cupboards now, as if to prove herself right. If it was vitamins she was looking for, she was going to be looking for a while, Lucy thought absently as she forked up the last of the baked beans and finished her second cup of tea.

"What day do you do your shopping on?"

Maura had a set day for everything: washing on Fridays, grocery-shopping and floor-washing on Saturdays, ironing on Sunday evenings and so on. Now she obviously expected Lucy to follow a similar path.

"I did a bit this morning."

"What! But there's nothing in the fridge. Did you not get any fresh stuff?"

Maura's own shopping, cooking and family eating routine followed a rigid pattern. Fresh things like chicken and salads and any soft vegetables that were likely to go off quickly were eaten at the weekend. Hardy things like turnips were relegated to the latter part of the week.

"There's no point in getting coleslaw and things – they only go off when I'm eating at work most of the time."

Why do I have to be so defensive in my own house? she thought.

"All the same, Lucy, you should make some effort. I know I might be old-fashioned but you'll have to learn to put a proper dinner on the table at some stage. You couldn't be feeding beans and waffles to a family."

Some chance of that, at the rate I'm going, thought Lucy. "Mam, I'm fine. I won't starve, you know."

Maura, warming to her theme, was not about to give up.

"I'm wondering if you'd be better off moving back home and renting this place out – you'd make a wonderful nest-egg. And you'd be eating properly, at least."

At this, Lucy drew the line. Whatever about moving home and eating properly, she certainly wasn't putting herself in the way of making any more money than she already had. Things were bad enough as it was.

"I'm fine here – it's near work and the shops and everything. Speaking of work, I'd better get going."

With that, to Maura's horror, she pulled the ironing board out of the spacious utility room and proceeded to iron a uniform for the night.

"Honestly, Lucy, you should do your ironing properly on your day off. It's not right to be doing it in dribs and drabs on your way out the door."

The idea of moving home again receded further into the back of Lucy's mind at this latest criticism. She could do nothing right this evening.

"I think I'll come over tomorrow while you're in bed and do a bit of cooking for you," Maura decided as she watched her daughter doing a slap-dash job on the navy trousers and tunic. "I could put a few quiches and shepherd's pies in the freezer and make a nice lamb casserole that'd do for the next few evenings."

Lucy pushed her hands through her fine, brown hair and made a concerted effort not to throw the iron at her mother.

"Your hair's got very shaggy lately," Maura pounced again, her attention having been drawn to the sorry state of the said hair by Lucy's gesture of frustration.

"I'm getting it cut next week."

"You'd want to," Maura instructed as Lucy escaped up the stairs to change out of her jeans and sweatshirt. "You'll never meet anyone and settle down if you don't start looking after yourself a bit."

Strangely, Maura Dalton seemed to be in no doubt that her daughter would eventually meet someone and settle down, despite the fact that she rarely went out socially and had never produced any evidence of a boyfriend. Maura got her own hair done every Friday morning and could never understand how her only daughter could look so unkempt all the time. Maura herself wouldn't leave the house without her customary dab of pressed powder and the same shade of lipstick that she'd worn for as long as Lucy could remember.

Maura was inclined to blame it on the crowd that Lucy had started to hang around with as soon as she'd started secondary school, all black jeans and black leather jackets with grubby black T-shirts underneath. Whatever fad it was that had turned her lively, pig-tailed little girl into a difficult and truculent teenager hadn't done her any favours, she always concluded.

Upstairs in the enormous master bedroom, Lucy sank down onto the king-size sleigh bed that had been left in situ by the previous owners, complete with matching double wardrobes, nightstands, dressing-table and two chests of drawers. The room resembled something out of the Hilton, with its plush, pale wool carpet and heavy ivory curtains.

The now familiar pang of bitterness assailed her as she took in her surroundings. Did her mother truly never wonder about the circumstances that enabled her only child to afford such a house? Or was it easier for her not to dwell on the subject at all, for fear that she'd actually come up with an answer?

The thought of her mother getting into the habit of coming over to check on her housekeeping was really too much for Lucy. Now that her husband, Paddy, had retired from the Department of Agriculture and was under her feet all day, Maura needed a new outlet for her boundless sense of industry and her daughter was as good a project as any.

Wondering if her uniform had shrunk in the wash, Lucy looked disconsolately at herself in the full-length mirror that stood between the two stately sash windows. She did look a bit bedraggled, she had to admit, especially as the buttons of her tunic were looking a bit strained and the trousers had started to cling to her bottom more than they'd done last week. Deciding that she had better order the next size whenever the uniform suppliers came around again, she pulled hard on the tunic to make it cover her bum before stepping into her flat, navy work shoes.

Sometimes when she was stuck in traffic on her way home from night duty, Lucy watched the skinny girls in their full make-up and smart suits walking briskly along the street to whatever civilised office they were working in and envied them their effortless elegance. Yet the thought of having to perform to that standard every single morning put the fear of God into her. At least in The Friary she wasn't being judged for her glamour or the size of her waist. The residents of the private nursing home had more to bother them than whether Lucy had a Burberry handbag or not.

"I'm after having a good look in the presses while you were getting ready," Maura greeted her at the bottom of the stairs. "You haven't even a bit of pasta or rice in the house. Even if you had a few chops or a bit of stewing steak in the freezer it would be something. And all the crisps!"

"But I eat a full dinner at work most of the time – even at night," Lucy lied in desperation, knowing where her mother was leading.

"Really – even at night?" This was said with scepticism before the inevitable, "Don't mind if you hear me making a bit of noise downstairs tomorrow. You sleep away and I'll have a proper dinner ready when you get up."

Beaten temporarily, Lucy ushered her mother out the door and down the stone steps before she was tempted to commit either grievous bodily harm or even matricide.

She was definitely going to have to put a stop to this.

"Honest to God, Cathy, she's driving me cracked. You'd think I was twelve the way she goes on."

It was gone midnight and the two girls were having their first cup of tea of the night, sitting in the two comfy leather armchairs at the Nurses' Station so that they could hear if any of the residents called out or rang their bell.

"My mother's like that as well, Lucy – always on about late nights and getting enough sleep. You'll just have to take her with a pinch of salt."

"You don't know my mother. She's landing every day of the week with little foil trays of shepherd's pie. It's like a refugee centre sometimes in my house."

"Can't you do a cookery course or something to head

her off? Tell her you have to practise," Cathy laughed, amused at Lucy's description of the mass cooking that Maura got up to.

"It'd be no harm anyway to learn how to cook for myself," Lucy admitted. "It would be healthier. I keep putting on weight even though Mam thinks I eat practically nothing." Secretly, Lucy was hoping that Cathy would tell her how to lose weight without her actually having to ask.

"You might just be eating the wrong things. Did you see that Absolute Beginners programme last night? The one about the cookery school?"

Lucy shook her head, never one to watch television once the soaps were finished Usually she spent her evenings curled up with a good book.

"It's a reality TV thing set in The Gourmet Rooms in Sunday's Well. Irene Lucas – you know, your one off *Afternoon Tea* – she's on it and Paul and Danny O'Sullivan. They're hilarious. That Lily O'Neill is on it as well – she's a right dose – and the fellow from the sports news."

Lucy wondered where all this was going but waited patiently, knowing that Cathy enjoyed the telling of a story before getting to the point.

"Anyway, Mrs Carter – she's the instructor – was giving the introduction the other night and it was all about eating the proper food. She reckons that if people ate fruit and veg and nothing out of tins or packets, there'd be no obesity."

"She's probably right," Lucy admitted, a vision of all the chocolate bars and crisps that her mother was giving out about appearing before her.

"Wouldn't it be gas if you did one of her courses? That'd shut your mother up!"

"What – with Irene blooming Lucas to look at? I don't think so."

Both girls burst out laughing at this. *Afternoon Tea* was the daily staple of the residents of The Friary, running five days a week from two o'clock until four. After years of listening to Irene Lucas pontificating, Lucy knew she couldn't engage in any activity that meant she'd have to look at her any more than she absolutely had to.

"But she's only on the celebrity show," said Cathy. "The normal courses run all year round."

"And they definitely have one for beginners?" Lucy was starting to warm to the idea.

"Yeah, but, Lucy, they cost a bomb. I can't remember how much but more than either of us gets paid in a month."

This made Lucy even more determined, although she was slow to let Cathy know that the price wouldn't be a problem.

"I could use my savings. It'd be worth it to have Mam stop going on at me."

"Listen, they do a re-run of the Absolute Beginners show at night. Go into the Day Room and get the *RTÉ Guide*. You could take your break at whatever time it's on. I'll do a quick round to make sure everyone's all right – Eithne McCarthy needed an extra blanket last night."

An hour later, Lucy was glued to the small portable television in the staff room. Lily O'Neill, the former lap-dancer, was mincing around a large, professional-looking kitchen in a very short skirt and a gold lamé top with a scandalously plunging neckline. The cookery teacher, a stern lady in her fifties, was trying to get her to fold flour into something but Lily was beating it vigorously despite the instructions. At another table, the two rugby players that Cathy had told her about were whipping cream and trying to decide whether 'holding a figure of eight' would do or if 'forming soft peaks' was required.

Enjoying it, Lucy was almost disappointed when the credits started to roll. Quickly she scribbled down the number that flashed up on the screen at the very end, determined to phone in the morning as soon as she got home. Despite Cathy's misgivings about the cost, Lucy was convinced that the Absolute Beginners course was exactly what she needed to sort her life out.

Chapter 8

Now that the time had come, Kate was really looking forward to the cookery course. Pamela Carter had placed a short note in with the order list the previous week advising her of the time and date and saying that she hoped Kate would enjoy it.

And I will, Kate told herself firmly as she turned the 'Closed' sign on the door of the shop and blew out the candle in the aromatherapy burner.

Since the day that the idea of the course had first been mentioned, Kate had started to look at her life with a more critical eye than usual and hadn't particularly liked what she'd seen.

She hadn't even been fully recovered from the accident when she'd shocked her parents and sisters with her decision to sell the house that she and Timmy had loved. She'd seen the advertisement for Good For You in one of the Sunday papers and something about the old-fashioned shop front with its bright red sign and the trailing window-boxes had appealed to her. The deal had been completed in record time and she'd suddenly found herself the owner of the small shop and the musty flat above it.

Hard work and the solitude of her new life had kept her going but now, looking back, she wondered if her self-imposed isolation had been gratuitous self-indulgence.

The fact that she'd never taken on an assistant, even when the business was well established, made her question whether she'd simply been refusing to face the future because she couldn't reconcile herself to the past. She knew now that the only thing holding her back had been the thought of having more time on her hands than she could possibly fill. She normally updated the accounts and ordered new stock after supper. If she was to get all the tedious stuff done during the day while someone else ran the shop, then her evenings would be even more bleak and empty that they already were.

Now that she'd finally put a small advertisement on the front window of the shop and another in *The Examiner* she was actually starting to look forward to having even a little time to herself.

It hadn't been much of a life, she thought now, studying the neat kitchen with its duck-egg blue presses and tidy breakfast bar in the small flat that she'd renovated over the years. Normally her enthusiasm for the shop overshadowed the deficits in the rest of her life but today everything seemed to be picked out in sharp detail. The fact that there was nothing else in her life but work was one thing. The fact that she'd refused to allow herself – she could admit this now, all of a sudden – to form any close friendships since her arrival in Cork ten years ago was another. Most bleak of all was the fact that, apart from the people who frequented the shop below, there was no meaningful human contact in her life at all.

Not for long more, she vowed as she made her usual dinner of stir-fried chicken and vegetables. She was determined that, as well as learning how to cook proper meals, she would soon have people in her life to actually share them with.

Agnes checked herself in the mirror and added another coat of lipstick. She'd set her hair in rollers that morning so that she'd be well groomed for her evening out but wondered now if it was her imagination that she looked like Margaret Thatcher. She'd tried a new hair colour as well – a softer brown that she thought was appropriate to her age.

She hoped that she wouldn't stick out like a sore thumb among the undoubtedly sophisticated people that she'd be mixing with for the next three hours. She knew that her coat looked good enough, especially since she'd sewed the Richard Alan label on. As long as she made sure to place it properly when she took it off, she reminded herself, knowing that making an impression was everything. If the other people on the course thought from the outset that she was a person of means, then they'd automatically treat her as such.

She'd parked her small Mazda in the shadow of a large tree at the far end of the street, well away from the imposing white townhouse, lest she be spotted alighting from it. Her tan court shoes made the kind of smart ring that she liked on the footpath as she approached the shallow steps that led up to the door of Number 5. Just as Agnes started to ascend, she was bypassed by an unlikely-looking girl in jeans and a checked shirt who shot up the steps and stabbed at the doorbell. Agnes wondered if she herself was at the right door at all, expecting a more gracious clientele than this gruff creature who barely acknowledged her polite greeting as they waited for the door to be opened.

It was Mrs Carter herself who greeted them and ushered them into the elegant hallway. Agnes recognised her immediately from the frequent appearances that she made on daytime television and the chat shows. She looked even more stern and in control in real life, her silver hair coiffed in its usual roll at the back of her head and firmly pinned in place. She wore a grey dress this evening, a variation on the usual scheme of navy or black.

"Come in, ladies. You're most welcome. I'm Pamela Carter," she said graciously.

Agnes nodded imperiously and introduced herself as if she were entirely at ease in such palatial surroundings. The other girl just mumbled her name.

"You may follow me to the kitchen and familiarise yourselves with the work stations. The others should be along soon."

Mrs Carter glanced at the face of an impressive grandfather clock as she said the last bit, her tone of voice making Agnes feel smug that she had been early rather than merely on time. Obediently, they trailed after her,

Agnes secretly thrilled to be in the company of such a prestigious woman in the kind of surroundings she always felt she should have been born to.

The kitchen was indeed impressive. Eight individual worktops were placed in a semicircle facing a single larger one, presumably to be manned by Mrs Carter. The back wall boasted a row of split-level ovens and three enormous fridges. The rest of the room was fitted with cherrywood units that blended magnificently with the large expanse of terracotta floor tiles.

On each of the work stations, Agnes noticed, there was a neat cardboard box. This, she supposed, contained the supply of starter items that were included in the price of the course.

Four of the work stations were already occupied. Farthest from the door was one of the most handsome men that Agnes had ever laid eyes on. Above average height with thick dark hair and the kind of tan that definitely had not been acquired in Ireland, he wore well-cut navy trousers teamed with a pale pink shirt and a navy sweater – most likely cashmere, Agnes thought, highly impressed.

The next three work stations were occupied by a group of young girls who seemed to know each other. They were already exclaiming over the contents of their boxes, which seemed to contain spice jars and some implements whose use they were trying to guess. Agnes smiled in their direction but elicited no response from the trio who were wholly engrossed in their guessing game.

"Please, make yourselves at home – you'll be spending a lot of time in this room over the next few months," Mrs

Carter told them as the peal of the doorbell reached them again.

This was the kind of tone Agnes had envisaged, the 'make yourselves at home' part. She placed herself next to one of the girls, directly facing the work station that Mrs Carter would be manning, and valiantly held herself back from opening the small box in front of her. It wouldn't do to appear too eager, as if she were down from the hills for the evening. Better to look a little blasé, as if she were used to this kind of thing.

The gruff girl had taken the space to Agnes's right and was already poking in her box, her head lowered as if she were avoiding having to converse. Agnes smiled grimly at her in case she was some famous actress in character for her latest film.

It was the thing nowadays, she knew, to stay in character all the while that a movie was shooting – like the film about the serial killer where the leading actress had put on stones in weight and even let herself get cellulite. It wouldn't do for Agnes to burn her bridges by being too snooty only to find out that the girl was someone important after all.

Agnes now turned to do a more detailed study of the room, eager to have all the details for Beatrice later. She was just trying to figure out what street the house backed onto when the door of the room burst open.

"Hi, everybody, I'm Rosa Mooney! And this is Kate. We just met on the doorstep."

Rosa bounded in, blonde and skinny, her hair bunched up high on the back of her head with wispy tendrils feathering down around her ears. Rich parents definitely, Agnes prognosticated, as an overpowering waft of perfume made its way over towards her.

Giddily, Rosa popped behind the nearest work station, next to the dour girl whose name Agnes hadn't yet found out. She started chattering immediately, distracting Agnes in her study of Kate, who smiled politely at everyone before taking her place at the last station near the door. While not particularly glamorous or expensively dressed, the petite lady in the embroidered caftan and beaded sandals had something elegant about her. She stood calmly by the work station, her face serene and her glossy chestnut hair pushed daintily behind her ears. Agnes wondered if she might be one of those health gurus that seemed to be all the rage these days, a celebrity one maybe, even though she couldn't remember actually seeing her on television.

Satisfied that she wasn't overdressed for a cookery class in her tweed skirt, the ivory twin set and the pearls that had been her father's wedding present to her mother in 1920, Agnes prepared to give her full attention to Mrs Carter. She was content now that what amounted to three months' typing income would be a worthwhile sacrifice for the opportunity of fraternising with such a gracious, if somewhat eclectic, social assembly.

Rosa was highly excited at the thought of learning yet another new skill, even though she'd almost missed the start of the class because of the complimentary makeover offer. What she'd really wanted was to meet some of the make-up artists involved in the film world so that she could network at the drinks party afterwards. Working in Customer Service did have some advantages, although she'd noticed that the girls working on the make-up counters were first up for the freebies while she'd had to contend with being experimented upon. Unfortunately, the make-up artist that she'd had the misfortune to be allocated to had been a complete windbag, pontificating about colours as if it was the Sistine Chapel she was painting. She'd had to sit through forty minutes of being a guinea pig while everyone else threw back champagne and mingled with the celebrities. She'd barely had time for a sip when her mother had phoned from her hotel room in the Cayman Islands to remind her of the cookery course. Accepting a liberal spray of a new fragrance from one of the leading fashion houses, she'd hightailed it across the city to Sunday's Well and screeched to a halt just outside the house.

Mrs Carter had looked askance at the shiny yellow Mini when she'd opened the front door but Rosa had already decided to disown it if there was a problem about parking.

Apart from a brief chat with Kate at the next work station, she hadn't had time to mix with the rest of the group. Mrs Carter, as she was always called, even by Rosa's own parents, was about to commence her introduction.

"As you know from the introductory brochure, this is a course for beginners. It's not just about recipes and menus, but about the buying of fresh ingredients, the preparation of wholesome, nutritionally balanced food and the idea that it's possible to cook economically with a minimum of effort and a lot of enjoyment. We'll cover a little about choosing wine throughout the course, as well as things like storing and freezing food."

She paused then, as if to see if everybody was paying attention.

Rosa definitely was. Her mother had warned her on more than a few occasions over the past week that she'd had to pull a considerable number of strings to get a place for her on the course and that it wasn't something that she could dawdle about it. Mrs Carter was a considerable force in Cork social circles and it wouldn't do for Rosa to change her mind after the first week or get ejected for not paying attention.

Rosa thought bitterly that it was typical of her mother to keep harping back to the Properties of Distinction thing, even though it had been almost two years ago. She'd really liked the idea of showing the elegant period homes to the type of people who could afford them – it just hadn't been made clear from the outset that the training course would be so boring and technical.

The job description had mentioned the selling aspects of it and she'd been convinced that she had the manner to do it justice – it was all the stuff about stamp duty and dry rot and engineers' reports that she'd got bogged down in.

Eventually, Andrew Hackett had had a word with her father and suggested that while he'd been delighted to give Rosa the opportunity to train as an auctioneer, he really felt that her particular skills would be better appreciated in a more 'people-centred' occupation.

Drawing herself quickly back to the present lest she be caught daydreaming, Rosa tuned in to what Mrs Carter was saying about simplicity and the ability to adapt the menu to suit the available produce. It was all about knowing what was in season, apparently. Alarmed that this was leading to yet another list of technicalities that she wouldn't be able to master, Rosa visualised herself sitting up at night with an inventory of seasonal vegetables and fruits, wondering what would be in full bloom and when.

Almost as soon as her moment of panic had begun, it was alleviated by the instructor's next announcement.

"It is appreciated that all of you are very much beginners and for that reason, I'd like to organise you into two groups so that each of you will have someone to consult with for your practice from one session to the next. This system has proved to be invaluable to previous participants on the course, particularly considering that each week I'll be expecting at least one of you to demonstrate an item covered in the preceding weeks."

A general silence followed this, with Rosa only dying to break it to find out who'd be in her group. This was as good as an introduction agency to Rosa's mind, the idea of consulting the stud at the end of the row about luscious desserts and the like appealing immensely to her.

To her dismay, the stud was paired off swiftly with the three glamour-girls at the far end of the row. Momentarily disappointed, Rosa glanced at the others, wondering what kind of group they'd make and whether they'd be any fun.

"Agnes, Lucy, Rosa and Kate," Mrs Carter continued,

nodding at each of them in turn, "you can make up the other group."

Lucy didn't look best pleased, Rosa noted – perhaps she too had been banking on the god with the Beckham aftershave. The demure granny in the twin set and pearls looked a bit put out too while Kate smiled encouragingly at Rosa and winked. She'd mentioned to Rosa when they'd met on the doorstep that she was living in the city so at least they'd be near each other if they had to confer on recipes and things.

Eager to find out the status of the rest of her group, Rosa turned to Lucy.

"Hi, I'm Rosa. I'm living in Bramwell Court, off Gilabbey Street. Are you in the city as well?"

"I'm in Bramwell Court too, actually," Lucy announced quietly, her tone almost reluctant.

"What! That's brilliant. I thought it was only all pensioners there," Rosa confided. Thrilled to know that there was at least one young person living near her, Rosa was ready for a getting-to-know-you when Mrs Carter called them to order, her disapproving gaze resting on Rosa for a little longer that it did on the rest of the assembly.

"That's settled then," she continued, still looking pointedly at Rosa who ceased her friendly overture to Lucy immediately. "Now let's get down to the business of cooking. Aprons first, please."

Rosa resurrected the blue and white striped apron from amongst the dangerous-looking knives and small unidentifiable jars in her box. Excitement surged through her as she tied the strings twice around her narrow waist, feeling completely positive about the prospect of a career in the exhilarating world of gourmet cooking.

Lucy felt like a pillar of salt being in such close proximity to the glamorous blonde on her right. Her make-up was flawless, her porcelain skin reminding Lucy of a china doll that her Aunt Sarah had brought her from America when she was seven. Her hair looked like a shampoo advert and she even smelled delicious.

Lucy never wore perfume, always thinking herself a little unworthy of it. Cathy, her night-duty partner, claimed that she wouldn't answer the door without a squirt of something and seemed to have a different cut-glass bottle in her handbag every night. Mrs Carter introduced herself briskly, as if there was no time to waste, informing the group that this was no wishy-washy evening class. No, she was determined that each and every one of her pupils would get full value for money and would finish the course a competent cook. In the weeks that followed, she told them, the value for money concept would become so familiar that they would quake at the idea of discarding food or being uneconomical with one's oven.

The moment Mrs Carter announced that they were to be placed in groups for the classes, Lucy's nerves had started to jangle. She'd been feeling comfortingly anonymous up until this, rummaging absently through the 'starter pack', a neat cardboard box containing a selection of basic items that would apparently enable the most culinary challenged individual to master a nutritious and appealing meal.

Lucy looked around in horror, terrified that she'd get paired with Kate, who she recognised from the health shop and who would probably presume that she knew as little about cooking as she did about essential oils. The skinny blonde with the cloying perfume and the three polished-looking girls at the other end of the row terrified her, as did the fellow who looked like something out of an aftershave advert. The woman with the heavily powdered face would be all right, she supposed, if it came to it. At least she was used to working with older people.

Suddenly, with very little ado, it was all sorted and Lucy found herself being quizzed by Rosa who was highly excited at the idea that they lived practically next to each other.

"I can't believe I've never seen you before!" she exclaimed, as if they were going to be great friends now that they'd found each other.

"I'm out a lot – on night duty," Lucy offered, by way of explanation, thinking the whole thing was a bit scary. She was only here to learn how to cook.

"Are you a nurse? Oh my God, I wouldn't be able for that at all!" Rosa gushed, her expression of awe annoying Lucy.

"I'm a care assistant," Lucy explained, wishing that Mrs Carter would just get on with the business of cooking.

As it happened, the tutor was just about to start, and Rosa was called to order.

Lucy felt a bit foolish in the blue and white striped apron that they'd all been supplied with but figured that if the rest of them were wearing one then she'd have to get on with it. Rosa looked like she was about to give a demonstration on a television show, making Lucy wonder suspiciously if she was as ignorant in the kitchen as she claimed to be.

Once they examined the contents of their boxes with a running commentary from Mrs Carter, the first menu was outlined.

"Spicy Stuffed Peppers to start, Creamy Mango and Mustard Chicken for the main course, followed by a Chocolate and Orange Cheesecake."

Lucy was stunned at the ambitious-sounding menu but was too shocked to say anything. Rosa, on the other hand, muttered that she'd thought it was going to be all scrambled eggs and French toast and queried whether it was for beginners at all.

"That's the whole point," Mrs Carter explained patiently. "It's about simple delicious cooking that seems deceptively sophisticated. Anything that I do with you will be, as one young man described it last term, 'eejit-proof'."

Timing was everything, she told them. The cheesecake must be made first in order to allow time for setting. The table should be set while the main course was cooking and any utensils used should be washed up and put away then.

Lucy thought it all made sense once you knew what to do. Rosa was terrified and whispered to Lucy that she'd be in a state of panic from the beginning of the class until the end. She wasn't too terrified, though, to notice Lucy's blunt-cut nails.

"You should go to that new nail-bar down that side

street where Le Coiffure is. That's where I go – you're in and out in minutes," she advised.

Somehow, Lucy didn't think so.

She found she wasn't as intimidated by the bubbly blonde as she'd normally be, despite her skinny build and stylish, expensive clothes. Rosa's exuberant personality made it almost impossible for her to keep her usual wary distance. There was something childlike about her that actually made Lucy feel almost protective about her as the class went on, especially when she threw out the cut-off tops of the red peppers instead of saving them to make 'lids' once the hollowed-out bodies had been stuffed with wild rice, porcini mushrooms and an array of herbs that neither of them would ever be able to remember.

"It's okay," Lucy heard herself whisper as soon as Mrs Carter was out of earshot. "Have one of mine."

"But we're supposed to have two each." Rosa was nearly crying

"I know. But one proper one with a lid might be better than two half ones."

"Thanks, Lucy." Rosa sounded nervous. "She'll probably eat us without salt."

"It's only a cookery class. We'll be grand," Lucy reassured her, surprising herself with her firmness.

"Everything going to plan, ladies?" Mrs Carter's serious eyes seemed to be everywhere in the room at once, overseeing her charges.

"Grand," Lucy muttered, making her way to the ovens to place her lone stuffed pepper in alongside the chicken fillet that was bubbling away nicely in its concoction of cream, mustard and mango chutney. Rosa followed her as soon as Mrs Carter had departed from her work station, guilt written all over her face.

"I'm sure she was wondering why I had only one pepper," she hissed anxiously.

"Right now, everybody, time for a well-deserved cup of coffee," Mrs Carter announced before Lucy had a chance to reply. "The peppers should take about fifteen minutes so don't forget the time."

As soon as the rest of the class started to make their way towards the drawing room at the front of the house, Rosa nudged Lucy.

"I'm going to investigate the sex bomb and see if he's single," she said under her breath.

Lucy didn't know what to say to this but there was no way that she was going to be involved. She'd be mortified if she even had to say hello to him. Rosa, on the other hand, had no such reservations and gave Lucy a little wink before taking off down the hall at speed.

"It's great so far, isn't it?" The lady from the health shop who Rosa had introduced earlier as Kate now fell into step beside Lucy.

She was smiling and Lucy noticed again how serene she looked.

Minutes later, they ended up next to each other in the drawing room. Kate chatted easily while Lucy awkwardly tried to balance her china cup and saucer while perched on the edge of a long sofa upholstered in a slippery gold material that she felt she might slide off at any minute.

Kate had an almost ageless beauty about her but the

small lines around her eyes told Lucy that she was probably in her late thirties. Envying her petite figure and shiny hair, Lucy was hesitant at first about disclosing just how appalling her cooking skills were but soon relaxed when Kate told her that all she ever ate were sandwiches and things like nuts and seeds from the shop that she didn't actually have to cook.

Reassured that she wasn't the only one on the course who relied on convenience foods, Lucy allowed herself to smile and tell Kate that she was doing the course to get away from beans and potato waffles. Kate laughed at this just as Mrs Carter clapped her hands to call them back for the second half of the class and Lucy left the plush drawing room with a wonderful sense of Kate's laughter floating around in her head. Maybe the other woman didn't see her as awkward and shy – maybe she'd just taken it that Lucy was a normal person.

Chapter 9

Agnes woke early the next morning with a sense of excitement and purpose. She'd stayed awake for hours reliving the first evening of the cookery course and the success it had been. By the end of the three hours, as well as coming to grips with all the new terminology Mrs Carter had outlined, she'd also started to get a handle on her classmates.

Kate, the lady in the unusual caftan, owned a health shop in the city and was originally from Dublin. Agnes had a good chat with her when they'd been paired off at the end of the class with a list of cookery terms which they had to explain the meaning of. She felt that she'd held her own with things like *roux* and *sauté* and hadn't felt a bit intimidated when Kate came up with explanations for *al dente* and *en croûte*. They'd exchanged phone numbers at the end of the class and Agnes felt that she was just the type of person she could phone if she really got bogged down with a recipe.

The two younger girls in her group were a little harder to fathom. Lucy, the girl she'd met on the doorstep was either shy or very bad-mannered, keeping to herself as much as possible, despite Rosa asking her a multitude of questions at every opportunity. Rosa, on the other hand, couldn't be stopped from talking. She'd told Agnes that she worked in Brown Thomas, something that interested Agnes greatly. She could only ever buy clothes or cosmetics in the sales at the high-end department store. Perhaps having an acquaintance with a finger on the pulse, or maybe even a staff discount, would be of assistance to her the next time she needed new shoes or some make-up.

While she hadn't had an opportunity to chat to the four people in the other group, Agnes had overheard Rosa whispering to Lucy at the coffee break that the handsome man with the pink shirt was a paediatrician at St Angela's and that she would find out more about him in due course as both her parents worked there as well.

The three girls in the same group as the paediatrician had stuck together giggling and making smart comments whenever Mrs Carter's back was turned. Rosa – now considered by Agnes to be a reliable source of information – said that they were in IT, whatever that was.

Resting cosily under the duvet for a few moments longer than she normally would, Agnes started to plot what she might have for dinner this evening that would suit Beatrice while still allowing her to practise one of the new dishes. She knew that the creamy mango and mustard chicken dish was out – it was far too rich for Bea to digest, not to mention the fact that her sister would question the extravagance of buying a whole jar of mango chutney for one recipe. After the coffee break, Mrs Carter had demonstrated three fish dishes and Agnes came to the conclusion that perhaps it was safest to try one of those first. If Bea actually liked it, then maybe she'd be more amenable to trying something more adventurous rather than dismissing all of it as nonsense.

Bea had been quite put out the previous evening when Agnes had arrived home from The Gourmet Rooms, griping about Agnes having left the heating on too high and the fact that she was dehydrated and had a headache from it. It had taken two paracetemol and a special concoction of honey, ginger and lemon juice in boiling water to settle her. Agnes had been well and truly chastised for the wastefulness of leaving on the heating when she knew full well that Beatrice couldn't reach the little thermostat in the hot press to turn it off. The only reason that Agnes had left the heating on in the first place was that she was afraid of Bea being perished if there was any delay with the class running over time.

Agnes had wisely decided to play down just how much she'd enjoyed the class, rather than upset Beatrice any further than was necessary. The day she'd phoned The Gourmet Rooms to book the course, she'd even asked if the cookery school was wheelchair accessible, although she knew in her heart of hearts that Bea wouldn't even consider it.

If her sister had been the type to consider trying out new things every now and then, Agnes thought, maybe they both would have had better lives. But as it was, Bea refused to leave the house, save to go on her trip to the GP every three months and in essence she expected Agnes to do the same. If it wasn't for the fact that she'd learned to drive all those years ago, Agnes imagined she'd have been housebound her whole life. The Mazda, decrepit as it was, was her lifeline.

"Agnes – are you up yet? I've pins and needles in my legs."

Startled out of her reverie, Agnes quickly swung her legs out of the bed, knowing by the tone of her sister's voice that she'd woken up in bad form.

"Coming, Bea!" she called out, wondering what it would be like to lounge around in her bed until ten or eleven o'clock just once in her life.

"You're very late up this morning," Beatrice complained as Agnes made her way to the kitchen to get the breakfast tray ready.

Bea always had her breakfast in bed, followed by a small nap so that she'd have the energy for the routine of washing and dressing that their mother had devised and later handed over to her younger daughter.

Five minutes later, Beatrice was propped up in bed by the plethora of pillows that Agnes always had trouble arranging to her satisfaction. Her silvery grey hair was loose around her shoulders, awaiting the customary roll that Agnes would dress it in later. It needed a trim, Agnes noted now. Mentally putting the job off until the weekend, she knew that Bea would soon remind her of it anyway.

As it was Wednesday, Bea's breakfast consisted of

porridge and honey, followed by a chopped-up kiwi and a handful of grapes. This was rotated on a daily basis to include brown bread, Weetabix, toast and various other fruits, all with Bea's poor digestion in mind.

"I suppose you'll be rushing off to Rathcabben the minute I'm out in the chair," Bea accused now. Her flinty grey eyes, almost the same colour as her hair, were suspicious.

"I'll have to go in for a few things but you could come as well. It's not cold out." Although the evenings had started to get a little cooler, there was still the autumn sun to warm the air. Bea would be fine if she wrapped up well.

"I'd be perished. And you'd have my arms pulled out of their sockets getting me in and out of the car. I wouldn't be right for the rest of the week."

This was true, Agnes had to admit. Even though she always made sure to ask her sister if she wanted to go to town with her, it was a relief when she declined. The effort of hauling Bea out of her wheelchair and into the car, stowing away the cumbersome chair in the boot of the Mazda, then getting her out into the chair when they got to town was enormous and she didn't blame Bea for considering it an ordeal. Once they'd perused the few shops that Bea had any interest in, the whole exercise had to be repeated again for the journey home.

"I won't be long. I'll just get something for the dinner and drop in my good skirt to the cleaner's."

"Well, don't be gone half the day like you were on Monday."

The day before the cookery class, Agnes had gone into town to collect her typing. Conscious of the fact that she'd be presenting herself at The Gourmet Rooms the following evening, she elected to have a look around the shops and maybe have something new to wear to make an impression. As it happened, she'd done a lot of typing that week and had a sizeable cheque on account of it.

After cashing her cheque, Agnes had taken the unprecedented step of heading for Cork city without having informed Bea that she might be a bit late. Despite the fact that she'd spotted the cream twin-set with small pearl buttons as soon as she'd set foot in Marks & Spencer's and had hightailed it back to the carpark with the minimum of delay, it had still been a quarter past one when she'd arrived home – fifteen minutes after their usual lunchtime.

If it hadn't been for the fact that she'd be wearing her new twin set to The Gourmet Rooms the following evening, she would have lost all pleasure in her purchase after Bea's diatribe. The man from the ESB had come to read the electricity meter but he'd been gone by the time she'd been able to get to the door. Because their meter was inside, this would mean an estimated bill, something that Beatrice would normally never countenance.

"I don't have much to do today so I'll be home early. Now, have your nap while I wash up these," she advised, taking Bea's tray and heading back to the kitchen to get her own breakfast.

An hour later, Bea was sitting out in her wheelchair, a heavy tartan rug wrapped around her legs. Thankfully, she hadn't opted for a bath, something that Agnes was finding it harder and harder to manage. Even the task of transferring her sister from bed to chair was becoming unmanageable of late, particularly as Bea seemed to have put on more weight lately.

"I have your flask ready and I left a few Ginger Nuts wrapped in foil as well. If you sit in here you'll have the sun coming in for another while."

If Agnes was leaving the house, she tended to set Beatrice up with everything she needed so that she was less at risk of falling out of her chair trying to reach for something. Once the television was on and she had her flask of tea and a few biscuits, she rarely needed anything until Agnes returned.

The freedom of just walking around Rathcabben was something that Agnes savoured. Even though it was only ten minutes' drive from their cottage on the Cliff Road, it represented a break from her usual routine. Today, the drive was glorious, the autumn sun glinting through the trees and lighting up the interior of the car. Main Street was as busy as ever but she eventually secured a parking spot outside the library, a godsend where Beatrice's weekly supply of books was concerned.

Her first port of call however was The Office Shop.

"You're in great demand, Agnes," Tony greeted her from behind a large cardboard box containing a photocopier.

"That's what I like to hear," Agnes retorted with a smile. The more work the better, especially now that she'd spent all her savings on the Absolute Beginners course.

"I think it's the fact that you have it back to them so fast. There's more here from Karen Kelleher for you. And there are a few bits from the convent as well – one of the Sisters is doing a course. Enough to keep you going until Friday!"

"The more the better," Agnes told him as she handed over the work she'd done since Monday and accepted the small white envelope that contained her cheque. "See you on Friday."

Now her day could begin properly, starting with her trip to the bank. Then it would be on to the library and finally a wander around the supermarket to check out the ingredients that Mrs Carter had used – although Agnes herself might have no call for them if Beatrice thought they were too expensive.

Queuing in the bank, she tried to remember exactly what books Bea had asked her to bring home. Without her being aware of it, the two people in front of her had moved to the various counters and Agnes was startled back to reality by the cashier calling "Next please!" in her direction. Mortified to be caught dreaming and holding up the queue, she shot forward to the desk.

"I'd like to cash a cheque please," she began, barely glancing up at the bank official as she rummaged for the cheque.

"Agnes Cotter?"

Taken aback, she ceased her hunt for the cheque and looked up, the deep timbre of the voice jogging something in her memory. The man before her was smiling, his face tanned beneath a thatch of silvery white hair. She recognised him immediately, the wide smile and piercing blue eyes the same as ever.

"Willie? My goodness, Willie Boyle!" Agnes's heart did a funny little jump and she hoped that the shock of seeing him again didn't show on her face.

"It's great to see you, Agnes. I wasn't sure you still lived around here."

"Still here," Agnes acknowledged, her cheque now forgotten. The last time she'd met him had been almost forty years ago. "I thought you were still living in Dublin, Willie?"

"Retirement planning," he told her, smiling. "We bought a house down here last year with view to moving back when I retired. I still have six months to go but the opportunity here came up when the manager took leave of absence. I decided to take it and make the move a bit earlier. I'm only settling in yet."

"You're the manager here?" Agnes had noticed his use of the word "we" and deduced that he'd married in the intervening years. It surprised her that after all the time that had passed she still felt a pang of disappointment to hear it.

"You'd hardly think it," he laughed. "We have three staff out sick today with that bug that's been going around so I had to abandon the paperwork and pitch in myself."

"Well, it's great to see you." Agnes was conscious of the queue building up behind her, especially when the bank was short-staffed.

"You haven't changed a bit, Agnes. Now, what about that cheque?"

Flustered, Agnes handed over the cheque, wondering how true it was that she hadn't changed much. She studied Willie now as he deftly sorted out her transaction. He had a little more weight on than she remembered but it suited him, making him stockier in build.

Agnes was glad that she'd made an effort with her own appearance that morning and knew that the deep red cardigan with the gold buttons looked well on her. The white blouse she wore under it was crisply ironed and her little red and white polka-dot scarf was tied at a jaunty angle that she'd practised after seeing it in a magazine.

"Now, there you go, Agnes," he concluded, handing over her money. "We must keep in touch. Miriam barely knows a soul in Rathcabben so she'd be delighted to meet you."

"Well, I'm in and out of here all the time so I'm sure we'll see one another again. Now, I'd better move on or you'll be here until midnight."

"See you again."

"Bye for now," Agnes smiled, departing the counter with as much grace as she could muster. It wasn't every day she met an old flame.

Agnes took a deep breath of the crisp September air as soon as she stepped outside the bank. Her heart was beating a little faster than usual after the chance encounter and she knew that she needed to sit down and take it in over a cup of coffee. Beatrice, she knew, would be impatient at her delaying over coffee in town when she could just as easily come home and have one but the last thing Agnes needed was home and indeed, Bea.

Thankfully, the morning rush in Carrie's Kitchen had died down and she secured a small table at the back of the shop. In case anyone would ask to share, she placed her handbag discouragingly on the remaining chair. Tucked away with her cup of milky coffee and an almond and raisin muffin that she felt she deserved, Agnes sat back and allowed the memories to flood over her.

The thing that she remembered most about that time was the anger that she'd felt at everyone. That and the sense that her life was over before it had even begun properly. Her mother, however, had been quick to point out that Agnes had lived quite a bit of her life already, more than Bea had been able to do.

The evening that she'd first met Willie Boyle came back to her as if it was only a week ago and she remembered now with painful clarity the day it had all begun. Agnes had been working in the Cork branch of the Department of Health at the time, having completed her advanced commercial course with honours. She even had a small flat and came home at the weekends to her parents and Beatrice.

She had a vivid memory of getting the phone call that Friday at work, mainly because phone calls were discouraged unless a dire emergency was afoot.

"It's Mother here, Agnes," she heard as soon as the call had been connected to her boss's office for privacy. Her heart was thumping wildly. Her mother had never phoned her at work before.

"Is everything all right? Dad?"

"Dad's fine," her mother reassured her, "but Beatrice has had a fall. She was going out the back for a bit of fresh air and the chair must have gone off the edge of the slope."

"Is she hurt?" Agnes was amazed that her sister had tried to negotiate the steep slope outside the back door alone. She was terrified that she was already dead and that her mother was trying to tell her gently. She'd bought Bea a lovely angora scarf earlier in the week and was looking forward to presenting her with it later that evening.

"She's in terrible pain. I think the leg might be broken. Dr Donnelly is coming as soon as he can. She's in bed now but she's crying. She's very bad, Agnes."

"I'll ask to get off early. I'll be home as soon as I can."

"No, Agnes, it's not that. It's the retirement night I'm thinking of. If the leg is broken, I'll never be able to leave Beatrice tomorrow night. You'll have to buy a dress and go with Dad. It would look very bad if he was on his own."

Thinking back on it now, it probably *would* have looked strange in those days for a man to arrive at his retirement function alone when he had a wife and two daughters at home.

"But I can stay at home – I'll be well able to manage," she'd protested, knowing how much her mother was looking forward to the rare night out.

"Not if the leg is broken. Beatrice might even be in hospital. I couldn't leave her there on her own."

Promising her mother that she'd do her best, Agnes had headed for Cash's on her lunch break and purchased the pink dress and a pair of white court shoes that had tiny pink bows at the back. She still recalled every detail of the dress and the way that the fitted bodice and flared skirt had set off her slim figure perfectly. She knew the deep pink colour suited her as soon as she tried it on and even though it cost almost all of her week's wages, she just had to have it.

In her more philosophical moments, Agnes was able to credit Beatrice with her meeting Willie in the first place. Their father had been the manager of United Bank in Rathcabben at the time that it merged with Allied Trust and he'd made the decision to retire, although it was still a little before time. The gala evening planned by management to celebrate the successful merger of the two banks would also serve as a retirement evening for James Cotter who'd given many years of dedicated service.

It was to be a glamorous affair and their mother Rosaleen had spent weeks touring the boutiques and drapery shops in Cork looking for the perfect outfit. She'd eventually come across a pale blue bouclé suit in Cash's, a suit that Agnes could still visualise in its plastic wrap long after the retirement night had come and gone. Even the smart navy shoes remained in their box, untouched for months until another occasion warranted their appearance.

Agnes could still remember the suppressed excitement that she'd felt that evening. Bea had sat white-faced in the bed as her younger sister had dressed up and put on her make-up and a pale pink lipstick.

"Very nice for you, going off to the dinner," Bea had piped up resentfully from her pile of pillows.

It was all Agnes could do to bite back the retort that it was Bea's fault that she was going in the first place.

By the time they arrived at Hollygrove Manor, Cork's most exclusive hotel, the whole good had gone out of Agnes's evening. She recalled feeling guilty about her mother not being able to go to the night out and guilty that Bea could go nowhere at all.

Everything had changed, of course, when she laid eyes on Willie Boyle. She'd noticed him immediately where he stood by the door chatting animatedly to an older, distinguished-looking man when she and her father arrived. His hair had been jet black then and he had dark blue eyes that lit up with interest as soon as he and Agnes were introduced.

Although she had been on dates with men that she met at work or at the dances in City Hall on Saturday nights, this was the first time that Agnes had felt a blush rising up her throat as soon as someone looked at her. Clutching her tiny white handbag onto which she'd tied a small pink ribbon to match her dress, Agnes had chatted as politely as she could, anxious to make a good impression on her father's behalf.

The dinner had flown by and she'd barely eaten a thing. The glass of champagne that she'd sipped to toast her father's retirement had gone to her head immediately, making the whole evening seem surreal and a little mystical.

Afterwards, Willie had asked her to dance and she'd been more than happy to oblige, especially when she caught the nod of approval that her father gave her when he was sure that no-one was looking.

After that, she and Willie had become an item. He got on well with the girls in her flat and most Friday nights they went dancing together, often with a few of his colleagues from the bank and Agnes's friends from the Department.

A year passed and Willie was even starting to talk to her about the future. Even though she still came home every weekend to help her mother, Willie was happy to collect her in his brand new Prefect and take her to Cork on a Saturday night. He'd even taught her to drive, something that Agnes was eternally grateful for to this very day.

Now, as she picked at the remains of her muffin and drank back the last dregs of her coffee, she wondered what her life would have been like if she'd had a chance to marry Willie before she'd fallen in for the task of looking after her sister.

It was Dr Donnelly who'd broken all the bad news to Agnes at once. Firstly that her mother was suffering from cancer of the womb, something that had been neglected for a number of years through her fears for Beatrice's welfare.

Agnes hardly had time to absorb this shock when he moved on to the subject of Beatrice.

"Time," he told Agnes gravely, "is not on your mother's side and it's important that decisions regarding your sister's care be made as soon as possible."

"But Dad will be there and I'll be home every weekend," Agnes had reminded him, shocked that this was coming without warning. She had always thought it would be years before any decisions had to be made.

"It wouldn't be seemly," he said delicately, "for your father to take over Beatrice's care. If you, Agnes, aren't prepared to take on the responsibility of your sister then it will be up to me to arrange a suitable institution."

To this day, Agnes wondered if it was his use of the word 'institution' that had made the decision for her. Perhaps if he'd said Care Home or even Welfare Home, she'd have been strong enough to tell him that Willie was now talking seriously about marriage.

It still hurt that her parents hadn't discussed the situation with her themselves. Instead, the doctor had been allowed to tackle the situation as he thought best. In those days, Agnes recalled, it was taken for granted that the wisdom of figures of authority like priests and doctors was bowed to unquestioningly.

In the weeks that had followed, Rosaleen's family saw her become weaker and weaker, to the point where she was no longer able to care for Bea at all. At one point, just before the end, Agnes had found herself caring night and day for both her mother and her sister.

Willie, to his credit, had been infinitely patient. Eventually, though, she'd had to make a decision. By the time her mother died, he'd been transferred to one of the Dublin branches, the only way to advance a career in those days. For months, he'd travelled back to Cork every weekend, spending the evenings chatting and playing cards with Agnes, Beatrice and their father. He'd even asked whether Beatrice would consider coming to live in Dublin if he and Agnes were to marry.

It was sadness now, more than anger, that she felt when she thought of Bea's reaction to that particular proposal.

"You'd expect me to move to Dublin? Would Willie not come back to Cork if he's so mad about you?"

"He has no choice at the minute – it's the way the

Bank works," Agnes had explained, suddenly finding that she had to defend Willie. "He has to go wherever they send him or he'll lose his job."

"Well, it's not fair expecting me to go to Dublin just to suit you and Willie. You go if you want." Bea had turned her head away then in a gesture that brooked no further discussion.

Eventually, after a short discussion with her father on what would become of Beatrice if Agnes were to marry, she did the only thing she could and broke the news to Willie that she wasn't in a position to agree to anything while she had Bea to consider. Tears were shed by both of them in the darkness of the Prefect that night but Agnes was adamant. If Beatrice wouldn't come to Dublin, there was no way that Agnes could leave and see her sister face life in an institution.

She'd seen Willie a few times after that when he'd called to see her on his trips home to Cork, always hoping that she'd changed her mind. The visits had stopped eventually, something that had broken her already wounded heart.

Seeing him today had brought back all the memories that she'd suppressed for so many decades. What was Miriam like, she wondered? Did they have children or even grandchildren? How long were they married? Like herself, Willie was sixty-five. Could this have been her life, moving back to Cork at retirement age with Willie, a cast of children and grandchildren in the background?

But Agnes had realised long ago that there was nothing to be gained by dwelling on the past. Pulling herself together, she shook away her memories. She had other things to think about now, like her trip to the library and the evening ahead when she would try out one of her new recipes, maybe one of the more adventurous ones after all. It wouldn't hurt Bea to compromise a little, for once in her life.

Chapter 10

Rosa resurrected her cream Burberry mackintosh from the small office behind the Customer Service desk and sighed deeply as she tied the belt neatly around her tiny waist. It was all very fine thinking that working in an up-market department store was glamorous and exciting but at the end of the day her ankles ached and her jaw was stiff with smiling politely while people dithered over the little cards that went with the gift vouchers. She'd even ventured a "Have a nice day!" to a few customers earlier, bored with the monotony behind the desk.

It was nearly five past six by the time she said goodnight to her colleagues, all of whom were lovely and the only thing that made the job tolerable at all. There was a slight drizzle coming down as she made her way to the carpark, the evening grey even though it was only the second week in September. Glad of an opportunity to use it, she popped up the little umbrella that was secreted in the base of her Burberry holdall. She'd bought the bag and coat together earlier in the season and had been dying for the weather to get a little cooler so that she could give them an airing.

Sitting patiently in the Mini twenty minutes later, she cursed the rush-hour traffic that always seemed to get worse at the slightest hint of rain. Not that it mattered, she reflected, when her parents were away anyway. Rosa normally drove over to Douglas and had her dinner with Bernadette and Maurice after her shift on Thursdays and, despite feeling cloistered by them most of the time, she always felt a sense of loss when they were away, even if it was only for a few days.

She was dying to fill them in on all the details of the cookery course, especially now that she'd be able to prove her intention of getting into the restaurant business in a tangible way. As soon as she had a few of the more manageable recipes off by heart, Rosa planned to invite her parents over and treat them to a delicious home-cooked meal.

Thinking on this, it occurred to her that it was two days since the opening night of the course and as yet she hadn't attempted any of the recipes. Perhaps a trip to Tesco might be an idea, especially as she had nothing else planned for the evening. Maybe she could even call to Lucy, who lived only two doors away, to share a practice run. Revving impatiently now that she'd decided on a plan, Rosa put the car into neutral and pulled out her mobile and the miniature Filofax that was like an extension of her arm.

"Lucy? Hi, this is Rosa Mooney here. From the cookery class?"

Wedging the phone between her ear and her shoulder, Rosa inched the car forward a little and explained to Lucy that she was thinking of practising one of the meals from their first class.

"Would you like to come to Tesco with me and pick out a few ingredients? We could cook over at my place. Unless you've had your tea, that is."

She hadn't thought of this when she'd decided to phone on impulse. After a slight hesitation during which Rosa started to feel a bit nervous about being thought of as pushy, Lucy said that she'd love to try out a few of the recipes.

"Brilliant, Lucy, I'll pick you up as soon as I get out of this traffic and we'll go to Tesco in Wilton. Will you bring the book so we won't forget anything important?"

Thrilled to have someone to share her newfound skills with, Rosa revved a bit harder, praying that she wouldn't see another green light come and go without the Mini making a significant move forward.

An hour later, following one of the most exhausting ventures to a supermarket that she'd ever experienced, Rosa was leading Lucy through the front door of 3 Bramwell Court. Laden down with shopping bags, the two girls made their way straight to the kitchen, eager to get started on their experimental meal as soon as possible.

"Your house is fabulous," Lucy commented, looking around the spacious kitchen with its painted cream units and hardwood counter. "Mine is like a barn compared to it."

"But they're all the same layout," Rosa protested.

"Yes, but mine's all hard and shiny. Yours looks lived in."

"My parents had to do this place up a bit when they bought it first so I offered to direct the traffic," Rosa grinned expressively. "It came out a bit more expensive than they'd anticipated but they thought it was worth the extra when they saw it finished. What kind of kitchen do you have?"

"I don't know exactly what the wood is – it's very pale and plain."

"Shaker, probably beech," Rosa said, sounding very knowledgeable. "Very hard-wearing."

Lucy by this time had unpacked all the groceries and was putting them in order for the two dishes that they were going to prepare. Rosa looked at the bewildering array of items and started to feel a slight tinge of panic. It was fine earlier in the supermarket – she'd felt like Anneka Rice in the TV show years ago trying to find all the items on Lucy's list in double-quick time. Now that the buzz of the shopping bit was over, she was less sure about the enterprise than she'd been earlier sitting in the traffic jam.

The stuffed peppers would be easy enough because they'd actually made them on Tuesday night in the class. The smoked haddock recipe would prove more challenging as they'd only watched Mrs Carter demonstrate it at the end of the class.

"Should we do the fish first, do you think?" Rosa said timidly, hoping that Lucy knew what she was doing.

"Well, the peppers take about twenty minutes to cook

so maybe we should get them into the oven and concentrate on the fish then."

"Which bit should we start with? Will I get the book out? We'll never remember it all."

"One of us could start preparing the peppers. We'd need to put on the rice first though."

"Will I do the rice? Did you see the look Mrs Carter gave me when she spotted the lids of the peppers in the bin the last night?"

Lucy smiled over at her and rolled her eyes. "We *are* supposed to be beginners!"

Feeling somewhat reassured, Rosa measured out a cup of rice and perused the cookbook again to see how much water it needed. "How am I going to measure two and a half cups of water?" Mrs Carter had advised them not to get too bogged down in measuring things in grams and kilos. It was less complicated if they could gauge the everyday things like rice and pasta in cups instead.

"Just put in two cups and estimate the rest. We can always add a bit if we haven't enough."

Rosa was heartened by Lucy's confidence with the complicated business of cooking but wondered how on earth someone so competent could have such an ambivalent relationship with her hair. Studying her now as she expertly scooped out the two bell peppers, Rosa could visualise Lucy's fine, lank hair cut into a soft wispy style and its mousy tones lifted by a mixture of copper and golden highlights.

"What?" Lucy said out of the blue, noticing Rosa's consideration of her.

"Nothing," Rosa conciliated, noticing the slightly defensive tone. "I was just thinking that you have great hair for a Cameron Diaz style – you know, short and wispy. Mine's too curly for it."

"Oh." Lucy reddened at the scrutiny and started to chop an onion, looking slightly annoyed at Rosa's assessment of her.

"You look like Cammy actually," Rosa continued, worried that she'd caused offence. "You've got the same eyes."

"Oh," Lucy said again, looking a bit anxious.

Rosa was just about to rush in with another comment about Cameron Diaz's assets when the lid started to clatter violently on her saucepan of rice. Turning swiftly, she attempted to reach the lid to lift it off, oblivious of the vicious spurts of steam escaping from under it until she felt the sharp sting of heat on her wrist.

"Jesus, I'm scalded!" she shrieked, loud enough to wake the dead in the surrounding counties.

Almost as quickly as it happened, Lucy grabbed her arm, simultaneously turning off the gas under the rice and turning on the cold tap. The bite of cold was nearly as shocking as the steam burn, causing Rosa to screech again.

"It's all right Rosa. This'll cool it." Steadily, Lucy held Rosa's wrist under the cool stream until the stinging eased. "Do you have a First Aid box in the house? You'll need to put something on this or it'll blister."

Rosa thought of the small biscuit tin her mother had

given her when she moved in and wondered if everything in it was out of date. She opened one of the presses and pulled it down nonetheless, then leaned on the worktop examining the small red patch that was already appearing on her wrist while Lucy examined the contents of the box.

"Here, this'll do," she said finally, and rubbed a toxic-smelling cream into the burn.

"Thanks, Lucy. I suppose the rice is ruined?"

"No fear of it – we'll just put it on low and it'll be fine."

"Did you do a First Aid course?" Rosa enquired, more interested in Lucy's skills than the meal.

"We have to do an update every year at work," Lucy told her, embarrassed at the admiration in her tone. "We'd better get cracking or it'll be all hours before we get it on the table."

Rosa giggled at this reference to Mrs Carter's thoughts on eating too late and the subsequent risks to their digestive health but pointed out that their combined metabolism was running on high after their supermarket dash so in fact they'd burn off all the calories in no time.

"I suppose so," Lucy conceded, examining the large piece of smoked haddock that they'd agreed on at the fish counter. "I'd say the rice must be done by now."

"It looks okay." This time Rosa turned off the gas flame before venturing to lift the lid. Having successfully drained it, she looked to Lucy for confirmation as to the next step. "Do I just mix it all together?"

"In it goes!" Lucy lifted the chopping board and added

the neat piles of chopped onion, chorizo, garlic and a small pinch of dried chilli to the rice. "There should be plenty there to fill the peppers."

Five minutes later, with the peppers safely roasting in the oven and their carrots and broccoli steaming gently, the two decided to tackle their first *roux*, the basis of all good sauces according to Mrs Carter.

"All this butter can't be good for us," Rosa commented, watching as Lucy plopped a full ounce into a stainless steel saucepan.

"Is it very fattening?"

"One hundred per cent!"

Lucy added the ounce of flour and started to stir the mixture vigorously. "The milk, Rosa, quick!" she instructed urgently.

Panicking at the immediacy in her voice and the fact that the thing was in lumps already, Rosa splashed in a large glug of milk from its plastic container, spattering the top of the cooker in the process.

"Gradually, she told us, remember?" Lucy kept stirring frantically with the metal whisk and miraculously the mixture started to resemble a thick sauce.

"Another bit," she encouraged.

Rosa obliged, less generous with the milk this time and fully in awe of Lucy's competence. She'd either been listening very attentively to the tutor on Tuesday night or studying really hard in the meantime, Rosa thought now, vowing to pull up her socks at the next class.

"What's next?" She was mesmerised at the way that Lucy could keep the sequence of the recipe in her head.

"We'll have to add the grated cheese as soon as this is done," Lucy told her.

Glad that she'd had the foresight to involve Lucy in her first foray, she grated almost the whole block of cheese, stopping only when her new friend reminded her that they only needed two handfuls.

"Just as well you stopped me – this is as bad as the butter."

"I thought dairy products were supposed to be good for us?"

"Not half a block of cheese! One portion is supposed to be the size of a match box."

"Tell me you mean a big match box?" Lucy looked incredulous.

"No, the small ones," Rosa insisted, wondering if this was why Lucy was a bit plumper than she needed to be. She was at least a size sixteen, although maybe the heavy grey sweatshirt that she wore over her jeans might be making her look bulkier.

"This must be very fattening then, with the butter *and* the cheese?"

"I got the low-fat cheddar so it probably won't be too bad. Anyway, the fish will make up for it. "

Lucy looked relieved at this, making Rosa wonder if she was trying to lose weight.

"Should I start chopping the fish up yet?"

"I think so. This is nearly ready." Lucy held the saucepan over so that Rosa could see the smooth cheese sauce. "I'll add the carrots and broccoli while you're doing that. I can put on the pasta while it's cooking."

A few minutes later, the smoked haddock and vegetables were simmering gently in the cheese sauce and the pasta was well under way.

"Do you think there'll be enough for the two of us?" Lucy enquired, looking anxiously at the two pots.

"Loads. Irish people eat portions that are far too big. It's to do with the famine, apparently."

"What is?" Lucy was by this time unloading the spicy stuffed peppers from the oven.

"You know," said Rosa, "this idea that we mightn't have enough unless we pile it up like Mount Everest. Hey, they smell fantastic!"

"They do, don't they? Here, tuck in."

Lucy looked chuffed and Rosa held up the glass of wine that she'd poured while Lucy had organised the pasta.

"A toast!" she called out excitedly, clinking her glass with Lucy's. "To Absolute Beginners!"

Chapter 11

Now their second class was looming and Lucy wasn't half as nervous about it as she'd been the previous week. She'd even told Cathy and the girls at The Friary about the cookery class and about her cookery session with Rosa Mooney. Under normal circumstances, she'd have been afraid that it might seem a bit grannyish but if a glam-bird like Rosa was doing it, not to mention the debonair Mark and the three IT-girls, then she didn't mind a bit.

Telling her colleagues about the course at The Gourmet Rooms, Lucy realised with a start, was the first time she'd ever had anything of a remotely social nature to talk about. The interest on their faces surprised her and she spent most of the morning coffee break answering questions about Mrs Carter, the house – a listed building according to Una Riordan – and the recipes that they'd covered. Cathy, needless to say, had quizzed her exhaustively when she heard that Mark Toland was also doing the course.

"How do you know him?" Lucy asked in amazement,

although nothing surprised her as far as Cathy was concerned.

"Lucy, you'd want to start looking at magazines. He's always at things like fund-raisers and art exhibitions. I think they take photos of him because he looks fantastic no matter what he's at."

Lucy knew that Mark was a paediatrician of some sort because Rosa had made it her business that first night to ascertain his credentials. He was the only man in the class and, despite the IT-girls clinging to him like limpets, Rosa was of the opinion that there was no reason they too couldn't be in with a shout.

While Lucy had been supportive of Rosa's foray into the other group to chat up the delectable Mark as she'd labelled him, she drew the line at being included in any attempt to seduce him. She'd been intimidated enough by Rosa's inspection of her nails the first night – there was no way that she'd be able to perform to the standard of glamour that a man like Mark would require in a woman.

Lucy had been inordinately pleased at the interest that the girls at The Friary had shown in her cookery course. It occurred to her that maybe the reason she'd always felt herself to be such a boring person was that she never actually did anything interesting that would merit talking about.

Cathy had an interest in almost everything that was going on around her. When she wasn't in the thick of organising staff nights out with Una, she was organising day trips for the residents to places like the Heritage Centre in Cobh where the Titanic had last berthed on its final fateful journey. She knew everything and the next time she got her on her own, Lucy was going to ask her who Cameron Diaz was.

Jessica, a mother of two young children, was on every committee known to man. If it wasn't the Parents' Council, it was the Girl Guides. She even did a Meals on Wheels run once a week and seemed to know everyone in the small village of Glenrahan where she lived.

Now that she'd made a start on kick-starting her life a bit, Lucy was actually beginning to get enthusiastic about it. She'd even thought about going back to Good For You to get a few more essential oils, now that she was less afraid of Kate after talking to her at the tea-break the first night.

Thinking on this now, Lucy decided to go to the health shop as soon as her shift ended. It might mean missing her weekly trip to Bookends but for the first time in years, she actually had something else to do.

Kate left Mrs Howard to her own devices, knowing that she liked to choose the flower remedies herself once she'd had a rundown of the various uses. A delivery of soya products had arrived and she was anxious to get the items sorted out and close up on time so that she'd be ready for her cookery class.

The loud jangle of the doorbell announced the arrival of another customer. Kate extricated herself from the collection of milk, cheese and yoghurt and popped her head over the counter, pleased to see that it was Lucy Dalton from her class at The Gourmet Rooms.

She'd been intrigued to see her at the opening session,

recognising her from her one visit to the shop. Again, Kate had been curious about her, the surly exterior strangely at odds with her presence in such prestigious surroundings. Even though she hadn't paid for her own ten-week course, Kate was aware that it was horrifically expensive and somehow Lucy's understated jeans and sweatshirt ensemble didn't fit the picture.

She looked better, Kate thought now, than she had the first time she'd seen her in the shop. Her light brown hair, despite its straggly cut, had a lovely shine to it and she looked livelier and less suspicious than she had on that first occasion.

Kate pushed the wayward strands of her silky chestnut bob behind her ears and greeted Lucy enthusiastically, interested to know if she'd started on the dishes that they'd covered earlier in the week. Kate herself had tried out a few of the recipes, managing them well considering that she hadn't cooked properly in years.

"Great," Lucy told her. "I went over to Rosa's on Thursday and Saturday and we tried a few of the recipes out. Did you do any of them?"

"The first night I tried the fish pie, which was great but I didn't realise how big it was going to be. I'll halve the ingredients the next time!"

"The cheesecake was huge as well. Rosa and I made it on Saturday and took half each."

"That's the thing about living alone. You're not inclined to cook because it seems like a big fuss for one."

So far, the course was proving to be something of a catharsis for Kate, reminding her sharply of how very isolated she was in the world but also of the family life that she'd missed out on since the accident. She'd started to allow herself to think about what it would be like to cook for a family as she'd stared at that enormous fish pie but somehow she couldn't visualise it.

The futility of spending the rest of her life imagining how her future would have worked out had hit her then, making her shake herself. She'd just have to start again and rewrite her future. Maybe she wouldn't be sitting around her table with a husband and children but she could certainly share her world with a circle of friends.

It was happening already, now that she'd decided to make a conscious effort. Almost as if divine intervention had inspired it, Agnes Cotter from the class had phoned just as Kate was staring at her fish pie.

"Agnes rang the other night to see how I was getting on with the recipes," she told Lucy now. "She came over here on Saturday evening and we did the cheesecake as well. Her sister has a sweet tooth apparently so she was thrilled to be going home to her with a treat."

Kate had really enjoyed the company of the older woman and had realised that, in her own case, it was only her refusal to move on that had held her back. Agnes, on the other hand, had had very little choice.

"It's great to have someone to practise with. I'd probably have been lazy and gone back to the beans and waffles if I hadn't had Rosa to buck me up this week. I think we're doing roast meats and steaks tonight so that should be interesting."

"No harm – every time my mother comes to Cork she

asks me how I do my roast beef on Sundays!" This was one of the few times, Kate realised, that she'd even mentioned her family since she'd moved to Cork, always preferring to maintain her privacy.

"Sounds like my mother – only she doesn't even hold out for a roast. She'd be happy with scrambled eggs at this stage. I think we'll be doing chocolate desserts tonight as well."

"So I read in the little book. It all sounds so ambitious but she makes it seem easy."

"That's the best bit. Actually, Kate," Lucy asked her now, "I wonder if you could tell me about omega 3 and 6, you know, fatty acids and that. My friend Cathy at work is always on about them. She seems to think eating enough of them might be good for losing weight."

Lucy looked almost embarrassed as she asked this so Kate kept her tone as brisk as possible. Weight was a sensitive subject for a lot of people.

"Do you mean as a supplement or in food?"

"I don't know really." Lucy looked sorry now that she'd asked at all.

Kate started to explain the particular foods that contained good sources of the essential fatty acids, like oily fish, as well as the various supplements that were available, loving this aspect of her job.

"But it's probably more economical to incorporate them into the general diet. A lot of people are buying a mixture of seeds like sunflower, linseed, pumpkin and sesame to include in breakfast cereals. Porridge mostly – because low GI foods are the best way to lose weight."

"What's low GI? I've heard Cathy on about it."

Kate was pleased that Lucy seemed to have gained a certain amount of confidence in her and went on to explain the Glycaemic Index.

"And how do you know which foods are low GI?" Lucy was interested to know, having begun to seriously consider the issue of her weight since she'd started the course in The Gourmet Rooms. Hearing Mrs Carter going on about reducing saturated fats and Rosa reading the labels for the fat content of everything before she'd put a smidgen of it past her lips had made her realise that it might be possible to lose a stone or two.

"There's a small book on it on the bottom shelf – I can photocopy it for you if you like."

"I might just get it and have a read of it at home, thanks. And I might get some of the seeds as well."

"They're all on the shelves over there so you can see what takes your fancy. The nuts have the essential fatty acids as well, if you think you'd like them as a snack."

Mrs Howard had approached the counter again, as usual presenting Kate with a selection of flower essences. She'd told Kate that the tiny bottles had been the saving of her since the sudden death of her husband earlier in the year. Developed for use as emotional healers, many of Kate's customers used them on a regular basis, from nervous Leaving Cert students to vulnerable post-natal mothers.

Kate herself used them regularly and was more than convinced of their value. In the aftermath of Timmy's death, her friend Daphne had suggested she try them. She could remember as if it was yesterday the time she'd discovered that pine was the remedy for guilt and how she'd slept for the first time in months after taking a few drops of it.

"Are the nuts not fattening?" Lucy enquired, approaching the counter again, the wicker shopping basket laden with bags of organic seeds. The book that Kate had recommended was tucked into the basket as well.

"You know when Mrs Carter talks about saturated fat? That's what people call 'bad' fat. The fat in nuts is considered to be 'good' fat. It's important to go for unsalted nuts, though, rather than the type of ones that you'd get in the pub which have a lot of salt added to them."

"God, everything that's nice is bad for you," Lucy joked as she paid for her basketful. "I might even have to give up the Kit-Kats once I've read this."

"I always think the ninety per cent rule is a good one," Kate laughed, amused at Lucy's stricken face. "As long as you're good ninety per cent of the time you're doing pretty well."

After she left, Kate considered the change in Lucy since her first visit to the shop. Maybe her gruff exterior was simply a cover for shyness, a means of warding off attention. Yet somehow she didn't think that it was just shyness that kept the guardedness in her eyes.

Wondering wryly if perhaps she should have studied psychology instead of becoming a health guru when she'd abandoned her life in Dublin to escape to a place where nobody knew who she was, Kate smiled another welcome as the doorbell jangled again.

Chapter 12

"I'm definitely going to find out more about him tonight," Rosa insisted to Lucy as they made their way to Sunday's Well in Rosa's yellow Mini Cooper.

"He spent most of the time talking to Agnes the last time. Maybe he's into older women."

Rosa had insisted on Lucy travelling the short distance across town with her, citing her need to go over the recipes in case Mrs Carter wanted her to demonstrate something from last week's menu as she'd warned that first night.

"I think maybe Agnes monopolised him a bit," she insisted. "He's probably dying to meet the likes of us."

She'd been obsessed with the gorgeous Mark earlier in the week and was convinced that most people met their life partners through mutual interests rather than in pubs or nightclubs.

Whatever about Rosa, Lucy wasn't convinced that she herself was exactly the kind of wife that Mark might have in mind – although she didn't think she looked too bad this evening. She'd noticed during the week that Rosa tended to wear neat cardigans with her jeans rather than the kind of jumpers and fleeces that made Lucy look like a barrel.

This evening, she'd been so exhilarated by her purchases at Good For You that she'd popped into Marks & Spencer's to get something nice to wear for her class. She'd spotted the teal blue cardigan and had decided to buy it to go with her jeans instead of her usual fleece.

"Well, at least you have something in common with him," said Lucy. "Did you mention that your parents work at St Angela's too?"

"I didn't get to it with Agnes hovering around. Maybe you could distract her a bit at the coffee break."

This was more like Lucy's territory. For a minute she had thought Rosa was going to ask her to help out with the chatting up of Mark Toland.

They bumped into Kate on the doorstep and Agnes was there before them.

Like the first week, Mrs Carter got down to business immediately.

"I'm going to look at roasting meat first and we'll talk about the different joints and their properties as soon as we have that underway. Tonight, I've used small cuts of lamb, pork and beef but the principles are the same no matter what the size of the joint."

"Something every girl should know!" Rosa said under her breath, giving Lucy a dirty wink.

Terrified that Mrs Carter had heard, Lucy lowered her

head lest the instructor see the grin that threatened to break out on her face. Rosa was desperate when she got going.

Ten minutes later, they were trying valiantly to trim the fat from the lamb before sealing it for roasting.

"This is gross. Imagine if it was cooked like this the amount of fat you'd be taking in."

"Jesus, Rosa, I'm going to have to start thinking in grams of fat the way you do. Is that why you're so slim?"

"That and the walking. I try to do a few miles every day, depending on the weather. Would you come with me sometime?"

"Definitely. I'd have to get a pair of runners first though."

"Sport Scene on Thomas Street have good walking shoes," Rosa instructed, ignoring the waft of smoke that had started to rise from the oil in her cast-iron frying pan. Fashion in any form always had the power to distract her from whatever it was that she was doing.

"Turn it down a bit maybe before you put the lamb in," Lucy suggested, noticing that the gas flame under Rosa's pan was practically roaring.

"It'll be grand – she said to have it red hot to seal in the juices."

With that, Rosa plonked the joint of lamb straight into the smoking oil, unleashing a shower of spatters that resembled a volcano erupting. To add to the confusion, she let out a shriek that would wake the dead as her arms and face got splattered with the red-hot droplets.

"I'll get it, Rosa." Mrs Carter, at the gas hob next to

her, came to the rescue. Mortified that she was making a show of herself, Rosa insisted on managing and tried to reach in to turn off the gas herself. The lamb was hopping around in the pan, still emitting bursts of juice and oil that showered Rosa as she attempted to get one slender arm to the controls while she used the other to protect her face.

"Honestly, Rosa, I'll get it," the tutor insisted, her voice taking on a sterner edge.

Capitulating at last, Rosa watched as Mrs Carter reached for the controls of the gas ring, small spots of grease beginning to speckle and spread on her pristine pale-blue blouse. The kitchen was full of black smoke.

Rosa stared at Mrs Carter's blouse open-mouthed just as the smoke alarm kicked into action with a piercing shrill. "I'm sorry. I'm so sorry!"

Her face a study in exasperation, Mrs Carter switched it off as Kate and Lucy darted to open the windows. Rosa continued her apologies while Agnes tutted fussily and the IT-girls and Mark gaped over at the commotion.

"I think we'll seal this batch as quickly as possible and get them into the oven," Mrs Carter called over the babble that had broken out. "An early coffee break might be the best option. We can do the theory in the drawing room and come back to our chocolate desserts later."

With this, Mrs Carter ushered them from the room, first handing a mortified Rosa a small tube of cream to rub on any burns she'd sustained.

"At least you know now what *not* to do," she said with a hint of a smile.

Chapter 13

After speaking to Kate on the phone yet again, Agnes had abandoned the Chocolate Mousse and cleared up as quickly as possible in case Beatrice would wake up from her nap earlier than usual and see all the ingredients that had been wasted. Two cartons of ruined double cream as well as the melted chocolate and the whisked eggs went into the bin, carefully covered with a scrunched-up newspaper.

Kate had been a wonderful support as usual. She'd advised her not to worry too much about getting something wrong and promised that she'd go through it with her at their cookery session on Saturday, now that they'd decided to make it a regular thing. She was so gracious and kind, Agnes thought, even to poor Rosa who seemed to make an exhibition of herself at every opportunity and had even ruined Mrs Carter's blouse at the last class.

Satisfied that her sister wouldn't notice her misdemeanour, Agnes closed the lid of the bin with a sigh.

Beatrice already thought it was a ridiculous waste of money to be going to a cookery class at her sister's time of life, and Agnes sometimes felt weak at the thought of her finding out the real cost of it.

She wiped down the worktop hurriedly and pressed the button on the kettle when she heard her sister stirring down the hall. As if on cue, Beatrice rang the little bell that she kept by her bed to summon Agnes. She'd want to see the Six O'Clock News before her tea was served, then have Agnes read to her before she had her cocoa at nine.

"Are you there, Agnes?"

Beatrice's shrill voice had begun to irritate Agnes a lot lately, especially since the day she'd met Willie Boyle in the bank. In the early days, she'd buried all the resentment that she'd felt at the loss of Willie and the life she could have had with him. The worst time had been in the immediate aftermath of her mother's death, when Beatrice had taken to her room, refusing to communicate with them. Agnes, heartbroken after Willie, didn't even have her sister's support and instead spent her evenings keeping their father's spirits up after the loss of their mother.

She remembered it as a terrible time in her life, the loneliness overwhelming her so much that she even fantasised about running away to America without telling anyone. She didn't do it, of course, but the idea that she *could have* kept her from losing her head altogether.

It was only when their father died the following year that Beatrice came out of her shell, setting the tone for the remainder of their lives together. Agnes had often thought that Bea was somehow happier once their father was gone, aware that Agnes was effectively trapped as there was nobody else to look after her. She'd felt enormous guilt for even thinking this but it was a thought that had come back to her on many occasions over the years.

If she didn't have her classes at The Gourmet Rooms to go to at the present time, Agnes felt that she might be very intolerant of her sister's demands. Meeting Willie had put her a little on edge, making her feel almost defensive about her life. She was nervous now of bumping into him every time she went into town, imagining Miriam as a glamorous, interesting woman who had much more to offer him than she herself had.

She was convinced that her own life would appear insular and paltry to someone like Miriam. Agnes, after all, had precious little to show for her sixty-five years. Despite her occasional anxiety over the reduction in her savings, Agnes was glad that she'd decided to go ahead with the classes at The Gourmet Rooms, the fact that she was involved in something interesting and worthwhile making her less apprehensive about the inadequacy of her life.

Shutting them out of her mind, Agnes took a deep breath and responded to her sister as kindly as she could, knowing that life wasn't easy for her either.

"I'm coming, Bea. I'm just putting the kettle on."

"Well, hurry up – I want to go to the toilet before the News. I hate to miss the beginning of it."

Agnes thought uncharitably that if her sister wanted to watch the News that badly, she ought to have announced it a bit earlier, considering it took at least ten minutes for Agnes to lift her into the wheelchair, bring her into the bathroom, lift her onto the toilet and then back into the wheelchair when she was ready. Now she'd be rushing the procedure, which Agnes was finding more and more difficult as the years went on.

She was perspiring heavily by the time Beatrice was finally settled in front of the fire, her legs wrapped in a tartan rug and the television positioned to best advantage. Agnes prepared the tea, longing to try out the minute steaks that Mrs Carter had demonstrated at the end of last week's session. The accompanying ingredients were fairly basic – just potatoes, onions, garlic, cheese and a little cream for the gratin potatoes and a few seasonal vegetables so Beatrice couldn't really complain about experimenting with expensive ingredients. She did however tell Agnes that there was no way that she'd be able to digest such a heavy meal in the evening – or at lunch-time for that matter when Agnes suggested the latter. Agnes hadn't even mentioned the lamb shank with garlic and rosemary, knowing that it would most definitely be out of the question. And it wasn't something that she could try on the quiet when Beatrice was having her nap, on account of the pungent aroma of garlic and rosemary, not to mention the timescale required.

No, Beatrice demanded that they stick with their usual supper of a boiled egg, a slice of ham and a half tomato each. She would have been shocked if Agnes had attempted to make two separate suppers, admonishing her for being extravagant with what was, after all, Beatrice's money.

Nowadays, Agnes fantasised constantly about the day that she'd start receiving her own pension. It was less than four months away and the thought of it made her dizzy with anticipation. Almost all her life she'd been dependent on someone – first her parents and then Beatrice, who'd inherited the house and a small amount of money that they both lived on.

While she had no idea of how much Beatrice's inheritance had been, she supposed that it had now dwindled to almost nothing. Most of Beatrice's old-age pension paid for their groceries and the everyday things. Whatever remained at the end of the week was kept by Beatrice for the yearly things like house insurance and filling the oil tank.

Agnes did get a small allowance, her spending money Beatrice called it, but it was the typing that allowed her to have a life of her own – that and the small savings that she made here and there with the grocery money.

As soon as the tea was finished and the washing-up done, Beatrice got ready for her book. Even though she had the full use of her hands, they tired easily from holding the book and even the wheelchair-mounted bookstand that Agnes had bought her the previous Christmas was no good as she still had to turn the pages herself. Anyway, she was so used to it being read out to her that it wasn't the same if she had to read it herself.

Agnes sat in the fireside chair facing her sister and gritted her teeth when Beatrice announced that she couldn't remember the part of the plot her sister had read the previous evening. Agnes would have to go back a bit. Already bored with the long-winded romance that seemed to be going nowhere, the thought of reading any of it twice almost brought Agnes out in a rash.

Thirty pages later, she noticed that Beatrice was starting to nod off so she paused a little, hoping that the session was nearly at an end. Perhaps Beatrice would suggest a game of draughts, something that would at least stimulate Agnes's brain a little.

"Why are you stopping?" Beatrice demanded, her eyes popping open crossly.

"You looked a bit sleepy. Are you sure you don't have enough for one night?"

At this, Beatrice went off into one of her rants about Agnes having no gratitude, and the fact that she hadn't had to do a day's work in her life. Instead, she'd lived off Beatrice since their parents had departed, without a care in the world.

As usual, she conveniently forgot to mention the fact that Agnes did all the housework, shopping and laundry as well as caring for Beatrice around the clock, even getting up at night to change her position from left to right a few times to prevent bed sores.

Not wishing to antagonise her any further, Agnes continued with the book, consoling herself with the fact that it would soon be time for the cocoa. Beatrice rarely stayed up later than half nine, giving her sister plenty of time for typing whatever it was that The Office Shop had placed in the padded envelope.

Sometimes, Agnes couldn't believe how duplicitous she'd become. Her sister still thought she was writing to one of the African pen-friends that she'd found in the *St Martin* magazine. Although she didn't fully appreciate the second-hand computer that Agnes had bought through the 'pink pages' of the *Evening Echo*, Beatrice was content that it kept her carer in the house most of the time, save when she got an idea about an evening course.

If it wasn't for the night courses that she so diligently saved up for every year, Agnes would have lost her reason years ago. The year that she'd done the Information Technology for Beginners had been one of the best ever because it had led to the buying of the computer and the subsequent work for The Office Shop. She'd been described as an excellent typist in her day and had easily picked up her speeds again once she'd mastered Microsoft Word.

At last Beatrice demanded the cocoa and Rich Tea biscuits that she always had before bedtime. Afterwards, Agnes helped her to change into her nightclothes, struggling with the corset that her sister insisted on wearing even though corsets had gone out with the ark.

"I need it to keep my kidneys warm," was her usual answer when Agnes questioned the need for it.

Finally, with her sister settled for the night, Agnes opened the envelope that she'd collected from the Office Shop earlier in the day. She generally went to town on Monday, Wednesday and Friday, with Beatrice unaware that she dropped off the pile of disks and reams of typed pages and collected another envelope of handwritten material and dictaphone tapes. She had never told Beatrice about her little job with The Office Shop, knowing that she would probably stop her meagre weekly allowance once she got to the bottom of how much Agnes was earning. Agnes had become an expert at keeping things to herself over the years and for good reason, as Beatrice's condition was inclined to take a convenient turn for the worst whenever her carer's life showed signs of becoming too lively.

On this occasion, most of the typing work was for a Mr Bailey who was doing some sort of thesis or study on the effects of waste incineration on the environment. Apart from anything else, Agnes felt that the typing gave her an opportunity to broaden her knowledge base on subjects that she wouldn't otherwise know about.

Only last week, she'd been able to tell Kate Lewis on the cookery course that so-called 'backyard' fires were a much greater threat to the environment than incinerators were, thanks to Mr Bailey's information.

She glanced at the clock now and wondered if she'd be able to finish all her work tonight. If so, she'd be able to make an extra trip to town in the morning on some pretext or other and hand it in to Tony, the manager, even though Beatrice would probably go on about the price of petrol. She could then afford the ingredients for the Chocolate Hazelnut Torte that Kate had suggested she try. She might even be able to afford the small Burberry scarf that had been down to half price in one of the shop windows. It would go well with her beige cardigan and surely Rosa Mooney would recognise it as a designer brand.

Setting to it, she knew that it would probably be midnight before she was finished but it would be worth it if she was able to collect her money and buy the required items. She had to keep up with the recipes at all costs — otherwise Mrs Carter would think she was an idler with more money than sense. Swiftly, she tapped away, satisfied that she'd look the part at the class the following Tuesday. She'd barely completed two hundred words when Beatrice's bell tinkled insistently.

"I can't sleep, Agnes. Will you get my things ready – I think I'll take a bath to help me nod off."

Groaning inwardly, Agnes tried to persuade her sister that a cup of hot milk with honey and a pinch of nutmeg would be the better option but Beatrice was having none of it.

"You're doing nothing else anyway," she added spitefully.

An hour later, Beatrice was again settled, having complained vociferously that she was perished because Agnes took so long over drying her. Now she was propped up in bed drinking the hot milk that she'd refused earlier.

"I'd ask you to read another few pages only you're so grumpy tonight," she told Agnes, peeved because she'd been told it was too late to have her legs massaged.

Thanking her lucky stars that she didn't have to endure any more of Clarissa of the heaving bosoms, Agnes bade her sister goodnight swiftly lest she change her mind and once again wearily faced Mr Bailey's dissertation on the finer points of dioxin breakdown.

Chapter 14

"I'm dying to hear what was on the menu this week," Cathy Rohan said, as soon as they'd left the nursing office.

Lucy had had her third session at The Gourmet Rooms the evening before and was bursting to tell her all about it.

"Okay, let's see – Balti Lamb in a creamy coconut and yogurt sauce, Thai green curry, Chicken Chow Mein . . ."

"What was the theme this week? United Colours of Benetton?"

"Something like that," Lucy told her with a grin as they started making the first of the two beds in the semi-private room while Mrs Grainger and Ettie Collins were out in the dining-room having their breakfast. "Cuisine from around the world, to be precise!"

"Is the lamb thing very fattening? Every Indian recipe I see seems to be full of butter and cream."

"You can adapt this one with low-fat coconut milk

and low-fat natural yogurt. Even Rosa thinks it's not too bad and she's a complete expert on fat content."

"Did I tell you I tried out the chocolate mousse on my sisters? Well, Barbara had it – Mags couldn't because of the raw eggs," she told Lucy, referring to her older sister who was in the latter stages of pregnancy.

"Did it set all right for you? We all had trouble with that in the class. Agnes tried it at home after and had to bin it."

"I thought it was dead easy," Cathy said with the kind of confidence that Lucy had always wished she could have even a smidgen of. "I'd love to try that lamb thing. What else is in it?"

Lucy started to explain the intricacies of the lamb curry as they completed their bed-making and stowed the linen trolley away in its press. It was a source of pride now to her that the others were dying to hear the recipes from the famous Gourmet Rooms cookery school.

To her amazement, she almost looked forward to work now. Before, she'd be doing the beds with Cathy or one of the others, all the while listening to what *they'd* been up to over the weekend. Now, she too had a hobby.

"Will we ask Nora Wallace if she'd like to have a bath before the hairdresser comes?" she asked now. "Her son is taking her out for lunch today."

"You're full of beans," Cathy commented. "Una bought a selection of nail varnish in Boots at the weekend. We could see if she'd like her nails done as well. It might cheer her up a bit."

The afternoon out would be the first for Nora Wallace since the loss of her husband Charlie. The two had shared a twin room in The Friary since a break-in at their farmhouse in Fermoy had left them too vulnerable to live alone.

As soon as the breakfast was over, Lucy approached Nora with her idea for a relaxing bath instead of her usual shower.

"It'd be nice to have a bit of pampering before you go out with Michael," Lucy cajoled. "You've lovely lotions and potions in your room that we could try out."

Nora's son was a regular visitor to The Friary and was married with four children. Owing to the fact that he lived in a two-storey house, he'd been upset that he hadn't been able to look after his parents at home and made every effort to give them as much help and attention as possible.

"I suppose I could," Nora agreed, not her usual chirpy self. Lucy and the rest of the staff knew that she missed Charlie desperately but were at a loss as to how to help her.

An hour later, the elderly lady was tucked up in her armchair with a cup of tea, dressed up to the nines for the arrival of her son.

"I've instructions to give you a professional manicure," Lucy told her with a smile, producing a shell-pink nail polish and a rich Royal Jelly hand cream from Una's stash.

"I'll be watching you," Nora teased with a hint of a smile. "I was always very fussy about my nails. Charlie used to admire them all the time."

"Really?" Lucy was glad that Nora was at least mentioning Charlie again. "I thought most men wouldn't notice things like nails at all."

"They'll always notice if you take care of yourself," she advised. "You have to make the effort, you know, or men lose interest."

"My mother's always telling me that I should make more of myself," Lucy told her, smiling at the consensus of opinion as she started on Nora's thumbnail. Unused to painting nails, she left far too much varnish on the tiny brush, creating a large blob that ran into the cuticle.

"Well, you should, Lucy. You're a lovely girl and very kind. Have you a fellow at all?"

Normally, Lucy avoided any kind of personal conversation at work but since meeting Rosa and Kate at The Gourmet Rooms, she felt able to open up a little. She'd always responded negatively to questions before, dreading having to admit to having no social life, hobby or boyfriend.

"I'm afraid not," she responded now, glad that Nora was engaging in conversation at all.

"You will have in time. Don't waste your life waiting around for him though. You'll have to go out and look, you know. I think you'll have to get the acetone," she added as Lucy tried in vain to repair the mess she'd made.

"I think you're right," she admitted, heading off to the clinical room to get the nail-varnish remover. Perhaps Nora was right about more than the acetone, she reflected, as she rummaged through bottles of Calamine Lotion and iodine to find it.

"Now," she announced to Nora when she arrived back with the acetone and a few cotton wool pads, "we'll start again and you can tell me how to do it properly."

"Only put a small bit on the brush and go in downward strokes. The bright colours are fine if you have good nails but, even if they're filed short for work, the clear varnish will polish them up a bit."

"How did you meet Charlie?" Lucy asked now, hoping to draw Nora out a little while they both focussed on the nails.

"He was doing a line with a girl I knew when I met him but it came to an end – I can't remember why now. He asked me up at a dance a few weeks later. I was going to say no on account of the other girl but I danced in the end because he was a nice fellow. I took a chance, as they say, and I was never sorry after. You have to take a chance now and again, Lucy."

"I suppose you're right, Nora. Now, how's that?"

Nora inspected her nails for a moment before sitting back and smiling gratefully at her carer. "Charlie would have been delighted with them."

"That's a compliment of the highest order," Lucy grinned, gathering up her things. "Now, I'd better have your coat ready so we won't delay Michael."

Nora's words of wisdom stayed with her for the rest of the morning. It was true what she'd said about wasting her life waiting for things to happen. Lucy had always presumed that she was a boring person to whom nothing exciting ever happened. It now occurred to her that people like Cathy and Rosa went out and made things happen.

Almost as if to prove Nora's point about taking a chance now and then, Cathy broached the subject of hair with Lucy in the canteen at lunch-time.

"I presume you're not interested but Barbara just texted me. They're looking for models at Hair Affair again."

Cathy was forever asking the girls at work to pose as models in the hair salon where her younger sister was training. To date, Lucy had always declined, terrified of looking foolish if one of the students made a mess of her already miserable hair.

"Are you going?"

"Definitely – just to get my fringe cut. One of Mrs Grimes' grandchildren told me I looked like Dora the Explorer yesterday."

Lucy giggled, much to Cathy's annoyance. With her glossy black hair cut in a thick fringe, she did indeed look like Dora.

"What kind of thing would they do on my hair? It's very fine."

"Something a bit shorter, kicked out a bit. You'd have to blow-dry it every time though."

Lucy thought of Nora telling her that it was worth it to make an effort.

"Go on then," she decided impulsively. "I can always grow it back if they do a mental job on it!"

Stunned, Cathy reached for her mobile to text Barbara before her generally cautious colleague changed her mind.

A few hours later, Lucy found herself sitting in a high chair in the glamorous salon with Cathy grinning at her in the mirror. Both of them had had their hair washed and were sitting back relaxing while the tutor gave final instructions to the trainees. At least, Cathy was relaxing. Lucy was too nervous of what was to come.

"Hello, my love. I'm Rocky. What can I do for you this evening?"

Glancing up from her daydream, Lucy was confronted – via the mirror – with the strangest character she'd ever seen. Even his voice, high-pitched and singsong, was a little ambiguous.

"Oh," Lucy responded, stunned by the closely cropped, bright purple hair and red and green velvet ensemble. As far as she could make out, he was dressed entirely in women's clothing, the long red coat decadent over matching palazzo pants and a green beaded tunic. Lucy wondered how on earth he was going to cut someone's hair dressed in a coat but could see that it was exactly what he intended to do when he placed two stretchy, metallic bands around the sleeves to hold them up.

"Mmm . . . very fine. Needs something to lift it a little."

Rocky leaned on the back of Lucy's chair while he considered the situation, all the while plucking at her hair as if checking that it wouldn't come out in clumps. Cathy, at the next station, was chatting amiably about her fringe with a normal-looking young girl with a blonde ponytail. How well I'd get the *artiste,* Lucy fumed, trying to catch Cathy's eye in the mirror.

"Okay," Rocky announced after a long pause. "Winona Ryder or Cameron Diaz – your call."

Considering that Lucy didn't actually know what Winona Ryder looked like and had only seen a picture of Cameron Diaz about a week ago when she'd asked Cathy about her, the choice was somewhat limited. But how odd that he had picked on Cameron Diaz, just as Rosa had done!

"Cameron Diaz," she blurted out, acutely aware that she was trapped in the chair with no real means of escape.

"Bravo!" Rocky commended as he wielded a small pair of scissors and waited for his tutor to move along the line.

"Have you long left to do?" Lucy was asking this for more than polite conversation. She was terrified that he was going to say that he was only in his first year.

"Nearly finished – about six months left to go. Then it's off out into the big, bad world for me. Thailand, here I come."

"You're going to Thailand?" Lucy wondered if there was a shortage of hairdressers there.

"Definitely. It's a much freer society than here. Don't worry, I won't ask have you any holidays planned."

He laughed merrily at this, tilting his head girlishly at her in the mirror. Lucy wondered what he'd be like in a 'freer society' if this was how he looked like in a conservative one. His face, she noticed, was beautifully made-up with long black eyelashes that she thought might be false.

"Thailand sounds lovely," was all she could think to say as the tutor approached and started to question Rocky. Cathy's fringe, she noticed, was starting to take shape.

"Right so," the tutor announced eventually.

Rocky, obviously raring to go, brandished his scissors over Lucy's head and lifted a bit of her hair.

"Ready to rock!" was the last thing she heard before closing her eyes and letting him get on with it.

Despite his chattiness earlier, when it came to cutting hair, Rocky was a man of few words. For twenty minutes, his face was a study of concentration, a deep frown marring his perfect features. Lucy used the time constructively, planning her future as a thinner, more interesting person.

On Rosa's advice, she was now walking the short distance to The Friary instead of hopping into her car at every opportunity. Today, she walked to Good For You after work, home to Bramwell Court for her dinner and back into Hair Affair to meet Cathy. The small Stepometer she'd bought in Sports Scene when she went to get her runners was now telling her that she'd done her 10,000 steps for the day – an amount she wouldn't have done in a fit a few weeks ago. Already, she noticed her work uniforms were getting a bit looser, something that gave her a great boost of confidence. A few weeks ago, she'd been planning to get a bigger size, now she was determined to aim for a smaller size when the uniform fitters came to The Friary in January. The thought of getting a Size 14 for the first time in years was as exhilarating to Lucy as a Size 10 would be to most people.

"Stunning!" Rocky announced eventually, although Lucy couldn't see how he could tell when her hair was still wet. "You'll have to come back in for a few highlights some evening though if you really want to carry off this Cameron Diaz thing."

"I'm not exactly sure . . ."

"Why not? You have the same eyes. Very few people

have that startling blue that she has. You could make a bit more of it with eye make-up though."

Lucy had been about to tell him that she wasn't so sure of his idea about the highlights – not wonder about whether she could turn into Cammy, as Rosa called her.

"Now, you're going to need a bit of volumising serum to hold this. I use this one," Rocky advised, holding up an electric-green tub.

Lucy wasn't convinced that what was good for Rocky would necessarily be good for her but decided to go with Nora Wallace's mantra of taking a chance now that she'd started.

Soon, Rocky was blow-drying away to his heart's content. Cathy, her own minor renovation complete, had parked herself next to Lucy to offer encouragement.

"You're amazing, Rocky," she flattered, obviously hoping for a freebie at some time in the future. "Lucy looks years younger. You do, Lucy, honestly. The shorter style suits you."

"More shape," Rocky agreed expansively, while Lucy started to study herself in the mirror. She did look younger actually. And her face looked a bit less round – although that could have been more to do with Rosa's obsession with grams of fat rubbing off on her.

"You go, girl!" Rocky stood back to admire his finished handiwork.

Cathy, eager to compliment her younger sister's workmate and boost Lucy's confidence, started to applaud excitedly.

"It's fabulous!" she declared, drawing the attention of the whole salon down on Lucy's head. A head, Lucy had to admit, that looked a lot better than the one she'd came in with.

"It's an excellent cut, Rocky," the tutor commented. Her protégé glowed with pride as the rest of the group joined in the scrutiny.

Lucy felt like a specimen under a microscope as the tutor took the opportunity to point out all that Rocky had done well with the haircut. It pleased her, funnily, to have a bit of positive attention when normally she'd have run a mile.

"We're definitely going for a drink after this," Cathy insisted as they paid their ? 10 and left Hair Affair a few minutes later, waved off by an ecstatic Rocky. Barbara was thrilled that her sister had brought a friend who'd consented to such a dramatic transformation and slipped Lucy a few tester-sized pots of the electric-green volumising serum to experiment with at home.

"I'll have some job recreating this in the morning before my early shift," Lucy sighed as soon as the two of them were settled in the front lounge of Jury's Inn, the nearest bar to the hair salon.

"Just set the clock a bit earlier. It looks great, Lucy. Barbara was always telling me that Rocky is really talented but I was terrified of trying him out before. I think he's right about the highlights – they'd look great."

"He's a bit flamboyant, isn't he?"

"He's definitely that – but really nice with it. Did he tell you he's saving up to go to Thailand for gender-reassignment surgery?"

"What? He mentioned Thailand but I presumed he

was going there to work. Is he going from male to female?" Rocky was such an androgynous character that it was hard to tell for definite what his true sex was.

"Yeah, he's always wanted to be a woman apparently. He's already started to take his oestrogen and everything. He's very open about it."

Lucy sipped her vodka and tonic and envied Rocky the ability to be open about his life, however traumatic it must be for him to live as a man when he so clearly wished to be a woman.

"Fair play to him – it'd be great to be like him" she said wistfully, thinking of the sense of freedom that honesty could bring.

"Jesus, Lucy, don't get carried away!" Cathy shrieked, missing the point. "You'd be desperate-looking with purple hair."

Chapter 15

Kate was going through the ordering process with Emma for the third time when the bell tinkled and Agnes poked her head around the door. On Mrs Carter's orders, the two of them were heading off to the Farmers' Market in Midleton to investigate seasonal organic vegetables in preparation for their fourth class at The Gourmet Rooms. For the first time ever, Kate would be leaving Good For You in the capable hands of her new assistant.

"Hi, Agnes, I'm nearly ready," she called out, admiring the older lady's sense of style.

Today, Agnes was wearing fitted navy wool trousers and a light green jacket with a navy trim on the sleeves and collar. As usual, she had a small silk scarf tied elegantly at her throat, this time a blend of navy, green and ivory to tie in with the cream wool top she wore under the jacket. Even her smart navy court shoes matched the outfit.

"No hurry, I'll just pop down the back for a minute to the books."

Kate turned her attention back to Emma, reminding her that taking the customer's phone number was essential so that she could phone them if there was a problem with their order.

"And if anything *really* drastic happens," she smiled, "you can give me a ring on the mobile – we're only going as far as Midleton."

"Grand so, Kate. Enjoy your lunch."

"I'd want to – seeing as it's the first Saturday I've had off in ten years! I'd better see where Agnes has disappeared to." She made for the little library at the back of the shop.

It still amazed her how much her customers loved the few bookshelves and the pair of comfy antique chairs that she'd set up from the outset. Kate felt that it allowed people to look up their ailments or concerns in privacy, especially if it was a busy time and they didn't want to broadcast their complaint to the whole shop.

"Before we go, Kate," Agnes said, looking up from a pamphlet, "I must ask you about antioxidants."

"Is it in relation to heart health?"

Kate liked to find out exactly what benefits a person was looking for before she overloaded them with unnecessary information.

"Well, no." She hesitated a little. "It's just Rosa. She was telling Lucy and me about them the other night. That they slow down the ageing process."

"They do actually. Take that leaflet with you and I'll photocopy a few other things for you over the weekend. Tomatoes are amazing, if you're thinking of increasing your food sources. All the red foods are good – beetroot, grapes, red cabbage. A glass of red wine is good as well."

"Really? I must remember that the next time I'm out anywhere."

"Vitamin E is another good one. You can pierce a Vitamin E capsule and rub it into your skin to make it more supple. I'll get you a few capsules to try out, if you like."

"Oh, that would be lovely, Kate." Agnes looked less embarrassed now, Kate thought as she went off to get a handful of the Vitamin E capsules and retrieve her handbag from under the counter.

Agnes was delighted with all the information on ageing, even though Kate took pains to reassure her that she showed very few signs of her sixty-five years. Considering that she cared full-time for her disabled sister, she looked super and was always groomed to perfection.

"You're so good to come and pick me up, Agnes – I really appreciate it."

Kate, sitting beside Agnes in the ancient Mazda, was grateful for the sedate manner in which the city streets were being negotiated.

"Did you ever learn to drive, Kate?"

"Years ago. But I had a bad car accident and I haven't had the inclination to drive since."

"That's terrible. Were you badly hurt?"

"I was in hospital for months," Kate admitted, taking a deep breath before telling Agnes the rest of it. "My husband was killed in the accident, Agnes, so I couldn't bear to get back behind the wheel. And when I moved to Cork, I had no real need for a car."

"I'm very sorry to hear about your husband, Kate. I didn't mean to pry."

"That's okay. It's thirteen years ago now."

"It's still hard, I imagine – things like that are. It doesn't matter how many years go by."

Kate glanced over but her companion's face was inscrutable. As far as she knew, Agnes had never been married but the wistfulness in her voice sounded very real and heartfelt.

"How is the new assistant getting on?" Agnes asked then, as if she were purposely changing the subject.

"Brilliant. She's a really fast learner and she knows nearly all the regulars now. I was a bit afraid of leaving her alone initially but she's well into the routine at this stage."

"It must have been hard to manage it all on your own," Agnes commented.

"When I opened first, I didn't have much choice. The business took a while to take off properly so I really couldn't afford an assistant. After that it became a habit."

"I know what you mean, Kate. It's easy to get into a rut. If I didn't have the cookery course to get me out of the house, I'd go mad."

"Does Beatrice get out and about at all? I know a lot of places have problems with wheelchair access."

"Don't talk to me about wheelchair access. You know that coffee shop in the Marble Island shopping centre? We used to go there after Mass most Sundays until they renovated it. Now they have state-of-the-art toilet facilities but there are three steps up to the front door so we can't even get into the place!"

Kate laughed at Agnes's comical telling of the story but was very aware of the frustrations that many wheelchair users encountered.

"There's a lady that comes into the shop – she's a public health nurse – and she's always talking about the lack of facilities for chair-users. She covers your area actually, so you probably know her."

"I don't think so. What's her name?"

"Catherine Tierney. She's very nice."

"We've never had a public health nurse visiting, to be honest. I remember a lady came once offering to help when Mother was alive but she was sent packing. I think Mother was afraid of Bea being put into a home if she couldn't manage her."

"I think things have changed a lot since then, Agnes. A good number of my customers have the public health nurse coming and they get great help. You should look into it."

"But what could they do for Bea at this stage? No matter what kind of therapies she'd get from them, I don't think it would make a difference, to be honest."

"I think it's things like respite care that they offer, rather than therapies," Kate explained, a little shocked that Agnes was receiving no help whatsoever. "You know the term, do you? Respite? Residential care to give people like you a break?"

"Yes, but Bea would never agree to it," Agnes stated vehemently. "I remember Dr Donnelly mentioning it a few years ago and there was murder because it was into the County Home that she'd have to go."

Kate had heard people speak of the dreaded County

Home before, an old institution that was long gone but one that still stuck firmly in the memory of many elderly people.

"But, Agnes, it's all these new Respite Centres now – purpose-built places where people can go for a holiday break with full-time care. I have one customer whose mother goes into Summer Orchard for a week every two months and she loves it."

Agnes mentioned that she'd seen a feature on the opening of Summer Orchard in *The Examiner* earlier in the year but had presumed that it would be outrageously expensive to stay there.

"It's free, as far as I know. Beatrice would love it, I imagine. I'll ask Catherine Tierney about it if you like, Agnes."

"Would you? I could put it to Bea if I knew a bit more about it and see what she thinks. She's very set in her ways though." Agnes indicated and turned left into Midleton. "I hope we're able to find this market."

"I think it's just off the roundabout. I can't wait to see if we can get the artichokes."

"God, Kate, I'm delighted you're with me. I'd be a right disaster trying to pick them out on my own."

Agnes negotiated her way into an empty space right next to the newly developed market area, exclaiming at their good luck at such close proximity to the row of open stalls.

"It's the cooking of them that I'm worried about, although I hope we're not too late for all the good stuff," Kate said, lifting her small wicker basket out of the back seat. Agnes took a similar one out of the boot and the two women joined the midday shoppers thronging the paved square. The market ran from ten until two every Saturday and it was already past one o'clock.

"Don't worry," Agnes reassured her. "We'll get as much as we can. This looks great, doesn't it, Kate?"

"Cheese heaven!" Kate grinned, making straight for the stand nearest to them.

It was indeed a cheese-lovers' oasis, the linen tablecloth laden with a mouth-watering selection. Small plates of testers were lined up at the front and Kate speared a tiny chunk of creamy goat's cheese straightaway.

"Try this, Agnes. It's gorgeous. I might get a bit and do the thing with the sun-dried tomatoes tomorrow."

Vying with the rest of the punters gathered around the stand, she identified her choice to the young girl manning the table.

"How much will I give you?" the girl asked, indicating the wheel with her knife. Kate loved the excitement of open markets, although she usually ended up with far more of the speciality breads and cheeses than she needed. This time, she decided to go for a small piece in anticipation of the other things she might come across in the course of the afternoon.

"I think I'll get some too," said Agnes. "I might inveigle Bea into having it with me later."

A few minutes later, Kate's cheese was joined by a rich jalapeno chutney. Agnes, in a burst of adventure, chose a blueberry relish from the same stand.

"Bea will think I'm trying to poison her," she joked

with Kate, holding up the jar for her to inspect the dark blue contents.

Kate was about to point out that Agnes was hardly likely to poison her sister at this late stage when a handsome man with silvery grey hair standing next to them made exactly the same comment. He was smiling broadly at Agnes as he said this, the familiar tone telling Kate that the two knew each other already.

"Willie!" Agnes exclaimed.

She looked a bit shocked, Kate noticed.

"It's good to see you again, Agnes," he continued, still smiling at her.

Kate stood back a little, observing the interaction between them. Agnes explained that she and Kate had taken the trip to Midleton to source organic vegetables for the next phase of a cookery class they were doing, introducing Kate in the process.

"I can't see that you'll have much to learn, Agnes. She was always a good cook," he added to Kate.

Reddening a little at the praise, Agnes asked Willie if he was a regular visitor to the market.

"Miriam comes nearly every week. Sometimes I tag along and stock up from the fellow who does the organic chocolate."

"It'll be the death of you yet, that organic chocolate."

This came from a small, rotund lady with closely cropped grey hair who'd just turned away from the Rosbeg Preserves stand with a large brown-paper bag in her arms. She was about the same age as Agnes and was dressed casually in jeans and a red cotton sweater.

"Miriam," Willie introduced enthusiastically, "this is Agnes Cotter, the lady I told you about. Agnes lives just outside Rathcabben. And this is her friend Kate."

"Hello, it's lovely to meet you both," Miriam smiled. "Isn't the market marvellous?"

Agnes, Kate noticed, looked a little bit pale but started to chat away in her usual lively manner to Willie and Miriam about the market and their classes at The Gourmet Rooms. Deducing that Agnes and Willie were old friends from the past, Kate was curious as to why Agnes appeared so nervous in his company.

Conscious that it was nearing two o'clock, she noticed that a few of the stall owners were starting to dismantle their awnings and pack up the remaining produce.

"If you'll excuse me," she interrupted politely, "I'll just go and investigate the vegetable stand. You stay put, Agnes, and I'll buy for both of us. It was lovely to meet you both."

Willie shook her hand firmly while Miriam pointed her in the direction of a dark green awning that had *Lorcan Reddy Organic* written on it in cream-coloured script. Agnes was still looking a little at sea but Kate felt it would have been rude to drag her away.

She made her way over to the far side of the square, a little alarmed to see the stallholder removing three large empty baskets from the front of the stand and stowing them in a dark green van with the same logo as the awning.

"Are you finishing up?" Kate enquired, addressing the man's back. He was tall, she noticed fleetingly, his shoulders and arms muscled from physical work.

"Just packing away the empties," he told her, turning around to address her properly. "I'm afraid there's not much left today."

"Oh . . . I . . ." Kate's breath caught in her throat and the words didn't seem to be able to come out. Starting to colour slightly at this failure of her vocal chords, Kate looked around the rows of neat wicker baskets, startled at the sudden increase in her heart rate.

"Were you looking for anything in particular?"

He was smiling slightly, towering above her even though he was leaning on the table in front of him. His eyes, ringed with the longest lashes she'd ever seen on a man, were somewhere between green and brown.

"Artichokes," she got out at last, dredging up at least one of Mrs Carter's requirements. Whatever effect this giant of a man was having on her, it certainly wasn't good for her.

"I have some in the back for the market in Macroom this afternoon. Hang on and I'll get them."

As soon as he'd turned his back, Kate took a deep breath and tried to pull herself together. She never behaved like this around men – especially ones that she didn't know from the back of a bus. Although she had to admit to herself that he was exceptionally handsome, she didn't think it was just his looks that had such an effect on her. It was the curiously gentle way that he'd spoken that had made her heart start to beat faster, as well as the feeling that he was standing much closer to her than he actually was.

The crowd in the market square had thinned out a

little by now but there were still a few customers examining the remaining selection of ripe beef tomatoes and bunches of carrots with the green leaves still on.

A thin man in a trench coat standing next to her was prodding and squeezing all the produce, reminding Kate of a Moore Street trader she'd seen on television telling a customer "They're not mickeys, love – they won't get any bigger if you squeeze them!". She smiled to herself at the thought.

"Are globe artichokes okay?"

He was back now with a full tray of artichokes and it occurred to Kate that she ought to have done a little more research. She and Agnes hadn't even decided how many they'd need. She glanced around but couldn't see Agnes.

"They're great," she said enthusiastically, hoping that she sounded as if she knew what she was talking about. "I'll take six of them."

"Grand so."

Realising that she was supposed to be shopping for both herself and Agnes, Kate looked around to see what else she needed to get. Butternut squash, for one thing, she thought as she spotted two remaining ones at the far left of the table.

"I'll take these as well," she told him, examining him in more detail as he placed the artichokes carefully in a brown-paper bag. His hair, cut short, was light blond with the golden streaks that came from working outdoors. His face and arms were tanned and despite the fact that it was early October, he wore a short-sleeved navy T-shirt with his well-worn jeans.

"I'll take a few of these as well," she said, indicating the basket of beef tomatoes in front of her. This would mean a trip back to the cheese stall for some of the delicious balls of mozzarella that she'd had to stop herself buying earlier, she realised, imagining the combination of sweet tomato slices and the creamy buffalo cheese with some of the basil pesto that Mrs Carter had recommended as one of their kitchen staples.

"They're lovely with mozzarella and basil," the vegetable man commented, as if he'd read her thoughts.

"I was just thinking that," she told him in amazement.

He smiled then, a wide grin that showed perfect white teeth, and told her the price.

Kate handed over ?10 and started to pack the vegetables away in her basket as he counted out her change.

"There you go."

Their hands touched as he placed the coins in Kate's extended palm. She looked up then and was startled to find that he was looking right into her eyes, his lips parted as if he was about to say something else.

"How much are these per pound?" This interruption was from the trench-coat man who was trying to elbow his way in between Kate and an older lady who'd been there first.

Forcibly moved out of the way, Kate thanked the vegetable man in a voice that came out in a sort of whisper and turned away from the stand, wondering if she was just imagining it or if something really momentous had just happened in her life.

Agnes sat in the car with her head in her hands, unaware

that Kate was wandering around the market looking for her. Realising suddenly that people were probably staring at her, she sat up straight and tried to pull herself together. She caught sight of herself in the rear-view mirror and noticed how pale she'd become since putting on her make-up that morning. Wishing that Kate would return to the car so that she could escape from Midleton as quickly as possible, she retrieved her handbag from the glove compartment and started to touch up her face a little.

She felt better once she'd dabbed her cheeks with pressed powder and renewed her lipstick. Thanking God that she'd been able to hold it together until she'd returned to the safe haven of the Mazda, she lay back against the seat and took a deep breath, unable to stop herself from reliving her conversation with Willie and Miriam.

She'd been pleasantly surprised to find that Miriam wasn't the sophisticated creature that she'd imagined Willie's wife to be and had even felt slightly glamorous compared to the other lady who wore oldish jeans and a red, crew-necked jumper that made her look barrel-shaped. Glad that she didn't feel inferior in the style department, Agnes had felt able to converse easily about the farmers' market and her cookery class without feeling defensive about her life as she'd imagined she would be on meeting Miriam.

The fact that she was actually a very nice person was also a surprise to Agnes. She'd even commented on Kate and how lucky Agnes was to have a wide circle of friends.

"I'm just getting to know the place at the moment but I suppose that's what I get for moving to the sticks at my time of life! I should join a class of some sort myself to get to know people."

"Well, I can certainly recommend The Gourmet Rooms. Are you from Dublin originally, Miriam?" Agnes was curious to know more about the life that Willie had led since she'd last known him.

"Yes – from Howth. I was adamant that we had to be near the sea if we were emigrating to Cork because I've lived on the coast all my life."

"Well, you're in the right place in Rathcabben. Are your children living in Dublin?"

"We haven't got around to having any yet," Miriam joked, laughing over at Willie. "We're only married a year."

Agnes nearly collapsed. Surely it wasn't possible that Willie Boyle had been single all these years?

"Late starters," Willie confirmed with a grin, "but better late than never."

"That's marvellous," Agnes enthused with difficulty, feeling overwhelmed by this new information but unable to stop herself probing further. "Were you working in the Bank as well, Miriam?"

"God, no, I'd be dangerous if I was let loose with all that money. I was a primary school teacher but I took early retirement a few years ago. I met Willie when I went in to pay off the last of my mortgage."

"You're making me sound very unethical, Miriam! We met again at an art exhibition a few weeks later and it went from there," he explained to Agnes.

"That's marvellous," Agnes repeated, her mind whirling with the idea that she might have been able to re-ignite her relationship with Willie at any point over the past four decades if only she'd been able to stand up to Beatrice. It was also occurring to her that she didn't deserve someone as decent and loyal as Willie Boyle if she had so little backbone.

At last she made her escape from the couple, her heart hard with envy at Miriam's luck in finding someone like Willie and having the freedom to enjoy it.

She started now as Kate's face appeared at the passenger side of the car.

"Sorry, Agnes, I spent ages looking for you. It only occurred to me a few minutes ago that you might have gone back to the car to wait."

"That's fine, Kate. Will we head off?"

She was terrified of breaking down in front of Kate, afraid that she might think her foolish for being bothered about Willie after forty years. It wasn't actually Willie that was upsetting her so much – it was the idea that so much of her life had been engineered by Bea who, despite her sacrifices, treated her like a hired housekeeper.

"Are you all right, Agnes? You're very pale." Kate looked concerned, making Agnes realise that she mustn't have made a very good job of her make-up after all.

"I'm grand – a bit tired," she countered.

"Let's forget the lunch and go straight home. You'll be able to have a lie-down for the evening."

Earlier in the day, they'd been planning to have a late lunch but the thought of sitting in a crowded restaurant didn't appeal to Agnes at all now. Nor, for that matter, did going home to Beatrice.

"Will we head back towards Cork and decide about lunch on the way?"

"Whatever you want, Agnes," Kate agreed. "Do you feel okay to drive?"

It was Kate's kindness and concern that made the two small tears squeeze out of Agnes's eyes and creep slowly down her cheeks. She brushed them away quickly, apologising for being so out of sorts.

"Sorry for being so miserable on our day out, Kate. I didn't mean to abandon you with all the vegetables." She'd only just noticed the basket at Kate's feet.

"That's fine, Agnes. It can be a bit much meeting people from the past. It's why I moved away from Dublin actually, to get away from people talking about Timmy all the time. You're the first person I've mentioned him to in years."

Agnes was surprised at how perceptive Kate was in knowing that it was meeting Willie and Miriam that had upset her. She was also pleased that Kate felt able to mention Timmy to her, considering how little they knew each other.

"We were supposed to get married, you see," she found herself saying, "but Mother got sick and I had to start looking after Bea."

Now that she'd started, Agnes was relieved to be telling someone about the life that she'd let go. She started the car and reversed out onto the street, glad to have a distraction while she unburdened herself. Kate listened silently, her presence calm and comforting.

Agnes was still talking when they pulled up in the

narrow lane at the side of Kate's shop and she felt lighter than she had in years. Normally, she'd have felt disloyal and bitchy talking about Bea and all she'd given up to care for her but today, for the first time ever, she felt justified. It wasn't caring for her sister that was the problem so much as the fact that she was expected to do it to the exclusion of everything else.

"Would you like to come in for a bit and have some lunch? We could both do with a cup of tea and you'd be able to recover a bit before you go home."

Kate should have been a counsellor, Agnes thought now. She spoke very little yet when she did, she seemed to know exactly the right thing to say.

"Are you sure you don't have things to do in the shop?"

"If Emma's managed this long, she'll manage another few hours. You go on up," she said, handing Agnes the key to the street entrance. "I'll pop in and tell Emma we're home. She can lock up as well – it'll be good experience for her."

Having a late lunch in Kate's house was exactly what she needed, Agnes realised as she let herself into the small entrance hall and ascended the narrow, sisal-covered stairs. A pang of envy struck her when she saw the cosy flat, its comforting mix of cream walls and soft blue furnishings reminding her of the little flat that she'd lived in before she'd moved back home all those years ago.

"Sorted!" Kate announced, arriving up from the shop below, just as Agnes was filling the kettle in the kitchen area.

"I'm making myself at home – I hope you don't mind."

"All assistance welcome," Kate smiled, starting to unpack her basket. "Look – I got the artichokes. The fellow on the stall asked me if 'globe' ones were what I was looking for. I couldn't show my ignorance so I took them. I got us a butternut squash each as well and some tomatoes. Will we have them for lunch with the cheese? I got some nice bread as well."

"Thanks, Kate, that would be lovely."

Agnes plucked two blue china mugs off the mug tree and thought how great it would be to have her own place to live with no interference from her sister.

"I'll be starting to draw my pension in the New Year," she told Kate now.

"You certainly don't look your age, Agnes. It'll be great to have your own income, though."

It was a relief to have told Kate about all the scrimping and saving that she had to do over the years.

"I've been looking forward to it all year but today really brought it home to me. I can't always be using Bea as an excuse for everything. If I'd stood up for myself years ago, I wouldn't be whinging and whining about everything here today."

"We all need to let off steam now and again. You should have seen me after the accident. I was like a banshee. I didn't even want to get out of bed. You were great to keep going, Agnes, despite all you had to give up."

"At the time, I thought I had no other option." Agnes was slicing the wholemeal loaf that Kate had picked up from the Alternative Bread Company stand on her way back to the car. She paused, the knife in mid-air. "From now on, Bea and I will have to come to a better arrangement. I'll have my own money soon and I'm going to make the most of it. I might even go on a holiday."

"So you should, Agnes. Maybe if you explain to Bea that you need more help at this stage, she'll understand a bit better. And I think you really should get in touch with Catherine Tierney about the Respite Centre."

"I'm determined to now," Agnes said firmly, accepting a delicious-looking tomato and mozzarella salad from Kate. "Things are definitely going to change from here on in."

"Good for you, Agnes." Kate raised her mug of tea in a toast to Agnes's future. "Cheers!"

"Cheers!" Agnes echoed, thinking of the delicious supper of stuffed artichokes that would be served in the Cotter household later that evening. There was no time like the present to introduce a new way of life.

Chapter 16

Lucy threw her jacket over the newel post of the stairs and brought her latest purchases through to the living room, detouring to the kitchen to put on the kettle first.

As well as some nuts and seeds, she'd bought a detox solution that she had to drink twice a day for a week to rid her body of any toxins that she'd built up from poor diet and lack of exercise. Kate had advised her that she'd be surprised at how much energy she'd have after the week, especially if she drank eight glasses of water a day as well. And the fact that she might lose a few pounds in the process Lucy considered to be a good thing.

It surprised her that she was already looking forward to telling Rosa about the detox programme. This was the same Rosa that she'd been terrified of on their first meeting but who she now understood a little better to the extent that she was more in awe of her than actually terrified.

Perhaps it was Rosa's childlike attitude to things that

made her so easy to get on with, Lucy thought now as she sat at the dining-room table sorting through the things she'd bought. She'd already started to nibble on the Brazil nuts, skipping her usual chocolate bar for a change.

Feeling slightly virtuous, she read the information slip on the large bottle of detox solution before smelling it gingerly and deciding that it wouldn't be too bad when it was diluted in the recommended pint of tepid water. Almost looking forward to taking it, she decided to hold off until a few hours after dinner when her stomach would be empty as Kate had suggested.

Next, she examined the small bottle of sweet almond oil she'd got to add her essential oils to. Since she'd started to take her pampering baths she'd become aware of how dry and coarse her skin was.

As if on cue, the doorbell pealed. Just as she reached it, another peal sounded, followed immediately by Rosa's face at one of the glass panels. She waved excitedly on spotting Lucy.

"I've all the ingredients. What do you think? Will we try out the vegetarian curry thing? We could make the banoffee if we put on the condensed milk straight away."

"Hello, yourself," Lucy greeted her pointedly, unable to suppress a grin. Rosa was the most exuberant person she'd ever met.

To Lucy's amazement, their unlikely union had started to strengthen, bound by the equity of their culinary ineptitude and by Rosa's diligent quest for a 'life path'. It seemed that both of her parents were in medicine, her father an Ear, Nose and Throat surgeon and her mother a psychologist. Rosa, aware that she was somewhat of a disappointment to them, said she had tried a selection of 'careers', all of which had been unsuitable for one reason or another.

Rosa tended to describe the story of her hunt for an appropriate career with a kind of upbeat nonchalance that suggested she really didn't care about failing to make the grade in the academic sense that her parents might like, yet Lucy sensed a slight sadness underlying the more outrageous tales.

Beauty Therapy had been one of her earliest endeavours. However, the idea of directing people towards the tanning booths and recommending the stylish nail treatments was soon overshadowed by the back-breaking labour of doing three or four full leg waxes in a row followed by the endless routine of electrolysis treatments and eyelash tints.

On that occasion, she'd persisted for almost a year, the vision of being the proprietor of a string of exclusive beauty salons holding her imagination until she realised that even managing an appointments system required a level of consideration that she wasn't prepared to give.

Lucy marvelled at her new friend's ability to bounce back and start again with whatever new project took her fancy but supposed that the financial cushion afforded by her parents must surely be all the incentive that she needed to start over.

The beginners' cookery course was to be the start of yet another opportunity for Rosa. She'd decided to take on the simple starter course as a precursor to an extortionately priced twelve-week course that would lead her into the realm of haute cuisine and the eventual opening of her own exclusive restaurant.

Watching her gingerly placing the two unopened tins of condensed milk in one of the large lobster pans that she'd found under the sink, Lucy had some doubts as to whether this latest venture of Rosa's would reach the desired conclusion.

"And we boil the tins for an hour for them to turn into toffee?" Rosa said over her shoulder, the gas blazing under the saucepan, even though the water from the kettle had already been boiling when she'd poured it in. "What if they burst?"

"I think she said to *simmer* them," Lucy told her pointedly as the lid of the saucepan rose menacingly and steam started to spurt dangerously from under it. "Though we'll only have to heat these ones through – I already simmered them for an hour last night."

"Grand so, I'll turn it down a bit. Do we have enough vegetables, do you think?"

Lucy figured that there were enough vegetables present to eradicate scurvy from the face of the earth and wondered exactly how many people it would take to eat the amount of vegetable curry that Rosa had in mind. Companionably they chopped away, placing the prepared items in a selection of matching glass bowls that Rosa had pulled out of one of the cupboards.

"How come you have all this state-of-the-art stuff if you didn't cook before?"

Rosa was hunting for a pot large enough to sauté

vegetables in prior to adding the selection of Indian spices and the tub of natural yoghurt that Lucy had at the ready. Lucy, shaken by the question, tried to answer in as blasé a tone as possible lest Rosa should question her on the fact that the house was a bit grand for a single girl who worked as a care assistant in a nursing home.

"Everything was here when I bought the house. I don't know how to use half of the things that were left. Here, give me that or you'll end up in traction."

Rosa gratefully handed over the large Le Creuset pot, amazed at its weight. They stared at it together, Lucy wondering practically how they were going to lift it when it was full of curry while Rosa had visions of having to enlist the help of the strapping engineer who'd moved into the house between her own and Lucy's.

"Do you think we should take the toffee out soon and let it cool while this is cooking? What if it's too hot and the cream melts?" Rosa asked after a while, looking up from the vegetables to consult the clock.

She was always anxious about getting things wrong, something she put down to never getting things as right as her parents expected. It amused Lucy no end that Rosa considered *her* an authority on cooking and kept checking that she was doing things properly before proceeding with the smallest step.

"Maybe we could put them in a pan of cold water after they're done to cool them down quickly. We could do the avocados for the starter while we're waiting."

Unable to credit that she was talking seriously about stuffing an avocado with prawns in a sour cream sauce,

Lucy hunted out the small, serrated kitchen knife that had come in their 'starter pack' and set to work while Rosa diligently tossed sliced bananas in lemon juice in preparation for the final stages of the banoffee.

"I can't believe our fourth week is over. And, you know, I always thought that vegetarian stuff would be all beans and lentils."

"So did I," Lucy admitted, "and I also thought all Indian food was extremely spicy. I'd never even tried it before now."

"The Italian class next week should be straightforward," Rosa commented, having got into a right state about the seasonal vegetables earlier in the week.

"The theory bit next week is going to be about setting up a catering business so you should enjoy that bit as well."

Every week, Mrs Carter did a 'theory' session towards the end of the class. They'd had a talk on buying and storing cheese the previous week and were due talks on organic farming, wines and herbs and spices in the coming weeks. Next up, however, was the session that Rosa had been looking forward to all along – the vagaries of setting up a small catering business.

"I hope it isn't too complicated," Rosa said anxiously. "I often get in over my head. If it came to it, I could hire a chef to get things off the ground but I'd really have to manage the rest myself."

This was, Lucy noticed, Rosa's first real admission that the opening of a restaurant in Bramwell Court might not be the easiest thing in the world to undertake. She hadn't mentioned things like insurance and permits at all, something that Lucy imagined must be a necessary part of the process. Not to mention health inspectors and restaurant critics. It would be interesting to see what Mrs Carter's 'expert' would have to say on Tuesday night.

"What kind of overheads would you have?" Lucy asked now, thinking of all the equipment that would be needed to upgrade the kitchen to a more industrial type one.

"I'm not sure, to be honest," Rosa admitted. "Mum and Dad would have to back me financially for a business loan for definite. I don't have much savings."

Lucy began to think that if Rosa's idea had been a little more solid and if she'd known her for a bit longer, the restaurant would have been an ideal venture to invest in. As it stood, however, she decided not to mention it. Maybe she could at a later stage, if the plan looked likely to come to fruition. Instead, she told Rosa that she was lucky to have parents who believed in her idea and were willing to support her.

"That's because they only have me to focus on," Rosa answered, crushing the biscuits for the base of the banoffee. "It's a bit claustrophobic sometimes – I suppose it's because I'm adopted that they're so overprotective."

"You're adopted?"

"Yeah – since I was a couple of weeks old." Rosa's chin jutted out a little as she said this, Lucy noticed, as if she were awaiting some kind of criticism. "They were oldish getting married and realised fairly quickly that they weren't able to have children. So they adopted me through some nuns that ran St Angela's at the time."

"Did you know from early on or were you told when

you were eighteen or something?" Lucy wondered how she herself would have felt to find out that her parents weren't really her parents at all.

"They told me from when I was really small – three or four, I think. It wasn't the done thing at the time but Mum felt that it'd be easier on me, less of a shock, rather than finding out as an adult."

"Did you mind – once you got older, I mean?" Lucy asked now, figuring that it was something that Rosa wanted to discuss, seeing as she'd brought it up.

"Not really, to be honest. It seemed normal to me because I didn't know any different."

"It's best to know from the beginning." Lucy wasn't sure what else to say.

"You know, Lucy ... you're the first person who hasn't asked me if I want to meet my birth mother."

"You're probably sick of being asked that. Although I can see why people would be curious," she added, sensing that Rosa herself was divided on the issue.

"I've thought about it, now and again. Mum and Dad have always been open to the idea but it's not something I ever felt I needed to do."

"Maybe it's the fact that your parents are open about it that lessens your curiosity. If it was something you weren't allowed to discuss, you might be more inclined to push for it."

"You're probably right, Lucy. Sometimes, I do wonder about things. Like if I was Mum and Dad's real daughter, would I be doing something in medicine right now?"

"God, Rosa, you should meet my mother! I'm no

more like her than the man in the moon. She organises things with military precision while I just sort of do things only when I have to."

"I suppose," Rosa conceded.

Observing Rosa, Lucy was in very little doubt about her feelings on finding her birth mother. Perhaps she was just afraid of what she might find if she did go looking, something that Lucy could appreciate.

"You never know, Rosa. You might change your mind in time," she said, sensing that maybe all that was needed was an opening to do so after years of declining the offer. Lucy knew all about missing the chance to say things and then not being able to find another opportunity.

As she told Rosa now, her own mother was always brisk and full of business, barely giving Lucy a chance to say a word without criticising her. Even Lucy's improved performance in the cooking stakes, something her mum had been harping on about forever, didn't quite meet with her approval.

It was hard to explain just how stunned Maura had been when she'd opened Lucy's freezer and found one of the drawers full of neatly labelled foil containers.

"Who did all these?" she'd demanded territorially, as if Lucy had secretly employed a third party to usurp Maura in her role as chief caretaker of her daughter's nutritional well-being.

"I told you, they're the things we do at the cookery class," Lucy had defended. "Mrs Carter's obsessed with freezing leftovers and doing things in big batches because it's more economical and you utilise the oven properly."

The proprietor of The Gourmet Rooms had great belief in economy and had drummed it into her class from Day One that it was almost a criminal offence to turn on a fan oven to cook only one item. Therefore a dish like lasagne should be served with roasted vegetables, followed by a baked dessert like the Chocolate Torte. Freezing leftover portions to avoid the necessity of buying convenience meals was another of her mantras, there being no excuse in her book for not eating wholesome, unprocessed food that could be prepared in minutes.

"I'm telling you, Rosa, it's impossible to please her. I'd have to open a restaurant myself before my mother would believe I'd be capable of minding myself. I think it's the curse of being an only child."

"You're right about that for sure. If they had someone else to focus on they wouldn't need to be so involved."

Lucy, as if to demonstrate her grasp of Mrs Carter's economic policies, had by now covered the extra portion of rice that she'd added to the amount they needed to serve with the curry, planning to use it for stuffed peppers the following evening.

Rosa had neatly segregated a batch of the vegetables that they'd prepared, eventually realising that there was enough to feed a small army, and had announced her intention of roasting them the following evening.

Finally satisfied that everything was in order, they set the table in Lucy's imposing dining room, conscious of Mrs Carter's constant warnings of the hazards of poor digestion caused by rushed meals in front of the television.

"Avocado with King Prawn in a soured cream sauce,

seasonal vegetables cooked in the finest Indian spices, followed by a rich banoffee pie!" Lucy announced triumphantly, her enthusiasm rubbing off on Rosa who immediately speared a succulent prawn and scoffed it before wondering out loud whether banoffee would freeze without the bananas going black.

Chapter 17

"Tell me again why I didn't have an assistant before now?"

Kate stood at the bottom of the stepladder taking the large bottles and jars that Emma was handing down to her before dusting them off with a damp cloth and handing them back up.

"You just didn't come across anyone as efficient as me before now, that's all," Emma replied, finally declaring the job finished and descending the ladder.

The shop was reasonably quiet for a Friday afternoon with a few people browsing before settling on purchases.

"It makes such a difference, you know, having you here. I used to spend all evening doing the accounts and putting through the stock orders. No wonder I had no time for anything else."

Kate knew that holding off on getting someone to help her in the shop had only been an excuse to avoid building a normal life, yet she could acknowledge that she just hadn't been ready for it. She'd known all along that people grieved in different ways but she'd never have believed that she was only now coming to terms with the past after thirteen years.

She'd been able to talk to Agnes about it the day that they'd went to the farmers' market in Midleton, opening up for the first time about Timmy and the accident. She'd even told her a little about losing her baby in the aftermath, something that Agnes had become quite emotional about. She too had lost her chance of having a family of her own and had seemed to understand the sense of finality that Kate had felt for years.

"I'm a bit like that at the moment," Emma said now, referring to Kate's comment about not having any time. "I've the reflexology class at half seven this evening so I feel I'm just tearing from A to B all the time."

Emma worked as a nurse in the Aged Care unit at St Angela's and had injured her back in a skiing incident a few years previously. She was acutely aware that if it continued to play up on a regular basis, her career in the hospital would no longer be viable. Hence, she'd cut down on her hospital hours to work two days every week in Good For You and was in the process of qualifying as a reflexologist. Her next step would be to qualify as an aromatherapist, with a view to starting her own holistic service in the future.

"Will you even have time to go home this evening after work?"

"I'll stay around town and have something to eat and swot up a bit on the theory."

"Well, Agnes is coming over at six so if you're not

afraid of being poisoned, you're welcome to have dinner with us. I could do with an independent observer!"

"That would be lovely, Kate – if you're sure I won't upset your concentration."

"Not at all. It'll be great to have another real live person to try it out on for a change."

"Surely you're not that bad?"

"Don't bet on it! I'll head upstairs for a while and get the orders out of the way. Come on up as soon as you lock up."

Kate made her way towards the counter at the front of the shop to retrieve the small file that they used on a daily basis to list any items that needed to be ordered specially for a particular customer. She was thrilled that she'd asked Emma to stay for dinner, considering it another step towards making a proper life for herself.

Her eyes were drawn to the window as the light was obscured momentarily by a dark green van parking on the kerb outside. She noticed immediately that it was the same van that she'd seen at the market, her heart going a little faster when she saw the cream script that read *Lorcan Reddy Organic* on the side.

Berating herself for being ridiculous, she nonetheless paused at the counter to see who would emerge, although she didn't actually have a view of the front of the van. She knew that there could be any number of similar vans belonging to the same company with any number of people driving them, yet she was unable to drag herself away until she was sure.

She continued to stare at the window, almost ignoring

the chime of the doorbell in her eagerness to see who would swing open the double doors at the back of the van.

Just as she started to visualise the man from the Midleton market carrying a tray of organic vegetables along the street to Galligan's restaurant just around the corner from Good For You, she looked up to greet her customer and found the object of her thoughts standing right in front of her.

"Hello," he said, seeming to recognise her straightaway.

"Hi," Kate greeted, trying to sound as professional as she could, despite her erratic heartbeat and the heat that was starting to creep into her face. He looked gorgeous again today, she noticed, this time in a checked shirt worn over jeans and a white T-shirt.

"I'm looking for Aloe Vera cream, if you stock it."

Admonishing herself yet again for acting like a teenager, Kate pulled herself together and told him that they had a few.

"I'll show you what we have in stock," she said, leading the way to where the skin creams and lotions were stored on the pine shelves.

"You were at the market last Saturday," he commented as she searched around for a cream that she thought was particularly good.

He was standing behind her now and Kate could hardly believe how aware she was of his presence. It had been years since she'd felt this conscious of any man.

"That's right. It's the kind of place that I get really carried away in. The artichokes were great, by the way."

"That's what I like to hear," he smiled as she handed him two types of Aloe Vera preparation. "Which one would be best? I think I'm a bit allergic to something I'm growing. My sister thought Aloe Vera would be good." He held out one of his hands, the back of which displayed a dry, flaky rash.

"This one is a bit more concentrated and there's a barrier cream in it. Do you use gloves for work, incidentally?"

"Not always. The odd day, depending on what I'm at."

"It might be a latex allergy, when it's just on your hands. See how you get on with the cream, though."

"I'll keep the allergy thing in mind," he said, taking out his wallet.

"On the house," Kate said spontaneously, surprising herself.

"Oh, that's not —"

"You *did* give me half of the artichokes that were destined for Macroom," she cut in.

"Thanks. I'm Lorcan, by the way."

"Kate Lewis," she answered, holding out her hand. His handshake, as she'd expected, was firm and warm, causing her heart to take another spurt of its own accord.

"It's years since I've been in this shop," he told her now. "My aunt used to have it years ago when it was a sweet shop."

"Was that Miss Staunton?"

"That's right. She was in her eighties when she finally retired. You've made a really nice job of it."

"Thanks. It needed a bit of renovation but it's in a great location."

He was just about to answer when the doorbell chimed and a group of teenagers arrived in, followed by a lady with a small baby in a buggy. While most of her customers were regulars who tended to browse for a while, the four girls in their school uniforms lined up behind Lorcan, immediately making the small shop appear crowded. Kate, normally delighted with a rush of business, was amazed at how disappointed she felt.

"I'll leave you to it," he grinned, turning to leave. "Thanks for the cream – I'll let you know how I fare."

"See you again," Kate smiled, reluctantly turning her attention to her latest customers as the door closed behind him.

"I'll take over here, Kate." Emma had arrived on the scene, noticing the small crowd.

"Great. Give me a call if you need anything," Kate told her, finally resurrecting the order list that she'd been looking for before Lorcan had arrived.

She needed to escape now to the tranquillity of her little flat upstairs to think. It was strange, but something about Lorcan Reddy made her feel that she was going to be seeing a lot more of him from here on in.

It took Kate almost an hour to finish putting through her online orders when it normally took far less time than that. Unable to stop herself, she'd Googled Lorcan Reddy Organic. But, to her disappointment, there was precious little of a personal nature regarding Lorcan Reddy on the website. The business had evolved over almost twenty years from a ten-acre plot of land on the Mallow Road to its present location on a hundred-acre farm near Blarney.

The site went on to outline details of seed catalogues and a range of related services. It occurred to Kate as she browsed the website, searching for clues about Lorcan, that if she had a daughter of thirteen, this was exactly the kind of activity she would most likely be engaged in at this very moment. Feeling juvenile and not a little surprised at her own adolescent behaviour, she exited the site smartly and sat back to contemplate dinner, pushing Lorcan Reddy firmly out of her mind.

She hoped that Agnes wouldn't mind that she'd asked Emma to join them for dinner. When Agnes had phoned the previous evening to cancel their Saturday cookery date on account of Bea having a doctor's appointment, Kate had suggested that she come over for dinner on the Friday evening instead. Realising that Agnes would be limited in the time that she could be gone, Kate had decided that it was time she went solo with a few of the recipes. Now, with the inclusion of Emma, she was going public with her skills as well.

It seemed to Kate that Agnes's whole life had to revolve around her sister, with Beatrice making no distinguishable effort to co-operate with her carer's needs at all. Even when she said anything remotely critical of her sister, poor Agnes immediately followed it with a guilty statement about how she shouldn't be giving out when she was so much luckier than Bea to have her health.

This evening, Kate's plan was to do roast butternut squash as a starter, followed by a vegetarian lasagne and the chocolate mousse that they covered in one of the first classes. Wanting to be ahead of the posse now that Emma was joining them, Kate started to get her ingredients and utensils in order. As soon as she opened the vegetable drawer of the fridge, she was immediately reminded of Lorcan Reddy.

Agnes had suggested at the class on Tuesday night that they revisit the market in Midleton so that she could get a proper look around, having been distracted by Willie and Miriam the previous week. Now that she'd met him in the shop today, Kate couldn't countenance the idea of meeting Lorcan so soon again, fearing that it would look a bit suspicious if she turned up at his stand a day later. Hopefully, Agnes would be so caught up with Bea's GP appointment that she wouldn't be able to contemplate the trip for another few weeks.

Snapping out of her incessant thoughts of Lorcan Reddy once again, she started to get the dinner underway. She was aware that Emma too would be on a fairly short timescale, considering her reflexology class at half seven.

The next hour flew by in a whirl. She chopped the squash into thin slices and layered them in three small ovenproof dishes after smearing each piece with a mixture of garlic and herbs. Next was the lasagne, done in individual dishes, the layers of pasta and finely chopped vegetables bubbling deliciously in the rich cheese sauce. The mousse, she hoped, would be as light as a feather.

Agnes and Emma hit it off immediately, chatting away happily as Kate tossed the green salad in the large wooden bowl that she'd bought earlier in the week. Her kitchen, always adequate for her limited needs in the past, seemed to be bursting at the seams these days with new pots and pans being required at an alarming rate.

Listening to the lively chatter of Agnes and Emma, Kate realised that in all her years in Cork, she'd never actually entertained before. When she and Timmy were first married, they'd had people around almost every weekend. She was aware now of just how much she'd loved the buzz of conversation and banter that had been a constant part of her life in the past.

It occurred to her that she hadn't even cooked a meal for her parents or sisters since she'd moved into the flat, preferring to visit them in Dublin every couple of months rather than have them descend on the oasis of calm that she made for herself. Perhaps that too needed to change.

"Come and get it!" she called over to Agnes and Emma now as she placed the big bowl of salad on the tiny kitchen table, followed by the crispy roast squash.

"You can't be a novice at this," Emma insisted once she'd tasted the first bite. "This is gorgeous!"

"That's the thing about the Absolute Beginners class — the whole point is to cook things that are really easy. I'm only disgusted I didn't think of doing it sooner."

"Same here," Agnes joined in. "I've been doing night classes for years but cookery never really occurred to me until lately. I live with my sister, Emma, and she's very set in her ways about what she eats so I used to think there wasn't much point."

"Well, at least you'll be able to introduce her to new things now. It's a fear of change that holds most people back."

"Well, Bea definitely has a fear of change," Agnes agreed. "I brought up the idea of her going for a week in Summer Orchard last night and she was horrified. I told her that we could go to see it first but she refused point blank. It was worth a try though, Kate."

Agnes went on to explain her home circumstances to Emma, telling her that Kate had gone to all the trouble of finding out about the Respite Centre from her customer, Catherine Tierney.

"I feel a bit cross with her, to be honest," Agnes admitted.

"Well, it was worth a try," said Kate. "What did Beatrice think about getting some equipment in for lifting her in and out of the chair?"

Catherine Tierney had been more than helpful when Kate enquired about services for older people in the area, even offering to visit Agnes and Beatrice at home if they wanted. She told Kate about things like a remote-controlled bed that would help Bea to sit upright and an electric hoist that would transport her in and out of bed without Agnes having to exert herself. She'd even mentioned the possibility of a Home Help who would assist Agnes and even stay with Bea when Agnes went out.

"She was very annoyed at the mention of a hoist. She wouldn't trust a machine to lift her, you see, because she's used to me doing it. I'll have to find a way to come around her at some stage in case anything happens to me."

"You're right, Agnes, about putting a back-up plan in place," said Emma. "Lots of people that end up in long-stay care do so because their carer has had an injury or become ill. You have to take care of yourself – for both your sakes."

Agnes looked very gratified at this.

"And part of that is making a point of getting out and about, Agnes," said Kate.

"Well, I've always tried to go to courses and meet people but it's difficult because Bea doesn't like me to have people back to the house. She's not able for it really."

It was on the tip of Kate's tongue to say that Beatrice was well able to control the purse strings and manage all their financial affairs but she didn't think it fair to openly criticise her. She was the only family in Agnes's world, after all.

"There's a Carers' group attached to St Angela's that you might be interested in when the cookery course is finished," said Emma. "It was set up by the Ladies' Committee a few years ago because a lot of the people who are full-time carers have no outlet at all. I'll give Kate the details for you if you like."

"That would be great. It's lovely to know that there is support out there if I ever need it, even though I know Bea won't accept anything right now. But we have to think about the future whether Bea wants to or not."

"It's a worry to have someone so dependent on you, Agnes," Kate agreed, placing a bubbling dish of lasagne on the table.

"My eyes have been opened since I started the cookery course, to be honest. I was telling Rosa about Bea the other night and she was saying that they even have counselling sessions in St Angela's to help carers with coping skills. Rosa's mother runs a group session once a month. I think I might go to that as well when I get time, just to stop myself getting totally burnt out."

"Is Rosa Bernadette Mooney's daughter?"

St Angela's was Cork's largest general hospital and had both maternity and mental health units attached. Despite its size, Emma's question seemed to prove that everyone knew everyone else there.

"Yes, Rosa's in our class at The Gourmet Rooms. Her mother's a psychologist, I think."

"She's a lovely woman. I've often heard her speak about Rosa."

"She sounds nice," Agnes agreed. "Rosa says she's very involved with fund-raising for the hospital as well."

"As far as I know, Mrs Carter is involved with the Ladies' Committee too," Kate said, remembering a conversation she'd had with Rosa the first week of the course.

"They raise thousands for the hospital every year," said Emma. "I keep saying I'll get involved but I've enough on my plate with the reflexology course."

"Not to mention two jobs! I feel guilty just watching how much you pack into a day, Emma," Kate laughed.

"It's easy enough when I have no real responsibility. You have a business to run and Agnes has Beatrice to look after."

"Well, it was hectic at the beginning when I moved here but the business runs itself at this stage," Kate had to admit.

"How did you come to settle in Cork, Kate?" Emma enquired.

In the past, Kate would have found a question like this invasive and would have shied away from any conversation that was remotely personal. Aware that it wasn't Emma's intention to be intrusive, Kate told her about Timmy being killed in the car crash some years previously and about her long stay in hospital afterwards.

"We didn't have any children so I had no real ties. I saw the shop advertised in one of the Sunday papers and I liked the idea of doing something for myself. So I moved to Cork to make a new start."

Sitting here at the small kitchen table with Agnes and Emma, Kate was acutely aware of how innocuous the edited version of her life sounded, even to her own ears. Emma was probably thinking of her as a tragic widow who'd been unlucky enough to lose her young husband in a horrific car smash, much as Agnes had done the previous Saturday when she told her about it. As far as the facts of it went, it actually *was* the truth, yet Kate wondered how her two new friends would react if they knew the whole sorry story of Timmy's death, and of her own part in it.

For a moment, it was as if the others weren't in the room at all and the familiar nauseating guilt assailed her as she thought of the innocent passenger of the oncoming car who'd lost his life so needlessly.

Stop this, she told herself, drawing in a deep breath. Almost as suddenly as it began, the feeling of panic abated.

"I'm sorry to hear about your husband, Kate," Emma said gently. "I think you've made a great job of starting again."

Kate had a sudden mental picture of Lorcan Reddy

telling her earlier that she'd made a great job of the shop.

"It's a long time ago now – thirteen years actually," she told Emma, amazed at how she was getting used to talking about Timmy in the past tense once she'd started to talk about him at all.

"Still, starting over is never easy – I should know, considering that I thought nursing would be a career for life. Now look at me!"

"You're only young ones, the two of you!" Agnes laughed. "Imagine being almost pension age and having to start looking at things differently!"

It was true, Kate told herself optimistically, that her own life was far from over and once again, a vivid picture of Lorcan Reddy's hazel eyes came to mind.

Chapter 18

Rosa knew that she was going about it all wrong, that she should have got all the ingredients together on the worktop first but she was just so excited at the thought of her parents' faces when they saw the tiramisu. So instead, she'd just pulled everything out of the presses in a rush and flung them up on the counter in no particular order. Now she was trying to get the coffee mixture together, rooting in the cupboards for a bag of ground coffee while the mascarpone mixture went warm in the mixing bowl. There seemed to be icing sugar everywhere and she cursed the fact that she'd been too lazy to go over to Lucy's house to borrow a sieve.

Mrs Carter had said to do the coffee and Marsala first and have it cooling while you arranged the sponge fingers. Then you could do the mascarpone topping at your leisure. Rosa however hadn't ever used mascarpone cheese before, except last Tuesday at the class, and had been dying to take it out of the container and mix it up with the cinnamon and icing sugar.

Now all the pleasure had gone out of it as she finally resurrected a bag of Lavazzo only to find that she hadn't washed out the percolator the last time she'd used it. More time wasted, she thought in a panic, spilling the ground coffee all over the worktop. Cursing violently, she glanced at the clock. Her parents were arriving for dinner in less that two hours and she hadn't even started on the chicken liver pâté that she planned to serve Italian style on thin slices of garlic crostini.

The whole routine had seemed so easy when she'd replayed it mentally for the last few nights. Last Tuesday, they'd covered Italian food and the simplicity of the recipes had made her believe that she'd be well able to carry off a dinner party to thank her parents for enabling her to do the Absolute Beginners course in the first place.

Her plan had been to make the tiramisu first and have it chilling, then she'd fry the half pound of liver that she'd purchased the previous day and whiz it up with the onion, garlic, mushrooms and port wine. That could also go into the fridge to chill until the last minute when she'd spread it over the already sliced baguette. Set on a bed of salad leaves dressed in a light basil and oregano vinaigrette, the authentic starter couldn't fail to impress.

The next part of Rosa's plan had involved her taking a long bath to de-stress and get ready for her parents' arrival. She wanted it to look as if she hadn't been slaving away over the meal all day – rather that she was a complete natural and had just dashed it together effortlessly.

Now she was plastered in mascarpone with her blonde curls falling over her face as she tried valiantly to take the percolator apart to wash it before getting started on the coffee. She'd had more than a swig of Marsala to calm her nerves and was already feeling slightly light-headed. Whether this was from the heady Italian liqueur or the thought of her parents finding both their daughter and her kitchen in chaos and no dinner to speak of was anyone's guess – either way it was all getting the better of Rosa.

Cursing as her fingernail snagged on the mesh filter, her thoughts turned to the simple pasta dish that she'd chosen as a main course. She'd bought fresh tagliatelle, which she was set to serve with grilled bacon, a little fresh cream and a crumbled gorgonzola cheese. They'd made it in class and it had taken only minutes, with the bacon grilling while the pasta cooked to *al dente*.

The beauty of this dish was that it could be made at the last minute. Rosa had had a vision of the tagliatelle bubbling gently as her parents relaxed and sipped their wine and complimented her on their delicious starter. Nonchalantly she'd stir in the cream and toss in the blue cheese and the crispy bacon that she planned to have keeping warm in the top oven, along with her warmed plates. Now, however, looking at the pig's ear she was making of the dessert, she wondered with a sense of dread if she wouldn't feel completely under pressure trying to pull this off.

The doorbell rang just as she burst into tears, her arms still enveloped in suds and bits of old coffee grounds.

"Oh God, no!" she wailed out loud, as she knocked over a jug of water in her attempts to grab a tea towel to dry her hands, creating a minor flood over the surface of the worktop. She hoped to God her parents hadn't got the time wrong. An early arrival would be the last straw.

"Fuck again!" she then screeched as the tributaries started to make their way towards the bag of coffee. Rescuing it and drying her hands simultaneously, she knocked over one of her favourite John Rocha glasses as she raced to the door. Pausing momentarily to mourn the shattered crystal shards, she dashed the tea towel across her face to remove at least some of the mascarpone mixture before swinging the front door open in a panic.

Lucy had called over to see if Rosa was free to go for a quick walk along the Carrigrohane road with her. To her surprise, she didn't even get time to say hello, never mind ask about a walk.

"Oh, thank God it's you, Lucy! You'll have to help me!" Rosa cried, tears of relief mingling with the earlier panicked ones.

"What's happened, Rosa? Tell me!" Lucy almost shouted at her, alarm coursing through her at the number of things that could have happened to someone as vulnerable as Rosa.

Rosa's face was blotchy with tears and her hair was tousled, something that Lucy had never seen in the weeks that she'd known her.

"It's desperate. I don't know what to do!" Rosa sobbed, unable to help herself now that her friend had arrived and there was a hope of deliverance on the horizon.

"Will I ring your parents for you?" Lucy asked frantically, sure that she wouldn't be able to deal with whatever it was that had caused this. Rosa was normally so sunny – a bit nervous and giddy, mind – but never hysterical like this.

"No, whatever you do, don't do that!" she screeched. "Just come in and help me, will you, Lucy?" she tailed off miserably.

This was said in such a small, pleading voice that Lucy started to feel more in command of the situation. At least she wasn't shrieking any more. Closing the door behind her, she guided Rosa towards the lounge, swiftly taking in the scene in the kitchen as she passed the open door. There was broken glass all over the floor.

A burglary she could cope with.

But what if something more awful had happened to her friend during the break-in? There were so many stories about deranged sex offenders who were released after pathetically short prison sentences going on the rampage as soon as they were free.

Lucy knew she wouldn't be able to help her friend through something like that and wondered again if she shouldn't just ring the Mooneys straight away and let them deal with their daughter – they were both doctors after all. But Rosa had been adamant and Lucy knew only too well how hard it was to tell something like this to the people that you trusted most.

Surprisingly, the lounge hadn't been touched. As usual, it was neat and tidy, with the furniture arranged to perfection. Perhaps Rosa had managed to fend off her attacker before something really terrible had happened. Or maybe Lucy had arrived in the nick of time and the doorbell had frightened him off. They sat next to each other on one of the sofas now, Lucy's arm resting awkwardly around Rosa's narrow shoulders.

"Look, Rosa, try to tell me. I'll understand, whatever it is."

Lucy knew she sounded wooden and stilted – she wasn't used to this kind of conversation. But she had to give Rosa the opportunity of telling what had happened – otherwise it might just get stuck in her chest somewhere, never to be spoken of again.

"I feel such a fool. This is so typical of me. It's all my own fault!"

"Rosa, nothing is *your* fault!" Lucy told her vehemently.

"Thanks."

Rosa's sobbing had subsided somewhat and it seemed that she was able to talk after all, to Lucy's relief.

"I just thought it was a good idea at the time. Mum and Dad called over on Wednesday and I was so excited after doing all the Italian menus the night before that I asked them over for dinner tonight."

Lucy was wondering where this convoluted conversation was leading but listened patiently anyway. Sometimes it took Rosa a while to get to the kernel of a story, even under normal circumstances.

"I was going to do the liver and mushroom pâté thing and the bacon and gorgonzola pasta but the tiramisu went completely astray on me. They're coming at half seven and I've nothing done. The kitchen's like a tip because I was trying to do everything together and I won't even get time to shower and change, the way I'm going. Do you think I should leave the tiramisu altogether and just take some ice cream out of the freezer?"

Shocked, Lucy just stared at her friend. Was it possible that all this was about a failed dinner party? About Rosa's parents finding out that their money had been less well spent than they'd been led to think?

Appalled at the way her mind had jumped to the conclusion that Rosa had been the victim of a sexual assault in her own home, Lucy tried to pull herself together and focus on the litany of disasters that her friend was now outlining between sniffles. Tales of asking her boss for a few hours off so that she could get home early and then having the bacon grilled at four o'clock so that she'd be organised. Now it was shrivelled to a crisp. And how Mrs Carter was always on about setting the table once everything was prepared, yet Rosa couldn't visualise there being anything to put on the table now that the dinner was a disaster.

Slowly, it began to dawn on Lucy that to Rosa, losing face in front of her parents yet again actually *was* a disaster. She wondered if Rosa's sudden loss of confidence had anything to do with Tuesday night's talk about the setting up of a small business and all that it entailed.

Rosa had been in a right panic coming home in the car, fretting about all the legalities and council requirements. The first of the two speakers had been from the County Council and had focussed on things like planning permission in the case of a building not previously used for commercial purposes and the need to register for income tax and VAT.

Then there was the process of contacting the Companies Registration office to register the name of the business and the requirement to pay council rates for all commercial premises.

Next had been an environmental health officer who spoke at length about food hygiene standards, staff training and ongoing assessment by the environmental health department. Rosa, by the end of it all, had been as white as a sheet and practically shaking in her seat.

"Would you have to do all of that, even if the restaurant was in a private house?" she'd asked the council official nervously.

"If it's being run for profit, yes," he'd stated firmly, putting the death knell on Rosa's aspirations.

Now her parents were arriving and she somehow had to prove to them that even if she wasn't actually going to be able to open a restaurant, at least she was able to cook a meal as a result of her expensive cookery course.

Why was it that they couldn't accept her the way she was? Lucy wondered crossly in Rosa's defence. A little bit unreliable and unfocussed she might be but surely they could see that she was helpful and enthusiastic as well, as Lucy had found out since she'd met her. Not to mention the fact that she adored both of them and was always talking about them, despite being nervous of letting them down.

Now that she didn't have to star in a victim support role, Lucy was all action. If it took a proper dinner to assure the Mooneys that their money had been well spent then she was more than willing to pitch in and assist Rosa in making a decent stab at it.

"Look, let's go out and see where you're at with it. You sound like you have most of it done." She led Rosa towards the chaos. "You probably only need help with the finishing touches," she added encouragingly.

The situation wasn't as bad as Rosa had painted it, or as Lucy had anticipated.

"Look here, Rosa. Put all that stuff in the dishwasher – we'll know where we're at then."

Obediently, Rosa sprang into action as Lucy swept up the shards of glass that littered the floor.

When all the dirty utensils – and there were a lot of them – were removed to the dishwasher and all the ruined stuff placed in the bin without comment, the place looked presentable again.

"I'll sort out the percolator and we can get the tiramisu finished anyway. The topping's perfect," Lucy praised, testing it with her finger.

The mascarpone topping for the dessert *was* actually made to perfection.

Now that she had Lucy to guide her, Rosa tackled the making of the strong black coffee that could be mixed with Marsala and poured over the sponge fingers that lay in waiting on the granite work surface.

"Would you consider doing that pasta dish with the olives and capers? We could make it now and have it on a low heat so you'd only have to do the actual pasta in front of your parents."

"I suppose I could. I have a jar of green olives that I got yesterday – I've no red peppers, though."

She looked so crestfallen at this obstacle that Lucy

immediately offered to walk to the small shop down the hill from their houses for a few.

"Would you? Oh, Lucy, thanks a million! I think I would have ended up ringing them and telling them I'd broken my leg or something if you hadn't arrived."

Happy that things were under control at last, Rosa went off in search of her olives, glad that she had a really good friend to show for her ten-week course, even if she wouldn't have a restaurant.

Lucy took off to the shop, leaving Rosa to halve the olives and skin a few tomatoes for the sauce. She was fine really once she was supervised and instructed, Lucy thought, although she did wonder if she herself was qualified to either instruct or supervise.

In a way, she actually envied the strange bond that Rosa had with her parents and the fact that they went to such lengths to indulge her, notwithstanding their apparently high standards.

Rosa's house in Bramwell Court was owned by her parents and from the way she talked, most of the bills seemed to be met by them as well. Even the fees for the classes at The Gourmet Rooms had been paid by the Mooneys.

Lucy felt somewhat detached from her own parents and certainly wasn't financially dependent on them. The money that she'd inherited from her Uncle Ned had made sure of that, she thought bitterly, the whole scene with Rosa earlier bringing the past startlingly close to the present.

Lucy always had a niggling sense of shame at the way she felt the need to take everything out on her parents, even though she was well aware that nothing had been their fault. If anything, they'd been horribly deceived and were still innocently ignorant of the full facts of Ned's last will and testament.

But she still had an almost childish anger that she'd been left to deal with proceeds of the sale of his two-hundred-acre farm and the slim likelihood of ever disposing of such an enormous sum of money. Despite buying one of the most expensive houses on the market at the time, she still had an unwieldy number of zeros on her account statement. When she had first been burdened with the money, she had naively thought she could somehow spend it. Now she knew better. Yes, the money could be spent but not if she continued to live as she lived right now. One of these days she would simply have to give it all away.

As always when she allowed her thoughts to turn to the events of the summer she'd finished primary school, it only took a few minutes for her brain to reach the turmoil stage.

She'd reached the shop in record time, probably because her mind was hammering away at such a pace that her feet just followed.

Glad of the activity in the busy little shop that sold everything from groceries to wine and beach balls to gas cylinders, she grabbed the requisite red peppers, adding a can of chopped tomatoes in case Rosa had had any unforeseen difficulty with the peeling of the fresh ones.

Then she started wondering if Rosa had the foresight to buy some wine to accompany the meal so she picked up a bottle of Chianti as a backup, even though the

Mooneys were probably used to something a little more expensive. Tough, she thought crossly, annoyed on her friend's behalf that her parents were so hard to please.

At least Lucy could say for her own parents that they'd never demanded much from her in terms of unreasonable achievement. The fact that both she and Rosa happened to be the only child in their respective families was where the comparisons ended.

Lucy knew she'd been a difficult teenager, going against her parents at every turn. She just couldn't help herself, even though she always felt guilty for disagreeing with them. Her father only ever wanted a quiet life and for Lucy to be happy, so he'd been delighted for her when it came to light that his older brother had willed her all his land and property. Ned had been mown down by a drunk driver at the age of sixty-two – a tragedy, it was said at his funeral, for all concerned. Surprisingly, despite the sudden nature of his death, he'd already made his will.

Lost in thought, Lucy didn't notice that the person in front of her in the queue had finished and that Mr Whiriskey was waiting expectantly for her to move forward towards the counter. At least not until the person behind her had tapped her gently on the shoulder and said "You're next!", causing her to start violently and drop her purchases.

Red wine splattered to the four corners of the tiny shop, creating pandemonium as the rest of the customers tried to jump out of the way of the advancing puddle. Lucy, blushing furiously at the scene that she'd caused, bent quickly to try and retrieve the tomatoes and red peppers, noticing as she did so that the legs of the person next to her, clad in cream chino-type trousers, were covered in dark red splatters.

"Oh, God, I'm so sorry!" she began, getting up from her crouched position to apologise properly.

As she did so, the owner of the wine-spattered legs was in turn bending down to assist her, himself apologising for startling her and creating the incident in the first place. In their haste, their heads bashed together with such force that Lucy finally realised where the term 'seeing stars' came from.

Mortified, she tried to apologise again as soon as she could speak, but was shushed by Mr Whiriskey who was descending on them with a mop and a yellow cone.

"Everyone outside for a moment, please," he instructed firmly, no doubt motivated into such swift action by the thought of the number of claims that could be made against his insurance on the strength of slippages on the drenched shop floor.

Shuffling towards the door, Lucy could visualise her face as the most alarming shade of puce as she looked around contritely at the small crowd.

"Sorry about this," she mumbled, aware that her voice was barely audible. Talk about a scene.

"That's all right," someone said jovially, "although it's a desperate waste of a bottle of wine!"

Finally looking up properly, Lucy was mortified to see that the speaker was the owner of the ruined chinos.

"Sorry about the trousers," she got out, trying to look contrite, a cold sweat breaking out all over her as she realised that the assembled crowd were watching with interest. He was about her own age, well built with short fair hair and a friendly, open face. Lucy found it hard to believe that he was so casual about it all and wondered if he'd looked down at the legs of his trousers properly yet.

"It's my own fault for rushing you. Anyway, it'll wash out."

Red wine? She didn't think it'd be that easy – but, before she had a chance to say so, Mr Whiriskey ushered everyone back into the shop.

"I've got no more of that wine," he told her gruffly, "but there's other stuff there if you want to have a look."

"It's fine, thanks, just take for that bottle and the peppers," she told him, landing the two unfortunate peppers up on the counter. She hadn't been able to retrieve the can of tomatoes from under the shelves but figured that the sooner she was out of the shop the better, regardless of how Rosa had got on with peeling the ones she already had.

Apologising yet again to Mr Whiriskey for the inconvenience she'd caused, she scuttled out of the shop as fast as she could, mouthing another 'sorry' at the fellow with the polka-dot legs. He grinned back at her and rolled his eyes before moving forward to the counter at last.

Lucy booted it up the road towards Bramwell Court, imagining that Rosa might have fallen apart again at her lengthy absence.

At least she'd had on her new Nikes and the navy jogging pants and pale blue polo shirt that made her look slimmer than she actually was, she consoled herself, thinking of the chino-man's smiling face. She was just rounding the corner into the cul-de-sac when she heard a familiar voice behind her.

"So what are you going to drink now?"

Please tell me he's not living in Bramwell Court, Lucy begged God silently, mortified that she'd have to encounter him again with the spectre of the red wine hanging over her. It was bad enough making a fool of herself in front of a complete stranger but having the whole neighbourhood thinking she was a disaster area was desperate altogether.

Sure as hell, he rounded the corner with her, looking at her expectantly for an answer.

"I'll think of something," was all she could come up, her face flaming. It was bad enough that he was good-looking but she really couldn't cope with the fact that he was nice as well.

Thankfully, Lucy's house was the first of ten so she was able to duck in her own gate almost immediately. Realising in embarrassment that she was supposed to be going into Rosa's house, she had to reverse and make her way to the third house, all the while thinking that she was doing a spectacularly magnificent job of making a complete ass of herself.

"Bye then," she offered weakly as she rounded the limestone pillars at Rosa's gate. Another smile and he was gone, leaving Lucy in a state of turmoil on the doorstep of Number 3.

"I had a great plan while you were gone," Rosa greeted her, as effusive as if nothing had happened earlier.

Only the fact that her hair was still in disarray gave any indication of how distraught she'd been.

"Go on," Lucy prompted her cautiously, imagining some complicated recipe that would entail Lucy going back down to the shop. And regardless of how much Rosa wanted to impress her parents, that much Lucy was not prepared to do.

"You can stay for dinner as well. Mum and Dad are always saying they'd like to meet you and we could do the dinner together. It'd be good practice," she added hopefully when she saw Lucy's sceptical expression.

Lucy was indeed sceptical about the Mooneys wanting to meet her. She couldn't visualise herself being able to make polite conversation with such sophisticated people – she'd have nothing to say and would no doubt look completely out of place between Rosa and her glamorous mother. She said as much to her friend now, galvanised by the thought of how intimidated she'd feel.

"I can't believe you're saying that," Rosa told her indignantly. "I'm always telling them how organised you are and how you have such a flair for cooking. They're dying to hear all about the classes so you can't say you have nothing to talk to them about."

Lucy finally gave in to Rosa's pleading and went home to change as soon as the pasta sauce was bubbling. The tiramisu had finally been assembled and placed in the fridge. Even the table was set. Lucy had almost kicked herself when Rosa opened the drinks cabinet in the dining room to expose a wine collection that would give the cellar of any vineyard a run for its money.

Upstairs in her bedroom she rummaged through the rails of the cherrywood wardrobe looking for something remotely dressy to wear to Rosa's dinner party. Eventually she settled on a pair of black trousers that she'd worn to her cousin's wedding the previous year. She remembered the trousers as being particularly uncomfortable and was surprised to find that they fitted better than she recalled. The only clean top that she could find among the chaos in the chest of drawers was also black, making her look as if she was off to a funeral instead of a sociable night out.

At the last minute she added a Newbridge silver pendant and bracelet that her mother had given her for Christmas. She hadn't worn them before, thinking the pendant was a bit big and flashy but now she was glad of it to take the morbid look off the rest of the outfit.

Realising that time was moving on, she pulled a brush through her hair, delighted that she'd taken Rocky's advice and had gone back to get the highlights done. Now, instead of a mousy brown mop that lay lankly around her face like a pair of old curtains, she had a lively, honey-blonde style that was short enough to flatter her face without making her look boyish.

She hadn't been able to manage the blow-drying technique at all until Rocky had advised her to buy a professional hairdryer instead of the miserable one that she'd found at the bottom of one of her drawers. Now that she'd mastered the art of it, she was almost fanatical about getting it right every morning.

Lucy had always looked on the myriad of hair-care products in the supermarket as gimmicks, never for a moment imagining that any of them could lift her own lank style into anything like a bit of body. Rosa had giggled at this, asking Lucy how she thought the television presenters managed when they had to do a feature in the Dublin Mountains.

"You don't see their hair blowing all over the place, do you?" she demanded.

Lucy had had to agree, hence the buying of the volumising serum and spray that Barbara had given her samples of that first night. Rosa and Cathy were inevitably right about these things, Lucy conceded as she admired her hair, making a mental note to pay more attention to their advice in the future.

She made her way back to Number 3 in time to stop her friend putting the fresh tagliatelle into a steaming pan of boiling water, despite the fact that it only took four minutes and that her parents hadn't landed on the premises.

"Well, they rang to say they were leaving and I got into a bit of a panic," she explained. In desperation, Lucy poured two glasses of wine and told her friend to take a few gulps to settle her nerves. Everything was under control.

"It's as well to have the water boiling, anyway," Lucy reassured her, turning the gas flame down a little lest the place be like a sauna when the guests arrived.

"Maybe we could fry the bread and keep it warm in the oven," she said then, more as a means of giving Rosa something to do than any need to be ahead of schedule. If they did any more preparation they'd practically have it eaten for them but her friend was like a hen on a hot griddle and needed something to keep her busy.

Rosa immediately poured enough olive oil into the frying pan to deep-fry an elephant, followed by the garlic that they'd crushed earlier. The crisp slices of garlic bread were safely placed in the oven at a low heat and the kitchen was full of a lovely garlicky aroma when the doorbell rang. Rosa raced to answer it, leaving Lucy feeling slightly sheepish in the kitchen.

She always felt intimidated by self-assured, glamorous people and she dreaded the thought of being under the demanding scrutiny of the Mooneys when she still hadn't recovered from the debacle in the shop.

Why was she always so terrified of people like the faceless Mooneys when in reality, they were only Rosa's parents? Why wasn't she like normal people, looking forward to meeting her friend's parents, instead of cowering in the kitchen in dreaded anticipation of being drawn into the limelight to be chatty and entertaining?

At that moment, Lucy saw her life for what it was and realised that it would take more than losing a few pounds and buying a raft of hair products to banish all the doubts that she had about herself.

So much for a new start, she thought dejectedly. Especially when it's all only on the outside.

Chapter 19

The night of Rosa's dinner party, it became clear to Lucy that she wasn't the only person in the world who felt displaced from everybody else.

Until then, it had never occurred to her that other people had issues in their lives that they had to deal with. It was just that, like her, they were good at covering up.

Once she'd met them, Lucy realised that Rosa's parents were perfectly normal people. It was only Rosa's desire to live up to what she imagined were their expectations that was the problem. As far as Lucy could see, Maurice and Bernadette were happy with Rosa the way she was.

It occurred to Lucy that much of her own distress at feeling different from everyone else was down to the way she thought people were critical and judgemental and that she could never match their expectations of how she should look or behave so it was better not even to try.

She'd been delighted to find that far from being a slightly older and more glamorous version of Rosa,

Bernadette had turned out to be comfortably middle-aged in a matronly sort of way and, despite her earlier misgivings, Lucy had taken to her warm smile and even warmer hug. Maurice, with ginger hair that was thinning on top, seemed to be the more reticent of the two, sitting back and eating all before him, praising the two girls warmly for the excellent meal. Lucy could hardly believe now that she'd been terrified of meeting them and of having nothing to talk to them about. They'd sat up drinking coffee until the early hours, chatting about anything and everything. Bernadette had been particularly interested in the people that Lucy looked after in The Friary, telling her of the many clients who came to her practice suffering from the stresses of caring for an elderly relative.

It seemed that psychotherapy was Bernadette's main field of interest and Lucy was fascinated from the outset by the concept that people's past experiences determined their behaviour.

After Maurice and Bernadette had left, the two girls had sat up for ages, dissecting the evening and the success of the meal. Lucy thought Rosa's parents were great, especially Bernadette with whom she'd felt totally at ease.

"I can't believe you were in such a tizz about getting the meal right! Your parents would have been happy if you'd served them dog food."

"I know. But I still wanted to get it right. I hate everyone thinking that I can't manage anything on my own. They might be sorry they ended up with me at all," she ended jokingly, although to Lucy her worry sounded all too real.

"They're delighted with you," Lucy insisted, reminding

her of how they'd hung onto her every word all evening, patently proud of every little thing about the meal. The delicate flavour of the mushroom and port in the chicken liver pâté. The luscious cream cheese topping on the tiramisu. The elegance of the table with the little burgundy candles placed evenly the length of the pristine damask table-runner.

"I wonder sometimes," Rosa said dolefully.

She looked like a small child as she said this and Lucy realised immediately where her fear of getting things wrong came from. Her real mother hadn't wanted her. What would happen if she didn't get everything right for her adoptive parents? Would they too not want her?

It seemed as clear as day to Lucy, but obviously not so to Rosa who seemed to have no idea of how much her parents adored her. It didn't matter that the Mooneys were thrilled with her no matter what she did with her life if Rosa herself kept feeling that she was a disappointment to them.

"But I must be," she insisted when Lucy pointed this out. "Loads of Dad's colleagues have daughters my age who are qualified GP's and the like."

"Yeah, and plenty more of them have children who are drug addicts only you wouldn't hear about it," Lucy retorted. "What about the fellow that your mother was telling us about, the neurologist's son? He must have been a right lunatic."

Maxwell Kennedy, it seemed, had been transporting cocaine between Cork and Galway in his brand new BMW, arrogantly confident of being the last person who'd be suspected of being a courier. When the guards finally did catch onto him at a roadblock outside Limerick, he'd foolishly taken off at high speed and had wrapped his car around a tree in the ensuing chase. It was unlikely that Maxwell would ever walk again, despite the expert treatment that his parents had been able to procure for him.

"I suppose you're right," Rosa had eventually conceded. "It's just that I always have these visions of people asking Mum or Dad what I'm doing with myself. I'd like them to be proud of me."

"But that's the thing, Rosa. They *are* actually proud of you only you don't realise it. You're too busy trying to get to the next thing that'll impress them for you to notice, that's all."

"Jesus, Lucy, you're starting to sound frighteningly like Mum."

"It'd be a nice job, wouldn't it? Figuring out why people are as daft as they are and getting paid for it!"

"You'd be good at it – you're very perceptive. Did you ever think about going to college?"

Now that Rosa had opened her heart about her feelings on being adopted, Lucy was suddenly tempted to tell her the whole story of how her secondary school years had gone by in a blur. Listening to Bernadette about the power of simply talking about a problem made her wonder now if it wasn't such a terrible secret after all. Maybe bringing it out into the light might take the horror out of it.

"Nor really. To be honest, I hated school. Well, not school exactly. I think I hated everything around then."

A small silence ensued and something about the

expression on her face alerted Rosa to the fact that all was not right in her friend's world.

"How come?"

Haltingly, Lucy told her of the summer when she was thirteen. How she'd gone to stay for the weekend with her grandparents in Kildare when her parents had gone to a wedding in Rome. How for the three nights her Uncle Ned had come into the small room beside the kitchen where she always slept. It was cosier than the large double room upstairs that her parents normally used when they went on their few visits to Kildare every year but, as Lucy found out to her horror, it was miles away from the safety of her granny and grandad.

Lucy wasn't able to tell her friend the details of that weekend, only that she'd never stood in the house in Kildare since. Even when her grandfather had died suddenly a few months later, Lucy had insisted on staying with her cousins in the village.

And when Ned had been killed a few years later, it had taken all her strength just to go to the funeral and stand between her parents accepting people's condolences, her expression grim in the face of their sympathy.

"Did you tell anyone, Lucy?"

Rosa was almost afraid to touch her, so still was she sitting with her arms wrapped tightly around herself.

"I didn't know how to. Mam and Dad wouldn't have understood – it's not like now where you see things in the paper every day of the week. I didn't even know properly what had happened until I started to see other people on television saying what had happened to them."

"But did they not notice? You must have been in a terrible state."

"I was starting in secondary school the following week so maybe they thought I was nervous or something. I was always in trouble, Rosa, I couldn't help it. I think I blamed them for sending me to Kildare in the first place."

"What about your grandparents? Did they never ask why you didn't come to visit?"

"They all thought I'd got in with a wild gang in school. I suppose it suited me. I often wondered if Grandad suspected that something had happened. He died very suddenly a few months later."

Lucy's face was bleak then, as if she was exhausted from the telling of her story. She glanced up at Rosa to gauge her reaction and was shocked to see her crying. Suddenly she was afraid that maybe Rosa was disgusted with what she'd just heard.

"Lucy, I can't believe you went through all that on your own. You're the most amazing person I've ever met."

The pride and admiration in Rosa's voice was unmistakable and for the first time ever, Lucy had a sense that maybe it hadn't been her fault, that maybe she hadn't actually invited it all in some way. She'd always thought that maybe she had — that she'd sent out some sort of signals that had made her uncle think she had wanted him to do what he'd done. Suddenly, it felt all right to cry and once she started, Lucy thought she'd never stop.

Rosa threw more logs on the fire and replenished Lucy's glass, then sat beside her, held her hand and let her cry, amazing even herself with the way she was able to just let Lucy be.

Eventually able to talk again, Lucy told her about the glorious moment when she'd heard that Ned had been killed.

"He was at the mart one Saturday and he had a car crash on the way home that night. A neighbour told Dad afterwards that he'd been drinking all day but that never came out at the time. It was covered up because he was friendly with a few of the local guards and the Super-intendent. There was a man killed in the crash as well. I know it sounds awful, Rosa, but I was delighted. I was always dreaming about killing him."

"You shouldn't feel bad about hating him, Lucy. He deserved everything he got. And he can never do that to anyone else, at least."

"I'm always thinking about it though. When your mum was talking about work earlier, I kept thinking that maybe I should go to someone like her to get it all out of my head."

"We could ask her about it, if you want. It's expensive though."

Lucy sighed deeply at this but forged ahead, wanting to get the full story out now that she'd started.

"Actually, Rosa, money is no object. The more expensive the better."

Seeing Rosa's quizzical look, she went on to tell her about Ned's will and how he'd left her everything: the land, all the livestock and everything he had in the bank.

"Guilt money," she ended bitterly.

"What did you do with it?"

"Granny didn't want to live on her own in Kildare after he died so she came to Cork to live with us. I asked the solicitors to put the farm up for sale after that."

"Is that how you came to buy the house here?"

Rosa was aghast at the story but still had no concept of the size of the farm or the price of land. Lucy just nodded.

"I hate the money but it's so hard to get rid of it without Mam and Dad finding out. They keep telling me I should invest it in something but I'd hate it to get bigger. There's still nearly a million left."

"A million! Good God!" For once Rosa was pretty much lost for words.

"I know it sounds bizarre but it's like a weight sitting on my shoulders all the time. It makes me feel like he paid me off or something."

"Lucy, sometimes if I'm upset over something, Mum asks me to try and look at it differently to see if it's still as bad. Often it isn't."

"Rosa, there's no getting away from it. I've done that for years and I'm sick of it."

"You know how you said you wanted to kill him? What if you looked at this money as being the least you deserve after the way he ruined your life? Use it to go to a counsellor, or to do something to help you recover. You could donate some of it to one of the organisations that help people who've been abused. It's better than wasting your life hating it."

"I suppose you're right. It's just that I couldn't think straight about it before. And I had nobody to talk to."

Lucy smiled then for the first time, a smile of gratitude that cemented her strengthening friendship with Rosa.

"It would be good to see a counsellor," said Rosa. "You'd be able to see things more clearly and decide where to start."

"What if I'm not able for it? I can't believe I told you. What if I'm not able to talk to a stranger about it?"

"I'm really glad you did tell me, Lucy. But it'll be better in the long run if you talk to someone who can give you the proper advice. You have to get it out of your system."

"I'd love if it was someone like your mother, Rosa. Would you be able to ask her if there's anyone really nice at St Angela's?"

"Of course I will – I won't have to tell her who it's for or anything. She'll definitely know someone good."

"Maybe it's all the wine but I just feel exhausted all of a sudden," Lucy said now, astounded that she was close to falling asleep when she'd just disclosed the biggest and most important secret of her life, the thing that had haunted her every single day since it had happened.

"That's very normal. Mum is always saying how sleep is good for emotional healing. Sometimes people even fall asleep in her clinic if they've talked about a really harrowing experience. You can stay here tonight, if you like."

"Can I, Rosa? I feel a bit wobbly about going home now, to be honest."

"I had the spare room made up anyway, in case Mum and Dad wanted to stay. I'll get you some pyjamas."

Gratefully, Lucy followed Rosa up the stairs. As a teenager, she'd avoided staying over in her friends' houses and had always been tense and anxious if someone even brought up the subject. Tonight, she was glad to be staying over in Rosa's. The thought of going back to her hollow, empty house wasn't at all appealing and she said as much to her friend now.

"You couldn't be on your own tonight, Lucy. Your head is probably spinning from all the talking. Here, I got all this Clinique stuff at work but I've never used it. You might as well try it out."

"It's not that," Lucy explained as she examined the miniature cleansing bar, clarifying lotion and moisturiser. "I've never loved my house the way that you do. For me it's just somewhere to sleep at night – I don't even feel it belongs to me."

"That's the thing, Lucy. You see the house as something that was bought to get rid of the money and you haven't tried to make it your own. Maybe now you'll be able to do that."

"I just don't have the same taste as you, for a start," she said, looking around Rosa's guest bedroom.

The walls and bed-linen were a simple ivory colour, broken by heavy suede-look curtains and headboard. A rich chocolate-coloured bedspread was folded halfway up the bed, layered with another, smaller one in ivory and chocolate. As well as the pillows, there were two chenille bolsters in the same rich brown as the curtains, accompanied by a few scatter cushions that matched the bedside lamps. Lucy was only dying to get into the bed, it looked so inviting.

"I do everything on a budget, Lucy. I'm always looking around for bits and pieces that match. Your house is fabulous, with all the white walls and timber floors. It's just a matter of softening it up a bit."

That was exactly what her house needed, Lucy thought. It was full of hard edges and bright, harsh light that made her feel exposed and vulnerable all the time. "Would you give me a hand if I did start to try and liven it up a bit? I wouldn't know where to start."

"Would I what! A chance to spend money that isn't mine is almost too good to be true!"

"Thanks, Rosa. What am I supposed to do with all this stuff?"

Rosa had added a Lancôme eye cream and a Dermalogica Daily Exfoliant to the collection of items that she thought Lucy might need for her overnight stay.

"Sorry they're not matching. They come in the special offers with a lot of the cosmetics."

"Rosa, I just use soap and water most nights," Lucy told her.

Rosa, her face incredulous, clearly didn't believe her. "What about moisturiser?"

"I use this stuff that Kate recommended for dry skin — she stocks it in the shop. My face gets very patchy at times." Lucy felt like a child having to admit that she'd been stealing sweets.

"That's because you don't exfoliate to get rid of all the dead skin cells. Use that little powder every night to scrub your face and it'll be as smooth as anything. Then go over it with the toner to close the pores before you put on the moisturiser. You have lovely skin anyway, Lucy – it'll just brighten it up."

At this rate, Lucy could visualise herself having to set her alarm clock for five a.m., considering that she was already getting up a bit earlier to do her hair the way Rocky had recommended.

"Rosa, thanks for all this. Really, I mean it – you've been so good to me."

It wasn't just the skin-care products and the pair of navy silk pyjamas laid out on the opulent double bed that Lucy was thanking Rosa for.

"You've been great to me too, Lucy. If you hadn't given me one of your red peppers that first night I would have left The Gourmet Rooms after the first session. I certainly wouldn't have got this far if you weren't helping me."

"You would, Rosa. It's just better fun to do it together."

"The more I think of it," Rosa sighed in a resigned tone of voice, "the more I realise that a restaurant mightn't be such a good idea here."

"Don't let all the regulations put you off. No matter what you do there will be rules and regulations. Once you get things sorted, you'll be up and running."

"It's not just that. I didn't think of things like parking and noise levels at night. It wouldn't be fair on the neighbours to have car doors slamming and people chatting in the street at all hours."

"The neighbours include me, don't forget."

"I know. Most of the residents here are elderly though.

It would be a bit much. And did you hear your man from the Health Board about all the regulations for toilets and wheelchair access. I'd have to gut the whole house."

"Well, does it have to be here? You could always rent a place." Lucy hated to see her friend's dream going down the drain so quickly.

"I thought about that as well but it's more expense. I hadn't really looked into it enough, to be honest, Lucy," she admitted. "Still, I have my job in BT's to keep me going until something more exciting comes up."

"And we actually know how to cook now!" Lucy was optimistic that their new skills might still lead to a career more suited to Rosa's needs.

"And we've made new friends. I really like Kate. That shop of hers is a goldmine."

"She's lovely," Lucy agreed. "You can ask her anything without feeling stupid. She's very good to Agnes as well."

"Agnes has it tough enough with her sister, I think. She won't even let her cook the stuff we do in class because it's too expensive."

"I was talking to her the last night at the break and she was telling me that she was nearly engaged once when she was younger. It never went ahead because she had to look after her sister. If that was me, I'd be livid but Agnes just says that Beatrice hasn't had it easy either."

Thinking about Agnes now made Lucy see how lucky she was in one way. Despite everything that had happened with Ned and the anger she still felt towards him, at least she was free to improve her life as best she could. Agnes had had no such choice and still didn't.

She told Rosa this now and vowed to try and make the most of her life, even though she knew that the counselling wouldn't be easy.

"You've done the hardest part, Lucy, in saying it out loud. I'll phone Mum first thing and get the name of a counsellor. Now you'd better get some sleep – it's nearly half three."

Life was series of new starts, Lucy realised, as she drifted off to sleep that night in Rosa's luxurious room. Bernadette Mooney had spoken about change and the fact that if people refused to change then the next ten years of their life would be the same as the last ten. If this was the case, then Lucy was determined that change would come sooner rather than later.

Chapter 20

Agnes was absolutely thrilled about doing the bread-making because she was confident that Beatrice couldn't complain about it. That meant she'd be able to practise at home to hone her skills, although it occurred to her now that she'd better not show too much skill or Beatrice would be asking her for fresh ciabatta day and night. Not that she'd be at her beck and call for all manner of things the way she had been up to lately.

Since the day that she'd met Willie Boyle and Miriam at the market in Midleton, Agnes had changed her tune. It was partly her own fault for letting Beatrice take over her life and she'd already spent almost forty years resenting it. It was hard for her to admit that a small part of her had actually *liked* being the victim of circumstance but she knew now that this was true.

Willie was a case in point. His own plans had been cut short when Agnes had declined his offer of marriage. It hadn't stopped him from getting on with it, even if he wasn't lucky enough to meet someone else in his younger years. The fact that he'd made a life for himself even at this late stage had galvanised Agnes even further.

Donning the new angora sweater that she'd bought in the January sales but had hoarded until she'd found a matching scarf, she sprayed herself liberally with Opium, loving its rich opulent fragrance. The perfume had been her latest little treat, acquired on her last visit to the city. Agnes always made the most of her trips, having a set routine depending on what she was looking for.

She'd been running low on perfume lately and had been bearing it in mind for a while to go on a shopping spree. Not that she ever paid for perfume. Usually, she decided on what she wanted from the scented page inserts in the glossy magazines that were always lying around in the GP's surgery when she brought Beatrice for her quarterly Vitamin B12 injection.

Once she'd settled on a fragrance, Agnes waited for a chance to go to Cork and proceed around all the chemists and cosmetic counters asking for a sample of the chosen scent. She used various little excuses – she'd smelled it on a friend and wanted to try it for herself or she was planning to buy it for a friend but wasn't quite sure. Sometimes she even told the truth, that she'd smelled it in a magazine and wanted to see if she definitely liked it. Generally, she came away with the equivalent of a 50ml bottle as most of the testers were between 5 and 10mls.

It was hard work certainly but worth it if she garnered enough of what she wanted to last a while. She tended to stick to the one fragrance until she'd used up all her testers

– that way people would identify her with a certain expensive scent.

It was Rosa Mooney who'd suggested that Opium might be a good scent for the mature lady, a choice that Agnes had concurred with immediately on smelling it. Rosa seemed to be a mine of information on all things beauty-related, even convincing her about the value of antioxidants in maintaining a youthful appearance.

Aside from the cooking, joining the Absolute Beginners class had turned out exactly as she'd hoped. Like all the evening classes that she'd attended in the past, the few hours out of the house were invaluable. But it was the connection with so many new people that was the highlight for Agnes.

She'd felt comfortable with Kate Lewis straight away, even though she was considerably younger and an independent career woman with her own business.

Rosa, despite annoying her a little in the early stages with her tendency to keep disrupting the class by not listening properly and then getting things wrong, had turned out to be engaging and generous. So much so that she often bungled her own dishes by coming unnecessarily to the aid of one of the others if she thought they were in trouble with something. She'd even offered Agnes her employee discount the next time she needed to buy something in Brown Thomas, something that made Agnes look forward to the sales more than usual.

Lucy Dalton, whom Agnes had thought to be rude in the extreme the first night that she'd met her, had again turned out to be a different character altogether. In the space of less than six weeks, she'd been transformed – heavily influenced by Rosa, Agnes suspected. Of all of them, Lucy was by far the most practical in the kitchen, taking everything in her stride and appearing to absorb Mrs Carter's instructions without having to rely as heavily on the Gourmet Rooms cookbook the way the rest of them did.

The other group, made up of the handsome paediatrician and the three computer experts – she'd finally found out what IT meant – tended to stick together, regardless of Rosa's efforts to snare the young doctor.

Agnes glanced in the mirror one last time and, satisfied with her appearance, left the safe haven of her bedroom to check on Beatrice before she took off to The Gourmet Rooms. She'd already made up a snack for her, in case she got peckish after the News. They'd had the supper early and Beatrice had been complaining about being left to starve the first few Tuesday evenings. Agnes had even read a few pages of the latest Silhouette romance to Bea after lunch so that she wouldn't be deprived of entertainment.

As usual, she was looking forward to getting into the city for the evening and sweeping up the steps of Mrs Carter's impressive residence. Agnes had read somewhere that Mrs Carter had been widowed at an early age and had started up the cookery course as a means of keeping up the large house that had been in her husband's family for generations.

Apparently, the young Pamela Hynes had come to work in the office at Carter's Grain Store and had taken the eye of Thomas Carter almost immediately. Thomas had married her, only to die shortly afterwards in a machinery accident. As far as Agnes knew from the many society magazines that she devoured, they hadn't had any children.

Agnes loved these little titbits of information as they made her feel that she had the inside track, as if Mrs Carter herself had told her these details. Even though she always tried to strike up an interesting and intelligent conversation with the tutor at the beginning of the class or during the break, she never seemed to be any closer to getting to know Mrs Carter any better.

Despite being slightly disappointed with her own lack of connection with Mrs Carter, Agnes had to admire the way that she tended to divide her time almost equally between all the participants of the course before leaving them to enjoy their refreshments while she returned to the kitchen to prepare for the second session.

In particular, she gave great attention to Rosa whose great enthusiasm was marred by an unfortunate lack of organisational skills. If left alone for a moment, Rosa tended to get all her ingredients mixed up and ended up having to be supervised by Mrs Carter if her companion, Lucy Dalton, was out of bounds.

Lucy, on the other hand, needed little attention, yet Mrs Carter made it her business to ensure that she was enjoying the course, encouraging her to experiment with the recipes for variation.

She seemed to interact comfortably with Kate Lewis, whose shop she frequented and whose products she recommended highly. Like Agnes, Kate didn't seem to have got to know Mrs Carter any better for all the years of her coming in and out of the shop.

Sighing with relief that she was finally free to leave the house, Agnes retied her scarf at a slightly jauntier angle and bade Beatrice goodbye for the third time. In the past five minutes she'd made two other attempts to leave but had been delayed looking for a particular romance book that she'd eventually found down the side of her sister's bed. After that, she'd had to refill the thermos flask with vegetable soup instead of the cocoa that Beatrice had decided on earlier but which she suddenly regretted in case she'd starve if Agnes was delayed.

Soon, she'd be independent of her sister. Her first pension payment would be through in the New Year and then Beatrice would see what side her bread was buttered on, Agnes thought firmly as she finally took her leave.

"Now, everybody," Mrs Carter greeted them as soon as they were all positioned at their various work stations, "we'll be doing various breads tonight, starting with a basic bread mix and branching out to various uses after that. Bread-making is yet another of the great mysteries of cooking but once you get the basic recipe, it's actually pretty simple."

"Will there be yeast involved?"

Rosa looked terrified but Mrs Carter smiled encouragingly at her anxious expression before assuring her that it was a good start that she'd actually heard of using yeast as a raising agent.

Agnes noticed that Lucy was also nodding at Rosa in

a satisfied manner, as if to say, "See, I knew you were more tuned in than you thought."

Once they'd all slotted their pages into the Perspex holder at the front of their work stations, Mrs Carter began to explain the vagaries of fresh yeast versus dried yeast and the importance of proving the dough twice before baking. As usual, all the ingredients for the first recipe were laid out on their work surfaces for them and the ovens were already pre-heating.

"We'll need to get cracking," she warned as the familiar exploration of the ingredients began. "The first proving will take at least thirty minutes at this room temperature. Then you'll be shaping it and allowing another thirty minutes for the second proving. Don't panic at all, Rosa, we'll have plenty of time if we move along smartly," she added kindly when she saw Rosa looking at Lucy, her face a picture of alarm.

Their instructor roamed calmly from one work station to the next as her charges heaped the flour and other dry ingredients onto the granite surfaces and made a well in the centre for the liquids. Dried yeast was being used in the recipe, much to Agnes's relief, in view of the fact that the fresh version was harder to source and considerably more expensive.

Agnes swirled the inside of the 'well', drawing in the flour gradually as instructed. To her gratification, Mrs Carter nodded approvingly before moving along towards Rosa who seemed to be having serious difficulty. The edges of her heap of flour had caved in and the liquid had started to run off the edge of the work surface. Lucy was trying valiantly to assist her partner, abandoning her own surprisingly neat effort to hand her a wad of kitchen roll.

"It's a bit like a volcano erupting," Rosa giggled nervously as the heap of flour collapsed once again, gaining her, to Agnes's bemusement, an almost indulgent smile from the instructor.

Eventually, after much kneading and pummelling, all six of them had a ball of dough settled into a greased plastic bag which they labelled and placed at the back of the room near the ovens.

"The next thing we need to do is decide on how to shape the bread and what toppings or fillings we might want to use."

Agnes was thrilled with the idea that she'd be able to practise the variations to her heart's content at home, although she knew it was unlikely that Beatrice would have any truck with the black olive and mozzarella foccacia. She'd be able to divide the basic dough in three parts, she decided, and make something with an exotic topping for herself while shaping the remainder into a batch of plain rolls or an attractive plait for her sister.

After careful examination and consideration, all of their efforts were deemed to have doubled in size when thirty-five minutes had elapsed. Out of the plastic bags came the lumps of dough, ready for further kneading and shaping. Agnes got particular pleasure from twisting the neat plait into shape, visualising the scrumptious golden creation that it would become.

As soon as that was settled onto its floured tray, she flattened the next portion of dough and dotted it evenly with stoned olives and little balls of creamy mozzarella, pushing each piece well down into the dough as instructed. A generous sprinkle of sea salt and that too went onto a flour-strewn baking tray.

The third portion she rolled into small balls and placed next to each other on a smaller tray, patting the tops of them gently into shape. It would be at least another thirty minutes before they were ready for baking.

"I think a cup of tea is in order after that little marathon," Mrs Carter praised, indicating the drawing room with a sweep of her hand.

Satisfied with her own performance, Agnes wiped down her granite worktop efficiently and washed her hands, noting the way that Rosa scattered bits of flour everywhere in her attempt to tidy her space before the break. Lucy and Kate didn't drop so much as a crumb between them.

"Sit in there, Agnes, and I'll get your tea. I have a plan that I think you'll like," Kate said with a hint of excitement as soon as they'd reached the drawing room. She'd indicated the comfortable chaise longue that was nestled in the recess of the large window, knowing it was Agnes's favourite place to sit.

The heavy burgundy drapes were open as usual. Since the start of the course, Agnes had loved sitting in this seat, imagining how elegant she must look to anyone passing in the street, perched on the edge of the gold upholstery as if she were mistress of the place. Now she was wondering if she'd been living in a sort of fantasy world for years – imagining a better life instead of going out and getting one.

Tonight, Rosa and Lucy were tucked away in the far corner of the room. Typically, Rosa was examining her complexion in the huge overmantel while Lucy lounged in one of the overstuffed armchairs looking more relaxed than Agnes had ever seen her. She was wearing a soft, baby-pink lamb's-wool jumper with a long denim skirt, an outfit that made her look much taller and slimmer than her old jeans and fleece ensemble.

"Chocolate and orange cookies," Kate announced, arriving back with two china mugs and a plate of biscuits. "I'd pay to come here for the tea breaks even if I never got a lesson."

"I love the ginger ones as well. We'll be doing them at some stage, Mrs Carter says. Now, what plan do you have for me?"

"Day care," Kate enthused, her large brown eyes alive with the brilliance of the idea. "Catherine Tierney was in the other day and she asked if Bea had changed her mind on the respite care at all. When I told her that she was very definite about not going, Catherine suggested that she try the Day Centre."

Kate had been more than helpful in trying to get assistance for Agnes, even liaising with the Public Health Nurse on her behalf. Catherine Tierney had offered, via Kate, to come out to the house to meet Agnes and Beatrice to explain all the services that were available but Agnes had been afraid of Bea causing a rumpus. She couldn't bear another week of the cold shoulder that she'd had when the respite at Summer Orchard had been brought up.

"What would it involve?" Agnes was more cautious

now after the last episode, although the idea of a day as opposed to an overnight stay sounded a little more viable.

"It sounds great actually. It's a purpose-built unit here in the city and there's even a bus that brings people there and back. It's like a social club really – they do painting, storytelling, bingo and that kind of thing. They have a book club as well so Bea might like that. I think she'd love it if she gave it a chance at all."

"You see, Kate, that's the thing. Bea always thinks that I want to get rid of her but it's not that at all. I'd love to see her going out to something that she'd enjoy instead of being stuck at home all the time. I think that's why she sleeps so badly as well – she doesn't use up any of her energy during the day."

"Well, you should talk to her about it. Catherine says the people who go there love it."

Agnes nibbled thoughtfully on her delicious biscuit and vowed that she'd be more firm with Bea this time, if only for her own sake. Neither of them was getting any younger.

"I think it's a wonderful idea, Kate. I might have a bit of a battle on my hands though."

"Well, it'd be worth it if it meant that Beatrice would be less afraid of getting help. Now, get that tea down you. We have work to do."

Agnes could see Mrs Carter approaching through the open double door that led out into the hall. She smiled now as Rosa was dragged away from an in-depth conversation with Mark Toland, the handsome paediatrician. Lucy caught Agnes's eye and winked, aware that she'd been employed by Rosa on more than one occasion to investigate whether Mark was single or not. To date, they'd all had limited success in the fact-finding department and Rosa was apparently on the point of relinquishing him to the three IT-girls. Placing her cup and plate neatly on the polished hostess trolley, Agnes winked back at Lucy and followed her companions back to the kitchen.

Next on the evening's agenda was traditional wholemeal bread and scones. Agnes's mind was already ticking over at the possibility of having a full day to herself every week. And perhaps Beatrice would make friends of her own if she tried, she mused as she measured the grainy heaps of pinhead oatmeal, bran and wholemeal flour into her bowl. She visualised herself taking a day-trip on the train with her free travel and wandering at her leisure around Kilkenny or Galway, enjoying the shops and tourist spots. As soon as she got home tonight, she would discuss the Day Centre with her sister.

As it transpired, Agnes never did get to broach the subject of the Day Centre with Bea. She knew immediately that something was amiss when she opened the front door at twenty past ten and heard the television blaring. Beatrice always turned it off straight after the news; otherwise she'd be too 'hyped up' to sleep, she was fond of saying.

Calling out as she closed the door nervously, she immediately heard a feeble groan from the direction of the kitchen. Instinctively, she raced to see what had happened but found herself unable to open the solid wooden door leading from the hall.

"Bea, what happened? Are you hurt?"

Agnes fully expected to hear her sister's robust voice answering her indignantly, chastising her for being late. Instead, all she heard was a feeble whimper. Panicking momentarily when she realised that she couldn't get at the phone to call for help, Agnes gathered her wits and called back to her sister in a strong reassuring voice.

"Stay where you are, Bea. Don't try to move. I'll go around to the back door."

Grabbing her keys again, she raced out the front door and around to the back of the house, the heels of her good shoes sinking into the gravel. Thankfully, the light outside the back door was on. Her hands shook uncontrollably as she tried to insert the key in the lock, every moment seeming like an hour in her haste to get to Bea. Finally the key turned in the lock and she pushed the door open gingerly, terrified of what she would find.

Beatrice lay ashen-faced on the tiles with the wheelchair partially on top of her.

"Oh God, Bea, what happened?"

Agnes rushed over to her and immediately lifted the wheelchair from where it was resting across her legs.

"I was trying to get the biscuits. I don't know how I fell over," Bea explained in a feeble whisper.

"Don't worry. I'll get you up. How long are you here?"

"You were just gone. I couldn't even reach the phone."

Once again, Agnes realised the extent of the mistake she'd made in trying to care for Bea herself. Only a few weeks ago, Kate had told her about the personal alarms that disabled people could access through their local health centre. But because it would have involved Bea signing a form with the Public Health Nurse, Agnes had known that Bea would never agree. If only she'd had the alarm, she would have been able to press a button attached to a wristband to alert the emergency services.

Once she'd straightened up the wheelchair and replaced the cushion, Agnes turned her attention to Beatrice. There had been many falls in the past but this was the first time that she'd seen her sister looking so pale and shaken.

"Don't, Agnes!" Bea yelled out as soon as Agnes tried to move her legs into place. The left one was rotated outwards like the limb of a rag-doll.

"It's okay, Bea," Agnes soothed, trying in vain to lift her sister under the arms instead. As soon as her legs moved at all, Bea screamed out in pain again.

"I think it's broken, Agnes," Bea cried. "What'll happen to me now?"

Agnes guessed that Bea had spent the last few hours lying on the cold tiles in the kitchen worrying, not about the fact that her leg might be broken, but about the idea of being hospitalised.

"We'll have to ring for an ambulance, Bea – you can't stay here."

Shakily, Agnes lifted the receiver and dialled 911. As best she could, she explained to the operator the situation they were in and called out the address as clearly as she was able.

"Please send someone as fast as you can," she pleaded, stories of people having to wait because the ambulance had gone to another emergency springing to mind.

"I'm perished, Agnes." Poor Bea had been lying on the

floor for three hours and probably hadn't even had the soup that Agnes had made earlier. Frantically, Agnes tried to think what was best to do in an emergency. You were supposed to give hot, sweet tea for the shock, she remembered, yet she recalled hearing that no food or drink should be given if a person might need surgery. And if Bea's leg really was broken, then the chances were that she would need to go to theatre to have it fixed.

"I'll get you a duvet and a hot-water bottle," she decided finally, her mind working overtime as to how she was going to get out to the hot press in the hall when Bea was wedged up against the door. First, though, she filled the kettle.

"I'll be back in a minute," she promised, racing out the back door. Back around the house she ran and in the front door. Gathering up a spare duvet, two pillows and their two hot-water bottles, she hurried back out and around the back again. Not used to this level of activity, poor Agnes was panting hard when she arrived back into the kitchen.

"Here, try and get this under you," she encouraged, tilting Bea as much as she could without hurting her.

As soon as she had her wrapped as best she could, Agnes filled the two hot-water bottles and tucked them in under the duvet, hoping that her sister wouldn't die before the ambulance got there. Bea's eyes were closing a bit, she noticed.

"Bea, you have to stay awake." All the films had this in common, the refusal to let someone who was injured to asleep. Bea wasn't even whimpering now. "Come on, Bea, don't go asleep," she insisted, shaking her a little to keep her awake. She hovered over the huddled form anxiously, trying to think of something to say that would stop her sister from going unconscious. Holding her sister's hand tightly she was shocked at how cold and feeble it felt in her own.

"We did bread-making tonight, Bea," she began, aware of how incongruous it sounded. "We did rolls, those nice soft ones that you like and brown bread. I'll be able to practise them while you're in hospital and bring them in to you. I'll be an expert by the time you come home."

Bea smiled feebly at this, encouraging Agnes to continue her monologue. Please let them come, Agnes prayed silently.

She resumed talking about the cookery class, telling Beatrice more about Kate, Rosa and Lucy that she had in the last six weeks put together. She talked about Rosa's ineptitude in the kitchen at The Gourmet Rooms, Kate's shop and how it was wheelchair accessible and the way that Lucy had blossomed since the start of the Absolute Beginners class.

The sound of the approaching siren sent a wave of relief flooding over Agnes.

"They're here, Bea. You'll be fine now. The ambulance is here."

"You won't leave me there, will you, Agnes?" Bea sounded terrified, as if her greatest fear was about to be realised.

"Of course I won't, Bea. But we'll have to get more help once you're home, that's all. We won't let this happen again, I promise."

Agnes could see the blue lights flashing through the kitchen blind and ran outside to alert the ambulance to where Bea was. Suddenly the kitchen was a hive of activity. The two burly paramedics examined Beatrice, talking her through the procedure gently as they placed her leg in an inflatable splint and manoeuvred her onto the stretcher.

"I'm afraid the leg looks as if it's broken, Miss Cotter," one of them said gently. The other one, Bill, placed an oxygen mask over Bea's mouth and nose, assuring her that it was purely routine.

The room took on a surreal appearance from the rotating blue light of the ambulance as it flashed outside the kitchen window and Agnes suddenly felt light-headed with all the activity. What if she'd been any later? Would Beatrice have died of shock?

"Will you be able to get to St Angela's later?" Bill enquired of Agnes now. "Or is there anyone you can ring?"

"I'll be able to drive," she told him, warmed by his concern. "What about a bag? Can you wait a few minutes until I pack her things?"

"Your sister won't need any clothes or anything for the moment. You can bring all that tomorrow."

Meekly, Agnes let go of her sister's hand for the last time as the paramedics popped the legs of the stretcher and wheeled Beatrice away from her. She was heartened to see her lift a hand feebly as the doors slid closed.

Agnes stared after the departing ambulance, terrified that it would be the last time she would see Beatrice alive, her mind dominated by one thought: what if *she herself* had been injured, say, in a car crash? Who would Bea have been able to call if Agnes hadn't returned home? How long would she have had to wait before anyone came? Either way, they were a crisis just waiting to happen.

The enormity of their isolation washed over Agnes and she sank down on one of the kitchen chairs and closed her eyes, alone for the first time in her life.

Chapter 21

By the time Lucy found a space in the vast carpark at St Angela's, she was already wondering if she was doing the right thing at all. On Wednesday, Rosa had given her the little card with Cora Nolan's name and qualifications on it and instead of taking her time to think about it, she'd picked up the phone and made an appointment there and then.

At the time, she'd imagined that it might be weeks before a slot was available but, trust her luck, the receptionist had informed her that there was a cancellation that very Friday. The fact that she wasn't working on Friday had cinched it for her, avoiding the need to ask Una Riordan for time off.

Now here she was in the car with her heart beating maniacally, terrified that she'd clam up as soon as she came face to face with the counsellor. If only it had been Bernadette Mooney that she was going to, she'd have felt more confident. As it stood, she was going to be meeting a complete stranger in less than five minutes' time.

Pulling herself together, she walked the short distance

to the front entrance of the hospital and followed the signs for the private clinic as Rosa had instructed. Suddenly, she was standing at the reception area in Suite 102, sweat breaking out all over her as she announced herself quietly to the middle-aged lady behind the desk.

"Just take a seat and Cora will be with you in a moment," she instructed, indicating a long leather sofa with a large pot plant at either end.

Lucy had never had any reason to be in a private clinic before and was surprised to find it was less intimidating than she'd expected. For one thing, she was the only person in the waiting room. This had been a big part of her anxiety all morning – the fear of meeting someone that she knew and of having to explain herself. Rosa had pointed out that if she did meet someone, then they'd be in the same boat and probably wouldn't question her for fear of having to broadcast their own reason for being there. As usual, she'd hit the nail on the head, calming Lucy just enough to stop her from cancelling altogether.

"Lucy?"

In a world of her own, Lucy hadn't noticed a door opening on the far side of one of the enormous pot plants. The girl in front of her couldn't be much older than herself, yet to Lucy she exuded self-assurance and confidence. Tall and slim with flawless skin, she looked like something straight out of a Pantene advertisement, with long, dark hair that fell straight down her back in a glossy mane. Her hand was already extended and Lucy jumped up and took it nervously, a bit perturbed at this latest development.

"Hello, Lucy, I'm Cora Nolan. You're very welcome."

Lucy had been expecting someone older, someone of Bernadette Mooney's vintage, rather than this young woman who wore fitted black trousers and a dark red shirt instead of the uniform that she'd imagined.

Even her voice was flawless, its tone calm and even, as if she would be fully in control of any situation that might arise. Her hand, when Lucy took it, was warm and dry.

"Hi," said Lucy, her voice coming out in a croak that made her wonder if she'd be able to get through the session at all.

Cora ushered Lucy into her room. "Now, make yourself comfortable," she invited, indicating a terracotta two-seater sofa with a matching footstool.

To Lucy's surprise, there was no desk in the room, just another matching sofa facing the one she sat on now. The floor, unlike the hospital environment that she'd expected, was covered with a springy cream carpet. She could see an aromatherapy burner sitting in the window ledge and recognised the scent of lavender and jasmine. The familiar fragrance, one that she associated with Kate's shop, made her feel comfortable straight away.

"Would you like to tell me a little about why you came today, Lucy?"

This had been another of her fears for the past two days – having to start her story as if she was telling a doctor about an ingrown toenail. Now, however, in the comfort and security of her squashy sofa, she'd been given an encouraging opening by Cora Nolan.

"I was abused when I was thirteen and I only told someone about it a few weeks ago," she blurted out.

Having rehearsed her opening line endlessly for two days, the relief of having it out was enormous. She came to a halt once she'd said it, her mind not having gone any further regarding what else she was going to say.

"And do you feel ready to talk a bit more about it now?" Cora prompted, her voice gentle, with no sign of shock or disgust.

Lucy took a deep breath and continued. "I think I must be. I think that's why I told Rosa, my friend, in the first place. I didn't tell her everything though. The details or anything." Lucy didn't know why she said this last bit as she didn't think she'd be able to tell Cora the details either.

"You don't have to tell me either, if you don't want to. Sometimes things come in stages."

"I think that's it," she agreed, glad that Cora didn't seem to be about to drag her story out of her. "It had a very bad effect on me," she continued. "Although I didn't know it at the time."

"In what way?" Cora settled herself in the sofa opposite as if she were about to listen to a friend telling a story about something completely normal.

Almost as if she were talking to herself, Lucy began. Once she started, she was surprised at the things she wanted to say – not about Ned and the horrible weekend in Kildare but about the way she'd behaved in school and the way she'd treated her parents over the years.

"Do you feel bad about that?"

"I do, to be honest."

Lucy's face was red as she described the way she'd been stubborn and moody, snapping at her mother if she so much as asked her a question about school or her friends.

"I always used to do the vegetable patch with Dad and I stopped that as well. He used to ask me about it at first – you know, what we'd plant and stuff – but I kept telling him it was boring. He stopped asking then and did it himself."

Lucy remembered this as a horrible time and closed her eyes briefly as she thought of the last time her father had asked if she wanted to thin out the lettuce with him. She'd shouted at him that she was sick of lettuce and spring onions and drills of potatoes. She still remembered the hurt look on his face and the way he'd said, "Grand so" in the mild, placating voice that he seemed to be using more and more with her.

"Did you mind when he stopped asking?"

Lucy thought about this for a moment. "I did, I suppose. Not so much about the vegetables but because he had nothing to talk to me about after that. You see, Mam hated the garden so I used to help Dad."

"Did you ever think about changing your mind?"

"Once I'd said all that, I couldn't," Lucy struggled to explain. "I was always looking at the plants when Dad was in work."

"Are you sorry you missed out on the gardening?"

"I am, I suppose. I used to enjoy it," she admitted, wondering if she was entirely mad to have come all the way over to St Angela's to talk about a vegetable patch.

"What else did you enjoy?"

"You mean before?" She couldn't even say "before what Uncle Ned did".

"Yes."

"I used to go out cycling with Jeanette next door. We used to spend the whole summer on bikes, you know, buying sweets and finding somewhere to eat them."

Lucy found herself reliving the long summer days when she and Jeanette Doyle would be gone from early morning until six o'clock when they had to be back at their respective houses for the Angelus. She'd almost forgotten about the bunches of lilac that they were fond of collecting along the way and how it was often dried out and wilted by the time they got home.

"And afterwards, what kind of things did you like doing?"

"That's the thing. I can remember hardly anything about secondary school. Rosa is always talking about things like dressing up and going to discos but I can't really think now what I liked. I only remember being horrible to Mam and Dad, to be honest."

"That seems to have affected you a lot," Cora commented.

"I think it did. It made me feel awful – it still does, actually."

"Did either of your parents ever ask you if anything was wrong?"

"I don't think I let them. I think I was *afraid* they might ask. I couldn't have told them."

"Did you think they wouldn't believe you?"

"It wasn't that. I wouldn't have known what to tell them. It was horrible and I couldn't have said it."

Lucy knew that her voice was rising but she couldn't seem to help it. She needed Cora to know that what had happened wasn't something small that could have been solved with a glass of hot lemonade, even if she had been able to tell her parents.

"It was huge, Lucy. It's a big secret to carry around."

This made Lucy feel like crying, something that had only ever happened to her once before, the night that she'd told Rosa. It was Cora's use of the word 'carry' that made her feel so overwhelmed.

"It *was* like carrying something. Here," she said, indicating her chest. "Something heavy."

Cora was listening to her intently, not pityingly at how daft she must sound, but with interest.

"The night I told Rosa, I felt as if someone had taken a big stone out and I could take a deep breath if I wanted to. Does that sound mad?"

"Not at all – it's very common in fact."

"I feel like that again now that I can talk about it."

"Do you think you could ever talk to your parents about it?"

"I don't want to. Ned's dead now so there isn't much point – it'd only upset them. I feel a bit better about going home in the last few weeks though." Lucy only realised this at the moment she said it.

"Really?" Cora looked interested again, prompting her to continue.

"I used to go home every Sunday that I was off, just for the sake of it. Mostly, though, Mam would come over to my house to tidy up and stuff. The last two weeks, I think I was a bit better. Not as short with Dad as I used to be. I even found it a bit easier to get on with Mam."

Now that she thought about it, Lucy realised that she hadn't felt inclined to be as obstinate as she normally did when her mother asked her a question. And she'd been more forthcoming about the cookery class than she had been at the outset. Initially, she'd felt that she was defying her mother in getting the better of her about being able to look after herself whereas last Sunday she'd wanted her to see how well she was doing.

"Not in a showing-off way," she explained to Cora. "Before, I used to almost try to annoy her. Now, I feel a bit sorry about that. I'd like her to see that I'm getting on well now."

"Why is that, all of a sudden?"

"I just don't feel as cross any more. It wasn't their fault that it happened. They didn't even know."

"It's easy to see that now. But when you were younger, could you see that?"

"No. And I think I was cross because they didn't cop on. I kept waiting for them to realise but they never did."

This was the crux of it, she thought, her heart sinking dismally. Despite the fact that the whole thing was Ned's fault, she'd been blaming her parents for not finding out and doing something. She thought of the bewildered expression that she used to see on her father's face sometimes and the exasperated one that her mother wore permanently. It dawned on her now that in all the years since it had happened, it had never occurred to them that there might be any real basis for her behaviour save teenage angst.

"I thought they should have been able to help me," she

said now to Cora. "But I think they genuinely didn't realise that something like this could happen, especially when it was Dad's own brother. If it hadn't happened to *me*, maybe I'd be as innocent as them too. All along, I felt that they *should* have known. Now, I'm not so sure."

"You're not as angry at them now?"

"No, I've let it go – I'm sick of it, to be honest."

"You seem to have sorted out a lot in your head already, Lucy."

To Lucy's mind, she sounded almost admiring of this.

"Some things I have," she admitted. "It's like my head is more organised now. Before I told Rosa about it, my head used to be churning but nothing made sense. Now, I'm thinking about things and asking myself *why* I'm thinking them."

"That's better than blocking it out the way you had to when you were younger."

"I just wish I'd been able to tell someone sooner."

Lucy had been thinking this for the last two weeks, about all the years she'd missed out on.

"It's great you're doing it now. Would you like to come again?"

"I would," Lucy told her, feeling a stone lighter already and smiling for the first time that afternoon.

Since her counselling session with Cora Nolan, Lucy had felt like a new woman. She had a day shift in The Friary the following morning, something that had never bothered her too much in the past. Now, however, she had an urge to be off for the weekend, thinking that it would be nice to go into the shops and look around. Rosa was working too, a full day as opposed to Lucy's half day, so she'd have had to go on her own even if she had been off.

Rosa's advice about spending some of her unwanted inheritance on herself had finally sunk in when she'd handed over the ?70 to the receptionist in Suite 102 the previous afternoon. Now she was wishing it cost more.

"You're dreaming," Cathy Rohan accused good-naturedly as they checked the controlled drugs together in the Treatment Room. It was nearly time for their break.

"Just thinking it's a shame to be working on a Saturday."

"Tell me about it," she yawned. "Leon had a work night out last night and I wasn't in bed until half one. I've to go into Marks & Sparks after work to change a cardigan for my mother."

"I'll come with you, if you like," Lucy announced, uncharacteristically inviting herself along.

"Brilliant. We can go for lunch somewhere first."

Cathy was the kind of person who made an occasion out of the opening of an envelope.

"Roll on two o'clock," Lucy grinned, signing her name under Cathy's on the medication register. It amused her that Cathy hadn't batted so much as an eyelash at her sudden decision to go shopping, even though she'd refused on almost every other occasion she'd been asked.

"Roll on eleven o'clock first so I can get a cup of coffee into me. Don't forget we have the nutritionist coming at twelve for the talk."

"We'd better get a move on then. I'll go and start setting up the Day Room."

Once a month, Una Riordan organised for a health professional to visit The Friary. Sometimes, like today, it was just for a talk while on other occasions it might be a physiotherapist or occupational therapist to make suggestions on special cutlery, walking aids or seating.

The Day Room, normally laid out in informal groups of armchairs and coffee tables, was usually rearranged so that all of the chairs faced the speaker. Lucy headed off to do this now while Cathy organised the lunch-time medications, making sure that there would be room for wheelchair-users.

She was looking forward to hearing what the nutritionist would have to say, having become interested in the subject from her many trips to Good For You. Not only was she determined to sort out the things that were happening on the inside, she'd also resolved to upscale her efforts to sort out her neglected façade and had been paying more attention to her diet that ever before. She'd been shocked to find that she was over twelve stone when she'd stood on the chrome scales in her clinical bathroom for the first time a few weeks ago. Up until then, the scales had remained carefully hidden in the pristine unit that surrounded the black marble sink. No wonder she couldn't get clothes to fit her properly!

Lucy was amazed that she'd already lost so much weight in the few weeks since she'd started the Absolute Beginners course. Almost seven pounds – despite the fact that Mrs Carter covered a dessert almost every week. She reckoned it was because she'd stopped buying all the chocolate bars, something that had happened almost unbeknownst to her. She'd always wandered around the supermarket aimlessly picking up the few items that she thought she needed, never really having a proper idea of what she would eat or when. But now, gradually, she'd become a more discerning shopper, with the chocolate bars and crisps going by the wayside, simply because she was too busy hunting for things like arrowroot and gelatine.

An hour later, Lucy was in a state of near shock as she started to realise how poor her diet actually was, notwithstanding all the changes she'd made already. Lauren Brady, whose first time it was to visit The Friary, started her talk with a presentation on the food pyramid – something that both Kate and Mrs Carter were always talking about.

Lucy's eyes were almost out on stalks when the trim redhead announced that they should be taking at least five portions of fruit and vegetables per day. If it wasn't for Mrs Carter, she'd hardly be getting even one.

"It's difficult to manage it," Lauren agreed when Nora Wallace expressed the view that her grandchildren were the devil for turning their noses up at vegetables. "Especially if you're eating processed foods that don't need a fresh vegetable with them. Frozen pizzas are a good example. Or if children are getting crisps and chocolate as snacks, then they won't be interested in fruit."

Lucy could identify with this, the mounds of buttery toast that she usually laid into on her morning break springing to mind. And the liberal topping of home-made jam from the residents' occupational therapy sessions didn't bear thinking about. Maybe it was time to swap the toast for a banana and kiwi as Cathy did.

Towards the end of the talk, Lauren offered to weigh each of the residents and advise them on what their ideal weight should be, according to their Body Mass Index. Lucy assisted each of them onto the scales, wondering if she too should have her dimensions plotted on the little graph that the nutritionist was consulting.

Deciding to go for broke, she stepped onto the scales and then under the height measure. She was relieved to see that she fitted into the 'overweight' category as opposed to the 'obese', a category she might well have fitted into a few weeks ago.

Cathy, needless to say, was in the 'healthy' category, something that Lucy now aspired to. Before she left, Lauren issued each member of her audience with a little disc so that they could measure their own Body Mass Index.

"Armed and dangerous," Lucy whispered to Cathy, wielding her disc. "This is going to be my new bible."

For the first time in her life, Lucy was actually enjoying shopping for clothes. Before, whenever Cathy asked if she wanted to go into town after a day shift, she'd have something akin to a panic attack at the thought of being under scrutiny and not measuring up. Having allowed herself to relax a bit with the girls at work, it surprised her that she didn't seem as intimidated any more.

Cathy, as soon as she'd changed her mother's dusky pink cardigan for an identical one in black, started to plough her way through the vast array of clothes racks.

"These are gorgeous, aren't they?"

She held up a pair of tweed trousers for Lucy to inspect.

"They're really nice – are you going to try them on? Give me your bags if you like and I'll hold onto them," Lucy offered.

"I meant they'd be nice on you. I'm practically broke after buying that dress that I wore last night. I'm on bread and water until pay day."

"They wouldn't make me look like the side of a house, would they?"

"No way – they'd be fabulous with a black top and high boots. We'll have a look for something with a V-neck," Cathy enthused, taking off with the trousers. Lucy followed cautiously, hoping that her friend wasn't going to get too carried away.

"What about this? You could get some nice beads to brighten it up." She tilted her head to one side, gauging Lucy's reaction to the black knitted wraparound top.

"Nice, actually. Will I try them on?"

"Do so. I'll go and look at the jewellery to see if there's anything to match."

Relieved that Cathy wasn't going to stand over her, Lucy escaped to the fitting rooms. Two minutes later, just as she'd figured out the ties on the top, she heard Cathy calling out to see what cubicle she was in.

"I have a necklace for you. Did they fit?"

Lucy emerged from the tiny cubicle, absolutely stunned at the fit of the trousers and the soft wool top. Cathy hadn't even asked what her size was yet the outfit was practically made for her.

"You look fantastic, Lucy. You *have* to buy them. Here, try the necklace – I think it's gorgeous."

The necklace was indeed gorgeous, a large aqua ceramic teardrop with tiny black flecks that rested just above her cleavage, covering what Lucy considered to be a vast amount of exposed flesh.

"Brilliant – those wrap tops are great with a bit of cleavage. Pity I don't have more to show off." She looked down at her own flat chest in disgust.

"Cathy, you're a genius! I'd never have picked these out if you hadn't spotted them. The trousers are really comfortable."

"They're lovely on. Are you going to get them?"

"Definitely. I'm useless at picking things," she confided, pulling the curtain closed to get changed.

"The only thing that holds me back is money," Cathy called back. "Otherwise I'd literally shop until I dropped."

"Well, if you spot anything else that you think would suit me, just shout. It'll be like having Trinny and Susannah with me."

"Are you serious?"

"Deadly serious," Lucy told her as she emerged from behind the curtain. "I hate clothes shopping. If you're not too wrecked after last night, I'd love to go to a few more shops."

Now that she actually had one nice outfit under her belt without the pain of actually choosing it herself, Lucy was raring to go.

"Well, hurry on and pay for those then. We've only three hours to closing time!"

MAIREAD O'DRISCOLL

"I'll treat you to lunch in BT's first to give us energy," Lucy decided, heading for the tills. "Rosa might even be able to take her coffee break and join us. Then we can get going properly."

"Done deal. Leon would love the idea of me going shopping and not spending any of my own money!"

Twenty minutes later, they were ensconced in a booth in the coffee shop at Brown Thomas with Rosa. To Lucy's delight, her two friends hit it off straight away and were now happily dissecting the latest Karen Millen collection while Lucy sat back and wondered who exactly Karen Millen was.

"If you spot anything you like, come up and tell me and I'll get the staff discount for you," Rosa instructed.

"I can't believe this!" Cathy exclaimed theatrically. "A blank cheque from Lucy *and* the chance of a discount!"

"There's new stock in Rock and Republic as well, if you're looking for jeans. And Coast have lovely greens and reds in."

"You're like a walking store directory, Rosa," Lucy said in admiration.

"One of the perks of the job," she admitted. "Although I'd better get back or I'll be fired. I'll call over to Number I later to estimate the damage to your credit card, Lucy."

"Bye, Rosa," Cathy grinned, "I'll see to it that she has a productive afternoon."

"Talk about a lamb to the slaughter," Lucy laughed, anticipation flooding through her. If Cathy meant business, then so too did Lucy.

"You look brilliant," Rosa enthused later that evening as

Lucy did a twirl to show off the boot-cut jeans that she'd teamed with a pale blue Lainey Keogh cardigan Cathy had insisted she buy.

"I love the boots – I just hope I'm not crippled after twenty minutes. I don't know how you wear them all the time," Lucy laughed, lifting the slim Roland Cartier heel for Rosa to examine.

"Mark'll be bowled over on Tuesday evening," Rosa giggled, referring to the suave paediatrician in their cookery group. They still knew nothing about him. They'd even tried to pump Rosa's parents for details the night of the dinner party considering that they all worked in the same hospital but to no avail.

"We'd better get going or it'll be closing time," Lucy remarked, leaving Rosa to lock her front door while she made her way out to the car. To celebrate the recent extension to Lucy's wardrobe, Rosa had decided they were going out for a drink in the Fiddler's Elbow, a pub she described as their 'local' despite the fact that she'd only ever been in there twice since she'd moved to Bramwell Court. Lucy, wearing the unfamiliar high-heeled boots, had insisted on taking the car.

Marvelling at the fact that Rosa had started yet another make-up job at the hall mirror, Lucy unlocked the car door, unaware of the footsteps approaching along the footpath.

"How did you fare without the wine?"

Lucy nearly jumped out of her skin when she heard the familiar voice behind her. She swung around abruptly, the embarrassment of the wine-spilling fiasco as fresh in her mind as it had been two weeks ago. Judging by the look of amusement on his face, it was still to the forefront of her victim's mind as well.

"No bother. How did *you* fare with the wine splashes?" she countered, surprising herself by returning his infectious grin. He had jeans on this time, coupled with a red and navy jacket that had a Great Outdoors logo on it.

"Nothing that couldn't be solved with a hot wash – or two," he said laughing, "although I've been too terrified to wear anything but jeans to the grocery shop ever since."

"That's what you get for trying to hurry me up," she reminded him.

As if on cue, Rosa finally deemed her make-up to be satisfactory and shot down her driveway at high speed.

"Oh, hello," she announced breathlessly, her surprise evident. She recovered fairly quickly and stuck out her hand, very obviously demanding an introduction to the handsome specimen Lucy was chatting to in the soft glow of the street light. "I'm Rosa."

Stricken, Lucy realised that she didn't even know his first name, never mind be in a position to introduce him. Stuck for words and with her earlier burst of confidence deserting her predictably, she opened and closed her mouth a few times, hoping that something would come out.

"Hello, Rosa, I'm Martin Kearney. Your friend here drenched me in red wine a few weeks ago." He rolled his eyes mischievously in Lucy's direction.

"Oh, my God, Lucy told me about that. It must have been a total comedy!"

"It was that all right," Lucy inserted dryly, her face reddening annoyingly as she recalled it once again.

"So are ye off out for the evening?" he asked now, obviously in no hurry to get wherever he was going.

"Just down to the Fiddler's Elbow," Lucy told him, hoping she sounded like someone who socialised on a regular basis.

"Good pub," he commented. "It's my local as well."

"Are you living in Bramwell Court too?" Rosa asked with immediate interest.

"I'm just across the green in Bramwell Crescent. I take a shortcut through here for the shop — although even that's getting a bit dangerous."

He grinned at Lucy as he said this, making her grateful for the cover of darkness as she blushed furiously yet again.

"Well, you can't be too careful these days," Rosa deadpanned.

"True enough. It was my turn to cook tonight so I had to venture out."

His eyes twinkling at Lucy, he held up a plastic bag bearing the name of the Chinese that was sandwiched between the pub and Mr Whiriskey's shop, the site of the wine disaster.

"We'd better let you go then — can't have people starving," Lucy said, smiling back at him.

"Well, enjoy the night out. I usually go down to the Elbow on a Saturday night with the lads, so we might see you there sometime."

"Bye then," was all Lucy could manage.

"We'll keep an eye out for you," Rosa promised as

Lucy gave a little wave and escaped into the car, her face still flaming from the encounter.

"He's a bit of a fine thing," Rosa remarked with a smirk as soon as the car doors had slammed. "And he fancies you."

"After practically drowning him in red wine and costing him a fortune in laundry bills? I don't think so."

More like me fancying him, Lucy reflected silently, a picture of the way his eyebrows shot up when he smiled lodging somewhere in the region of her chest.

"Lucy, he couldn't keep his eyes off you. I'm telling you – he definitely likes you."

"He was only being friendly."

"I bet you're glad you had the new gear on, all the same," Rosa countered perceptively. "We'll have to make it our business to be in the pub next Saturday for definite."

"We couldn't!" Lucy cried, horrified. "It'd be too obvious."

"It *is* our local," Rosa reminded her archly. "You won't get anywhere waiting for him to knock on the door. And he mentioned 'the lads', if you hadn't noticed, so there's more where he came from. Now hurry on – we're wasting precious drinking time."

Chapter 22

The night that she and Lucy had gone down to the Elbow, the subject of Rosa's birth mother had come up again. Now as she got ready for her class at The Gourmet Rooms, their conversation was still preying on her mind. Maybe Lucy was right in surmising that her mother could have spent the last almost thirty years regretting the fact that she'd given up her baby. Maybe she'd only been a child herself and had been pressurised into it by her parents.

All along, Rosa had had a vision of someone cold and stern giving her away because she hadn't been a good baby, one who'd cried too much or wouldn't feed properly. But perhaps it hadn't been like that at all. She tried to visualise her mother as a young girl, pale-faced and frightened, being led to the convent by her ashamed parents. Would she have been glad to hand over the baby and get back to her old life, hopefully without anybody having realised her situation? Perhaps her parents would have told people she was staying with relations for the summer, considering that Rosa had been born in late August. Or would she have dreaded leaving her baby in the care of the grim Sisters, terrified that she wouldn't go to a loving home?

And Rosa *had* wound up in a loving home, as it happened. Maurice and Bernadette had made sure that she'd had everything she wanted, and had spent hours playing with her. They'd sat up nights when she'd had the slightest of colds, never leaving her with anyone else if she had so much as a sniffle.

And they'd loved her enough to offer her the chance of tracing her birth mother on numerous occasions. They'd never been told whether Rosa had been born in Cork or not, only that there was a baby expected in the next few days which they could have if they were willing to accept it. They hadn't known if it would be a boy or a girl but it hadn't mattered to either of them. They'd fallen in love with Rosa the moment they'd laid eyes on her, they'd often told her, and had kept the name that her birth mother had given her.

Whenever her parents had brought up the subject of tracing her birth mother, Rosa had always refused, having an idea in her head that maybe she might do it when her own parents were no longer with her. Now she realised that her birth mother might be dead already or could be by the time she decided to make a move towards tracing her. How would she feel then, to not ever have the chance to hear her explanation?

Rosa pondered on this as she changed. She'd tried to

explain to Lucy on Friday night the way she felt every time the idea of tracing her mother came up, either with her mum and dad or even recently with Lucy. Fear was probably the best way of describing it — a fear of losing Maurice and Bernadette and of being left instead with someone that she couldn't identify as being her mother. Maybe it was a childish fear, she thought now, of falling between two stools and being left with nothing.

Trying to push it out of her mind, she started on her make-up but the moment she looked at herself in the mirror she started to wonder who it was that had given her the soft, white blonde curls and her slightly upturned nose. She'd never thought of herself like this before, as the diluted sum of two other people.

Shaking herself, she tried to focus on the cookery class. Mrs Carter was doing a full class on snacks and suppers tonight and she was having palpitations already about rubbery quiches, curdling omelettes and other unforeseeable disasters. Although now that she'd given up on the idea of opening a restaurant, she was actually beginning to relax a bit more.

Rosa had come to the conclusion that it wasn't so much that she was actually bad at cooking — in fact she actually enjoyed it once she got organised. But it was the getting organised that was the problem. It was fine at the class when Mrs Carter was hovering around or at home if Lucy happened to be there to remind her about things like turning on the oven first.

Left to her own devices, Rosa just panicked. Lucy thought it was just her lack of confidence that made her feel that she needed someone to keep an eye on her. Rosa herself thought it was a comfort thing, that she needed someone to enjoy the experience of cooking with. Either way, it seemed that she wasn't safe to be let loose with an array of ingredients in an unsupervised environment.

Thankfully, she had Lucy to help her out when it got stressful. Pulling on the denim jacket that she'd bought in Laura Ashley over her cream linen pants, she raced to the door when she heard the bell going, dying to see what her friend looked like in the new Hilfiger jeans that she'd bought on her shopping spree on Friday.

Lucy was the first person of Rosa's acquaintance not to make her feel inadequate for having achieved, as she saw it, very little in her life to date. She seemed to take things at face value, encouraging Rosa constantly but never getting exasperated when she got it wrong as had been the pattern through her school years and into her working life, such as it was.

Somehow, they'd just clicked. To her amazement, Lucy was continually saying that Rosa was the best thing that had ever happened to her, particularly in terms of making a start on revamping her image. Rosa thought that Lucy just needed a bit of encouragement to try new things and she never seemed to be offended if she suggested something.

"Oh my God, they're fantastic!" she enthused now, taking in the dark blue jeans that seemed to elongate Lucy's legs by about six inches.

"What do you think of the shoes? When I put them on first, I thought I looked like Minnie Mouse."

Lucy held up the legs of her jeans to show Rosa the dark purple, suede shoes with their quirky, rounded toes. The heels, despite being three inches, were so comfortable that Lucy felt as if she were still wearing her boots.

"They're gorgeous. I love the bows. You'll be able to wear them with skirts as well, they're so dainty."

"That's the first time 'dainty' has ever been in a sentence about me!" Lucy laughed, as they made for the car. "Cathy was sick that she couldn't afford a pair. She and Leon are supposed to be saving for a house."

"We should go out with them some night – Cathy's great fun."

"She is nice, isn't she? I felt a bit underhand in the shops, having all this money to spend. Everything she picked out looked nice on me and in the end she was telling me not to get too carried away or I'd be broke for the rest of the month. I had to tell her I was putting everything on my credit card."

"It's only the fact of knowing the money's there that makes you feel conscious of it. Did Cora Nolan say anything about the charities the last day?"

"I didn't get around to asking her but I will the next day. I'd love to give some of it to pay for counselling for people. I was able to tell you about it and I can afford to pay for counselling. Imagine what it would be like to have nowhere to turn!"

Rosa looked over at Lucy in the dim light of the car and was astounded at her strength of character. "You're something else, Lucy. Here you are only getting back on you feet and you're actually thinking of the fact that other people mightn't be as lucky as you. And I'm such a wimp, I'm afraid to find out about my birth mother in case she's not what I expect."

"You're not a wimp," Lucy insisted vehemently. "What happened to me *was* a big thing but looking for your birth mother is a big thing as well. You have to be one hundred per cent ready before you do anything. Look at how long it took me to tell someone."

"I'm thinking about it all the time, Lucy."

"Well, that's good. You can't keep ignoring it for years the way I did."

"If I did decide to look her up, would you help me?" Rosa asked tentatively, her face a picture of worry.

"Of course, I'll help you but how do we go about it? Is there some kind of register or something?"

"I'm not sure. The nuns at St Angela's organised it for Mum and Dad at the time so they should have some kind of record, shouldn't they? But will they want to tell me, Lucy?"

"You should ask your parents if they can remember which nuns they dealt with at the time – hopefully they're still alive."

"But I don't want my parents to be upset or think I'm not happy with them. I was always telling them I didn't need to meet her but now I'm thinking she could be dead by the time I find out who she is."

"That's fairly unlikely. She was probably very young herself when she found herself pregnant. She might only be in her fifties."

"I suppose I could ask Mum and Dad," Rosa conceded

reluctantly, as they pulled up outside Mrs Carter's house.

The now familiar scene was unfolding outside The Gourmet Rooms. Mark was taking the steps two at a time and Agnes could be seen scuttling along the street from where she'd parked under the trees as usual. Lucy and Rosa could never understand why she parked so far away from the house but were glad of the older lady's eccentricity tonight as they squeezed into the last remaining spot next to Mark Toland's Mercedes. The navy Saab convertible on the other side of it meant that the three IT girls were on time for a change.

Kate was already studying the format for the evening when the rest of them filed in and took their places at the work stations, all mumbling apologies even though it was still only five to seven. Mrs Carter seemed to have the effect, Rosa noticed, of expecting just a little more than enough from her class in every way.

"Now," she began, brisk and businesslike as usual, "this evening we're going to look at the nutritional content of food and whether we're really getting what we should be getting from our diet. While most people eat a dinner or main meal almost every day, what about the small meals and snacks that we eat in between?" Pausing to see if all her audience was with her, she continued. "Suppers and lunches are something that become wholly neglected in the race to get things done in the average busy day, so we're going to look at snacks and small meals that are nutritious as well as quick. For the second half of the class, we have a few people coming in to talk to us about the quality of the food we're buying and how we take it for granted that products are of good quality once we buy them in a reputable store."

Rosa was delighted with this. Sometimes the three hours of cooking and the wide range of dishes that they did each week got a bit overwhelming for her, even though she loved the creative challenge of it. A bit of light relief would be just the thing. Now, however, she'd have to pay attention to what their instructor was saying about quiches and omelettes and pizzas. Mrs Carter had already made up the basic bread mix that they'd covered the previous week and had laid a ball of it out on each work station to be moulded into pizza bases.

"This is great," Rosa whispered to Lucy twenty minutes later when Mrs Carter had moved down the line towards Kate and Mark. "I always looked on pizza as junk food but now I have an excuse for eating it."

"I wonder who the speakers will be later?"

"I was talking to Mrs Carter at the break the last day and she said there was to be a nutritionist and an organic vegetable grower. I can't remember who else."

"Everything going well, Rosa? Lucy?"

This was Mrs Carter's way of letting them know that she'd prefer it if they concentrated on their toppings instead of launching into a full-scale chat. Rosa smiled innocently at her to let her know that she was completely serious about her pizzas while Lucy started slicing pepperoni as diligently as she could.

The following hour flew by in a whirl of rolling pastry, beating eggs and grilling strips of bacon. Next up was a selection of salads that included freshly made dressings and a mouth-watering array of options for open sandwiches and stuffed wholemeal pitta breads, with relishes and chutneys incorporated to improve taste in all the choices. White breads and processed fillings were of course anathema to their instructor.

Finally, the coffee break was announced, much to Rosa's relief. Her head was spinning with trying to remember the names of all the different types of lettuce, not to mention trying to memorise the percentages of oil versus vinegar in the salad dressings. In an attempt to get it right, she had started to write the recipe down in the little notebook that was attached to the page holder on her workstation.

"Don't worry about writing it down, Rosa," Mrs Carter told her kindly. "It's all in the cookery book and once you've done it a few times, it'll start to come more easily."

Of course it was in The Gourmet Rooms book, Rosa thought now, annoyed at herself for getting hassled over nothing. She smiled at Mrs Carter in relief, her head feeling lighter immediately. She'd always had the impression that the cookery teacher was cold and severe but somehow Rosa felt that a lot of her stern demeanour was a front, a sort of professional persona that she wore.

When she'd first got the idea of doing The Gourmet Rooms course, Rosa's mother had been doubtful about her actually getting a place on it, so great was the demand. However, Bernadette had taken the liberty of phoning Mrs Carter herself to see if Rosa could be included, having met the great lady on a few occasions through the voluntary work that she did for the hospital.

Surprisingly, she'd been able to accommodate Rosa at

short notice, which was why Bernadette had been so adamant about her daughter not changing her mind at the last minute. Mrs Carter's reputation as a person not to be trifled with was legendary and Bernadette had been loath to alienate her lest she withdraw her support for the many charity events that the St Angela's Ladies' Committee organised throughout the year

Now, however, as they made the short journey to the drawing room together, Rosa reflected on the way that Mrs Carter's reputation preceded her and how far from accurate the general impression of her actually was. Despite her stern exterior, she was never critical when one of them bungled a recipe and certainly did her best to ensure that all of them kept apace of the classes as they developed.

Even her way of including everybody equally in whatever she was saying was an art in itself, Rosa noticed. She often asked Rosa little things about herself, like where she'd gone to school or whether she still lived with her parents, her way of showing an interest and making everyone feel comfortable.

As soon as all six of them were settled with their refreshments, she proceeded to outline the agenda for the second half of the class. First, there would be a master butcher, then a grower of organic vegetables, followed by a nutritionist.

"Each presentation should take about twenty minutes and you'll have a chance to meet with each of the speakers afterwards and discuss any areas that are of particular interest to you. Like where to source foods and where to get information. Meantime, enjoy your break."

"This is great," Lucy enthused when she heard about the nutritionist. "I sat in on a talk at work a while back and it was brilliant. Honestly, Rosa, half the time most of us are eating complete rubbish. I know I was, anyway," she said emphatically, thinking of the bags of mini-bars that she used to work her way through.

"I think I might talk to Mum and Dad at the weekend," Rosa blurted out, her mind very obviously still dwelling on her birth mother and how she'd go about finding her.

"I think that's the best thing to do," said Lucy, "and it'll mean that they're in on it from the beginning. You don't want to make them feel left out of this or they'll be really hurt when you do find her."

"Thanks for being so supportive about this, Lucy – I know I wouldn't even be able to consider it if I didn't have you as a sounding board."

"I don't mean to put a damper on it, Rosa," Lucy said gently now as they collected their coffee from the trolley, "but you have to think about the fact that your birth mother mightn't be in a position to come forward. Sometimes, people's circumstances are difficult." She hated the thought of her friend thinking that her birth mother would reject her without good reason.

"I've thought about that," Rosa said reflectively. "It might be a thing that she hasn't told her husband about having me. But there's no harm in trying, is there?"

"None at all. And I think you're right to be doing it now. A lot of nuns are getting on in years so the sooner the better."

"All I can do is try," Rosa decided, heading for the

window seats to join Agnes and Kate, her mind already whirling with the very real possibility of coming face to face with her real mother.

Agnes and Kate were already deep in conversation by the time Rosa and Lucy joined them. Agnes, as usual, was sitting on the chaise longue by the window but for the first time ever she was unaware of her surroundings and the view of the trees in the park opposite.

"She's terrified of getting a wound infection," she confided to Kate, amazed at the amount of knowledge she'd gained in the week since Beatrice had fallen out of her wheelchair.

As soon as she'd arrived in the Accident and Emergency department, an X-ray had confirmed that the neck of Beatrice's femur was indeed broken and would have to be surgically repaired the following day.

Bea had sat meekly on her hospital trolley as the doctor explained everything to them, including the risks of anaesthetic intolerance, haemorrhage and infection. Agnes, on hearing the pitfalls of the surgery that her sister would have to undergo, had asked if it was necessary at all considering that Bea was unable to walk anyway. The orthopaedic surgeon had explained that the risks of ongoing pain would be high if the hip wasn't repaired and eventually they'd decided to go ahead with it.

Now Beatrice was sitting up on Unit 10 like a Queen Bee, ringing her bedside bell as if the nurses were at her beck and call the way Agnes had been. Thanks to a little morphine pump attached to her wrist, she was blessedly pain-free and was making the most of the attention of the other patients who were encouraged to walk and were happy to do her little errands for her.

"Who's afraid they'll get an infection?" Rosa asked, pulling up a plush upholstered pouffe next to Kate's chair. Lucy settled herself on the chaise longue with her cup of camomile tea.

"Poor Beatrice fell out of her chair last Tuesday," Kate told them.

"She broke the neck of her femur," Agnes added. "She had surgery on Wednesday to repair it and she's doing great."

The fright of the Tuesday night had faded and now Agnes was left with a sense of trepidation about the eventuality of Beatrice coming home. Kate had been a great support during the week, cooking dinner for Agnes nearly every evening so that she wouldn't have to go all the way home to Rathcabben and come back in again for evening visiting.

Agnes had called in to Good For You on the Wednesday while Bea was in theatre, her nerves in tatters after a broken night's sleep in an armchair in the A&E. Emma had immediately insisted on holding the fort while Kate and Agnes went upstairs to put the kettle on. In the days that had passed since, Kate had been a tower of strength.

"That's terrible," Lucy said, touching Agnes's arm sympathetically. "She must have been in awful pain, the poor thing."

"It was desperate to come home and find her on the floor. The ambulance crew were brilliant, though. But I don't know what'll happen when she gets home."

"Surely the hospital can organise some help." This was from Rosa who was nearly in tears over Agnes and the shock she must have got.

"She might be able to go to a nursing home for a few weeks," Lucy told her. "I know we get a lot of people coming to The Friary for convalescence after surgery."

"I have to meet the Discharge Co-ordinator tomorrow. I'm terrified that she'll say Bea's not fit to be at home."

One of the ward sisters had already suggested to Agnes that it might be time to consider long-term care for her sister, something that Agnes was sure she'd never agree to. She told the others about it now.

"I couldn't put her in anywhere at this stage. She's the only person I have left in the world."

After all the years of resentment, it was only when there was a risk of losing her that Agnes had started to think about how lonely her life would be if she didn't have Beatrice in it. Even managing the bills seemed over-whelming to her and she didn't have a clue of where to start.

"What time are you meeting the co-ordinator?" Kate asked now. "I could go with you for support if it's before lunch."

"I hate being a nuisance, Kate." Kate had been brilliant and she didn't want to abuse her kindness.

"It's no trouble. When Timmy died, I'd never have managed to keep going if it hadn't been for my sisters. What time will it be at?"

"Half nine," Agnes said gratefully, relieved that she'd

have Kate to back her up if they really didn't want to let Bea come home.

"Fair play to you, Agnes," Rosa said, squeezing her hand. "Bea's very lucky to have you. Do you think she'd like it if we called in to see her? She must be getting bored in there."

"That's a great idea," Lucy enthused. "We could keep her company some evening if you'd like a break."

"I'd say she'd love to meet you. I'm always telling her about you."

"That's that, then. Lucy and I will drop in tomorrow evening. Right, Lucy?"

"Sure."

"It's great to have so much support from everyone," said Agnes, "and it'll be good for Bea to meet people – she sees nobody at home."

Beatrice had already met Kate the previous evening when she'd called in with a flask of coffee and a gooey chocolate hazelnut torte. She'd even brought plastic plates and forks and had passed slices of the rich, dark concoction around to the other three ladies in the ward, to their delight. It had been a lovely evening, one that made Agnes wonder why they hadn't involved people in their lives before now. Bea had chatted and laughed as if she'd known Kate forever, even asking her for advice on what she should take to bolster her sensitive digestion.

"Great," Lucy said. "I'm really looking forward to meeting her."

Just then, Mrs Carter arrived and told them that the first speaker would be arriving in five minutes.

Agnes straightened up in her seat in readiness for the talk, delighted that Kate had persuaded her to come tonight. She hadn't been going to but Kate had brought it up in front of Bea the previous night.

"I wouldn't be happy to leave Bea here on her own," she'd begun guiltily but Kate had interrupted her gently.

"Of course you'll come, Agnes. I'm sure Beatrice wouldn't expect you to miss it after paying for the ten classes," and she looked at Bea expectantly.

"Of course not," Bea had given in grudgingly. "Won't I have Maureen, Frances and Christina here to keep me company?"

The other three ladies had nodded their assent, having heard all about The Gourmet Rooms when Kate had arrived with the chocolate dessert.

God worked in mysterious ways, Agnes thought now as the portly figure of the Master Butcher appeared around the door. Maybe Bea would be more open to change, now that she'd seen a different side of life.

Chapter 23

Kate's heart nearly stopped when she saw Lorcan Reddy being ushered through the door of the drawing room by Mrs Carter. She was sitting next to Agnes, making a plan for the consultation with Beatrice's Discharge Co-ordinator when she looked up and caught his eye.

It had occurred to her that he might well be the speaker but she had dismissed the idea as just too coincidental. Nonetheless, she'd slipped the Lancôme Juicy Tube out of her handbag and gave her lips a quick slick as soon as the butcher had made his exit, just in case Lorcan Reddy did appear.

Just as well, she thought now as she tore her eyes away from him and tried to concentrate on what Agnes was saying. Lorcan, she noticed out of the corner of her eye, had taken a wad of paper folders out of a grey document box and was starting to hand them around to those nearest to him.

"Here you go, ladies," Kate could hear him saying to

Rosa and Lucy who were over at the trolley getting fresh coffee. "It's just a few notes so you can relax and take it all in."

Still watching him surreptitiously, Kate could see him smiling at the two girls. Rosa giggled and told him cheekily that she liked a man who came prepared while Lucy glared at her for flirting. Kate tried to bite back a smile at Rosa's antics, her heart jittering away madly as he now approached herself and Agnes.

"Hi, Kate," he greeted her, his eyes meeting hers and causing the same kind of electric shock that she'd had the day she met him at the market.

"Hello again. I didn't realise you were going to be the speaker."

"I do it every couple of months – although I'm not sure what I'll be like when someone I know is in the audience!"

"You'll be grand," Kate grinned, half delighted that she might be having some effect on him if he was nervous of speaking in front of her. "It's not as if you don't know your stuff."

"What's the cookery course like? I keep saying I'll do it sometime."

"It's brilliant, especially if you start off not being able to boil the proverbial egg, like I did. This is Agnes Cotter," she added, noticing that her friend was watching their interaction with interest.

"Hello, Agnes. I'm Lorcan Reddy, purveyor of fine vegetables." He shook her hand formally and gave her a folder of notes, handing the last one to Kate. "I'd better make a start, I suppose, or I won't be called back again.

Maybe I'll talk to you afterwards?" While he addressed this to both of them, his eyes were on Kate.

"Sure," was all she could squeak, her throat becoming strangely constricted.

For the next twenty minutes, Kate sat and stared at Lorcan Reddy without understanding a word of what he was talking about. Like watching television with the sound turned down, she studied the relaxed way that he sat back in his armchair with his long legs stretched out in front of him, his face animated as he spoke about his passion for organic food. Occasionally words like 'pesticide' and 'insecticide' floated into her consciousness but in such a disjointed way that she really couldn't absorb what he was explaining.

"But why are they so ugly?"

Lorcan laughed in response to Rosa's typically direct question, a deep, sexy laugh that jolted Kate out of her study and made her sit up straight in her chair. She was practically ogling him, something that she hoped nobody else had noticed. She watched as he explained to Rosa about the way that chemicals could be used to make vegetables look plumper and brighter in colour, and the way that they could be genetically modified to be a certain shape and size.

"We've become so accustomed to looking at 'perfect' products that when we see the plain and simple organic version we're almost disappointed. And I have to agree – some of them are a bit unfortunate looking."

Kate laughed along with the rest of the class, a feeling of something like pride coming over her at how nice he was to Rosa and the straightforward way he was able to explain things. Once again, she berated herself for being ridiculous. It wasn't as if he was hers in any sense of the word.

As soon as he'd finished answering a question for Lucy about the nutritional content of non-organic food versus organic and one about the side effects of the chemicals from Mark, the gorgeous paediatrician, he arrived back over to Kate and Agnes.

"I'm always glad when it's over," he sighed. "I always have this terrible fear of there being a militant supporter of genetic modification in the group."

"I think everyone here is safe enough," Agnes smiled, getting up from her seat. "Can I get you a cup of tea or coffee while I'm over there?"

"That'd be great, Agnes. I'm gasping for a strong, black coffee."

"Coming up," Agnes said perkily, heading off in the direction of the trolley.

"My hands are cured, by the way," Lorcan said now holding them out. The rash was indeed fully healed.

"Good for you!" said Kate. "It's funny that you actually came into the shop that day. A lot of people tend to go straight to a doctor or dermatologist with these things."

"You mean like the way people go to the supermarket for their vegetables? It's the easy way out, I suppose, to get a prescription for a bunch of chemicals. I usually try to solve things the natural way first."

Agnes arrived back with a mug of black coffee and a plate of ginger and lemon cookies but excused herself again, citing a mission for Rosa. Kate rolled her eyes and explained to Lorcan about Rosa's fixation on the fabulous Mark, who seemed to have no interest whatsoever in any of the women in the class.

They talked easily about anything and everything until Mrs Carter appeared at the door to remind her students that they still had another speaker. It was nine o'clock already and she also needed to give them their orders for the following week's class.

"That's my notice of eviction," Lorcan said, rising from what Agnes called a Queen Anne chair.

"And I'd better get back to the grindstone too." Kate stood also and was suddenly overwhelmed by his presence as he towered above her.

"I wonder if maybe . . ." He hesitated, causing Kate to look up. "Would you like to go out some weekend – for something to eat maybe?"

He looked at Kate expectantly, his face suddenly anxious. She could hear Mrs Carter in the background, clapping her hands to get Lucy and Rosa detached from Mark Toland.

"That would be lovely."

"This weekend or . . ."

"Saturday would be good," Kate told him, not sure exactly what kind of thing he had in mind. She could take the afternoon off and leave the shop in Emma's capable hands.

"I'll book somewhere nice then. Will I pick you up around eight?"

"Perfect."

They were smiling at each other now as a slim young girl with a shock of curly red hair entered the room. The rest of the group quietened down immediately.

"See you Saturday," Lorcan said quietly.

"Bye," Kate whispered, smiling foolishly at his departing back before catching Agnes's quizzical look. Wiping the smile swiftly off her face, she settled into her chair, any interest that she might have had in the nutritionist now suddenly gone out the window.

"She was the same girl who gave the talk in The Friary a while back," Lucy told Rosa on the way home, highly impressed with Lauren Brady's talk on the nutritional content of both fresh and processed foods. She'd even gone up and chatted to her at the end, eager to find out how one qualified as a nutritionist. "You know, Rosa," she said excitedly now, "if I do go to college, I think that's what I'd like to study. It all makes so much sense."

Immediately snapping out of her musings about her failure to make an impression on Mark Toland, Rosa sat back and studied her friend.

"You'd be great at that. You could phone UCC for a prospectus and see about what courses are available."

Rosa was an expert on getting information about courses and careers considering the many attempts that she'd made at various times since she'd left school. And now that the course at The Gourmet Rooms was into its latter stages she was going to have to make up her mind about what to do next.

She'd envied Lucy's enthusiasm earlier in the evening

when they'd had an opportunity to talk to each of the three speakers after their respective talks. Her eyes had been shining with interest while all Rosa could think of was chatting up Mark.

Rosa wished she could be like the people who had a very real connection with the job that they did, like Kate with her little shop. Every aspect of health seemed to fascinate her – she'd spent almost fifteen minutes in deep conversation with the vegetable grower earlier, obviously totally caught up in the health benefits of going organic.

It wasn't that Rosa wasn't enjoying the course. She *had* actually learned to cook a bit but now that she'd realised that her dream of opening a restaurant was just that – a dream – she felt a bit of a fraud. It occurred to her that maybe she could join Lucy and do a degree in nutrition and dietetics but then she didn't actually have an interest in nutrition the way that Lucy did, nor could she visualise herself being able to speak authoritatively on the subject the way that the speaker had earlier.

She sighed to herself as Lucy continued to extol the virtues of Lauren Brady. Was it possible that there actually was no career that could hold her interest *and* that she'd be good at?

Maybe I am useless, she thought now, her self-doubt giving way to fear. No wonder someone would give me away.

Chapter 24

Agnes sat stiffly in her chair in the small 'quiet room' at the end of the orthopaedic ward. She was glad now that she'd let Kate come with her for the appointment with Regina Manly, the Discharge Co-ordinator.

"You'll be fine," Kate said now, reaching over to squeeze her hand. "There isn't a chance in the world that she'll try to put Beatrice into a home. It'll be all about getting her home."

"I hope so."

Agnes looked up in trepidation as the door of the tiny room opened suddenly. She knew her cheeks were flushed from all the anxiety but she hadn't even bothered to powder them again. It was hard to believe that, after all her years of wanting a break from her sister, she was now preparing to go into battle to get her home again.

The lady that appeared before them was almost everything that Agnes had expected. Taller than average,

Regina Manly was as solid as Ayers Rock with severely cut, short dark hair and a navy suit that looked as if had been manufactured with its owner already in it.

She swooped on Agnes before she got a chance to rise and introduce herself.

"Agnes, I presume?" she began abruptly. "I've heard a lot about you from the ward staff – and not all of it good."

Agnes nearly fainted.

Kate hopped up from her chair and stuck out her hand, at a disadvantage in comparison to Regina's substantial bulk.

"I'm Kate Lewis and my family and I will be giving Agnes and Beatrice every assistance when they get home," she said with spirit, impressing Agnes immensely with her announcement of an imaginary family.

"Well, good for you. We'll need every bit of help we can get if we're to make life a little easier for the good lady beside you. From what I hear, she'd been masquerading as the Lone Ranger for forty years." She smiled suddenly at this little joke.

Agnes, white as a ghost in the chair, breathed a sigh of relief. Regina Manly wasn't criticising her at all.

"Now," Regina began, wedging herself into a neat armchair opposite Agnes and Kate, "we have a lot to do if we're to have everything up and running before Beatrice returns to Rathcabben. No more lifting, for a start."

Agnes and Kate remained speechless as the impressive woman before them outlined the plan that she'd devised. First, Bea would go to The Friary for a period of convalescence. Meantime, the occupational therapist and public health nurse would visit Agnes at home to decide on what equipment Agnes would need. As soon as it arrived, they would demonstrate the procedures to Agnes, in readiness for her sister's return.

"How about that for a plan?" Regina Manly looked at Agnes expectantly.

Poor Agnes, even if she'd wanted to refuse, decided that there was no way on earth she could possibly refuse such a formidable lady. As it stood, however, the plan was exactly what she had hoped for.

"I think it's marvellous!" she breathed, visualising a hospital bed similar to the one that Bea currently occupied. "We have a friend working in The Friary so I'm sure Beatrice will be delighted too. And Kate here knows the public health nurse."

"You'll have to have a home help, mind. No more pushing and pulling on your own."

Giddy with relief, Agnes smiled from Regina to Kate and simply said, "Yes – to everything!"

Regina, another startling smile breaking out on her serious face, nodded and rose to leave.

"That's all sorted then. I'll let you know when the room is available at The Friary. And I'm sure you'd like to tell Beatrice all the details yourself."

With a brisk shake of their hands the whirlwind that was Regina Manly disappeared, leaving Agnes and Kate stunned in her wake.

"I hope Bea will agree to it all," Agnes said anxiously as soon as the door closed behind her.

"Don't worry," Kate told her firmly. "We'll just have to put it to her nicely."

Relieved to have the support of such a good friend, Agnes looked up and smiled wickedly.

"And if she needs persuasion, we'll just give Regina a call!"

Chapter 25

Lucy felt good heading off to her second counselling session, the aura of fear gone now that she felt comfortable in her surroundings and with Cora Nolan. The counsellor had an air of calm about her that belied her age and an aura of glamour that would normally have intimidated Lucy immensely. It was a sign of how far she'd come lately, Lucy thought, that she didn't feel at all shy in Cora's company. Instead, she was actually eager to get to the session, having thought of all sorts of things during the week that she wanted to talk about.

"So how are you, Lucy?" Cora enquired as soon as they were both settled in the comfortable sofas.

"Great actually. I was looking forward to seeing you all week, to be honest. I know it's only the second session but I really feel as if things are coming together in my head."

"How so?" Cora questioned, her manner interested and encouraging.

Lucy loved the way that Cora was able to prompt her

gently without actually asking her the kind of intrusive questions that she'd often imagined a counsellor might ask.

"I always used to think that I was different from everyone else, because of what happened. That's why I didn't want to get to know anyone properly, in case they found out. I really thought that everyone else had no problems, that everyone I knew was lucky to be normal and have an easy life."

"Do you think differently now?"

"I do really. I think it was when I started the cookery course and I looked at the others the first night and they all seemed so confident and sure of themselves. It was only when I found out that Rosa was adopted and that she had loads of hang-ups about her parents that I realised I wasn't the only one carrying something around."

"Did that make you feel better?"

"Not better. Just more normal – as if I was the same as her in lots of ways. That I wasn't a freak," she finished, looking at Cora to see what she thought of this last admission.

"Has feeling normal made a difference, Lucy?"

"It has actually. It made me confident enough to open up to Rosa and I'm delighted about that. I feel I can make friends now."

Lucy had surprised herself recently by the way she'd started to accept invitations instead of doing everything in her power to avoid them. Her shopping day with Cathy had been one of the best days that she could remember and only the previous night at the cookery class, she'd agreed to go visiting Beatrice in hospital with Rosa. They'd agreed to meet after Lucy's session with Cora and have something to eat in the hospital coffee shop before heading up to the orthopaedic unit. She told Cora about this now, trying to explain how differently she was behaving of late.

"You see, Cora, now that I don't feel so strange about myself, I'm able to talk to other people. I feel very comfortable with Kate as well – she's in the cookery class too."

With Cathy and her new friends in the Absolute Beginners course, she didn't feel defined by the fact that she'd been a victim of sexual abuse. In her own head, everything in her life had always revolved around it and it surprised her a little that others seemed to see her as a person with a personality and a life ahead of her.

"What about going out? Do you feel any different about socialising?"

"That's getting better. The last time there was a night out at work I pretended it was my parents' wedding anniversary so I wouldn't have to go. But I feel that I'd be able to go to whatever comes up next. I went out for a drink with Rosa last Saturday and it was great."

"Really?"

"You know Cathy that I've mentioned? She was always on at me to go shopping with her after work but I dreaded the thought of it. Last Friday, she brought it up again and I agreed. We went to BTs and Marks and a few other places and met Rosa for coffee."

"Did you buy anything?" Cora smiled at Lucy's enthusiasm over her impromptu shopping trip.

"I did, actually – a load of stuff. Cathy's brilliant for picking out things that I'd never picture myself in," Lucy told her proudly, having told Cora the previous week about her embarrassment at trying things on in front of anyone.

"You seem to be getting on well with her?"

"I always got on well with her to work with – it was just the going out that I hated. I was afraid to get too friendly with any of them or they'd be at me to go places."

"Do you see people at work differently now?"

"Absolutely. I was completely wrapped up in my own thoughts all the time. Like what people thought of me and if they were talking about me being odd. I probably *was* odd," she smiled. "But now I can see things from other people's perspective."

She'd been shocked when Cathy had told her on Friday that Una Riordan's husband suffered from the early stages of multiple sclerosis. Lucy had seen him arrive to pick Una up from work on a few occasions and had been struck by what a handsome couple they made. Brian was a company director and travelled the world, often taking Una and the children on extended trips with him. Like the other people that she'd thought had happy, carefree lives, Lucy had often admired Una's affluent lifestyle and the fact that both she and her husband had successful careers and gorgeous children.

Lucy was glad that she'd been able to see these things now and admit them out loud. She'd wasted so much of her life envying others and letting her own life dwindle away meanwhile. Nobody was without their problems, she'd realised — it was knowing how to deal with them that was the important thing.

Explaining this to Cora made Lucy feel as if this was yet another strain of negative thinking that she was now finished with.

"That's a good way of looking at it," Cora commended. "What other negative things do you think the abuse instilled in you that you need to move on from?"

"One of the biggest things for me has been the fact that Ned left me all his land and money. As well as hating the fact that I have anything belonging to him, I've always felt it was another thing that I was hiding. I was always afraid that Mam and Dad would wonder why he left it all to me but at the same time I was mad with them for not working it out."

"So it's been a double burden?"

Lucy nodded her agreement.

"And what do you think might make that better?" Cora continued.

"Getting rid of the money for a start."

"And what about telling your parents?"

"I'm not sure that I'll ever be ready for that, to be honest. He's dead now and I don't see what good it would do. I used to want them to know so that they'd stop talking about him as if he was some sort of saint but now I don't care about that."

"Is it that the anger is gone?"

"Mostly. Not just the anger at Ned but the anger at Mam and Dad. I don't blame them any more."

"Do you feel your relationship will improve now?"

"I think so. I used to almost hate going over on Sundays but I'm not dreading it any more. I know it'll take a while for things to come right."

"It's great that you're even thinking about it. What about the money and everything?"

"I ended up selling the farm that he left me. I used some of it to pay off the mortgage for Mam and Dad but most of it is still there. Although the shopping on Friday did make a bit of a dent in it!"

"Do you feel better about spending it on yourself now?"

Lucy explained about Rosa's logic of looking at it as a means of getting herself back on track – like paying for the counselling and buying things that made her feel better.

"And *is* it making you feel better?"

"To a certain extent, it is. But I was thinking of giving a certain amount of it to a children's charity – to pay for counselling maybe. What do you think, Cora?"

"I think it's something that only you can decide. You have to look at whether you might regret it later. When you have your own children you might be sorry that you hadn't kept it to give them a better chance in life, for instance. That's just an example but what I mean is that you'll have to be sure."

"Maybe doing something drastic might not be a good idea. If I did it gradually – a bit here and there – I could see how it made me feel."

"You could look into the different charities as well, to see which ones appeal to you. You'll get a list in the phone directory. It might give you more of a sense of control rather than rushing into something."

"I think that's a good idea. Rosa's mum is involved with a few charities as well so I might ask her." Lucy felt satisfied with this somehow, as if yet another loose piece of thread had been tied up.

"You're going to visit Agnes's sister," Cora said now, revisiting what Lucy had told her earlier.

"I'm meeting Rosa and we're going for something to eat before visiting time starts. It'll be my first time meeting Beatrice. I think Agnes has a hard enough life with her."

"You have great empathy, Lucy," Cora commented.

"I didn't used to have," she admitted, "but that's because I thought that I was the only one with problems. The first night I saw Agnes at The Gourmet Rooms, I thought she was a bit snooty – she's very genteel and proper, you see. But she was just covering up, the same as I was. I understand people a bit better now."

"Well, I hope you enjoy the visit. And if you'd like to come again you're very welcome."

That was another thing about Cora, Lucy realised. She had a way of not making her feel that she *needed* counselling, that it was an option that she could avail of only if she wanted to.

"I'd like that," she said with feeling, her heart lifting yet another notch as the bleakness that she'd carried inside her receded a little more.

Chapter 26

Kate checked herself in the mirror for the fortieth time and wondered if she didn't look like some kind of Eastern guru. She'd decided on the beaded turquoise top and matching linen trousers because people kept telling her it was her best colour. Now she wondered if she should change into jeans or something more casual.

She glanced nervously at the clock, wishing that Lorcan would arrive, even though it was still only five to eight. She hadn't been on anything remotely resembling a date for years and still wasn't exactly sure if this *was* a date. Maybe the rules had changed unknown to her. Maybe going out for something to eat, as Lorcan had suggested casually on Tuesday night, wasn't meant to be anything significant.

At least they had plenty in common, she reassured herself, happy that they'd at least be able to converse without awkward silences. There was something about him – it was as if she knew him already. Even the fact that his aunt had owned the shop before she did was another bond.

They'd talked a little more about it on Tuesday evening and he'd been highly amused that she lived in the upstairs flat.

"But it's tiny up there. It used to be like a rabbit warren when we visited there as children."

"There's only me there and I must admit that I've knocked out a few walls since I arrived," she'd laughed, amused at his incredulity.

Now she was like a hen on a hot griddle waiting for him to arrive, already looking forward to seeing him again. She stopped herself from dashing to the intercom the moment the bell rang downstairs, not wanting him to think she'd been standing waiting for the bell to ring.

"You look lovely," he greeted her almost shyly and Kate speculated as to whether he'd ever been married. She didn't think so and wondered then what he'd think if she told him about Timmy and the baby and the man that she'd killed after the wedding thirteen years ago.

Snapping out of her reverie, she smiled as he exclaimed admiringly at the transformation in the room. The neat pale blue kitchen area with its shiny worktop of dark blue Louis Mulcahy tiles was tucked away at the back, separated from the rest of the room by two solid oak upright beams. One of the two comfy Laura Ashley sofas stood between the beams with its back to the kitchen while the other one rested opposite it in the alcove of the small bow window at the front of the house.

Kate loved the calming effect of the blue and cream colour scheme and Lorcan evidently shared her enthusiasm.

"There used to be a 'front room' but we were never

allowed in there. We kids were relegated to the back kitchen. Was the green lino still here when you arrived?"

"It sure was," Kate laughed, remembering the hardship she'd incurred scraping the decades-old adhesive away from the floor before she'd had the carpet laid.

They were still laughing about the lino when Kate collected her handbag from the coffee table and preceded him down the stairs, still not quite sure where they were off to.

"I booked us a table at Galligan's. Is that all right? I thought we could walk over."

"It'd be a bad job if we couldn't," Kate laughed as they set off up the street for the little restaurant known for its excellent seafood.

Even though it was only around the corner Kate had only been there a few times and was looking forward to it already. She was glad now that she'd made an effort, noting that Lorcan looked great in well-cut navy chinos and a crisp shirt with small navy, red and white checks that bore a logo that she, never one for labels, didn't recognise.

Inside Galligan's, they were directed to one of the plush leather banquettes where they were invited to peruse the menu while they waited for their table. Lorcan seemed to know everyone by name and ordered drinks while they talked easily and enjoyed the ambient buzz of the busy restaurant. The menu, Kate noted as she ordered, was varied in the extreme, making it a joy to choose.

"This is just gorgeous," Kate commented as they were settled into one of the booths that lined the back of the room.

"It's kind of quaint, I suppose," Lorcan agreed, adding, "I'm not big into these really modern, stark places."

Kate was pleased to hear this as she herself never felt comfortable in the type of large open restaurants with their minimalist décor and stark furniture that were everywhere these days. Galligan's had been in Cork city for years and its décor certainly hadn't changed much to accommodate the emerging trends, she observed as she let her gaze wander around the arrangement of discreet booths and small tables that were expertly placed with tall potted plants and the occasional oriental screen as subtle dividers.

They ordered, and chose a bottle of wine.

Then, when the waiter had filled their glasses and departed, Lorcan said, "Leaving Dublin must have been a big move?"

"It was at first, because I didn't know anybody, but I needed a change."

Her heart was pounding now but she'd already made up her mind to tell him the whole story. It seemed important somehow that he should know the whole thing from the outset. She'd trusted him almost as soon as she'd met him and couldn't bear to have him find out later what kind of person she was.

Admittedly, a busy restaurant wasn't the ideal place – she'd imagined talking to him back at the flat, sitting opposite him on one of the blue sofas in her own little territory. But it had come up now and she didn't want to shy away from it any more as she had for years. He was looking at her expectantly now so she ploughed ahead.

"I was working in the Department of Health before I moved to Cork. My husband and I were at a wedding in Kildare, it's thirteen years ago now, and we had a bad crash on the way home. Timmy was killed and so was the man in the car that we hit. I was driving."

"God, Kate, that's terrible. Were you hurt at all?"

She hated to see the concern in Lorcan's face – it only made her feel more guilty than she did ordinarily.

"I had loads of leg fractures and a broken pelvis. I had to go to the Rehab in Dún Laoghaire to learn how to walk again." She told him a little then about being unconscious and Timmy being buried before she woke up.

"Did you have any children?" Almost as if he knew.

"I was pregnant at the time but I lost the baby. I was only three months so we hadn't told anyone. I'd avoided drinking all day but people kept offering. Eventually I took a glass of wine and sipped on it for the evening."

She looked at him intently then, looking to see if she saw any condemnation in his eyes but he was just looking at her with interest, as if he knew she hadn't finished yet.

The waiter arrived just then with their starters and Kate picked absently at the mixed leaves in their tangy dressing while Lorcan started on his pancakes in sweet chilli sauce, giving her space to continue in her own time.

She put her fork down. "I remember driving home that night," she said in a low voice and he at once abandoned the food and gave her his complete attention. "There were a good few cars on the road because the races were on at Punchestown. I don't really know what happened. I just remember the car coming towards us and not being able to swerve out of its way. I was knocked out and only remember the hospital after that."

"Kate, that's horrendous. I'm so sorry."

"I bet you're sorry now that you asked about me moving to Cork," she said, smiling weakly.

"I'm glad you told me," he said gently, taking her hand where it lay on the starched linen tablecloth.

"I always feel that if I didn't have the wine, I might have been able to get out of the way of the other car. The man was a farmer – he'd been at the mart and was on his way home. It said on one of the newspapers that he lived with his elderly parents. Imagine what it was like for them to lose their son like that. And Timmy mightn't have died. Or the baby."

"Jesus, Kate, you're not blaming yourself, are you?"

"I suppose I keep thinking that I might have been sharper, more alert if I hadn't had a drink at all. Especially when I was pregnant."

She remembered the inquest, hearing about her own blood alcohol levels being well below the limit but it hadn't mattered to her. She'd never know if it would have made a difference and it was a bit late to be sorry after the event.

Losing Timmy and the baby had been her own punishment for her carelessness. The death of the other man was what drove the relentless guilt that she felt every time she allowed herself to think about it.

"Kate, you have to let go of it. I know that better than anyone."

The waiter was hovering so Lorcan signalled to him to

remove their plates. Then he took Kate's hand again and looked into her eyes with the calm intensity that she'd already become used to.

"Kate, I've been in this situation too, you know. Guilt can make you waste your life or you can try to get past it."

"Easier said than done," she responded wryly.

"I know this isn't the best time for telling you this but it seems to be the night for it."

"It can't be any worse that mowing down people in the dead of night."

"It probably is," he told her frowning. "I was a bit of a lunatic when I was younger. I've calmed down a bit since," he added when he saw her disbelieving look. "My parents wanted me to stay on at school and go to college like my sisters but nothing would do me only leave after the Inter Cert and train as a mechanic. I was mad into cars, the faster the better. I had this old Daihatsu Charade and I used to spend the whole time tinkering at it."

He broke off when their main course arrived.

"We'd better make more of an effort that we did with the first course!" he said after the waiter had left. "Do eat up, Kate – I don't want to spoil your meal."

"Never mind the meal, Lorcan – your story is more important than monkfish. Please go on."

"Okay. I suppose I'd better get it off my chest. Well, the car was like a rocket in the end, a powerful engine in a tin-can sort of body. I was a complete lunatic in it. Mam and Dad used to be up half the night waiting for the guards to come to the door telling them I'd been killed. As it transpired, I wasn't killed myself."

Kate couldn't believe what she was hearing. Lorcan was so calm and gentle and easy-going – she couldn't imagine him as a boy racer in a souped-up car.

"I was coming home from a disco one night. I think I must have been going about eighty miles an hour on a minor road. Needless to say I came to a bend that I couldn't take and the car went completely out of control. I hit a middle-aged couple who'd just left their son to the airport. The two of them were killed straight away. I was in bits – two legs broken, pelvis smashed, fractured skull. It wasn't half enough for me."

At a loss for what to say, Kate just squeezed his hand gently so that he'd continue.

"I was in hospital for five months, in the Orthopaedic in Cork. I know now that I was completely depressed when I came home but nobody called it that. They all just thought that I'd learned my lesson. Then the case came up and I got a year in jail and was banned from driving for ten years."

"What age were you?" Kate's chest was tight at the thought of the teenager that he'd been facing the terrifying prospect of imprisonment and tears sprang to her eyes.

"Nearly eighteen. I was lucky. If I'd been over eighteen I would've been sent to a mainstream prison. I ended up in an open prison in the midlands which was the best thing that ever happened to me."

"How so?"

"It was a farm, really, and there was this old man there who did the gardens, Mick Lawlor was his name. I think he saw how low I was and felt sorry for me. That's how I got into the vegetable growing. I used to spend the whole day with him, which was fine by the prison officers because it kept me out of harm. Some of the lads were doing computers and stuff but I wanted to be outside so they left me off."

"How long were you there?"

"Nine months in all. Good behaviour for the first time in my life. I was nearly sorry to leave because I hated the thought of coming home and everyone talking about me. I remember Mick telling me that I'd be wasting a third life if I carried on like that. I'd already ruined two, more if you think about the family of that couple. After that I started to get a bit stronger."

"How was it when you did come home?"

"People were a bit sorry for me, I think. The lads that I used to go around with didn't appeal to me any more and I wasn't interested in the cars after that. I gave up the apprenticeship in the garage and got a job in a garden centre."

"When did you get into the growing?"

"A bit of land came up for sale near home – only ten acres. I had most of the money and Mam and Dad helped me out with the rest. I think they were delighted to see me having an interest in something again."

"Lorcan, you were so young to go through all that and come out sane on the other side," Kate said now, admiration in her voice for the man he'd become.

"It didn't just happen – I caused it," he said firmly. "There's never a day that I don't wish I could be seventeen again but I can't go back. Mick Lawlor got me to write to the Cullitons' family through the guards before I left Castlebeg but I don't know if they ever got the letter."

"They never replied?"

"I didn't expect them to. They probably thought I was trying to get some kind of forgiveness from them so I could get on with my life. I didn't really deserve that and I didn't expect it."

"You're amazing," Kate told him truthfully.

"Not exactly amazing but thanks for listening and not judging me."

To her surprise he lifted her hand from where he held it across the small table and brought it to his lips, kissing it slowly, his lips grazing across her knuckles igniting feelings that had been hidden somewhere in the depths of her for years.

"How could I judge you?"

"You're pretty good at judging yourself," he reminded her.

"I suppose it's a bit selfish. It doesn't do anything only make me feel as if I'm doing something to atone for it all."

"Kate, even if you were to blame, beating yourself up can't help anyone or bring them back. And you've lost so much."

"I can see that you're right. This is the first time I've talked about it properly since it happened, even though it's thirteen years ago. I feel lighter now."

"I'm glad."

She smiled at him across the table, her heart lighter than it had been in years.

"Our food is stone cold – I'm sorry, Kate. My timing for my confession could have been better!"

She smiled. "I started it! Never mind – let's eat!"

Strangely, now that she'd managed to tell him her story, Kate felt ravenous and was dying to get started on the succulent, if somewhat cold, monkfish that had been placed before her. Soon she'd eaten everything on her plate and Lorcan had done likewise. The waiter was back again, clearing their plates and topping up their glasses. They both grinned when he asked if they'd like the dessert menu.

"Definitely," Kate told him, her heart lifting at the thought that she was going to spend the rest of her life with the man sitting opposite her.

Later that night, she didn't ask Lorcan to come up to the little flat over the shop, knowing that if she did, she'd want him to stay. Too much had happened that she needed to assimilate. Something that he'd said had struck her, about writing to the family of the people that he'd hurt, and she wondered if it wasn't what she herself needed to do. A future with Lorcan was what she wanted now but first she needed to let go of the past.

Chapter 27

Once Rosa discovered that Martin Kearney and a group of possibly eligible friends lived within shouting distance of Bramwell Court and socialised in the Fiddler's Elbow, she couldn't rest.

"It's only a matter of targeting them," she insisted to Lucy.

"You make it sound like an assassination attempt," Lucy complained, trying to put Rosa off the idea of shamelessly chasing them.

"We go there all the time – he knows that," she smirked. "It's just a wonder we haven't bumped into them, that's all." The fact that they had rarely stood in The Fiddler's Elbow since they'd lived in Bramwell Court didn't bother her in the least.

On Saturday night she had Lucy armed and ready in her new black broderie anglaise skirt, a black top with a deep V neckline and a pair of black wedge-heeled sandals that apparently made her legs look at least a foot longer.

These were the same legs that Rosa had insisted on tackling with a bottle of St Tropez the previous evening, having made Lucy go for a torturous leg wax on the Thursday. To Lucy's horror, the night out was beginning to take on the tone of a military expedition.

Lucy's heart was thumping solidly from the moment they left Bramwell Court until they entered the dimly lit interior of the pub. Rosa, in her usual skinny jeans, strappy top and impossibly high heels, insisted on picking a table in the middle of the floor, rationalising that there was no point in their being in The Elbow if they weren't going to be seen.

"Get that into you and start acting casual," she'd instructed, planting a pint glass of something very green and very putrid-looking in front of Lucy. She'd got the same for herself and they'd clinked glasses skittishly before taking a good gulp each. Relaxing a little, Lucy looked around to see if there was any sign of Martin, thinking it would be just her luck that he'd go into town instead. Satisfied that he wasn't in the pub at that very moment, she checked the neckline of her top yet again and gave it a little hitch up, ignoring Rosa's exasperated look.

"You barely have half an inch of cleavage showing!"

"Well, if he does turn up, he won't want to be looking at my belly-button."

"Give it time," Rosa advised wisely, giggling at Lucy's description of the depth of her décolletage.

"It's a bad job when you're on the Fat Frogs at this hour of the evening," Lucy heard behind her almost immediately and turned to find Martin looking down at her. Terrified that he'd heard them talking about him, she immediately started to redden.

"Is that what they're called?" Lucy responded, trying to recover her composure. There were two fellows standing behind him, she noticed. Out of the corner of her eye, she could see Rosa starting to preen.

"I suppose we'll all have to have one now that you've put them in mind," one of the friends said making for the bar.

After that, the evening took on a life of its own. One of Martin's friends, Lar, owned the house that they shared in Bramwell Crescent. Lar worked with an accountancy firm in the city while Gerry was a primary school teacher. Martin, it transpired, was a dentist and was in the process of buying a house in Bishopstown.

Lucy wondered fleetingly whether any of them was surprised that she owned the house in the Court, considering that they were detached and much bigger than the rest of the development but dismissed the thought quickly as a vestige of her former obsession that everyone must be thinking that there was something suspicious about her. Rosa effectively owned her house too, she reasoned, and there was nothing suspicious about her.

Apart from that one moment of anxiety, Lucy, for the first time ever, allowed herself to relax and enjoy the easy-going and friendly people in her company. It was the first time in her life that she'd actually been out with a group of friends like a normal person and she was determined to enjoy herself and put all the missing years behind her.

Almost as soon as they'd settled with their drinks, Lar

and Gerry started to give Lucy a serious teasing about the wine-spilling incident. In the past, she'd have been mortified at having any attention focused on her but now she was able to see it as the good-natured banter that it was.

"I'd say poor Paddy Whiriskey thought he was going to be cleaned out with lawsuits," Martin laughed, when Lucy described the speed at which the proprietor had launched the yellow danger cones.

"And it was all in aid of getting me out of a fix with a disastrous dinner party," Rosa commented.

The discussion immediately moved on to the cookery class and Rosa's valiant attempt to throw an independent soirée.

The three lads had insisted on hearing all about the cookery course, laughing at the many hilarious incidents Rosa described. They seemed to be highly impressed with the exotic-sounding dishes that the girls mentioned, until Rosa insisted that they wouldn't be half as impressed if they actually had to eat some of the failures.

"We'd be willing to try," Lar had said hopefully, his eyes on Rosa's flushed face with the soft golden curls escaping from her scrunchie as usual.

"We'd bring plenty of wine to wash it down – only we'd give it to you, Rosa," Gerry quipped. "We wouldn't trust Lucy with it."

"Do you really think you deserve a slap-up meal after that comment?" Lucy countered.

"Maybe I could come over and assist or something. Peel the spuds, maybe," Martin put in.

"Okay so, next Saturday at eight," Rosa announced decisively. "Lucy's house is best. She has millions of fancy pots and pans. Yokes for lifting lobsters and everything."

"Will we be getting lobster?" This came from the three lads in unison, causing them all to burst out laughing.

"Definitely not," Lucy said firmly, thinking of the days when she'd hear people laughing over something that she didn't think was funny at all. Now every little thing seemed funny, making her realise how little she'd laughed in the past sixteen years.

It was closing time when they finally left the pub and then the three lads had treated them to fish and chips from the Golden Grill alongside.

"We have to start stocking up in case the food is desperate next Saturday," Gerry joked.

"That's it! The invitation is withdrawn!" said Rosa.

"You didn't invite us," Martin pointed out seriously. "We invited ourselves."

They laughed the whole way up the hill, with Martin and Lucy falling into step behind the others as they neared Lucy's house.

"Very convenient," she commented as she threw the remains of her chips into the litter-bin on the corner. For all her dieting, she'd enjoyed the greasy stodge but promised herself that she'd go back to being good the following morning.

"Lucy, what do you think of Duke Special? It's just he's on in The Savoy on Friday night and I have tickets. Would you like to go?"

Predicting that Lar and Gerry probably had tickets as

well and were in the process of asking Rosa, she tried to act as casual as she was able.

"For a start, I've never heard of him. But I'll definitely go."

"You'll love him. He's from Belfast, I think. Will I put the album through your letterbox in the morning? It'll be early, mind, because I'm getting the train to Dublin for the match in Croke Park."

"That'd be great!"

"It's on at eight but we'd want to be there around half seven to get good seats. Will I pick you up at quarter past?"

It was beginning to dawn on Lucy that there didn't seem to be anyone else involved in the equation. "Grand so," she stuttered, the realisation that the trip to the Savoy might be some kind of date washing over her suddenly.

At that moment, Rosa, Gerry and Lar came to a halt outside Lucy's house. All three turned to face Lucy and Martin who were almost upon them.

"We'll wait 'til you're in," Gerry said to her, holding the gate open.

"And we'll make sure Rosa gets home safely," Lar promised, obviously now aware of the proximity of Rosa's house.

"See you Friday," Martin said quietly, touching her arm.

"Okay so," was all Lucy could get out.

"Make sure to start planning the dinner, won't ye?" Gerry seemed to be oblivious to the fact that Lucy and Martin would be seeing each other before the promised dinner party.

"See you Saturday," she told him and Gerry, smiling quickly at Martin before opening her front door. Rosa, full of beans now that her machinations were bearing fruit, waved happily at Lucy and made a telephone signal with her fingers to say that she'd phone her.

Lucy grinned broadly and watched as they strolled off towards Rosa's house, happier than she had been in years when she closed her front door.

"You are now joking!" Rosa was almost apoplectic when Lucy phoned her the following morning.

"There's no need to shout and have them hear you over in the Crescent," Lucy laughed as Rosa's enthusiasm rubbed off on her.

"In the Savoy, you said? We'll have to get on to the website and see what kind of gig it'll be. You'll need to be prepared."

"I'll be well prepared. He dropped in a CD on his way to work – through the letterbox because he was on his way early to a match in Dublin."

"This is looking good. What'll you wear?"

As usual, the discussion of what she'd wear started to take on epic proportions, with Rosa deciding almost immediately to come over and go through Lucy's things.

"Good idea. You can help me throw out all the old stuff. The place is bedlam with all the shopping I've done lately."

"Can't think of anything I'd rather do. See you in a while."

Lucy sat back with her mug of tea and thought about

the speed at which her life was changing. One minute she was Mrs Bored and Boring, the next she was socialising left, right and centre.

She could hardly believe that Martin had asked her out but now that he had, she was determined to do it in style. She'd let Rosa have free rein for the next few hours, she decided, to rid her wardrobe of all signs of the old Lucy Dalton. None of the old stuff fitted her anyway now that she was on the way to her target of being in Size 12 clothes for Christmas. She shuddered at the idea of all her Size 16's now and knew that the only way to avoid revisiting them in the future was to send them all to the Sin Bin, as Rosa called the recycling bin near the Elbow bar.

As well as a wardrobe clearout, she'd have to ask Rosa about her goal of making Number 1, Bramwell Court a little more comfortable. Like when she brought Cathy on the shopping trip, Lucy knew that once she got going, she'd get a bit of confidence and take off in earnest.

As it stood, the only furniture in the house was the stuff that had been left by the previous owners. At the time that she'd bought it, Lucy had been glad to accept the deal of a fully furnished house. The fact that it had added considerably to the cost hadn't bothered her in the least and the sellers, relocating to Saudi Arabia, had been delighted to avoid the hassle of storing everything.

She'd barely finished her tea when Rosa appeared, looking fabulous as usual in a patterned wrap dress that would have made anyone else look like a farmer's wife in a pinny.

"Right – I'll make more tea while you get the bin liners ready."

"There's not *that* much." Lucy started to root under the sink for the black plastic bags anyway knowing that Rosa was at her best when on a style mission.

Ten minutes later, all she could see was her friend's pert bottom as she delved into the depths of the wardrobe and flung things over her head to her. She was supposed to put the items in the black bags without question.

"Could navy fleeces be described as fetish material?" she questioned, pulling yet another from the pile in the bottom of the wardrobe.

Lucy grinned but kept quiet, knowing better than to start a debate.

"Hangers, Lucy," Rosa demanded eventually.

Obediently, Lucy passed her a bundle of hangers that had been retrieved from under the mountain of clothes in the early stages.

"All these will have to be ironed," Rosa cautioned seriously, indicating a sizeable heap of clothes that had been allocated to the bed. The remainder, laid out across a chest of drawers, she now hung carefully.

"Now?" Lucy was shocked – the bed was almost hidden under the number of things to be ironed.

"Well, we can't hang then up otherwise. I'll help if you like – it's very therapeutic, you know."

Lucy could think of other words for it but suspected that she'd have to give in. "You're beginning to sound like Mam – next you'll be looking in the fridge to see if I've done a grocery shop!"

"Are you going over home today?"

"Yeah – but we've loads of time left. What are you at for the afternoon?"

"Mum and Dad are in Kerry for the weekend. I was thinking of trying out a few of the breads. She's doing scones and sponges and things the next night so I don't want to get too far behind."

"Tell you what. We'll make some of the breads together and you can come over to Mam and Dad's for dinner with me. They'd love to try out some of the fancy ones."

"I can't go at this short notice," Rosa protested.

"Course you can. I'll ring home in a minute. They'll be delighted to see I have a civilised friend at last!"

Lucy had told Rosa all about the gang that she'd hung around with at school and the fact that her parents had never understood them. She'd already mentioned Rosa and suspected that her mother thought there was yet another failed Goth on the scene.

"Okay, so. We'll make something nice to take with us."

For the first time in years, Lucy now felt genuinely optimistic about her Sunday trip home. Cora would be proud of me, she thought as she headed down to make another round of tea.

"Don't forget to plug in the iron!" Rosa called after her, obviously not going to let her off the hook. There were already three plastic sacks ready for the recycling. God only knew what would happen when Rosa got loose on the rest of the house.

Maura took one look at Rosa and immediately started to

treat her like the Queen of Sheba. Paddy, delighted with the soft white bread rolls and the nutty brown loaf, shook hands with Rosa and went off to check on the dinner.

"Did you get your hair cut again?" Maura quizzed. In the past, Lucy thought she might have considered all the questioning a sort of criticism. Today, she decided she was going to take it as a sign of interest instead.

"Only a trim. He's trying to get the layers a bit longer, you see."

"It's lovely, isn't it, Mrs Dalton?" Rosa, as usual, was supportive, knowing how much Lucy's mother irked her.

"It is indeed, Rosa – but you're to call me Maura," she instructed as she led them into the sitting room. "Lucy always had lovely hair – she had it in pigtails for years, you know."

"Until I was about ten," Lucy corrected, smiling.

"Paddy always gets the dinner on a Sunday," Maura commented now. Settling herself into one of the fireside chairs, she now started to enquire about the previous week's class. "I was even thinking of doing it myself. I have plenty of time on my hands since Paddy retired. And now that Lucy's managing on her own I'm at a loose end half of the time."

Suddenly it occurred to Lucy that maybe it was only her own paranoia that had her thinking that her mother was checking up on her all the time. It made her feel almost guilty that she'd been shunting her out of the house and telling her she wasn't wanted when she probably just needed something to do with her days. In future, Lucy thought now as she listened to Maura and Rosa chattering, she'd let her mother come and go a bit without resenting all the interference, as she'd looked on it before.

Suddenly, her dad was calling them to hurry on or the dinner would be cold. In honour of the fresh bread rolls, he'd opened a can of Campbell's soup, telling Rosa vehemently that he would have made it fresh if he'd known in advance.

"Potato and leek, that's what I'll make the next time. I grow everything, Rosa, so you only have to shout if you need any fresh veg to practise with."

"That would be great, wouldn't it Rosa?" Lucy commented. "Mrs Carter is always on about free range this and organic that."

"Well, I'll poke around after dinner and see what's there. I'll make two boxes."

Paddy's enthusiasm was palpable once he got some interested feedback about his beloved vegetables. Lucy, for her part, was delighted that this was an opportunity to renew her interest in the garden after all the years.

Rosa, as ever, was just great with Maura and Paddy, filling them in on their project to modify Lucy's house a little.

"I haven't bought anything since I moved in," said Lucy. "I'm going to get a few rugs and cushions – that kind of thing."

"You're right," Maura told her. "It all adds to the value of it."

"We're under a bit of pressure though, Maura," Rosa confided. "We're having a dinner party for a few friends on Saturday."

Lucy looked at her horrified, and reddened, terrified that Rosa would blab about her date on Friday night. After a good kick on the ankle, Rosa tailed off her spiel about the dinner party, finishing with a lame comment about practising their cooking skills.

Whereas normally her evening at home dragged on interminably, the hours flew by. Maura was fascinated by Rosa's tales of the glamorous and interesting people she met in Brown Thomas and pumped her for details of the famous faces she met at the up-market department store. Paddy, as good as his promise, sent the two of them home with a box of vegetables each. And for the first time ever, Lucy left her parents' home without a cloud of guilt hanging over her.

Well-known...Chapter 28...marked out from

Chapter 28

On Monday evening, Rosa finally spoke to her parents about the possibility of tracking down her birth mother. Typically, and despite Rosa's anxiety that it would devastate them, they responded with the equanimity that she'd been accustomed to all her life.

She'd called over for dinner after their weekend in Killarney and had broached the subject in the kitchen as her mother was preparing the vegetables and her father was doing his usual study of *The Examiner* at the scrubbed pine table.

Expecting them to be a little shocked, she began gently by reminding them of all the times they asked if she wanted to look up her birth mother.

"I've thought about it lately and I'm wondering if I should."

"If it's what you want, then we'll help you in any way we can," Bernadette said firmly, stopping her scraping of the carrots to give her daughter a hug.

"We'll leave no stone unturned," Maurice assured her, getting up and kissing the top of her head the way he'd always done if she was upset over something.

"And we'll still be here, no matter what happens," Bernadette reminded her.

"Mum, can you tell me the whole story again, please? With as much detail as you can remember?"

So, starting right from the beginning, they told her the story of her adoption once again.

Considering that most of Bernadette's friends had married in their early twenties, she'd actually looked on herself as being quite old when she met Maurice at thirty.

"Time moved on, Rosa, and there was no sign of a pregnancy. We went for tests and things but nothing showed up and there weren't the options in those days that people have now with IVF. So we talked to Mother Bridget – she was the Superior at the time – and she said she'd keep us in mind if anything came up."

"It was as simple as that back then," Maurice added. "Now you have to have social workers involved and everything. The Sisters knew us, you see, so they knew a baby would get a good home."

"And I did," Rosa said softly, just to remind them that she wasn't looking for her birth mother because she was in any way unhappy with them.

"A few months went by and Mother Bridget called over to me in work. Unit 4 was called the Psychiatric Wing then. She just said that there was a baby expected in the next week or so and asked whether we'd be ready to take it."

Bernadette had tears in her eyes now at the memory and when Rosa looked at him, so did Maurice.

"In those days," Bernadette continued, sniffing back the tears, "there was a thing about 'not leaving your post' so I had to wait until five o'clock to tell your father – imagine I couldn't leave the unit to go over to ENT and tell him the news!"

"She came over as soon as the last patient left and we went straight into Cash's to buy everything."

Maurice smiled at the memory, telling Rosa about the Silver Cross pram that was too big for the car and had to be delivered the next day in full view of the neighbours.

"We didn't know whether you were going to be a girl or a boy so we bought loads of white and yellow matinée coats and bootees. It was all terrycloth nappies at the time and we were all week practising how to fold them in triangles!"

Bernadette smiled over at her husband as she told Rosa this, remembering a time of great joy in their lives. "And the big nappy pins with the pink and blue tops," she said.

"Yes, your mother would be folding the nappy and I'd be trying to get the pin in. And that was before you even arrived!"

Rosa could imagine the two of them preparing for the arrival of the baby, glowing with excitement the way they still did when she handed one of them a birthday card or a Christmas present. The thought of them buying all her baby things in Cash's, the most expensive shop in Cork at the time, made her feel like crying. No wonder the nuns had thought she would be going to a good home. And even though now Cash's had changed its name to Brown Thomas, Rosa knew she would never walk through the nursery section of her workplace again without picturing her parents standing there among the cots and changing units.

"So I had no pink stuff?" Rosa observed.

"Not at the beginning. Although you had that little embroidered dress and pink matinée coat on you the day we got you – the one I still have."

Rosa had always taken her mother's generosity of spirit a little for granted but she now saw her in a new light. It struck her now that the fact she'd kept the baby clothes another woman had dressed her baby in told her something more about the kind of unconditional love that Bernadette had given her for as long as she could remember.

"We waited anyway and got ready as best we could. Then we got a phone call one evening to go down to St Angela's at eight o'clock to collect you," Bernadette said, two tears escaping from the corners of her eyes.

"I had to put the carry-cot in the back seat of the car," said Maurice. "I even put a hot-water bottle in it so you wouldn't get cold. We went up to the main entrance of the convent and I parked right up at the steps. We didn't know whether to bring the carry-cot in or come back out for it." Maurice sniffed loudly and started to rummage in the pocket of his tweed jacket for a handkerchief.

"I was afraid the mother would be inside a window looking out at us," Bernadette went on, "so we left it in the car. Mother Bridget came out to the door herself –

normally one of the maids would answer the door – and brought us into the parlour. We were there for ages talking and drinking tea before a young nun brought you in."

"I thought they were after changing their minds about giving you to us, we were there so long," said Maurice. "And we were afraid to ask. There were sandwiches and everything for us but no sign of a baby. Eventually the young nun arrived with you in a blanket."

"I was afraid to get up until they brought you over. It was nearly like an interview and I was terrified that if I made a show of myself, Mother Bridget would think I was too unstable to look after a baby. That was the way it was back then, Rosa."

"I was the same. Even when they gave you to Bernadette I didn't go over to look at you. Imagine, I was there sitting up eating a slice of sponge cake rather than make a scene. We had to pull in at the gates of the Christian Brothers' school on the way home so I could look at you."

Bernadette smiled at her husband and Rosa could see exactly why she'd never had a need to look for her birth mother. The love between them was steady and unchanging, the same now as it was the day their family had been made complete.

"I had to ask the young nun what your name was to find out if you were a boy or a girl," said Bernadette. "I was afraid to ask in case they thought I was being a choosy madam. The young nun said you were Rosa and Mother Bridget gave her a look that would sour milk, I remember."

"That's right," Maurice commented with a grin. "Mother Bridget said we might want a more suitable name for you – a family name was how she put it. It was a kind of snobbery, I suppose, Rosa. The fact that we were doctors and that your Grandfather Mooney was a surgeon in his day."

The emotion that both of her parents were displaying even just talking about it made Rosa realise just how much they loved her, even though she was here in front of them asking to meet the woman who'd given birth to her.

"We asked about your mother, darling, but Mother Bridget said she was gone already. I was glad of that, you know, that she didn't see me carrying you out of the convent."

Once Maurice and Bernadette started to open up about the early days of Rosa's life with them, they couldn't stop.

"Because I didn't get much notice about you arriving, I couldn't take time off work at the drop of a hat. The board of management wouldn't let me stop work without a month's notice so I had to resign my permanent post. That was considered a big deal in those days, Rosa, so there was a major fuss about it. Do you remember I went back to work when you were seven?"

"Was it that long before they gave you a permanent job again?"

"I didn't care a bit. I had a ball at home with you."

"So had I in the evenings," said Maurice. "We were always aware, though, love, that you might want to find your real mother. And maybe even your real father if it came to it. Of course, they could be married with other children now – that happens a lot."

"I know. Lucy said that as well. But I'll just have to face it if that's the way it is." If Lucy could deal with the horrendous thing that she'd had to face, then she'd have to deal with whatever came her way. "And you're still my *real* parents, you know."

"I know, Rosa," Maurice said, stroking her hair.

Bernadette was taking a roast out of the oven at this stage, one that was a little dried out now that they'd become carried away with their memories.

"It might be a little hurtful if it is the case that the young couple were able to marry after a while but I wouldn't let it put you off. If we love you this much, your mother will love you even more. It's just that it might be hard for her to show it."

"You mean if it's a thing that she doesn't want to meet me?"

"I can tell you, Rosa, if it comes to not meeting, it won't be that she doesn't *want* to, it'll be more that she *can't*," Bernadette said as she drained the potatoes. "I meet women every day of the week who have lost a child. They never forget. But sometimes it's hard, especially if they hadn't told their husband about having a child that was adopted. That kind of thing could break up their marriage."

"It's great to be able to talk it out," Rosa said with feeling. As usual, the big bright kitchen was awash with the evening sun pouring in. The familiar smell of cooking and the warmth of the Aga surrounded her in a way that felt totally familiar and secure, making her wonder for a moment if she really wanted to shatter the idyll that her present life was.

"I think it's the right thing to do, love," Bernadette said now as she placed the roast beef dinner in front of her daughter. It was almost as if she'd sensed the moment of doubt. "I was always a bit worried that you might leave it too late and then have regrets. At least this way you'll know – one way or another."

"How are we going to go about it?" Maurice, quietly authoritative, was ready to start the process as soon as possible to avoid any further waiting for his beloved Rosa.

"We'll start by getting this into us. Then we can make a plan."

Over dinner, Maurice and Bernadette said that they doubted if the adoption had been registered with any state agency – it had all been done privately, with a sum of money agreed to facilitate the proceedings and to assist the mother in starting a new life.

"How much?" Rosa asked, more out of curiosity than anything else.

"I think it was £500 at the time. It doesn't sound much now, Rosa, but it was considered a lot then. It wasn't like putting a value on a baby or anything," Maurice reassured her, "It was more of a practicality to cover costs and help the mother out."

That was how things had been done then, they told her, in the days when people of a certain standing liked things to be organised discreetly. Rosa's birth mother had most likely been of a well-to-do background, they'd told her, not having had to stay to work off the costs as was the practice in the religious institutions of the day. No, it was probable that she'd been taken advantage of at a young age and her parents had approached the Sisters in their distress. She might have been closeted at home for as long as possible, then sent on a short vacation before returning to resume her normal life.

Girls from the poorer families who might have nothing to return to often lived out the remainder of their lives in the convent once their babies had been adopted, working as maids or cooks. Rosa, who had read some of the harrowing accounts of Magdalen Laundries, was terrified of finding that her birth mother had lived and maybe even died in such a place while she herself had been living in the lap of luxury.

"Thankfully, that kind of thing had died out by the time you were born," Bernadette consoled her. It was most likely that Rosa's mother had been given a certain amount of money by the Sisters to start a new life.

"I'll call to Sister Ignatius over in the convent in the morning and she'll be able to tell us where to begin," Bernadette promised as Rosa served the luscious chocolate mousse that she'd made to welcome them back.

"And whatever happens, we'll always be here for you, the same as ever," Maurice repeated.

Rosa looked at her parents with pride as they sat around the table. Nothing had changed in her life except the way she looked at it. Feeling like a grown-up at last, she tucked into her dessert, eager to begin the journey on which she was about to embark.

Chapter 29

Kate took great care with the letter, even down to the minute detail of what kind of paper to use and whether it should be typed or handwritten. She decided on a thick cream vellum eventually and tried out several pens once she'd settled on it being handwritten.

The only person she told about it was Lorcan. They'd met almost every day since they had had dinner at Galligan's the previous weekend. Then on Sunday he phoned to see if she wanted to go for a walk along Ballybrannigan Strand, a long stretch of unspoiled beach a few miles outside Midleton. They talked easily as they walked along in the blustery east wind, the sharp gusts whipping Kate's hair around her face. Tentatively, she told him about needing to write the letter and her belief that she might be able to move on from her past if she did so.

"How will you feel if you don't get a response?" Lorcan wanted to know, reminding her that a reply was something that he didn't get.

"I don't know. I definitely think that I have more of a need for acknowledgement than you did but that's not to say that I expect one. All I can do is send it and hope for the best."

"Have you thought about what you want to say?"

"In bits and pieces only. Mainly how sorry I am and maybe a little about how I still don't really know how it happened. I'll probably be months writing it, at the rate I'm going."

She'd made a few attempts at it that morning but to very little avail. Now that she was out in the fresh sea breeze with Lorcan, she was more convinced that ever that it was what she needed to do.

They had lunch at Ballymaloe House after their walk, with Kate feeling a little underdressed in her jeans and walking boots. As soon as she tucked into the fabulous buffet, she was hooked for good.

"Maybe we could come here for dinner next weekend? I'd be able to wear something civilised, I promise."

"I'd have to dress up too then," Lorcan laughed, looking down at his own jeans. "But I'll look forward to it. The food here is fantastic. We can book now for Saturday night, if you like."

"Great — I've just wangled myself another dinner date!"

"Not exactly wangled. Anyway, I really enjoy your company, Kate. I feel like I've known you forever."

"Same here," she told him, adding, "You know the worst bits about me now so it can only go uphill from here."

"There are no 'worst bits', Kate, just things that happen that we might not do again if we had our time over."

"Lorcan, you've no idea how good it feels not to be hiding any more. I used to feel so guilty about it that I couldn't even talk about Timmy or the baby. The guilt even overshadowed the grief."

"That's probably why it took so long for you to accept it at all, Kate."

"You're right there. But being able to tell you about it very honestly has been amazing."

The hustle and bustle of the busy country house restaurant continued around them as they gazed at each other across the table, oblivious to everyone else.

"You're amazing, Kate, and you don't seem to realise it."

"You're fairly amazing yourself," she told him, almost shy suddenly.

"I know we only know each other a few weeks but I keep thinking that . . ." He paused.

"That what?" Although somehow she knew exactly what he was going to say.

"That I feel we were meant to meet, that we're going to be together. Is that totally mad?"

"Only as mad as me thinking the same thing at the Farmers' Market in Midleton. Poor Agnes was having a crisis the same day and here I was having a figary over the vegetable man!"

"Well, I'm glad you were," he grinned, tucking into his smoked eel salad.

Later that evening, Kate sat down in earnest to write

her letter. Slowly but surely, it came together for her. She hoped that she sounded contrite and not too maudlin or self-seeking in it. In the morning she would finish it and go out and buy proper notepaper to transcribe it onto. And as soon as she was ready, into the post it would go, for better or for worse.

Chapter 30

As soon as she arrived at The Gourmet Rooms, Agnes was practically accosted by Lucy, Rosa and Kate. Their concern for Beatrice and their interest in what was happening in her life threatened to overwhelm her as she answered the barrage of enquiries.

Yes, Beatrice was improving every day. No, her wound wasn't full healed as yet so she'd need to stay on the orthopaedic ward a little longer. Yes, she'd agreed to go to The Friary for a period of convalescence, although she wasn't so sure about having to use the hoist on an ongoing basis.

"The first time she used it in hospital, she gave the nurses an awful time. But they're so patient with her. Carol, one of the day nurses, told her it'd be a shame to miss *Coronation Street* just because she didn't want to use the hoist! I always gave in! But as soon as she knew that she wouldn't be able to get into the chair to go to the television room unless she used the hoist, she was into it like a bullet out of a gun!"

"It must be difficult for her to get used to all the changes, though," said Lucy.

"Not half as difficult as it was for me to be lifting her! I didn't mind years ago when I was able but when I think that I needn't have been doing it at all, I see red. The nurses on the ward are not allowed to lift a thing in case they hurt their backs."

"Too right," Kate commented. "Look at Emma – she has an awful time with back pain."

"So when do you think she'll get to The Friary? I have everyone told to expect her."

"It all depends on her wound," Agnes explained. "It could be a week or more."

"Pay attention now, everyone," Mrs Carter called, interrupting the conversations that had sprung up around the room.

The four of them scuttled back to their work stations in anticipation of the culinary delights ahead of them. Agnes was particularly interested tonight, now that she'd decided that she and Beatrice were going to have a whole new life soon. As well as the changes in her care arrangements, Bea was going to have to get used to changes in her dietary routine as well. Since she'd been in hospital, Agnes had noticed that her sister ate everything that was put before her with barely a word about her digestion. She'd laid into Kate's chocolate hazelnut torte with gusto and was too busy chatting to complain about it being too rich and heavy for her. Well, she'd be seeing more of such things soon, Agnes vowed as she cocked her ears to hear what Mrs Carter had to say on the subject of biscuits.

An hour later, there was a vast array of produce cooling on the large wire racks at the back of the room. Lemon and ginger were Agnes's personal favourite but she'd also made a batch of chocolate and orange. Kate had tried her hand at orange and ginger while Rosa did cranberry and white chocolate chips. Lucy had experimented a bit with all of the ingredients, eventually concocting a small batch of chocolate chip and Bailey's Cream and another of rum and raisin.

"We'll do a simple Victoria sponge now so that the biscuits will be cooled in time for the coffee break. They're much too tempting to steer clear of."

This was high praise indeed from Mrs Carter, whose compliments were so few and far between that they were relished when they did come. Tonight she had a tweed skirt and a soft cashmere sweater on instead of one of her usual neat, knee-length shirt dresses. She looked softer and more feminine in the fine ivory wool top and even the scarf that she wore was an addition that made her look less severe than usual.

Agnes imagined that she wasn't much more than fifty years of age but somehow her austere presentation made her look older than her years. Tonight was the first night that Agnes had noticed her looking any bit younger and she wondered fancifully if perhaps the proprietor of The Gourmet Rooms had a new man in her life.

It was another forty-five minutes before their sponges, some more and others less successful, were lined up on the wire racks to cool, the biscuits having been removed to a series of dainty china plates. Carrying them through to the dining room, Agnes commented to Kate that she thought Mrs Carter must have a man in her life.

"I did notice that she's started to put on the style a bit the last few weeks. The dresses were very severe, like a uniform. She looks well, though."

"I think so too," Agnes agreed. "And speaking of men, did you see any more of Lorcan since?"

Kate had told Agnes about Lorcan asking her out when they'd met with Regina Manly in the orthopaedic ward the previous Wednesday but hadn't had an opportunity to tell her how it had gone. Adding milk to the two mugs that Agnes held out to her, she filled her in now on all that had happened since they last had a proper chat.

"The Saturday night in Galligan's went great – we must go there some evening with Beatrice once she gets settled at home. He called over on Sunday and we went to Ballybrannigan Strand near Midleton for a walk. We went to Ballymaloe House for our lunch afterwards, which was gorgeous. I only saw him for a few minutes yesterday when he put his head into the shop – he was delivering to Galligan's again."

"God bless us, Kate, things are moving very fast," Agnes said, sitting forward on the edge of the chaise longue. She was delighted for Kate and thought that Lorcan was very handsome.

"Well, I suppose neither of us are exactly spring chickens. Lorcan is just gone forty."

"He's a fine-looking fellow," Agnes told her, biting into one of Lucy's cookies, "You'd want to hold on to him or you'll wind up like myself and Beatrice."

"You've plenty of time, Agnes. And you'll be getting out more once you get into a proper routine – I'll make sure of that."

"You're very good to me, Kate. Imagine – I'd never have met you if I didn't do the course here."

"Well, I'm very lucky to have met such lovely people too. And that includes Lorcan."

"Is that the fellow who was talking to us about the vegetables?" Rosa enquired suspiciously, arriving over with Lucy.

"It sure is," Agnes told the two of them proudly. "And he's mad about Kate. They even went on a date."

Soon the four of them were in a huddle, hearing all about the trip to Galligan's and the subsequent day out on Sunday.

"Speaking of dates," Rosa piped up eventually. "Lucy has one on Friday night, too."

"Go on," Agnes breathed, impressed. Lucy had changed out of all proportion since the start of the Absolute Beginners class only eight weeks ago. She'd shed at least two stone in weight and had a snazzy new hairdo and what appeared to be a completely changed wardrobe. Now, it seemed she had a man.

"Well, it's not exactly a date," Lucy began self-consciously, suddenly afraid of making a fool of herself if it didn't work out.

Rosa rolled her eyes, putting her at ease again so that she was able to explain a bit about meeting Martin and the hilarious episode in the grocery shop. Kate and Agnes were laughing uproariously by the time she'd finished.

"And not only that – we invited him and his friends to dinner next Saturday!" said Rosa. "We still haven't decided what to cook!"

"All opinions welcome," Lucy invited.

Agnes thought they should do something complicated to let their guests know exactly the type of refined girls they were.

"But it'll have to be something eejit-proof so we won't make a complete show of ourselves," Lucy warned.

"Something wholesome," Kate giggled and prodded Agnes. "So that they'll definitely know what kind of girls you are."

"In that case it'll have to be something spicy," Rosa chimed in.

"They'll also like something that'll soak up plenty of drink," Lucy added, remembering the three had promised to bring plenty of wine.

Eventually they decided on Italian as having all the attributes that the evening seemed to require. After that it was only the finer details, like the shopping for ingredients and getting their timing right so that they wouldn't be flustered and red-faced on the night.

Agnes parted from her friends that evening and wondered at the way her life had changed in a few short months. Before, she'd always pictured her future trailing away into oblivion with only Beatrice and her needs for company.

Now this bleak prospect had been replaced by a new hope, one that included Beatrice as an active part of her life rather than as a jailer that kept her on a string. There was a lot to look forward to.

"I asked Mum and Dad about finding my birth mother yesterday evening," Rosa confided to Lucy as soon as they set off on their journey home from The Gourmet Rooms. Lucy had been working a double shift on Monday and a nine to five shift on Tuesday so that she could take time off for her counselling on Wednesday and get a half-day Friday to prepare for her night out in the Savoy with Martin. She and Rosa hadn't had a proper chat since Sunday evening.

"How did they take it? Were they upset at all?" Lucy asked, worried that Maurice and Bernadette would feel that they were losing Rosa.

"They're great really. They said straightaway that they'd do everything they could. Mum told me that she'd always felt a bit guilty about having me when my real mother must be out there thinking about me every day."

Lucy could visualise Bernadette saying this, her concern always for the other person. She always understood whatever it was that her daughter was going through.

"So what did they think was the best thing to do?"

"Mum called over to Sister Ignatius Bradley – she's the Superior – this morning to see if there were any records kept."

"And?" It was Lucy's turn to drive and even though she couldn't see Rosa's face in the darkness of the car, she could sense that Bernadette's visit to the convent hadn't been as productive as her friend might have liked.

"Sister Ignatius told her that there weren't any formal records kept. That was their way of protecting the mothers' names. It was all organised by a Mother Bridget but she's in Africa somewhere now. Sister Ignatius promised Mum that she'd write to her tonight but she says it could be months before we get a reply."

"Months!" Lucy found it hard to believe that her friend would have to wait months for the most important news of her life.

"I know. It's desperate. Wherever they are is so remote that they need a boat to get to the mainland. With the shortages of fuel and the weather it's often five or six months before they get any post from the mainland. Then Mother Bridget would have to try and get a reply back. It could be ages," she finished miserably.

"Well, at least the process is started," Lucy said supportively. "I know it's hard to wait but hopefully it'll come a bit sooner than you're expecting."

"It's just that once I decided, I thought it'd all happen fairly quickly. I didn't think it out properly."

"Well, fair play to you for taking the first step. We'll just have to do our best to keep occupied until you get news."

"You're right. There's no point in wrecking my head about it for months on end. It's in motion now so I can do no more. And we can start getting ready for the weekend if we really want something to occupy us."

"And we'll have to go shopping for cushions and things," Lucy reminded her.

In the past few weeks, Lucy had really started to get a figary about her house and the fact that it resembled a stark and modern warehouse. Now that the dinner party was imminent, she was taking it as a sign that it was time to take action.

"It's only that you haven't bothered to put your own stamp on it yet," Rosa told her. "A bit of moving and shaking and a few cushions and Bob's your uncle. There are all your books as well – we can put those on the shelves and use some of those stone ornaments for bookends."

Lucy thought it would take more than a few cushions to take the hard corners off her sitting-room but she knew that with Rosa's flair and ability to spend they'd be able to make some improvements.

"Late shopping on Thursday, then," she said decisively as they pulled into the driveway. It was almost half ten and she had another early shift in the morning so that she could be off at two for her session with Cora.

"That'll be great – I'll be off at three and we can blitz around. We can concentrate on the food nearer the time."

Waving her friend goodbye, Lucy laughed to herself at Rosa's use of the word 'blitz'. The girl obviously didn't realise that almost everything she did was in blitz form.

They hit Brown Thomas at three o'clock on Thursday and didn't stop going until the sales girls around the city were almost evicting them.

It was almost midnight when they finished their renovations, having rearranged all the furniture in Lucy's large sitting-room. The soft brown leather sofas were pulled in facing each other on either side of the fireplace which was now decorated with a startling array of candles of varying height. Rich brocade cushions from Past Times softened the room and picked up the cream in the heavy curtains and the patterns in the Oriental rug that Lucy had purchased in Holland's in Douglas for a price that she thought people only paid for Ferraris or Porsches.

They'd pulled into Mooneys' for tea and creamy cakes on the way home at the insistence of Rosa's mother and then proceeded to raid the garden of anything that was left in bloom. Bernadette, caught up in the girls' enthusiasm, had started plucking greenery at a serious rate to complement the hasty bunches that they seemed to be putting together.

Lucy's house was full of arty-farty vases, Rosa had told her mother, convinced that they'd be able to achieve an effortless-looking elegance with the minimum of stress. In the end, they wound up arranging everything haphazardly and hoping for the best.

On the night, Lucy planned to pick out a few of her favourite essential oils to burn, secretly hoping that the combination of ylang ylang, jasmine and rose would have some sort of aphrodisiac effect on Martin. Needless to say, she didn't tell this part of the plan to Rosa, who was sure to blurt it out at an inopportune moment.

She almost cried when the two of them finally sat down with their glasses of red wine, the new candles glowing in the fireplace so that they wouldn't look new and artificial on Saturday night.

"Rosa, it's fantastic. I can't get over how different it looks. I really love the rug."

"You'd bloody well want to," Rosa exclaimed, having

been shocked when she realised that Lucy was actually going to buy it.

The sales girl in Holland's hardly knew her luck when Lucy's newly acquired credit card had been produced and she announced that she was taking the stunning rectangular rug as well as the beautiful Turkish runner for the hall. The two items had come to almost ?5000, a sum that didn't bother Lucy in the least.

"Well, I think it's gorgeous," she insisted, stroking the rug almost reverently.

"It's time you treated yourself. And thanks for my treat as well, by the way."

On impulse, Lucy had pulled into The Sanctuary, a luxurious health and leisure spa on the Rochestown Road and booked the two of them in for a full day of treatments.

"No bother. We'll have a great day. It's a pity I didn't get a chance to do a bit of pampering before tomorrow evening."

"You look great as it is. Rocky is the business, isn't he?"

Lucy had nipped in to get her hair trimmed on Wednesday after her counselling session and Rocky, as usual, had come up trumps. Lucy's hair was now looking thicker and in better condition than ever, thanks to the hairdresser's insistence on her using a conditioning treatment once a week.

"He's fabulous," she giggled expansively in much the same way as Rocky himself would.

"Did you decide on which top to wear?"

Lucy had decided to wear her new jeans and high

shoes to the Savoy but had been deliberating over what top to wear. Finally, she'd decided on a jade green silk one that she'd bought in Next a few weeks previously.

"I'll wear the green one, I think. It's more comfortable."

"Did you listen to the CD?"

"Of course I did. I've had it blaring all week. It's brilliant, actually. I'll give Martin back his tomorrow night but I might buy another one the next time I'm in town."

"Duke Special will be delighted with you and your romance!"

"Would you believe, Rosa, that I've never actually gone to a gig or seen a band live at all before?"

"Well, it's time you started. We might even try and go to the Electric Picnic next year if we can get tickets. What do you think?"

"I'm on for anything," Lucy said happily as Rosa stood up to go.

"Don't let Martin Kearney hear you saying that," Rosa giggled, the red wine taking effect.

Lucy waved her off at the door, wondering just how close Rosa's words were to home.

Lucy was on a high when Rosa landed at the door at half six the following evening.

"I just came over to make sure you weren't panicking."

"Well, I am," Lucy told her in agitation as she tried to spray a bit of hair that was curling in instead of sticking out.

"What can I get for your present relief – a glass of

wine perhaps?" Rosa mimicked in a perfect study of Colin Firth in *Pride and Prejudice*, a film they'd got out on DVD a few weeks ago.

"Just a half one," Lucy said distractedly.

Rosa took off down the stairs, glad she had a role in the proceedings.

If it had been anyone else but Rosa with her, Lucy would have felt a right eejit, getting excited over a first date. But for Lucy, it really was a first date, never having been in a relationship at all.

She supposed that other people had gone through this when they were in their early teens, the rush of fancying fellows and getting ready for discos and dressing up but she had bypassed it all and was really only getting used to it now.

She remembered wondering at the others in her class at school when they were huddled together in the bike shed at lunch-time on Mondays, whispering about who was 'a good shift' and who wasn't after their Saturday night out. Lucy could hardly bear to listen to them, dreading the idea of someone kissing her and putting their hands all over her. The others seemed to be delighted with all of this – so much so that it had compounded her feeling that she really must be abnormal in some way.

Everything had changed as soon as she'd told Rosa about the horrible things that Ned had done to her. Now, the idea of someone touching her or wanting to kiss her didn't seem like such a disgusting prospect, particularly when she thought of Martin's open, smiling face.

"What took you so long?" Lucy chided her when Rosa eventually arrived back with the wine.

"Jesus, go easy," Rosa cautioned in mock horror as Lucy took a slug from her glass.

"I'll be grand now after that," said Lucy. "Is my hair all right?"

"Gorgeous. That foundation is great on you."

It was only in the past few weeks that Lucy had started to experiment with make-up and as soon as she had, Rosa had directed her to one of her friends on the Lancôme counter at work. Now she was fully fitted out with a natural foundation, translucent powder and a selection of eye-shadows and lipsticks.

"My eyes aren't too green-looking, are they?" she asked anxiously now, terrified of looking like Coco the Clown as soon as she stepped out the door.

"No!" Rosa shrieked in exasperation. "You look fabulous. Now come on down and finish your wine. I'd better go in case he thinks I want to go as well. Good luck!" she called out, already clattering down the stairs.

Alone in the house, Lucy studied herself in the mirror and decided she didn't look bad at all.

At exactly a quarter past seven, the doorbell went again. This time, she took a deep breath and made her way down the stairs, grabbing her coat and bag off the newel post. This was it.

Chapter 31

"Agnes, I wonder if I might have a word?"

Both Agnes and Beatrice looked up as the Ward Sister approached the bed. Bea was in ball order after the hospital hairdresser had been around to cut her hair and was telling Agnes all about the experience and the fact that she'd even been offered a free blue rinse.

"Of course, Sister," Agnes said, standing up.

"Do please call me Marie," the nursing sister insisted. She was only a young girl, barely out of college as far as Agnes could see, although her name badge said that she was also a qualified midwife.

"Marie, then," Agnes tried.

"It's something personal, Agnes – nothing about you at all, Beatrice," she reassured her patient. "It's more to do with the voluntary committee here at St Angela's actually."

Wondering where all this was going, Agnes sat down again.

"The Ladies' Committee organise what we call a

'visiting service'. It's really to help out people who have a relative in hospital but who may not have the transport to visit them, especially now when a taxi is so expensive. I was just wondering if you might be able to help us out with a lady who lives quite near you in Rathcabben?"

"Of course I would, Marie!" Agnes was just relieved that the visiting committee weren't going to be sent out to check up on her as she'd suspected at first.

"That would be marvellous. Her husband is on the men's side of the orthopaedic ward and she'd be delighted with a spin now and again. She's in visiting at the moment, so whenever you're ready to leave, I'll bring you down to meet her."

"I'll call up to the desk, if you like."

An hour later, Agnes made her way to the nurses' station, having dissected the ins and outs of Bea's plans to get the blue rinse before she left St Angela's. She'd always had good hair and had worn it in a thick roll at the back of her head for years. When it did need a cut, Agnes would trim it with a little hairdressing scissors that she'd bought in the local pharmacy, saving Bea the trouble of having to go to a salon.

Tonight, Bea was sitting up in bed with her silver grey hair cut in thick waves around her face. The blue rinse was just the thing to set it off. Agnes, predicting ongoing trips to the hairdresser and the hardship of getting her in and out of the car, didn't quite know whether to encourage her or not.

"Lovely, Agnes," Marie greeted as she approached the desk. "I'll bring you down to meet Mrs McCarthy this minute."

Little did Agnes know as she followed Marie down the highly polished corridor that she was setting off on a journey that would shape the rest of her life.

It was almost a surreal experience for Lucy to find herself dressed up to the nines heading off to town in Martin's car. She'd been in bits opening the door to him, wondering if she was in the right clothes for the night out, even though Rosa had endlessly assured her that she was. Martin confirmed this as soon as he saw her.

"Hi, Lucy, you look lovely!" Almost as if he noticed her sudden moment of shyness, he followed it up by saying that they'd better make tracks or they'd miss out on the decent seats.

"Off we go then," Lucy said happily, feeling a bit more settled now that she was no longer under scrutiny. "I have your CD in my bag – remind me to give it to you."

"Why don't you put it in?" he said, indicating the CD player in the car. "So we can get revved up."

"Good idea." Lucy put on her seat belt and rooted in her handbag for the disc. Slotting it in, she relaxed immediately when the now familiar strains of "Freewheel" filled the car.

"I love that one. It's a great album."

Again, Lucy had a surreal moment where she thought it must be a dream that she was driving along with this gorgeous man, chatting away about music as if it was something she was used to.

"I'd never even heard of him," she laughed, allowing herself to enjoy the moment, "and now I'm his number one fan. I can't wait to see what he looks like in person."

"The hair is a bit mad all right," Martin laughed, referring to the performer's rather strange image. "He sounds more tame than he looks."

"What about parking?" Lucy asked now. The Savoy was on Patrick Street, the city's main thoroughfare and there certainly wouldn't be parking right outside.

"I was thinking of Paul Street – we should be out before it closes."

Soon they were pulling into the multistorey carpark and Lucy was again hit by the normality of it all. Just a few short weeks ago, she wouldn't have had the confidence to go out to a gig with Cathy or one of the others at work and, if she'd been forced into it, she'd have been thinking that she stuck out like a sore thumb. Now, as a young couple stepped out of the car opposite then, Lucy could see that she didn't look all that different from anyone else.

"Level 2A – don't forget," Martin warned. "The lads are always slagging me for forgetting which level I've parked on."

"I'm glad to hear that men do that as well. Rosa nearly reported her car stolen a few weeks ago – we were going mental in Merchant's Quay until we remembered that it was City Hall we parked in."

"Remind me to give her a doing about that tomorrow night," Martin grinned.

They were making their way along Patrick Street towards the Savoy and Lucy thought for a moment that the world had never seemed so perfect. Although it was cool enough, the evening was crisp and clear and the city street looked clean and welcoming under the fancy new streetlights that had been installed as part of a recent makeover.

"*The smell on Patrick's Bridge is wicked, how does Father Matthew stick it?*"

Lucy burst out laughing at Martin's concerned rendition of the old Cork rhyme. The enormous statue of Father Matthew stood facing them at the end of the street, overlooking the bridge that spanned the Lee at the top of Patrick Street.

"I haven't heard that in years. Although Agnes, one of the ladies at the cookery class, tells me that the rhyme is meaningless now that the Cork Main Drainage scheme has cleaned up the river."

"Is she on the council or what?" Martin asked as they passed through the front entrance of the music venue.

"No, she does typing for an office centre near her and she's a mine of information. She must have a microchip for a brain because she's able to absorb details of all sorts of things as she types."

"Women and multitasking."

Lucy smiled at this and followed him down the centre aisle, delighted when they got seats halfway down.

"All we need now is our popcorn," Martin joked as Lucy shrugged out of her coat and settled in beside him.

After that the evening took off in earnest. Lucy was mesmerised by the performances of both the support act and the main act of the evening. Before she knew it, she was singing along, totally enraptured by the music. The next thing she knew, the 1,000-strong crowd were calling for an encore. Two songs later, she was rising from her seat, dismayed that the show was at an end.

"I'd definitely go to see him again," she said to Martin's back as she followed him along the aisle towards the exit.

"I think he's playing the Opera House later in the year so it'll be something to watch out for." He turned to face Lucy then in the foyer. "Would you like to go for a drink somewhere – it's only half ten?"

"That would be great. It's a shame to go straight home without dissecting Duke Special."

"Grand so. What about the Parliament? We'd get a seat, at least."

Lucy had never been in any of the pubs around the city so it didn't matter a jot to her where they went. Agreeing with the suggestion, she buttoned her coat and followed him out into the street, already imagining Rosa's face when she got all the details of the evening.

A few minutes later, they were cosily ensconced in a large, squashy leather sofa in a quiet corner of the luxurious city-centre hotel.

"I can't believe we actually got the last seats," Lucy commented as she added Diet Coke to her Tia Maria.

Martin, because he was driving, had ordered a non-alcoholic beer.

"No harm. I was really busy at work today – I was wrecked by five o'clock."

"I always had this idea that dentistry was nice, civilised work that didn't need too much exertion!"

"You must be joking. You start the day with a very civilised client list but by the end of it you've seen about five or six extra people. I think it's because we're right in the city that we get people dropping in with toothaches who need to be seen there and then."

"I never thought about that side of it. Are there a few people in the practice?"

"Only John Leyland, who started the practice, and me. We have two dental nurses, Isabel and Amanda, and the receptionist, Hilary."

They talked easily about Martin's work for a while and then Lucy told him a little about her own job at The Friary. Surprising herself, she also told him about her plans to go to college the following year and the fact that she'd phoned UCC for a prospectus.

"It will definitely be easier as a mature student," Martin insisted when Lucy admitted that she was worried about whether she'd be able for it or not. "We spent the whole time on the piss and only studied coming up to exams. The mature students in the class were doing a bit all the time so they did miles better."

"Thanks for the vote of confidence!"

"You'll be well able for it. Now, what about this dinner tomorrow night? Is it still on?"

"Of course it's on! We have to practise on somebody!"

The evening flew by after that. The night that she and Rosa had met him in the Elbow, he'd told Lucy that he was in the process of buying a house in Bishopstown. Now, he told her that the deal had fallen through and that he was back to the drawing board in the search for a property that would also be suitable for setting up a dental practice.

"The one in Bishopstown had a separate apartment attached with its own entrance so it was ideal. But there you go," he said with resignation.

They were just finishing their third drink when Lucy thought of the carpark.

"God, Martin, it's five to twelve – we'll be locked in!"

Horrified at the time, Martin jumped up in alarm. Shrugging quickly into her coat, Lucy grabbed her bag and raced after him.

"Come on," he urged, holding out his hand. As if it was the most natural thing in the world, Lucy took it and they ran along the streets of Cork as if the devil was after them. It was 11.59 when Martin hurriedly stuck the ticket into the machine. Lucy had her purse open in anticipation and slotted in the coins as quickly as she could, hoping the machine wouldn't close down in the middle of the transaction.

They both burst into gales of relieved laughter as soon as the car finally passed out under the barrier.

"Thank God you had change. I only had two fifties!"

Imagining the machine delivering forty-two one euro coins in change for him to lug home in his pockets, they both started to laugh again as he turned the car for home.

Chapter 32

Lucy and Rosa spent the best part of Saturday morning dissecting Martin and his attributes while they were out for their walk in Glenbower woods in Killeagh. Lucy had bought a small book detailing a selection of walks in the East Cork vicinity and they were slowly but surely working their way through it.

Lucy, high from her evening out with Martin, had been up at the crack of dawn. Knowing that Rosa wouldn't entertain her until at least half nine, she'd busied herself making bread for the dinner party that evening and had even put a picnic together for the walk that they had planned for themselves.

She kept reliving the evening, remembering every last minute in sharp detail. She'd been scared about how she'd cope if Martin kissed her or wanted their evening together to progress to sleeping together. Lucy didn't have a problem with other people jumping into bed with each other as soon as they met – it was just that she knew in

336

her heart that it would be a while before *she* was ready for it yet.

As it transpired, she needn't have worried about him pushing her into anything that she wasn't ready for. She'd invited him in for coffee and they'd sat talking for another hour. As he was leaving, he'd asked her if she'd like to go out the following weekend and had kissed her lightly on the cheek when she'd agreed.

If anything, she was a little disappointed that he hadn't wanted to proceed a bit, wondering if it meant that he wasn't overly interested but dismissed this thought when she recalled how pleased he'd looked when she agreed to go out with him again. She'd just have to wait and see what happened, she told herself firmly, banishing the familiar doubts that someone would find her attractive.

By the time she and Rosa had done a full circuit of Glenbower woods they'd exhausted all aspects of the Savoy, the wonderful Duke Special, the Parliament and all that came after. It was one o'clock when they finally threw off their small rucksacks at one of the picnic tables and sat down to the lunch that Lucy had prepared that morning.

"This is fantastic," Rosa enthused, scooping up a large dollop of Lucy's home-made hummus with a chunk of sesame bread.

Munching her way through the tangy olives and feta in her Greek salad, Lucy couldn't remember ever feeling so contented.

"I didn't get you tell you yesterday evening but I rang UCC about the Nutritional Science degree yesterday," she told Rosa now. "They're going to send me out a prospectus and details of how to apply."

"Did they give you any information about points or anything?"

Rosa knew that Lucy was worried about her Leaving Cert and whether she'd be eligible for university or not. She'd been afraid that her Leaving Cert results wouldn't be good enough to get into college considering the half-hearted way she'd dragged herself through the exams at the end of her schooldays.

But, as she told Rosa now, it seemed that she would have enough points for the course, unless there was a great demand for it and the points were raised. She prayed fervently that this wouldn't happen as her heart was now set on doing it.

"Will you give up work if you go to college next year?"

Lucy had thought about this too and decided that she might as well use up some of the money in the bank and make life a little easier for herself if she got the course. It would be difficult enough to study full-time, having been out of it so long, without killing herself trying to keep on her shifts in the Friary.

"I know it's almost a year away but I've been thinking about that side of it a lot. It would be best to give work up altogether and concentrate properly if I do go to college. Otherwise I'd only end up falling behind."

"You're so lucky, Lucy, to know what you want," Rosa said bleakly, opening one of the plastic containers that Lucy had filled with the strawberry smoothies that she brought for afters. She'd had to admit defeat when it came to the idea of opening her own restaurant having realised that there would be more to it than just the food. And she could barely manage that.

She was fine once she had someone to support her and her natural exuberance and friendliness made her ideal for any people-centred job. It was just finding something that didn't require too much in the line of organisational skills. As it stood, she found her job in BT's monotonous in the extreme, with no sign yet of the transfer to the Cosmetic Department that she'd applied for ages ago.

"I know something will turn up. We'll just have to think harder," Lucy counselled, sure that there must be a career out there somewhere that would suit her friend.

Rosa slurped the last of the smoothie noisily. "I think it's hitting me now that the course is almost over – I'm not sure what I'll be doing next." Sighing, she started to pack up the plastic containers and stow them away in the rucksacks again.

"Come on," Lucy said, giving her friend a hug. "Something will turn up, I promise. But first of all we have a dinner party to organise."

Chapter 33

"Lucy, would you be able to get Room 29 ready for an admission as soon as the breakfast is finished? We have a Miss Beatrice Cotter coming from St Angela's after lunch."

"No problem," Lucy responded brightly to the nursing manager, thinking how easy it was to be bright and breezy nowadays. Martin, for one thing, had put a spring in her step and she was already looking forward to eating out with him in Galligan's the following weekend. No wonder she didn't mind the fact that it was Monday.

"We'll need a raised bed with a monkey pole and an Air-Flow mattress," Una Riordan continued. "Miss Cotter is after a broken hip so she'll need quite a bit of help."

"I'll get it organised straight away, Una. She's the lady I told you about last week – Agnes's sister."

Later that day, Lucy welcomed Beatrice to her new, albeit temporary, abode and filled her in on how to use the controls on the bed as well as the call bell and the television.

"This is luxury," Agnes commented, having accompanied her sister on the short trip from St Angela's.

The room was indeed pretty, not a bit like a hospital room, with its fresh yellow walls and the bright floral duvet and matching curtains. Even the regulation floor covering was blue to pick up the colours in the soft furnishings.

"It's a pity I didn't have one of these beds at home," Beatrice said, gleefully raising the top section to get into a sitting position, already used to the controls from her time in the orthopaedic ward.

"You can raise the foot end as well if your ankles are swollen," Lucy reminded her. "And this triangle here is for pulling yourself up if you slide down the bed."

Agnes glanced at the metal triangle suspended from a tall pole attached to the head of the bed and thought tiredly of all the times that she'd heard Bea's bell chiming during the night, calling her to lift her up in the bed.

She said as much to Lucy who reminded her that there would be no more hardship now that the public health nurse and occupational therapist had been drafted in.

"You know, Beatrice, breaking your hip was a terrible thing to happen but hopefully when you get home again, life will be a little easier for both of you."

To Agnes's surprise, Beatrice agreed.

"I couldn't believe it when the nurses and carers in the hospital wouldn't lift me. There had to be two of them every time and even at that they used the hoist."

She'd been horrified at first when one of the carers had produced the sturdy nylon sling that attached to a frightening-looking lifting machine. However, once she'd got used to the idea of being mechanically lifted into her chair she realised what a trauma all of her sister's pulling and pushing had been for both of them.

"Well, hopefully there'll be no more of that," said Lucy. "Now, it's nearly time for the afternoon tea. You could have it in your room today until you get to know the place a bit."

"That sounds good," Beatrice chortled, in great form now that she had her own private room.

"You'll have to come up to the Day Room after tea, Beatrice. There's a card game on this evening that you might enjoy. If Agnes is gone you can ring the bell and someone will come and get you."

"That sounds great, Lucy."

Beatrice was delighted at the idea of investigating the rest of the nursing home and its residents while Agnes was glad that Lucy had mooted the possibility of her going home and someone else attending to her sister's needs for once.

"Are you looking forward to the wine lecture tomorrow night, Lucy?" Agnes asked now.

"I think it'll be great – I haven't a clue about wine. Up to now I only picked up the first thing in front of me in Tesco."

"It's been a lovely course," Agnes said wistfully. "It's a shame it's nearly finished."

"It was good value as well," Lucy commented, thinking how far she'd come in both knowledge and confidence.

"For two hundred euros it'd want to be good,"

Beatrice put in sceptically, causing Agnes to look at Lucy in alarm lest she give her away.

The course had cost many times the figure that Beatrice thought it had and even at that she thought it was too expensive. Copping on immediately, Lucy told her with a grin that it was extortionate but to think of all the exciting recipes that Agnes could tempt her with.

"You might even get a taste for fine wines now that I'll be an expert," Agnes quipped, thrilled with the fact that Lucy was willing to abet her in the conspiracy.

Lucy was still smiling when she reached the kitchen with the order sheets for the afternoon tea.

"You're in ball order this last week," Cathy Rohan commented as they started to sort out the list according to those who would have their tea in the communal dining-room and those who would dine in their own quarters.

Lucy smiled again and rolled her eyes, feeling confident enough now to tell Cathy about her date with Martin. The other girl would have given a blow-by-blow account of it had it been the other way around.

"Wait until coffee and I'll fill you in," she promised, laughing at Cathy whose eyes were nearly out on stalks.

"I'll say nothing until I hear more, so. Did Una tell you about the Halloween night out?"

Una Riordan was The Friary's social secretary as well as its nursing manager. With the agreement of the rest of the staff, twenty euro was taken from each person's monthly salary for the social fund that she administered. She then organised events at various intervals throughout the year including a summer barbecue, the Christmas knees-up and a pub night out every Bank Holiday.

Lucy had rarely gone to these gatherings, always feeling ill at ease among the others who dressed up to the nines and brought friends or boyfriends to make up the crowd. This time however, she was raring to go and thought she might even bring Rosa, whom Cathy had enjoyed immensely the day they'd met in Brown Thomas for lunch.

"When is it on?" she asked Cathy, her mind already working on what she'd wear.

"On the Sunday night. It's in The Fiddler's Elbow this year because they have music on so it should be good. Una was thinking of booking the Thai in Regency Lane beforehand if there are a good few of us. We've loads left in the kitty."

Later that day, Lucy put her name down on the list that Una always left out when there was something coming up, feeling exhilarated as she added a "2" after her name to denote that she'd be bringing someone with her.

She called in on Beatrice at the end of her shift to see if she was settling in.

Agnes was still there, busily tidying her sister's clothes into the beech fitted wardrobe. Lucy noticed that she was much less stressed now, almost gleeful as she chatted about all the people she'd met on the ward in St Angela's.

"I've even been asked to join the Ladies' Committee," Agnes announced importantly.

She went on to tell Lucy all about the lady that the Ward Sister had asked her to transport in and out of the hospital. "That was only last Friday. It was no bother at all – she's a lovely lady and she's only down the road from us. This morning before I left, Marie asked me if I'd like to join the Ladies' Committee. They're always looking for helpers, especially ones with a bit of experience."

"They do fund-raising as well, I'm sure. Rosa's mother is very involved," Lucy told her.

"Bernadette Mooney?" Beatrice piped up. "She's the lady organising the big New Year's Eve Ball that all the nurses were talking about." In the short time that she was on the orthopaedic ward, Beatrice had picked up almost everything that was going on under the roof of St Angela's.

"They're having their weekly meeting in the morning," Agnes went on, "and Marie asked me if I'd like to go. It'd be great for meeting people and getting out and about so I think I'll go and see if there's anything I can be useful at."

"Good for you, Agnes," Lucy commended, getting ready to leave. She noticed that Beatrice wasn't too encouraging about the Ladies' Committee. She was probably scared that Agnes would get too tied up with the voluntary work and that she mightn't have enough energy or time for her main job.

"See you tomorrow evening, Lucy," Agnes smiled, clearly delighted with this new direction that her life was taking and determined that she wouldn't slip back into her old timid ways when Beatrice got home.

Chapter 34

Rosa was itching for Lucy to hurry up but knew that she might as well settle until she heard the hairdryer cutting out. It was her own fault for persuading her friend to spend more time on her grooming.

She'd promised her mother that she'd be well able to make up a table of eight for the New Year's Eve Ball and was now anxious to get to The Gourmet Rooms and ask the others. It was the second last night of the cookery class and if she didn't invite them this evening someone else just might.

Lucy and Martin would be definites, as well as Lar and Gerry and Gerry's girlfriend Shona. Now that Kate had started her romance with Lorcan from the vegetable market, she thought she'd invite her as well. She was jolted out of her considerations now as Lucy arrived down to the sitting-room.

"Well, what do you think?"

Lucy seemed to be announcing her arrival in this

manner almost all the time now, Rosa thought with a burst of pride.

"Fabulous!" Rosa enthused, taking in the military style skirt that her friend wore with a fitted black shirt and matching black and khaki wedge-heeled sandals.

Rosa herself was dressed to the nines in a fitted black dress, fishnets and red killer heels.

"Come on then!" Lucy insisted with a grin, as if it had been Rosa who'd been holding up the show.

Mrs Carter was all business when she stepped into the kitchen. As she seemed to expect, most of her charges were there before her, lined up at their work stations.

"First of all, we'll have Dan Paulson from Coolgreena Cheese to talk to us about the various types of cheese, the cheese-making process and some of the uses and accompaniments. Then we'll have our wine expert, Molly Lacey, who operates Corked, a wine bar here in the city. The last session will really be a recap of all the classes in preparation for our final night next week."

"Hope we'll be able to sit down with a cuppa for the talks," Rosa whispered to Lucy, her new heels beginning to hurt from the few minutes standing on the terracotta tiles. She'd worn them in order to break them in but now she wasn't so sure if it had been a good idea.

"So we'll all proceed to the drawing room now," Mrs Carter announced as if she'd heard her, "and please make a cup of tea or coffee to relax with."

Ninety minutes later, the two speakers had come and gone and Kate, Agnes, Rosa and Lucy gathered in their usual spot for the most important part of the evening – their chat.

"I'm in a bit of a pickle," Agnes announced as soon as they were all settled with their tea and cookies.

The rest of them looked at her expectantly, wondering if something had gone wrong with Beatrice.

"Tell us, Agnes," Kate encouraged, feeling a little guilty that she might have neglected Agnes since she'd become so tied up with Lorcan.

"You know I told you I was going to go to the Ladies' Committee meeting this morning?" This she directed at Lucy, who nodded. "Well, they were on about this 'make-over' that they were going to do for charity this Friday evening but the main sponsor pulled out at the last minute. They were talking about cancelling it but I, like an eejit, opened my big mouth and said what about getting some of the girls at the make-up counters in the pharmacies to volunteer to participate instead. They'd have loads of samples and things. The next thing I knew, the chairwoman was congratulating me on a great idea and telling everyone that it was marvellous I was contributing. Now I have to get enough make-up artists to do forty women or the whole thing will be cancelled."

"But do you know any make-up people?" Lucy queried, trying to get to the bottom of it.

"I went into town this afternoon and went to three of the pharmacies on Patrick Street so I have three lined up. But I think I'll need about ten. Eight for definite or it'll be going on all night."

"I'll ask some of the girls in BT's," Rosa said

immediately. "Lucy bought loads of make-up at the Lancôme counter a few weeks ago and Karen got a huge commission – she'll definitely do it. And the Mac girl will probably do it as well. Don't worry, Agnes."

"That'll be five. There's Kelly's pharmacy next door to the shop," Kate said, "and the girls in there are lovely. I'll ask them in the morning. I'm sure they'd love to do something for charity."

Now that there was hope on the horizon, Agnes recovered a bit. "I know a few of the girls in that place on Oliver Plunkett Street as well, come to think of it. I mightn't do too badly."

"We'll do a blitz tomorrow, Agnes," Lucy promised. "I need loads of things so I can buy a heap of stuff to sweeten them up before you ask for their services."

"Oh, thanks, Lucy. Are you not working?"

"I'm on a day off tomorrow so I'll be free in the morning. I'll meet you at the front door of BT's if you like and we can have coffee with Rosa. The two of you can tackle the girls there first."

Wednesday afternoons had become sacrosanct on account of her counselling sessions, something that nothing could force her to miss. And if she had to spend a load of money to further Agnes's charitable cause then so be it. She and Rosa had prepared a list of children's charities that she planned to go through with Cora on Wednesday to see which ones would benefit most from a cash injection. The ISPCC was one that appealed to her on account of them covering all sorts of different services, including counselling.

"I'm delighted now that I can relax a bit," said Agnes. "I was sick thinking about it all day."

"Well, don't panic for the moment," Lucy smiled, and stood up to get another cup of tea for everyone.

"How's the romance going?" Rosa asked now, hoping that it was going well enough for Kate to bring Lorcan to the New Year's Eve Ball in six weeks' time.

"Flying," Kate grinned. It was obvious from her smile that she was totally smitten.

Rosa pounced. "What would you think about coming to the New Year's Eve Ball at Hollygrove Manor then? It's in aid of St Angela's and I'm trying to get a table together."

"Sounds good – count Lorcan and me in anyway. I presume it's formal?"

"Very. You'll probably be at one of the committee tables, Agnes."

"Not if I don't pull off this 'makeover' thing!"

"You will, Agnes," Lucy said, arriving back with the fresh tea. "Did you ask Kate about the Ball?"

"Full house," Rosa exclaimed proudly, thrilled that she now had her eight people lined up. Planning for the ball, she felt, would be another way of distracting herself until she heard some news from either Sister Ignatius or Mother Bridget. She was thinking about her birth mother more and more as the days went by, wondering in particular if she'd ever tried to look for her child.

She'd been awake for ages last night trying to picture what her face might be like but all she could picture was either her own face or Bernadette's. The ball would be a good distraction until she heard something. And now that the cookery course was looming to an end, she was back to the reality of her uninspiring job and the fact that she still had no real plan for her future.

"Ready, everyone?"

All four of them swallowed the last of their tea hurriedly and stood to follow Mrs Carter back to the kitchen, wondering what was in store for the rest of the evening.

Chapter 35

Finally, it was the last night of the course and Rosa was bursting to get to The Gourmet Rooms. She'd been a bit shocked the previous week when Mrs Carter had outlined the details of their final class. They would each be given a menu, and enough ingredients to accommodate the class would be left out at the back of the room. After that, it would be up to the individual to manage her own recipes.

Although she was nervous about the pressure of cooking a full meal on her own, she knew that Lucy would help her if she really got stuck. She would miss the camaraderie of the class after the ten weeks but knew that she'd still be in touch with her new friends. She was dying to hear all the details of Agnes's 'makeover' night although her mother had given her a pretty good gist of it.

Bernadette's account of it was that Agnes had done as much fund-raising in the past week as many of the volunteers had done in months, on account of happening to know almost everyone on the cosmetic counters of Cork city.

Agnes, in the face of a near disaster, had offered to do the rounds of the beauty consultants in the city herself to ask if they'd accommodate the prestigious 'makeover' event being held in the Kinsale home of Cornelius Price-Canning, one of the plastic surgeons at St Angela's.

Clutching at anything that might save the day, the committee had agreed to see what Agnes could come up with, settling on a deadline of twelve midday on Thursday to cancel the event if the make-up artists couldn't be sourced.

Always perfectly groomed herself, it appeared that Agnes had approached a number of cosmetic departments in the larger pharmacies around the city, asking each make-up adviser for a few hours of their time in aid of St Angela's. The very mention of Mr and Mrs Cornelius Price-Canning was enough to have them running for their vanity cases, many of them already familiar with Agnes on account of her regular quest for samples. Almost all of them were surprised that she was connected to the celebrity plastic surgeon.

The evening was a roaring success with each of Marjorie Price-Canning's chosen guests laying out ? 200 for a personal makeover. Marcus Haverty, the celebrity photographer, was approached to photograph the event. The subsequent two-page spread in the *Evening Echo* had generated even more valuable publicity for the cause.

To the delight of the make-up artists, Cornelius had

appeared towards the close of the evening, wowing them with his legendary charm and his assertions that any one of them could achieve as much with a lip brush in five minutes as he could with a scalpel in an hour.

Agnes was cited as the brains behind the idea – the Price-Cannings' magnanimously insisting that they had merely facilitated an event that would never have happened if Agnes hadn't stepped in.

This was the official version and Rosa, Kate and Lucy had insisted that Agnes should not reveal the assistance she'd had. Now, according to Bernadette, Agnes was the new best thing on the fund-raising scene in Cork.

Rosa was delighted that Agnes was getting a bit of acknowledgement at last, after all the tireless work that she'd been doing all her life. She hopped into the car now and drove the few yards to Lucy's house, beeping to get her friend's attention.

"I can hardly believe the course is finished tonight," Lucy commented as soon as she was settled into Rosa's yellow Mini. "Going for a drink will be a nice way to finish up."

The previous week, the four of them had decided to go for a drink after the final session. Rosa, the chief organiser, had picked The Front Lounge to start off with in deference to Agnes, imagining that she'd feel more comfortable there than in one of the newer wine bars or clubs around the city. She and Lucy could always move on to somewhere livelier if the others headed home early.

"I can't believe that I'll have to cook a three-course meal with nobody to help me."

Rosa had been wound up on this all week. Even though they'd be able to consult their notes, the two girls had gone through most of the basics during the week, eventually calling on Martin, Gerry and Lar to critique their efforts on Sunday evening. Now she was wondering if all the cramming hadn't just confused her further.

Lucy could hardly believe how Martin had become such a part of her life in the few weeks that they'd known each other. But she felt comfortable in his presence and had come to adore his two trusty friends. Even the way he encouraged her about going to college told her that he was the kind of person who completely respected her plans.

"Mature students always do better because they're not out drinking every night," he reminded her again on Sunday evening as they'd tucked into the eclectic meal that she and Rosa had prepared. "And you could do an evening course in computers if you wanted to get a head-start. You can even have my laptop to practise on if you do the moussaka for me again."

"God, Martin, you make it sound like an exotic dance the way you say it," Lucy had giggled.

Lucy hadn't thought about this aspect of her impending college course. At The Friary, she had no need to be computer literate and at home she had television and books to fill her evenings. But now that the classes at The Gourmet Rooms were coming to an end, it would make sense to do a beginners' course.

She'd decided there and then to phone the local VEC to see if there were any vacancies on their courses after

Christmas. She might even ask Martin to come with her to purchase a laptop of her own the next Saturday that he was free. He worked every second Saturday morning at the dental surgery in Tuckey Street while his boss, John Leyland did the alternate ones.

"It's been a great ten weeks, hasn't it, Rosa?"

"Brilliant. Mum was telling me that Agnes got great praise for the 'makeover' evening, by the way."

"Good for her – I'd say this is the first time in her life that she has the freedom to get out and about. She's been minding Beatrice since she was in her twenties. She even had to give up her job."

What Lucy didn't add was how demanding Beatrice was in having her needs met. This was fine in The Friary where there was plenty of staff to do things for her but Lucy couldn't imagine how Agnes had managed alone for years with no support.

"The course has done wonders for almost everyone in the class," said Rosa as she screeched up beside Agnes near Mrs Carter's house.

"All set for tonight?" Rosa called out, dolled up to the nines for the drinks later. "*I* can't even think about it until we have the exam done."

"Exam?" Agnes sounded vague.

"Well, it's almost like an exam. The pressure of having to do it on our own and all."

"Don't panic, Rosa!" said Lucy. "It won't be the end of the world if we burn the whole lot." Then, noticing that Agnes looked a bit tired this evening, she added, "We heard the 'makeover' went great!"

Agnes smiled with pleasure as she followed the two girls up the steps.

Rosa was in the grip of serious anxiety as Mrs Carter started her opening spiel.

"Welcome, everybody," she began, smiling at the anticipation on the faces in front of her. "Before I hand out the menus, do try to remember that this is not any kind of exam. Look on it more as an exercise that will prove to you all just how far you've come in ten short weeks. Now, there you go, Rosa."

Handing her the small slip, she passed on to Lucy. Rosa was nearly in tears with anxiety as she scanned the slip of paper. Alarmed, she glanced up to see how the others were taking it.

Kate looked serene as usual, with no hint of the panic that Rosa was feeling. Agnes looked a bit flustered, her hands fluttering as she exclaimed about whether she'd have time to marinade a steak as well as doing a chocolate and orange cheesecake. Lucy, practical as usual, was marking the relevant pages in her cook-book.

"Is yours okay?" Kate whispered over. "I've been given a selection of breads to make."

"Just breads — nothing else?" Rosa was aghast at how easy this sounded.

"I'm delighted — at least it's straightforward. No marinades," she added with a grin in Agnes's direction. "What did you get?"

"The smoked salmon starter, then the mango and mustard chicken. I have to do a banoffee for dessert.

"Not bad," Kate reassured her. "Just take your time."

Kate smiled to herself as she made her way to the back of the room to pick out the ingredients she needed. She had good reason.

Lorcan's proposal of marriage on Sunday night had stunned her but she'd accepted immediately, having no doubts at all as to how happy they'd be together.

They'd walked over to Galligan's for dinner and as soon as the waiter had removed their dessert plates Lorcan had quietly said that he wanted to ask her something. The seriousness of his expression alarmed her briefly until he took her hand across the table and laid the little red velvet box in front of her.

"Kate, I love you and I'd love us to be together all the time. Will you marry me? Please?"

"I'd love to," she told him, leaning across the table to kiss him, her face wreathed in the broadest smile she'd smiled in years.

"I was terrified all day," he admitted in relief. "Aren't you going to open it?"

Kate had forgotten all about the box in her excitement. She opened it slowly, tears in her eyes at the fact that Lorcan had gone out and deliberated over something so special with her in mind.

"Lorcan, it's so beautiful!" She could hardly breathe at the sight of the ring that nestled in its navy velvet bed. The large square-cut diamond was flanked by two slightly smaller ones, perfectly proportioned above the gold band.

She lifted it from the box, admiring it in the light before

handing it silently back to him and extending her left hand. She'd sensed somehow that it would fit perfectly and it did, feeling as familiar on her finger as Timmy's rings had for years. She'd taken them off that first evening that she'd talked to Lorcan at The Gourmet Rooms, a premonition of things to come settling around her after he'd asked her out.

Now she was sieving her ingredients for the bread, her mind full of the plans that she and Lorcan had sat up late into the night making, their clothes strewn on the floor of Kate's bedroom.

"I imagine it's ready for the liquids now, Kate," Mrs Carter prompted, obviously having noticed her repeated sieving.

Back to earth again, Kate re-engaged with her bread-making, all the while wondering if the others would notice her new ring. If they didn't, she'd tell them later in The Front Lounge.

Over at her own work station, Lucy was whizzing up the pine-nut kernels, basil and Parmesan for the pesto that she'd serve with the strong goat's cheese for her first course. She was delighted to have got an Italian meal and was actually looking forward to starting the tiramisu, which she planned to put in the fridge to chill before starting on the creamy basil and pepperoni sauce that she'd serve with fresh tagliatelle.

Italian food always reminded her of her first meeting with Martin the night of Rosa's ambitious dinner party. She glanced over at her friend now to see if she could help her while Mrs Carter was assisting Agnes.

Despite her tutoring, Rosa had taken out all the ingredients for the three courses in a misguided attempt to be organised and was now boggling at the sight of all the jars and tubs littering her work station.

"I've no room to manoeuvre with all this stuff around me," she complained in a loud whisper.

"What are you doing first?"

"Well, I have the condensed milk on the boil for the banoffee. But that'll take another hour. I was going to start the chicken dish next."

"Well, why don't you get rid of all the rest of the banoffee stuff? Put them down the back near the cooker. You'll have more room to do the chicken then."

Rosa obeyed immediately, delighted with Lucy's management plan. By the time she'd resurrected a casserole dish from the deep shelves at the back, her friend had wiped down the work surface for her and arranged the cream, wholegrain mustard and mango chutney beside the chicken fillets for her. She glanced over gratefully and Lucy winked back but Mrs Carter was now approaching and Rosa was at a loss as to how to proceed.

"Do you need a bowl to mix the ingredients for the sauce, Rosa?"

This mild reminder was enough for her and she went off in search of the said bowl, the simple routine of mixing the cream, mustard and chutney and pouring the mixture over the chicken fillets coming back to her.

Lucy noticed the gentle way that Mrs Carter directed Rosa without appearing to admonish her and was glad. She'd also given her the least complicated menu of all –

the smoked salmon roulade was foolproof, just spreading on the cream cheese and chives and rolling the whole thing up. She'd be well able to manage the cutting of it into short lengths and the presentation on a large white plate, decorated with fresh chives.

"Is it too soon to put the chicken in the oven, do you think, Lucy?"

Rosa's main course would be burned to a crisp if she put it in the oven now, Lucy reckoned. "Why don't you leave it to marinate a bit and start on the base of the banoffee?"

"Good idea," Rosa said happily, settling a bit now that things were underway. The worry of not getting her certificate at the end of the class was beginning to recede as well. Even though it wasn't an exam as such, she was still terrified of Mrs Carter saying that she hadn't proved herself a competent cook and refusing her the piece of paper.

Lucy watched her friend teetering around the terracotta tiles in her stilettos and thought that she looked like something out of a 1950's advertisement for the perfect housewife. Rosa had so many good points – it was just a pity that her attributes weren't suitable to the more conventional forms of employment.

Lucy thought briefly about her own future then and marvelled that she actually had one. Her life had been pretty aimless up to now, she'd realised, with no goals or ambitions at all. Now she had plans for everything – her career, the house, her clothes, even for Martin, all going well.

Even though it had only been a few weeks since they'd

met, they'd already become close. He was exactly what she needed – easy-going and uncomplicated with a great sense of humour that often made her laugh despite herself. He was interested in everything about her and had been enthusiastic and encouraging about her plans to go to university the following year.

To her wonderment, Lucy had very few fears now about the physical side of their relationship, something she'd always thought she'd hate or at least only tolerate if she ever did get married. Instead, she loved the way Martin touched her, his hands gentle and slow when he'd stroked her and held her face as he kissed her after their night out in Galligan's at the weekend.

She'd invited him in again when he left her home and as soon as he'd kissed her properly, all the doubts that she'd had were dispelled. She'd made it clear though that she wasn't ready for an intense relationship – that she needed to get to know him a bit first. She'd been a little anxious talking about it, knowing it was a bit much in this day and age to be so prudish about sleeping with someone that she actually liked and trusted. Martin was unperturbed, telling her that they had plenty of time.

"You can let me know as we go along," he'd told her, kissing the back of her neck and nibbling her ear as she lay back against him on the sofa. She knew that some day she'd be able to tell him about her past but not just yet. She had to come to terms with it fully herself first.

She was thinking about just how far she'd come in the past few months when another panicky whisper from Rosa broke into her consciousness.

"I think I whizzed the biscuits too much – they're gone into powder nearly."

Lucy examined the contents of the bowl surreptitiously, hoping that there was another packet of Digestives to hand. The packet that Rosa had been crushing with the food processor had been ground to a small dusty heap in the bowl.

"I'll see what I can do," Lucy promised, noticing Mrs Carter's absence gratefully.

A search of the cupboard revealed two packs of Lincoln creams and half a pack of custard creams. Kate too was rooting among the meagre biscuit collection and spotted Lucy's rummaging.

"I'm looking for more Bourbon Creams for Agnes," she explained. "What are you after?"

Lucy giggled as she explained the situation and the level of Rosa's anxiety. Kate understood perfectly, having been paired off with Rosa one evening to make a batch of dough. It was like rubber in the wind-up because poor Rosa was so anxious that she kept taking it out of the plastic bag to check it instead of leaving it alone to prove properly. Now Agnes had also been a bit heavy-handed with the food processor and had ground to nothing the chocolaty biscuits that she needed to give her cheesecake its rich chocolate base.

"Look, we'll crush up the Custard Creams and the Lincolns and halve them," Lucy decided. "You can melt a bit of chocolate to mix in with Agnes's."

"There won't be enough for two in that," Kate commented as she replaced her own leftover ingredients in one of the cupboards. "What about a bit of oatmeal to boost it up? I have a load of it left over from the brown bread."

"It won't kill anyone, I suppose," Lucy laughed, swiftly purloining the bag of pinhead oatmeal and shaking out a bowlful.

"I'll do the biscuits and send half over to you for Agnes," Lucy promised, setting off with the ingredients before their tutor returned.

"Grand so, only don't let Mrs Carter see you or Agnes'll be afraid of getting put out for cheating."

Five minutes later, Rosa had a delicious, if wholesome, base for her banoffee and Agnes was exclaiming at the richness of her cheesecake base now that it contained the expensive chocolate that Kate had spotted among the array of ingredients. Lucy and Kate were grinning at the success of their improvisations by the time Mrs Carter re-entered the room.

"I'm aware that you all may be at different stages so feel free to take your coffee break whenever it suits," she told them, eliciting a relieved sigh from Rosa who was becoming increasingly stressed.

"Are you ready, Lucy?" Rosa prodded immediately, conveniently forgetting about the two tins of condensed milk that were bubbling on one of the cookers.

"Do you want to take the tins out and have them cooling?" Lucy, just like Mrs Carter, had a mild way of directing Rosa that never seemed to fluster her.

"Good idea."

Lucy smiled as she abandoned her own work station and headed for the drawing room.

When Kate arrived into the drawing room, Lucy was

tucking into the crumbly home-made biscuits and planning the remainder of her menu.

"How did the banoffee base turn out?" Kate asked, amused still at their improvisation.

"Brilliant. I tell you, I'll need more than one drink after this."

"You can sing it," Kate giggled, more stressed with Agnes than she was with her bread-making. "I might have to get a lift home with Agnes if I have a few too many."

"So, how's it going, Kate?" Rosa said breathlessly, noting Kate's grin as she arrived into the drawing room.

She meant the bread-making but Kate was unable to resist spreading her good news.

"Flying," Kate said laughing. She then held out her left hand proudly.

Rosa wouldn't have made as much noise if somebody had been murdered on the premises. Agnes arrived on the scene, followed by Mrs Carter to see what all the commotion was about. They all crowded around Kate to admire the ring and hear the story of the proposal.

Mrs Carter, having a soft spot for Kate, offered her warmest congratulations and suggested, to everyone's glee, that perhaps a glass of sherry was in order.

Kate was glowing by the time the coffee break finished and wondered at the God that she'd railed bitterly against for the past thirteen years who now saw fit to bring her such happiness. She reflected now on the day that Mrs Carter had come into the shop and offered her a place on the course. Strangely, it had been the day that she'd finally decided she needed to get out and make a life for herself.

The cookery course had been the start of that process and the means of her meeting Lorcan.

She had finished her letter to the family of the man who'd died that night along with Timmy and their baby. Like Lorcan, she didn't expect a reply to exonerate her from her guilt – she'd simply let it go as soon as she'd handed the letter to her solicitor, who she'd hoped would be able to place it in the correct hands.

A lightness had come over her at that moment and she'd felt free to move on fully and see things as they really were, not as she'd allowed herself to think all those years. Perhaps she'd have been able to avoid the oncoming car if she hadn't had that glass of wine. But she had to accept that there was no way of ever knowing.

Even accepting Rosa's invitation to the New Year's Eve ball was an acknowledgement of the fact that she deserved as much as anyone to enjoy her life and the new people in it. Tonight in the drawing room, she'd wanted to shout her happiness from the rooftops. Although, she thought with a smile, Rosa had done just that for her.

"No wonder you're smiling," Lucy said, giving her another quick hug when they met at the back of the room a few minutes later. "I'll have to hear all about it later."

Lucy was thrilled for Kate. She looked on her as a friend now and hoped that it would continue beyond The Gourmet Rooms. She'd trusted Kate from that first day in Good For You when she'd tried to dissuade her from rushing into buying the aromatherapy burner, something that Lucy had never experienced in a shop before.

How angry and suspicious I must have looked, Lucy thought now as she put the finishing touches to her tiramisu. She had been angry, she could acknowledge now, at everybody for not noticing what had happened to her, for not trying to help.

Now that she was getting past that anger and taking control of her life, Lucy was determined to catch up the many things that she'd lost out on. Going to the New Year's Eve party was almost like experiencing her Debs again, only this time she'd actually be going to it. Leaving school had been a relief to her and she hadn't had any desire to celebrate it. The thought of having to buy a dress and ask someone to accompany her had seemed appalling at the time and she'd simply made excuses to get out of it.

She'd spoken about this to Cora Nolan at her last counselling session and came to the conclusion that the intense anger she'd been feeling was a direct result of feeling cheated out of all the normal milestones of growing up. She was able to talk about why she was so excited now about the New Year's Eve do, telling Cora that it was as if she was getting a second chance at launching herself as a proper adult.

It seemed to her now that she'd been stuck in a sort of confused childhood for years, not fitting into the grown-up world in the easy, comfortable way that other people seemed to.

But this time around, she'd be secure in the company of her own circle of friends and she planned to make the most of it. Martin had been enthusiastic when she'd asked him if he'd like to go, especially when he heard that Rosa was planning to ask Lar, Gerry and Shona as well. Now all she had to do was start looking for a dress, although she still had a few pounds more to lose.

"Are these all right?"

Rosa was anxiously displaying her salmon roulade starter, holding a chive aloft while trying to decide how to place it by way of a garnish.

"It looks fantastic – a bit like the little symbols on the monuments at Newgrange."

Rosa beamed at this compliment, even though she'd never actually seen the three spirals that connected to make a triangular shape etched on the centuries-old monument.

"Should I put on the rice, do you think?"

Lucy glanced at the clock to work out how much time they had left. The plan was to test all of the dishes in a buffet-style meal, starting at nine fifteen.

"I'd say so. I'll leave my pasta for another few minutes, I think."

The aromas in the kitchen were delicious by this stage and all of them had come hungry in anticipation of the feast of flavours that they'd experience.

"Ten minutes to the first course," Mrs Carter announced, putting Rosa into a frenzy of panic until Lucy reminded her that she was actually completely up to date.

Agnes, hovering near the ovens, peered anxiously through the glass to see how her Loaded Potato Skins were doing.

Kate was arranging her selection of breads on the

platters that Mrs Carter had left out for her, having first supplied Lucy with a warm, crusty loaf on which to present her goat's cheese and basil pesto starter.

Rosa decided to carry her first course through to the dining room while Lucy supervised the wild rice accompaniment to her main course.

In customary fashion, Mrs Carter clapped to draw their attention and announced that it was time to dine. The table in the enormous formal dining-room had been elegantly set, complete with crisp white cloth and linen napkins. The overhead lights had been dimmed to allow the soft glow of a silver candelabrum to dominate the table.

The sense of excited achievement was palpable as the offerings were sampled and commented upon, with Rosa basking happily in the compliments received for her artistic presentation.

For Agnes, the aura of fine dining in such civilised surroundings would normally be enough to sustain her for months. At any other time, she would have been able to contribute to the lively conversation and good-natured banter going on around her but after the shock she'd had earlier in the evening, she couldn't focus properly on what was being said, never mind join in.

Kate, with her usual good nature, had practically dragged her through the evening, enquiring gently at one stage if she was all right but not pressing her when she declined to explain her distracted humour. Perhaps she might have an opportunity to speak to her in the car on the way home and ask her opinion on how best to proceed in the circumstances. She felt so hopeless and alone and couldn't bear to think about the future now.

"I think it's fantastic of you, Agnes," Kate was saying.

Agnes just nodded, not sure exactly what she was talking about.

"Especially with all you've had to cope with lately," Lucy added.

Agnes looked at her sharply, wondering if she knew already – maybe everyone in The Friary had known before she did.

"Is it really your first foray into voluntary work, Agnes?"

Mrs Carter sounded impressed and Agnes realised it was her work at St Angela's that they were talking about.

"Yes, indeed," she answered, acknowledging the Ward Sister's part in getting her involved.

"Mum says they're talking about turning the 'make-over evening' into an annual event. It raised a lot of money apparently and they could have sold loads more tickets if they'd realised what a hit it'd be," Rosa enthused.

Agnes, her mind obviously elsewhere, just murmured some unintelligible reply.

Lucy thought that Agnes must surely be sickening for something. Normally, she'd have been thrilled to bits with all the praise. Instead she was barely keeping pace with the conversation, her mind obviously elsewhere.

Once the first course had been tested and tasted to everyone's satisfaction, they retired one by one to put the finishing touches to their main dish.

Lucy took the opportunity of asking after Agnes's

welfare as they stood side by side at one of the cookers. Lucy was watching her pasta while Agnes melted a knob of garlic butter in which to reheat the cooked potato that she'd scooped from their skins earlier.

"It's not something with Beatrice, is it?"

Lucy hadn't been working this morning but Beatrice had been fine on her shift the previous day.

"Well," Agnes said enigmatically as she added a dash of cream to the potato, "there's nothing wrong with Bea. It's me that has something to worry about."

"Is there anything I can do to help, Agnes?"

Lucy wondered if she'd perhaps run into financial difficulty while her sister was in hospital. This sometimes happened to women whose husbands managed the finances when they were left to do unfamiliar things like paying bills. It seemed to Lucy that Beatrice had control of the purse strings in this particular household and she wasn't sure if Agnes even had her own pension yet.

"I'll tell you about it in the hotel later," Agnes promised, studiously placing the garlic mash in the centre of a warmed plate and topping it with her medium rare steak.

"Okay. And you know I'll do whatever I can to help."

Lucy drained her pasta, ladled it into a large ceramic bowl and carried it to the table with the bowl of rich tomato sauce laced with cream and spicy pepperoni. Agnes smiled gratefully and followed her. Perhaps Lucy would have some know-how on what the procedure might be now that things had changed for her and Beatrice.

Rosa had arranged her chicken fillets on a large oval

plate, diagonally sliced to perfection and placed on a pool of the rich creamy mango and mustard sauce. The wild rice she'd placed in six tiny Le Creuset bowls topped with dainty matching lids. These were actually miniature soup tureens and again, everyone was impressed with her innovative presentation.

Relaxed now that the actual cooking was done with, they enjoyed the rest of their meal, gorging themselves in an attempt to try each luscious dessert. They finished with coffee and a selection of exquisite petit fours.

Lucy was glad to see that Agnes seemed to have regained some of her spirits as she chatted to Mrs Carter about her fund-raising and the upcoming charity ball.

"That means that all of us here will be there on the night," Rosa commented when Mrs Carter told them about her own involvement in the Ladies' Committee. Each year The Gourmet Rooms donated three spot prizes whereby Mrs Carter would come to the home of the winner and cook a meal for six. She was also involved in the homeless hostel attached to St Angela's, something that had been close to Bernadette Mooney's heart for years. Rosa's mother spent a few hours there every Monday night offering what she called a gateway counselling service for any of the clients who might later accept referrals to alcohol or substance abuse services.

"Most of the food left over at the end of the classes here is boxed and taken over to the hostel afterwards. Although sometimes it's safer to discard it," she said with the hint of a smile.

The stately hall clock chiming ten times broke up the

leisurely gathering, to Lucy's disappointment. She was enjoying every minute of the relaxed meal but was also wondering what it was that had Agnes in such a state of flux.

She said as much to Kate now as they lined up to receive their Gourmet Rooms scrolls from Mrs Carter who was unusually flushed, probably due to the glass of wine she'd consumed with her guests. Kate too had noticed the fact that Agnes wasn't herself and told Lucy that she was almost glad she hadn't invited Lorcan along to meet everyone if there was a crisis on hand.

Rosa in particular received her little Gourmet Rooms scroll with unprecedented excitement. The others tucked theirs away in pockets and handbags as they expressed their thanks to their tutor for such a vibrant and edifying ten weeks but Rosa stood gloating over hers for ages.

"I wonder if I might have a word, Rosa, before you leave?"

Mrs Carter said this so quietly that even Lucy, standing next to her friend, didn't hear her.

Rosa's heart sank immediately. She knew that getting the scroll like everyone else was a bit too good to be true. Once again, she hadn't been up to scratch but at least the others wouldn't have to know about it.

White-faced, she insisted that Lucy take a spin into town with Agnes and Kate, promising that she'd catch up in a few minutes. Whatever it was that Mrs Carter had to say could surely do without an audience.

Chapter 36

"I hope I'm not holding you up, Rosa," Mrs Carter began, her voice its usual calm, even tone.

Rosa was heartened that she at least wasn't cross over something. "Not at all," she reassured her. "We're only going for a drink to celebrate the end of the course. We all really enjoyed it."

"I'm glad to hear it. I must say, you were a very united group. Sometimes the class members just don't gel. It's a much more enjoyable course when people enjoy the company as well."

Rosa was still wondering where all this was going. If she was going to be admonished for something, then so be it. The sooner the better, she thought bravely.

"Now I won't delay you," Mrs Carter continued. "As you know, the cookery school has become so much busier since the Absolute Beginners series was aired on television. Hence, I've had to take on a bit more help for the Intermediate and Advanced courses. Now, I do like to concentrate on the Beginners myself – that's what the school is all about, after all."

"I see," Rosa mumbled, totally at a loss.

"As well as two assistants for the more advanced courses, I now find that I'll have to take on a personal assistant as well." She paused.

Rosa continued to look at her, mesmerised. Mrs Carter was wearing a very light foundation and powder this evening, she noticed absently. This was new, an extension of the slight shift in image that had happened over the past few weeks. It made her less severe-looking, Rosa decided, tuning back in to what her tutor was saying.

"Now I know you mentioned that you're working part time in Brown Thomas. If I might ask, are you hoping to get more permanent hours there or would you be interested in coming to work here at The Gourmet Rooms?"

"Here?" Rosa was dumbstruck. Panic struck her at the thought of supervising students in the classes when she was barely able to cook herself. "I'm not sure that I'd be able to keep track of all the recipes," she began, utterly confused. What was going on? She must have misheard.

"It wouldn't be in the actual kitchen," said Mrs Carter, "although there would be some involvement. It would be more here in the office in the morning, taking calls and bookings for the courses, sorting out the starter packs and preparing for the courses before you'd leave in the evenings. There would also be media appearances, at which I feel you'd be excellent."

"Media appearances?"

"As you may have noticed, the profile of the school has changed totally since the television series. Now we're getting a much younger clientele. 'Yuppies' – I believe they used to be called, although I'm told that word is gone out of fashion now. We need a younger face now, I'm afraid."

"And you think I'd be able for it?" Somewhere at the back of her mind, Rosa knew that she was probably shooting herself in the foot by questioning her own abilities when Mrs Carter clearly thought she was up to it but she could hardly believe that she'd been picked when someone like Lucy would be so much more competent.

"Of course you'd be able for it. I've been observing you in recent weeks and I'm convinced you'd be excellent at promoting The Gourmet Rooms – people want to see a stylish, vibrant young lady these days instead of a sort of matriarch figure. I feel that you'd attract a younger set – people in demanding jobs who have lost the art of cooking altogether. What do you think?"

"I'd love it," Rosa said finally, breaking into a smile after all her anxiety earlier. Lucy was right when she'd said that something would turn up for her.

"Are you happy to finish up with your present job?"

"Definitely. This will be absolutely great, Mrs Carter." Now that it was cleared up that she'd be having precious little to do with actual cooking, Rosa was beginning to feel a bit high on it all.

"Pamela. You'll have to call me Pamela if we're going to work together."

Mrs Carter extended her hand and Rosa took it

firmly. This was going to be her new start and she was determined to make it work.

"Thank you, Pamela, for asking me. I'll do my very best to be an excellent personal assistant."

"Marvellous, Rosa. I'll contact you over the next few days and we can make proper arrangements. Now go and enjoy your night out. You deserve it after all the hard work."

"Thanks again, Pamela. I'm really looking forward to starting again at The Gourmet Rooms."

Although she'd promised herself that she wouldn't get upset, Agnes started to cry almost as soon as she'd started to tell Kate and Lucy about Bea's decision to reside permanently at The Friary.

"Everything's in her name, Bea says. The house will have to be sold to pay the fees. She says she's determined to stay and she wants me to move in there too. She says it's safer there for both of us."

"Agnes, I can't imagine that Beatrice would see the house being sold," Kate reassured her, not convinced that Agnes could be evicted by her own sister and forced into a nursing home when she was in the full of her health.

"Bea says she couldn't go back there now that she's got used to the constant attention. She says I'll be well able to survive on my pension, that I can get a flat for myself if I won't go into The Friary."

Lucy reminded Agnes that many of The Friary's residents had spouses who remained living in the family home. Surely the same rule would apply to a sister?

"Have you spoken to your solicitor, Agnes?" Kate wanted to know.

"I've never had a solicitor," Agnes sniffled, her dainty handkerchief crumpled for once.

"I mean the family solicitor. Is there someone who may have sorted out your parents' will and that kind of thing?"

"Barrett and Co in the South Mall did all that. But I don't see what they can do now."

"Sometimes there are clauses put in that say a person can live there for their lifetime, even if the house is left to someone else."

Lucy was an expert on this as Ned had put such a clause in his will to ensure that Lucy couldn't sell the house while her grandparents were still living there. As it happened, her grandfather had died fairly soon after his son and her granny had decided to move to Cork, allowing the house and farm to be sold together.

"Do you think? I couldn't imagine living in The Friary – not that there's anything wrong with it," she added hastily for Lucy's benefit. "It's just that I don't feel old enough yet."

"At the very least you'd have some sort of squatter's rights," Kate advised. "I think you need to see a solicitor as soon as possible to clarify things."

"I'm sorry for spoiling the evening," Agnes apologised after a long discussion had convinced her that it was unlikely that she could be evicted or forced into The Friary.

She looked better now that she'd had a few sips of her

hot port. Kate had offered to go to see the solicitor with her if she rang for an appointment the following day. She'd repaired her lipstick and re-powdered her face by the time Rosa burst through the door, her eyes wild as she looked around excitedly to locate her friends.

"Guess what?" she announced, not waiting for a response before broadcasting to the whole lounge the best news that she'd had in years. "I have a new job. I'm going to be Mrs Carter's personal assistant at The Gourmet Rooms!"

Lucy was the first on her feet, congratulating Rosa with a gleeful hug.

"I told you it'd all work out. Anyone can see how good you are at dealing with people."

Agnes was astounded that such a serious and grave woman as Mrs Carter should have chosen such a young and inexperienced girl for a post that obviously required a certain degree of responsibility. But, despite her more pressing troubles, she congratulated Rosa warmly lest she should think her ungenerous. Rosa was genuinely nice in a very innocent sort of way and had been brilliant to Agnes the previous week in her crisis over the make-up artists.

Kate was genuinely thrilled, having been aware for some time of Rosa's chequered employment history. All she needed was direction and her new boss would guide her with a firm hand and an ever-watchful eye.

"So go on, tell us what happened?" Lucy demanded. "What will you be doing?"

Rosa basked in Lucy's encouragement and the admiration of Kate and Agnes. "First she started to talk about how successful the Absolute Beginners course was becoming and how she felt that it was drawing a new, younger clientele. I suppose it is, when you look at us," she added, making Agnes giggle coyly.

"Go on," Kate prompted, dying to hear what Rosa's duties would be.

"Anyway, she said that she was looking for someone young and vibrant to take over some of the work on that course so that she could concentrate on the other courses. I'll be dealing with bookings for a start and media enquiries once I get acquainted with the courses."

"Media enquiries?" Agnes was fascinated, considering her penchant for daytime television.

"You know, things like the morning television shows and that. Apparently Mrs Carter – actually I have to call her Pamela now – is always getting asked to feature on them but she feels that The Gourmet Rooms needs a new face, more modern or something."

Lucy and Kate were ecstatic for her. Rosa was a style icon in the making if ever there was one. Even first thing in the morning, Lucy pronounced, Rosa still looked great.

They all clinked glasses at her good fortune.

"Don't forget, we have to have a toast to Kate and Lorcan as well," Rosa said with characteristic generosity.

They all clinked glasses again, this time to a chorus of "To Kate and Lorcan!".

"Now, settle down, everyone," Lucy instructed as soon as the toast was finished. The bubbles had gone to her head and she was in glorious good humour. "We have to hear how Kate managed to snare a man in four weeks.

This could be of benefit to myself and Rosa, you know. You too, Agnes," she amended in deference to the fact that all three of them were single ladies.

"Well, to start at the beginning, I'd never have met him if I hadn't started the cookery course."

Kate went on tell them all the details of meeting Lorcan at the vegetable market, wishing that he was here with her to experience the good wishes of her friends.

"Agnes was there right at the beginning," she grinned, remembering their day out in Midleton. "Then he turned up to give the talk at one of the classes and we got chatting. He asked me out that night."

"Do you know what? I always thought that a class like this would be a great way to meet a man." Rosa didn't elaborate to include the fact that, despite having had her sights fixed on 'the delectable Mark', as she and Lucy privately referred to him, she'd made no progress and would have to write him off now that the course was finished.

"Well, I wasn't exactly setting out to find a man!" said Kate. "I thought I was finished with men, to be honest, after my husband died. But there you go," she ended with a grin.

"So when'll the wedding be?" Rosa wanted to know. "And where are you going to live?"

"We've decided on early next year for the wedding, maybe March. We're neither of us getting any younger! We'll live in Lorcan's house for the moment but it's not very big. It's a cottage that came with the farm when he bought it. So we'll have to think about building something bigger next year."

She smiled happily, delighted that her friends were so happy at her wonderful news. Spontaneously, the group of them clapped, all caught up in Kate's excitement.

"This calls for champagne," Lucy announced, heading for the bar and wishing that Martin was with her to share in the wonderful evening she was having. She was bursting with pride that Mrs Carter had offered Rosa such an excellent job – that she'd singled her out from the many people that she met on a daily basis through her work.

Maybe I'll organise a surprise celebratory meal for Rosa, Lucy planned now as she stood waiting for the barman to come back with the champagne. She could book somewhere nice and invite Rosa's parents as well as Martin, Gerry and Lar. Lucy suspected that Lar had a soft spot for her friend but was too intimidated by her exuberance and apparent confidence to do anything about it. Maybe it was time to encourage Rosa to see the possibility of Lar being more than a friend, now that she'd given up on Mark Toland. Lar would be good for Rosa, steady and dependable like her father. And the fact that he was an accountant might ensure that some level of control was exercised over her credit card into the future.

All three of them held out their glasses eagerly when Lucy returned with the champagne. The delicious meal that they'd had before leaving The Gourmet Rooms had been just the thing to soak up a couple of bottles. They were in high spirits and Lucy sat back contentedly and watched these new people in her life, these friends, and thought how lucky she was. She didn't feel at all as if she was on the outside of the group, even thought she wasn't talking to any of them right at that moment. A couple of months ago, she would have felt like a spare part, always on the fringes and never fitting in.

The evening that she'd forced herself to go into Good For You had been her time for change. She could see now that she'd been on the cusp of it – she'd been sick and tired of her old life and was ready to start anew. She knew that she wasn't there yet, that there was more to life than a simple destination. But she was content for now to enjoy the journey.

Chapter 37

On Kate's insistence, Agnes phoned the offices of Barrett and Co on Wednesday morning. She was determined to sort out the mess that she'd found herself in and was somewhat heartened to find that Kate, Rosa and Lucy weren't at all convinced that she'd have to leave the house in Rathcabben.

It was disappointing therefore when the receptionist at Barrett and Co informed her crisply that Stephen Barrett, the solicitor who dealt with "The Misses Cotters' interests", was on holiday and wouldn't be back for another ten days. If it was just an enquiry, then perhaps one of the other partners might be able to help. Knowing that her present situation was more than just a minor query, Agnes reluctantly made an appointment for the day that Stephen Barrett would return. In the meantime, she'd just have to resign herself to waiting for news of her future.

Kate too was disappointed when Agnes phoned her to say that it would be a week and a half to her consultation with the solicitor.

"How long more will the convalescence period in The Friary last?" she enquired.

"Well, they said it would be four to six weeks before everything at home would be sorted out," Agnes told her. "The occupational therapist is supposed to be calling on Friday to assess Bea's bedroom and the bathroom but I'm not sure now about the best thing to do. Should I cancel her, do you think?"

"Talk to Beatrice tonight, Agnes, and see if she'll change her mind. And remind her that you still have a few weeks to make up your mind about what you'll do."

"At least the Health Board is paying for the convalescence. It'll only be if she does decide to stay there full time that we'll have to start paying. It's ?700 a week, Kate."

"That's outrageous. How on earth is Beatrice planning to pay for it? Surely her pension wouldn't cover it. And if the two of you were to be staying there, goodness knows how you could afford it!"

"That's why Bea thinks the house should be sold. A few of the houses on the Cliff Road went for massive prices, even though they were much smaller that ours. Even the rundown cottages are selling for ?400,000 because of the views."

"Well, I think you should say as little as possible for the moment until you talk to the solicitor. You could phone the occupational therapist and postpone the visit for a week or two to give you some breathing space."

Agnes took Kate at her word. She visited Bea as usual that

night but said nothing about her planned appointment with Stephen Barrett. There was no need to antagonise her sister until she found out exactly what her rights were.

"Did you think any more about booking in here?" Bea asked as soon as Agnes was settled in one of the comfortable armchairs in the Day Room.

"I didn't really," she answered mildly. "It'll be weeks before we have to decide anyway seeing as the Health Board are paying for you here for the moment. We have loads of time."

"You've changed your tune since yesterday evening," Bea accused suspiciously.

Unable to resist rising her just a little, Agnes told her enigmatically that she got a bit of advice on the subject and that she wasn't too bothered.

"What kind of advice?" Bea looked alarmed now.

"Just from the girls at the cookery class. There are lovely little ground floor flats over on Lambert Street, near St Angela's," she lied, hoping to call Bea's bluff a little.

"But that's miles away," Bea protested, obviously thinking of what a loss Agnes's visits would be, despite the fact that she was treating her sister so badly.

"It is a bit, to be fair," Agnes continued, starting to enjoy Bea's irritation. "But I'll be so tied up with the Ladies' Committee and everything. Did I tell you they've asked me to help Bernadette Mooney with the New Year's Eve Ball?"

Blithely changing the subject, Agnes filled her sister in on the latest activities of the St Angela's Ladies' Committee. Although the ball itself was fully organised, the charity auction still had to be finalised.

At the last meeting, a sub-committee had been set up to garner items that would bring in even more funds for the hospital's charitable intentions.

"Marjorie Price-Canning suggested that I might be able to help on account of the fact that I knew so many people the last time. Some of the Beauty Consultants might offer, say, a personal make-over as a prize, for instance."

Agnes wanted to let Bea know that she had a purpose now and that it wouldn't be feasible for her to settle into The Friary at this early stage of her life.

"And who else would *you* know that would be any addition to the auction?" Bea said disparagingly, trying to take the wind out of her sister's sails as usual.

"Well, Kate for one – she might be able to give a little basket of natural products," Agnes threw back bravely. In truth, she didn't know anyone else who might be able to assist her.

"Will you sort out my knitting for me as you're here," Bea demanded bluntly, not at all satisfied with her sister's upbeat attitude. "I dropped a stitch about twenty rows back. I'll need it for the knitting class at six."

"Twenty rows! It'll take ages to fix that up!" Agnes exclaimed, looking at the complicated pattern of intertwining cables in the Aran sweater that Bea was wading through.

Annoyed at being taken for granted even as she was practically being evicted from her home, Agnes announced that she was going to make some tea. Leaving Bea stewing over whether she would or wouldn't sort out the knitting before the Arts and Crafts teacher arrived at six, she took off towards the little Visitors' Kitchen beyond the Nurses' Station.

"Agnes, there you are!" Lucy called from the desk. "I saw your car outside earlier. Any luck with the solicitor?"

"Nothing yet. I'll be meeting him Monday week so we'll see what happens after that."

"Rosa tells me you're up to your eyes with the Ladies' Committee these days. Her mother is up the walls as well."

"I'm supposed to be getting items for the auction but I don't know of anyone who'd be able to give me anything of any real value," she admitted dolefully, hoping that she hadn't bitten off more than she could chew.

"What about Mrs Grainger? Would she be able to do anything for you?"

"What could she do?" Agnes had met the elderly lady on a few occasions when she was sitting next to her in the Day Room. She didn't, however, appear to be the type of person who'd have anything to donate to an auction.

"What planet are you on, Agnes?" Lucy laughed incredulously. "She's Alasdair Grainger's granny!" Noticing Agnes's blank expression, she filled her in. "He plays with Arsenal – earns a fortune! He's always donating things to charity. Mrs Grainger might get you a signed jersey or something."

"I couldn't possibly ask her."

"I'm telling you, she'll be all for it. She's out in the sunroom, if you want to see her now."

Ten minutes later, it was all organised. Mrs Grainger assured Agnes that young Alasdair would be only too delighted to contribute something to such a good cause. It seemed he'd been brought into St Angela's as a child complaining of a sore knee that had transpired to be a tumour. The whole family, she said, were of the mind that if it weren't for the care and attention that he'd received when he was five, Alasdair Grainger might not be alive to be the superstar that he was today.

Gratified beyond belief, Agnes made a pot of tea and invited Mrs Grainger to join her and Bea in the Day Room. The knitting would just have to wait.

A few days later, Agnes got an excited phone call from Lucy to say that Mrs Grainger wanted her to come into The Friary at lunch-time to meet her favourite grandchild. Alasdair, to his credit, did not arrive empty-handed. As well as a jersey signed by his team-mates, there was a signed ball and a pair of tickets for the FA cup final.

Agnes was so ecstatic that she almost cried, prompting Alasdair to offer to attend the ball on the night with a few of his soccer friends if she thought it would raise the profile of the charity.

Over the moon, Agnes insisted on fetching Mrs Grainger and her grandson a tray of tea and scones from the kitchen, encouraging them to relax and enjoy it while she sped off to St Angela's to collect a wad of complimentary tickets for the football heroes.

Needless to say, the Ladies' Committee were highly impressed at Agnes's efforts. Three items for the auction and the possible appearance of four world-renowned soccer players was unprecedented in terms of exposure and would be a major draw for any of the patrons who were soccer fans or had teenage children.

The ten days dragged on interminably as Agnes awaited her appointment with Stephen Barrett. Kate had organised for Emma to come in and relieve her in the shop so that she could accompany her to the solicitors and, as the appointment approached, Agnes was glad that she would have her friend there for moral support.

She'd been feeling guilty for not telling Bea about the appointment but knew it was the right thing to do. She needed to know exactly what cards she held before allowing any decisions to be made that would affect the rest of her life.

She collected Kate at nine o'clock as planned and they walked the short distance to the offices of Barrett and Co on the South Mall. Kate squeezed her hand and wished her luck when the receptionist finally arrived to usher her into Stephen Barrett's plush office.

The solicitor couldn't possibly be more than twenty, Agnes thought in alarm, taking in his closely cropped hair and clean-shaven face. He looked like a schoolboy and she shifted nervously in her chair, perturbed that such a young man should hold her whole future in his hands.

"Now, Miss Cotter, I hope I'll be able to help you. Sandra gave me an idea of the kind of thing you need to know," he began as soon as the introductions were over.

Agnes had told the receptionist a little of her dilemma on the phone, hoping that she'd be able to have the relevant files at the ready to speed things up a bit.

Now all the worries that she'd had for the past almost two weeks flooded back to her. But, as it transpired, she needn't have had any such worries. Shocked to the core, she listened in silence as Stephen Barrett explained that Mr and Mrs James and Rosaleen Cotter had willed their house, in equal measure, to their daughters Beatrice and Agnes along with a sum of money that had grown considerably in the years since their death.

To date, he informed her, a monthly sum had been paid into a separate account, in the name of Beatrice Cotter, for household expenses.

"So you're saying that we've been living on the proceeds of this inheritance since our parents died?"

"That's just it. The sum of money remaining has been invested carefully by this firm over the years, which is why the account balance is more than healthy."

"Is half of the money mine?" Agnes was incredulous that Beatrice could have kept this from her for all these years, pretending instead that she was subsidising her sister from her own meagre pension.

"Absolutely. As is an equal share in the house in which you now reside."

"But can the house be sold if I'm still living there?" Even though it seemed that she was now a woman of considerable means, she was terrified of having to leave the home that she'd lived in all her life.

"Thankfully, no. Miss Cotter — Beatrice, that is — may wish to fund her care from her share of the money. In the event of this running out, there might be the possibility of the Health Board recouping any outstanding fees from her estate. But this would only happen in the event of your own demise."

A mixture of emotions had flooded through Agnes at that moment. Relief at the fact that she wouldn't be evicted as Beatrice had suggested at one point, annoyance at herself for not having enquired into the state of affairs years ago instead of blindly allowing Beatrice to control her – but mostly there was the sense of betrayal.

For all these years, her own sister had treated her like a slave, beholden to her for almost every penny. She'd lived a life of fear, terrified that she'd have no means of survival if anything happened to Beatrice before she herself reached pension age. All that time, she could have been an equal partner, could have had a few small luxuries instead of scrimping and scraping to make the housekeeping money cover her own small needs.

And what, she wondered now, had Beatrice been doing with her own pension money all along when it was now obvious that their living expenses had been covered by the monthly withdrawals from the inheritance? Was it possible that Beatrice had been squirrelling away her pension week after week while Agnes had been typing at all hours of the night to pay for a pair of tights or a tube of foundation?

Almost light-headed from the news that at least she wouldn't be evicted or have to sign herself into The Friary, Agnes thanked Stephen Barrett sincerely for the information.

"Your affairs are in a very healthy state, Miss Cotter," he reassured his white-faced client. "If, however, either you or Beatrice wish to make any changes to the current arrangements, I'd be happy to consult with you at any time."

"There may well need to be changes," Agnes told him, barely keeping her temper. "Would it be possible for you to visit the nursing home? My sister is quite debilitated."

After what she'd just heard, Agnes was damned if she was going to haul Bea in and out of the Mazda to get her to the South Mall.

"Absolutely no problem at all," the young solicitor confirmed. "I do hope I've been of assistance."

Back out in the street at last, having blurted the gist of her discovery out to Kate, Agnes struggled to take it all in. Gently, Kate took her arm and guided her along the street to the Imperial Hotel. Once inside, Kate settled her into a large comfortable armchair in a secluded corner and headed off to the bar to order tea and biscuits, convinced that Agnes would go into complete shock at the betrayal.

"I really can't believe that she would do that to me. My own sister, the only one I have in the world. To keep so much from me!" She was crying now, tears falling silently down her cheeks at all she'd missed out on to care for a sister who had no regard for her at all.

Kate put both her arms around her and held her tightly as she cried.

"I've wasted my life. There was plenty of money there for us to have had a lovely time. Why did she want to have me like a slave, Kate? There was no need."

"Maybe she was afraid of losing you," Kate said, trying

hard to figure out Beatrice's reasoning. "Maybe she thought if you knew you had plenty of money you'd just have taken it and left, bought your own house even. As it stood, you thought your choices were limited."

"But if I was that mad to go, I'd have gone years ago! I'd have married Willie Boyle and let her take it or leave it."

"You were too loyal, Agnes, that was all."

"Too much of an eejit, you mean!" Agnes retorted bitterly. "Imagine! I never even asked about money. I just believed everything Bea told me. And I was even grateful sometimes that she was so good at keeping things together."

"It's not a crime to have a trusting nature, Agnes."

Kate poured the tea that the waitress set down before them and handed one of the delicate china cups to Agnes.

"Take a drink, Agnes," she instructed. She pushed the plate of biscuits nearer to her as well.

"Oh, that's better," Agnes sniffed, a weak smile breaking through as she sipped her tea.

"I know it has all come as a shock, Agnes, but it's good news. You know for definite that you can stay on in the house and that there's enough money for The Friary if Beatrice really wants to stay."

"Well, she'll have to stay now. There is no way that I could look after her knowing all this."

"Are you going to tell her you know?"

"I'm so cross, I can't think straight. But I'll tell you one thing. I'm not going in there for the afternoon tea today or I'd surely explode." Since Bea had been transferred to

The Friary, Agnes had gone in every afternoon at three and had stayed until the *Nine O'Clock News*. The thought of it sickened her now – all the hours of keeping her sister company a waste.

"You're right. You need a little bit of space right now to think straight. We'll relax here for a while and we can have lunch back at the flat, if you like."

"Thanks, Kate. I don't know what to do with myself all of a sudden."

"Well, whatever happens, you have your friends to help you and the Committee to keep you occupied. I know you'll be fine."

The afternoon that Stephen Barrett had made Agnes aware that she was to all intents and purposes a wealthy woman was the first that she didn't visit her sister in The Friary. Instead, after leaving Kate's flat, she made her way towards Rathcabben and went on a shopping spree to the supermarket.

My home is my castle now, she told herself as she filled her basket with all the things that she'd never been able to afford or hadn't been allowed to buy for fear of Beatrice criticising her. Smoked salmon, Brie, Gorgonzola, pâté, fancy crackers, herbal teas, handmade chocolates as well as a large sirloin and two bottles of the most expensive red wine she could find all went into her basket along with a few tubs of Ben and Jerry's that she'd always wanted to try but which Beatrice disapproved of on account of it being ridiculously expensive as well as unhealthy to eat something as cold as ice cream.

Rationally, Agnes knew that she'd never be able to eat the vast amount of food that she brought home in the boot of the car. There might even be the possibility that some of it would go off and have to be thrown out, she admitted guiltily to herself. But for once in her life, she'd needed to just go out and buy whatever it was that she fancied right at that moment instead of having to plan every purchase with military precision lest she be short if they needed milk or bread at the latter end of the week.

That evening, she watched the juicy steak spitting and sizzling on the cast-iron frying pan that had been in the kitchen since her parents' time and promised herself one of the stylish Le Creuset grill pans that hung in the kitchen at The Gourmet Rooms.

After her luscious dinner, Agnes lay in the bath, almost smothered in Elizabeth Arden bubbles, sipping a glass of wine as she planned her future. Beatrice and her treachery aside, she was able to enumerate the positive things.

The fact that her own pension would be commencing on her birthday, New Year's Day, would take care of her everyday expenses, meaning that she would only have to touch her inheritance money for big things. Like changing her car – something that she intended to do as soon as the car showrooms opened their doors for the New Year. Her own little Mazda was on its last legs and she'd been worrying for months about how much longer it'd keep going for.

Her charity work, she decided, would be the main focus in her life now that Beatrice had decided to opt out of it so abruptly. It was ironic that she loved the voluntary work so much considering that she'd actually been doing what amounted to charity work within her own family for years with no recognition whatsoever.

And it was charity work, she realised as she dried herself and layered on a rich body lotion that she'd splurged on earlier in the day. If she'd actually been working in a nursing home, she'd have been paid a decent wage. As it stood, she'd worked the equivalent of a lifetime without the pension entitlements that came with a career.

Anger surged through her again as she drained the deep cast-iron bath that had been in the house since the year dot. All the times that she'd filled it for Bea and the stress of getting her in and out came back to her.

There was no way she could just calmly let her get away with the treachery that she'd perpetrated. Agnes wrapped her well-worn dressing-gown around her and strode purposefully to the bedroom. A trip to The Friary was on the cards.

Agnes was as high as a kite by the time she drove through the gates of the secluded nursing home. Its elegant period façade almost mocked her. Here was Beatrice, planning to live in the lap of luxury while Agnes was expected to survive on a pittance elsewhere.

Lucy was just leaving, her evening shift completed.

"Agnes, we were expecting you for the Male Voice Choir performance this evening. They're nearly finished now."

"I got a bit held up," she fibbed, unable to get into the whole saga with her friend. There would be plenty of time to tell her over the coming days.

"Go on in anyway – there are a few free chairs at the back that we put out for the late-comers." Smiling, Lucy headed off, oblivious to the showdown that was facing Agnes.

The choir was in full swing as Agnes made her way down the corridor. As she entered the Day Room, they were just bringing "Galway Bay" to a finale. Anticipating a gap in proceedings, she spotted Bea on the edge of the group, her wheelchair too cumbersome to fit amongst the lines of armchairs.

"Agnes," Bea began in a loud whisper as the deep male voices trailed off, "it's desperate you're so late. Una Riordan was keeping a chair for you all evening."

Her sister's admonishment was all that Agnes needed to raise her hackles again. Without a word, she released the brakes on the wheelchair and whizzed her smoothly away from the group just as the choir began a powerful rendition of "Down by the Sally Gardens".

Her protests smothered by the twenty-strong male voices, Bea was in her own bedroom before she was even finished giving out.

"I can't miss the choir – it'll be six weeks before they'll be back again!"

"Well, you won't miss them the next time – I can assure you of that."

"What do you mean?"

"I had an appointment with Mr Stephen Barrett today."

She paused for effect, gratified to see Bea's mouth open wide in horror. Knowing that she was badly caught out in her duplicitous dealings, Beatrice started to bluster.

"You had no right –"

"Well, it seems I had every right, according to him," Agnes flashed. "In fact, I had as much right to be wheeling and dealing over the years as you had!"

"Don't be silly, Agnes," Bea patronised, "you'd never have been able to manage the bills and all that."

"I'll be having to manage now, won't I, seeing as you'll be staying here? And it wasn't all bills, was it? What about all the investments they made for us? Do you know there is nearly a hundred thousand in the bank account?"

Bea looked even more shocked now, horrified that young Stephen Barrett had disclosed everything. His late father, she imagined, might have been more prudent.

"It's all very fine saying that we have plenty of money," she countered stubbornly. "What about a rainy day? Did you ever think of that?"

"Well, you have your own rainy day well sorted out anyway. The two of us were living on Mother and Father's money. And in that case, where did your pension go to?"

"That's none of your business!"

Bea had raised her voice now, determined not to be outdone by Agnes. It was just as well, Agnes thought, that the Male Voice Choir were in full flow – otherwise the whole of The Friary would have heard them.

"No more than it'll be any of your business when I withdraw my share of the money from the account," she smirked triumphantly. Let Bea see what she thought of that.

Beatrice was belligerent now as she played what she thought was her trump card. "In that case, I'll be wanting my share of the house. We'll just have to sell it. Then you'll know all about getting your inheritance."

"Actually, Bea, you can't do that. Well, you can – but only after my demise. That's how Stephen Barrett put it."

The fact that Beatrice was a full fifteen years older than Agnes wasn't lost on either of them. If Agnes maintained her current good health it would be years before her demise. Beatrice would most likely be well over a hundred before she would be able to claim her half of the house.

"You don't know what you're talking about, Agnes!" Bea spat out, antagonising Agnes further with the implication that she was stupid.

"All I know is that I gave the best years of my life to a witch! You even stopped me getting married!"

Finally it was out. It had seethed and boiled inside her for years, festering like a poison.

"Are you still on about Willie Boyle? You'd think you'd give it up, at your age!"

Shocked at the way her sister just sneered at the loss of such an enormous part of her life, Agnes knew that there was no going back.

"You know, Bea, I always gave you the best I could but I was never enough. Well, I hope you're happy here from now on because we couldn't possibly go back to the way we were."

Open-mouthed, Beatrice stared at her sister, aware that she'd gone a step too far.

"What do you mean?" she demanded, still not willing to back down after all her years as the dominant force in their relationship.

"I'll ask Stephen Barrett to start the paperwork. He said he'd come in here to see you if needs be."

"You can't just finalise everything at the stroke of a pen!"

"Yes, I can, Bea. You're on your own now."

With that, Agnes left the room, closing the door quietly behind her.

Chapter 38

It was two weeks to Christmas and the annual ward meeting was taking place in the staff room. Una Riordan was trying to get her staff to settle down so that she could make a final decision on which staff would be covering the Christmas and New Year shifts.

"As long as I'm off on Saturday the 23rd, I don't care what else I work," Cathy announced. "Leon's work do's are always all-night affairs so I'll have to have the Saturday off after it."

"That's grand – nobody else has requested it off," Una murmured, filling in the date on the large roster sheet.

"I'd love Christmas morning off – if there's a chance of it. This is the first year that Rory actually knows what Santa is." Jessica had three small children and even though she was job-sharing, her 'week on' fell over Christmas.

"That should be fine. I've fitted in a few written requests as well."

"I'd love to be off for New Year's Eve, if that's

available," Lucy chipped in before someone else did. In all her years at The Friary, she'd never had a request for a particular night off but she'd die if she was rostered to work the night of the New Year's Eve Ball.

"I'll give you two days together," Una said generously. "New Year's Day as well."

"Brilliant, I'll have time to recover."

"What are you going to wear?" Cathy wanted to know as soon as the meeting had disbanded.

"I've been trying to lose the last few pounds before I buy anything but I suppose I'd better buck up. It's only a few weeks away."

"Plus all the good stuff will be gone soon. Will we go shopping at the weekend? I have to get something for Leon's night out as well."

"Brilliant. What about Friday afternoon? We're both off at two."

"Done deal," Cathy declared, heading for the Treatment Room where Beatrice Cotter was awaiting her Vitamin B12 injection.

Lucy headed off to the Day Room to ferry Mrs Grainger down to the hairdressing room for her weekly appointment. As soon as she had her installed in front of the mirror, she went in search of Beatrice. She'd surely be finished with her injection by now.

It was Lucy's intention to get Beatrice to go down to the hairdressing room when Mrs Grainger was finished. Another lady had cancelled because she had a head cold so there was a free place. Despite the best efforts of all the staff, Beatrice had been miserable since her falling-out with her sister. Lucy felt particularly bad for her, knowing that Agnes too was very hurt about the whole situation.

Earlier in the week, Lucy had met Kate and Rosa for coffee to discuss the matter. They were all sorry for Agnes, who'd gone into a slump after the row. Even though she'd asked the solicitor to put the wheels in motion to dissolve the financial partnership that existed between her and Beatrice, her heart wasn't really in it.

"There you are, Beatrice," Lucy greeted now. "There's a vacant appointment in the hairdressing room if you want to get your roots tipped up."

"My roots are fine. They'll do for another week."

"That's the thing about getting a colour," Lucy commented, trying to get through to the taciturn Beatrice. "Once you start getting it done, you have to keep going. I'm holding off on getting mine done until nearer to Christmas."

"It looks fine," was all Beatrice said, her face glum.

"It's not bad, I suppose. But with the ball coming up and all, I want to have it right." She was hoping that the mention of the ball would draw Beatrice out a bit about Agnes. If Lucy knew that Bea was amenable to reconciliation, she might be able to persuade Agnes to come in and visit. It was almost two weeks now and there had not been any contact between them and Beatrice was pining away before their very eyes.

"I suppose that's why Agnes hasn't time to come in," Beatrice said now, surprising Lucy.

"The ball?"

"I suppose she's too busy for me now," she said desolately.

"I don't think it's the ball, to be honest. She's still a bit upset about you not coming home, I think." Lucy wasn't supposed to know about the finer details of their financial arrangements.

"She won't miss me a bit. She'll be gallivanting here, there and yon now that she's rid of me."

"Do you really think that, Beatrice? As far as I can see, Agnes is in a terrible state over you. She has nobody else, remember, and it's hard for her to manage on her own after all the years."

"Why won't she come and see me then?" Bea had been obstinate all her life and it was difficult for her to change her ways now.

"Well, maybe she thinks *you've* had enough of her. You *did* opt to stay here instead of going home to her."

Lucy knew she was taking a bit of poetic licence but Agnes was every bit as miserable as Beatrice.

"I suppose," Bea gave in grudgingly.

Heartened at her progress, Lucy pushed on. Una Riordan would be only delighted if she made progress with their elderly client who'd been doing so well in their care initially. Una had made several attempts to talk to Beatrice, afraid that she would go into a depression.

"Would we ring her, do you think? We don't have to make a big deal out of it. You could ask her if she wants to come in tomorrow night for the Celtic Queens."

The Celtic Queens were a trio of mature ladies with wonderful soprano voices. They were a particular favourite with the residents of The Friary when they visited.

"I suppose I could."

Beatrice sounded a bit unsure but Lucy persisted.

"Look, why don't you come down with me and get your hair done. I'll bring you some tea afterwards and you can phone her from your room. She'll be thrilled."

"Okay so," Beatrice gave in, a small smile lighting up her face for the first time in two weeks.

Agnes had just arrived in from an extraordinary meeting of the Ladies' Committee when she heard the phone ringing. Throwing off her new coat, she raced for the phone, as always worrying that it was the Friary ringing about Bea.

Since the evening that she'd stomped out on her two weeks ago, she'd felt inordinately guilty. She'd effectively cut off her sister's chance of coming home and was worried that the stress of it all would kill her. It had dawned on her afterwards that Beatrice was over eighty – no age to be shouted at by her younger sister.

The fact that she could have given her sister a stroke wasn't lost on her but now that she'd declared her intention of separating from her altogether, she couldn't back down. Apart from the whole money fiasco – .which was bad enough in itself – it was the fact that Bea didn't care a whit about her that had really hurt.

"Hello," she said now.

"Agnes, it's Lucy here."

"Oh, Lucy, hello. I thought you were working this evening."

"I am. It's just I had an idea I wanted to run by you."

"Is everything all right with Bea?"

"Great," Lucy reassured her. "Actually, it's Beatrice I'm ringing about. She was going to ring you later to ask you to come in for a concert but I had a better idea."

"Go on," Agnes said, surprised to hear that Bea had been about to ring her. If her sister had been going to phone her to apologise, it would be a first for her.

"The minibus is free this evening. What would you think if I brought Bea out to Rathcabben for a visit instead? That's if she'll agree."

"She'd be more than welcome," Agnes answered stoutly, aware that they couldn't keep up their vendetta forever. "I was just about to put the fire on. We could have our tea together."

"Don't get too prepared in case she doesn't want to go out in the cold. I'll ask her and ring you back."

Gratified that Bea might be holding out an olive branch after their two weeks of stalemate, Agnes lit the fire and tidied the house a bit for the possibility of her sister's visit. If she did decide to come, and Agnes wasn't sure that she would, then it wasn't going to be all sunshine and light. Beatrice couldn't just expect to land in and brush everything that had happened aside.

Twenty minutes later, Lucy rang.

"We're on our way."

It occurred to Agnes that Bea must be in a bad way altogether if she was putting herself out to this extent. Perhaps she was only now beginning to notice all the little things that Agnes did for her.

To assert her new-found independence, Agnes prepared a simple supper of garlic bread and a roasted pepper pasta dish. Now that *she* was mistress of the house, Beatrice would have to take things as she found them.

The pasta was just about *al dente* when Agnes heard the minibus from The Friary pull up outside the front door.

She made her way out slowly, not wanting Bea to think she was all over her straightaway. Lucy waved at her from the driver's seat, thrilled with herself to be bringing about a reunion. Just seeing her sister emerging from the back of the bus on the mechanical lowering device brought it home to Agnes just how much hard work she put in over the years. As soon as the wheelchair rolled off the ramp, Agnes walked out, knowing that Lucy would find it difficult to manage the chair on the unfamiliar gravel.

"Welcome home, Bea," she said levelly, meeting her sister's eyes squarely.

To her shock, Beatrice started to cry.

"I'm very sorry for everything, Agnes," she sniffed. "Lucy here thought it would be a good idea to come and see you. I hope it's not too late."

Agnes was speechless. In all their years together, Bea had never given in on anything. Goodness only knew what Lucy had said to her.

"We'd better get in out of the cold. Come on in, Lucy."

"Thanks, Agnes, but I want to go out to the kitchen shop at Ballymaloe. Rosa got a stainless steel zester there a few weeks ago and I want to see if there are any left. I'll call back for Beatrice later. Is that okay with you, Beatrice?"

Beatrice, still sniffing, just nodded. Silently, Agnes released the brakes of the wheelchair and caught hold of the handles, the familiar rubber grips reminding her of her years of care for her sister. Beatrice, looking small and much older than Agnes remembered, waved goodbye to Lucy as she made her way back to the minibus.

"I have the tea ready," Agnes began as soon as Lucy pulled out of the yard.

"You're very good, Agnes. It's lovely to be home again."

Agnes wondered if this meant that her sister had changed her mind about staying in The Friary. As it was, Agnes had cancelled the appointments with the public health nurse and the occupational therapist, not wanting to waste their time.

The smell of the garlic bread assailed them as they entered the kitchen and Agnes was just wondering what Bea would think of it when she announced that she'd come to love garlic since she'd broken her hip.

"Good," Agnes said, the wind taken out of her sails a bit. "I'll put it out and we can have a chat."

Pushing Bea in to the table as she'd always done, Agnes took her warmed plates out of the oven and placed a generous helping of the delicious pasta mixture on each.

"I thought you might up and go if you knew about all the money we had," Beatrice blurted out as soon as Agnes sat down.

"Well, if I didn't take off to Dublin with Willie Boyle

I was hardly going to do it afterwards," Agnes said mulishly.

"You might have met someone else and I'd have had to go into a home."

To Agnes's mind, Bea did actually look contrite but she didn't want her to think it was as simple as all that.

"I didn't get much of a chance. We could have had a better life, Bea. There was nothing to stop us going out for a spin in the car. Or to a concert or a play."

"I was always afraid that you'd get fond of going out and meeting people. Then you'd take off."

"There was never a question of me taking off. You could have come to Dublin if I got married to Willie that time."

"I didn't want to be dragging around after you and Willie all my life. At least I was in my own home."

"Why did everything have to be your way, Bea?"

Agnes was cross now at how awkward Bea was being. She picked at her pasta and waited to see what she'd have to say.

"Well, *you* had everything anyway. You had your job in the Department and you could go wherever you wanted. I was stuck at home all day."

"Were you jealous of me? Is that it? I was only doing the normal things – and you could have done normal things too, if you'd wanted. We could have had a better car, for a start, to go places. Did you never think of that? And you could have had special equipment in the house."

"I really am sorry about that, Agnes. I was afraid if the District Nurse came and saw how bad I was that she'd want to put me in somewhere."

"Did you not care at all about how I was managing it all?"

Agnes had to ask. Bea needed to answer all the hard questions that had been boiling inside her for the past two weeks.

"I did. I felt guilty all the time. But I was so afraid of being put into a home that I couldn't stop myself."

"But now you're in a home anyway and suddenly you can drop me like a ton of bricks! What about what I want? Do you not care if I'm here on my own in the house? Do you not think I might be afraid?"

"I never thought of that, Agnes." Bea looked genuinely shocked.

"Well, there you are." Agnes wasn't actually afraid in the house at all but was determined to make her sister see that she'd treated her appallingly.

"Would you not come and stay in The Friary if you're afraid here?"

"There you go again, Bea. You'd want me to move if I was afraid here. It wouldn't be a case that you'd upset yourself and come home to keep me company. You're so used to getting your own way and it's my fault for letting you away with it for so long."

Beatrice looked at her pasta bleakly and tasted a forkful. "This is lovely, Agnes. You were always a good cook. I know I was very awkward to manage and I'm sorry. I *was* jealous of you," she admitted at last.

"Did you not want any bit of a life for yourself at all, Bea?"

"I couldn't think of anything but keeping you at

home, to be honest. Even when you went to the night classes I used to be afraid you'd meet someone and go off with them."

"A man, you mean?" Agnes was incredulous.

"I suppose so."

"I never even went out on a date, Bea!"

"Well, you were always dressing up and putting on make-up."

"You could have too. I was always asking you to go to the night classes but you were never interested."

"Una Riordan in The Friary thinks I should see the counsellor. She says I might not have ever come to terms with being paralysed. I wonder would she be right?"

Agnes sighed. Maybe Una *was* right about that. Although she'd never actually appeared to be depressed, it was true that Beatrice had never accepted the fact that she was paralysed to the point of incorporating it into her daily life. She'd never really talked about how she felt to Agnes, even after all the years that they'd lived together. Perhaps a counsellor might be a good idea although Beatrice had been so bitter for so long that she might find it hard to adjust to the fact that other people were paralysed too.

"Maybe she's right," Agnes acknowledged.

"Will you forgive me, Agnes? I know I don't deserve it but I'd hate if you never came in to see me again."

There it was again – all about herself. It was just Bea's way, Agnes realised. She really did think that the world revolved around her needs. But perhaps it had been the fault of those around her. By the time that their mother had died, Bea had been completely brainwashed into thinking she was helpless.

Agnes had heard the word 'institutionalised' used on television recently and wondered if it applied to her sister. Maybe Beatrice was only acting out the role that their mother had expected of her – that of an invalid, instead of a person with a disability that could be overcome to some degree. Maybe it wasn't as much her fault as Agnes had been inclined to think.

"Oh, Bea, of course I'll forgive you," she sighed, sick of the fighting.

"I really am sorry, Agnes. About Willie more than anything."

Even to have Beatrice acknowledge the loss of her chance of marriage all those years ago was a salve to Agnes's hurt. She felt sorry for her sister now that she'd had such a poor life with precious little joy. She wasted all her years trying to hang on to Agnes, not realising that she might love her enough to want her in her life as a friend as well as a sister.

"Thanks Bea. Will we try and put it all behind us? You're happy in The Friary and I'm happy here. And you can always come out for your tea now and again."

"But are you not afraid on your own?"

Agnes was bowled over by this show of concern. Usually, Bea would dismiss her anxieties with her characteristic scoffing noise and forget all about it. This was a new departure indeed.

"I'm fine – really. I might even do the place up a bit in

the summer." It was still Bea's house too, she realised. "If that's all right with you?"

"Of course it is," Bea said, smiling at last. "We'll have a bit of comfort when I come out of a Sunday. Now eat up, Agnes," she said bossily. "I'm nearly finished and your plate is still half-full."

Chapter 39

Lucy lay back in bed admiring her dress where it hung on the door of the wardrobe. She'd placed it there specially the previous night so that she'd wake up to the sight of it hanging there. As she'd imagined, it had the effect of getting her immediately revved up for the evening ahead.

She was glad now that she'd opted to work part of the Christmas period at The Friary so that she'd be sure of having New Year off. Everything had been planned with meticulous detail. She and Rosa had had their leg waxes, highlights and spray-on tans well in advance, ensuring that there was no scope for disaster on the evening.

Rosa had been thrilled that she'd been able to fill the eight places at her table and had spent most of the weeks in the run-up fretting over it in case someone cancelled at the last minute.

Padding downstairs in the fluffy slippers that she'd won

in the Christmas raffle at The Friary, Lucy savoured the smell of the large pine tree with its tiny white lights. The whole house was pine-scented and she hated the thought of having to throw the tree out on the sixth. Martin had cheerfully lugged it into the boot of his car and hauled it into its stand in Bramwell Court. He'd even helped her to decorate it and despite the bottle of wine consumed during the evening it managed to look breathtaking to Lucy's eyes.

It had saddened her a little that this was the first time she'd looked forward to Christmas in years but once she'd talked it through with Cora at her last few counselling sessions, she'd made up her mind not to dwell on the past as much as she'd done in recent years. She'd also started to put into perspective the enormous burden of guilt that she carried for giving her parents such a terrible time over the years, her way of punishing them for not protecting her enough.

Feeling that she had nothing to gain by exposing the monster that her uncle had been now that he was dead, Lucy had decided not to tell her parents about the sexual abuse that she'd endured. From Cora's perspective, the fact that the perpetrator was deceased removed the responsibility to report the abuse to the Health Board – something that she would have been obliged to do in the interests of child protection if Ned had been alive.

Somehow, things with her parents had automatically become easier once she'd started to open up to Cora about the abuse. She still called over home on Sundays if she wasn't working but since the day that she'd brought

Rosa with her, things had improved out of all proportion. She was making more of an effort now – small things like phoning her mother to say that she'd bring dessert or bringing her father a book that she thought he'd like.

She brought Rosa now and again and Maura treated her like the Queen Bee every time, crediting her with the new groomed Lucy. Nowadays, conversation around the table flowed easily, making Lucy acutely aware of the strain that Ned's legacy had placed on all three of them – not just on her.

It was Rosa who'd hinted to Maura and Paddy that Lucy was in a relationship, something that must have been a pleasant surprise after half a lifetime of not knowing what was going on in their daughter's life at all. Maura had launched an enquiry immediately, not giving up until Lucy promised to introduce them to Martin over Christmas.

As far as Maura was concerned, things were finally looking up. For years she'd been trying to persuade her daughter to go to college and get what she termed a proper job. Now, of her own volition, Lucy was mad about the idea and was even dating a dentist, a bonus that Maura could hardly credit. She was even cooking these days, something that Maura would never have believed possible a few months ago.

Bringing her cereal through to the sitting-room, Lucy curled up on one of the sofas and allowed herself to think about the evening and night ahead. The heating had clicked in and she savoured the cosiness of the room that she'd hated almost from the time she'd moved into the house.

Now that she'd put her own stamp on it, the starkness was gone. Her books, always her best friends before she met Rosa, were everywhere, filling the mahogany bookcases and lined up under the window between the two mahogany bookends that had been Rosa's Christmas present. With the curtains still closed, she felt cocooned from the outside world, an amazing concept in a place where she'd always felt like an alien.

The space over the fireplace, formerly occupied by a stark abstract in black and white, was now home to a beautiful oil painting that Martin had presented her with on Christmas Eve. He'd watched her anxiously as she'd opened it – fearful of her not liking it as much as he had when he'd spotted it at the Shanagarry Art Group's winter exhibition.

He needn't have worried. Lucy had burst into tears as she'd gazed at it, marvelling at the richness of the colours and the tranquillity that it evoked. Martin had hugged her tightly when she'd eventually been able to tell him how much she liked it. She immediately took down the black and white painting that suddenly seemed to be all sharp angles and asked Martin to hang her present in its place.

She realised now with something like glee that she was actually looking forward to the New Year and all it would bring. She'd always hated the idea of making New Year resolutions but suddenly it seemed that there was no end to her plans. She still had another few pounds to lose, something that she was determined to achieve over the next couple of months. As soon as it opened after the holidays, she was going to join the gym that Cathy was a member of in order to tone up and get fit. Applying for her college course was a little down the line but already she was looking forward to it. She'd be sorry to finish up at The Friary in one sense but she also knew that it was time to come out of hiding and move on with her life.

Mostly, Lucy was excited about Martin and the way that they'd gradually become closer, almost without her realising it. She felt a frisson of anticipation now as she thought about the evening ahead and the fact that Martin would be staying the night.

She'd mentioned it the night before, as casually as she could, and he'd agreed, equally as casually while continuing to load the dishwasher for her. Lucy knew that she was ready to take the next step and could hardly believe that she was looking forward to the aftermath of the ball as much as the ball itself. She'd always had a sense that sex was something furtive and terrifying, yet in a few short weeks she'd come to a stage where she thought about Martin most of the day and longed for him to touch and hold her.

The biggest thing for Lucy was that she trusted him implicitly and knew that he'd never do anything to hurt her. She hadn't yet found the right time to tell him about the horrific experience of her childhood but she knew she'd be able to when the time was right. And she certainly wasn't going to let it mar what she hoped would be one of the best nights of her life.

She studied her new painting again, amazed at Martin's uncanny knack of getting it right every time. Entitled simply "Reflection", the Deirdre O'Donnell painting depicted a night-time streetscape reflected in the river Lee. The dark blues and deep reds and glowing yellows reflected from the streetlights threw the buildings into sharp focus, while the mirror image on the water was slightly blurred, reminding Lucy of the way that her memories were getting diluted as her future became clearer.

She knew that she was probably being fanciful in her interpretation of the painting but she couldn't deny the way she felt when she looked at it. It was like a tangible reinforcement that the past was indeed behind her and she considered it prophetic that Martin had chosen it for her.

The doorbell pealed sharply, breaking in on her thoughts about the future. Lucy grinned and uncurled her legs from the sofa when it pealed again almost immediately. For Rosa, everything would be an emergency until she had all seven of her guests seated around the table in Hollygrove Manor.

"Put on the kettle. I've got news!" Rosa spilled out breathlessly as she sped through Lucy's hall, skidding on the new Turkish rug that Lucy had made a return trip to Holland's for in the run-up to Christmas. The first one that she'd bought for the hall was now residing on the landing.

"Jesus, you could be killed around here!" she shrieked, righting herself in the nick of time before landing into the kitchen and starting to put on the kettle herself.

This was a new level of agitation and Lucy prayed fervently that someone hadn't pulled out at the last minute. That would be a disaster of epic proportions, Lucy knew.

"Calm down and tell me, will you?" she instructed, her mind already running through the possible solutions if that were the case. Perhaps Cathy and her boyfriend Leon could be persuaded to step in.

"I got a letter. From the nun about my mother."

"Today?"

"Mum called over after Mass with a pile of post that had come for me yesterday. It was all late Christmas cards and New Year cards and the letter was in the middle of them."

"What did she say? Had she any information?"

"Mother Bridget says that she's definitely alive and that she has reliable information that she's still living in Cork."

"My God, Rosa, that's brilliant!" Lucy hugged her warmly, delighted that something was happening at last.

Rosa had been like a new woman since she'd started her job at The Gourmet Rooms but the long wait for news of her birth mother had been lurking in the background, taking the edge off the happiness that she felt at finally having a job that she was proud of.

"I'll have to wait a while before anything else happens. She's written to my birth mother at her last known address to ask if she wants to meet me. It could be ages before Mother Bridget gets a reply and then ages again for her write to me with her name and address. If that's what she wants," Rosa added darkly.

"I know it's hard, Rosa, but thank God she's still alive and that the Sisters had kept some kind of records, even if they were fairly rudimentary. And even if she's not ready to meet you yet, maybe you could write to her and pass it on through Sister Ignatius or one of the nuns at St Angela's."

"It *is* good news, I suppose," Rosa conceded, her face brightening a little. "I'm worried that she won't want to meet me though. If she's been living in Cork all these years, you'd think she'd have tried to trace me before."

"We don't know her circumstances," Lucy reminded her.

"I know – I'll just have to face it when it comes. What's that you're giving me?"

"Rooibos Tea. Kate gave it to me."

Lucy handed the delicately painted canister to her friend, admiring again the African designs and the bright colours that broke the stark black and white of the kitchen.

"The container's fabulous. What does it taste like?" Rosa was sniffing the deep red tea suspiciously.

"Try it. I love it. And Kate says it's full of antioxidants – they keep your skin young-looking."

As expected, Rosa immediately took a large slug, almost scalding herself in the process.

"How many cups a day would you have to be drinking?"

"I don't know. Three or four maybe. We can ask Kate tonight."

"God, Lucy, I can't wait to see your dress on," Rosa said now, excited at the thought of seeing her friend all dressed up.

Lucy had gone shopping with Cathy one Friday afternoon and had bought the midnight blue dress almost as soon as she held it up against herself. Cathy had been on the lookout for something to wear to Leon's Christmas night out for ages so it was an ideal opportunity for her and Lucy to go on a proper shopping spree.

Lucy could hardly believe that the Size 12 fitted her, the rich folds of the heavy silk swirling around her legs when she did a twirl in the fitting room. Never before had she felt so glamorous and sexy. The dress had a halter neck and left a large expanse of her back bare, something that she knew Rosa would be able to enhance with a rub of her St Tropez mitt.

Cathy had been almost as excited with Lucy's find as she was with her own purchase of an elegant, strapless dress in black satin. After a reviving coffee in Norma Jean's on Patrick Street, they returned to the fray for jewellery, shoes and underwear.

Lucy had been thrilled to find a pair of navy sandals with diamante beading and even more thrilled with the results of her new underwear when she tried on her dress at home. The silk body had an invisible panel that flattened her tummy while the under-wired cups and halter-neck strap made her breasts almost as neat and pointy as Rosa's were. The dress fitted like a glove and was set off beautifully by the small creamy-white fur cape that Cathy had practically squealed about in Debenhams.

"I hope it'll still fit after all I've eaten over Christmas. Did you try on yours again?"

"Last night – and I still love it!"

Rosa, always prone to changing her mind about what she was wearing at the last minute, had stuck steadfastly to her choice of a slim–fitting, strapless number in a deep red embossed satin.

"I wonder what Lar'll think of it?"

"Honestly, Lucy, you're imagining things! He's never actually said he fancies me. He's only coming tonight because the whole gang'll be there and it'll be a bit of *craic*."

Rosa and Lar had inadvertently been paired off for the evening due to their being the only two singles at the table. Gerry was bringing Shona, his girlfriend of three years, to whom he'd become engaged over Christmas.

"I'm telling you, he's always watching you and smiling when you say anything. The last night we were out he said 'Rosa says' eight times. Martin and I were counting!"

"Very smug," Rosa muttered, trying to hide the smile that was threatening to break out on her face. She wondered if it was possible that someone as serious and intelligent as Lar would fancy her.

"We'll see tonight," Lucy told her with an air of wisdom. "What time is the taxi booked for?"

The plan was for all six of them to congregate in Lucy's house for drinks before setting off en masse, something that she herself had suggested in the planning stages. The only reason that the house felt so foreign and alien to her, she'd realised, was that she acted like a lodger instead of its rightful owner. Having a lively gang of friends calling around before a night out was something that most people took for granted but which Lucy was only now learning to appreciate.

"Half seven. We'll have loads of time to relax before we

set off. Lar said he'd collect me at half six and escort me over. Imagine," she said, rolling her eyes dramatically, "escorting me two doors down!"

"Imagine," Lucy retorted dryly, starting to laugh then at the expression of scepticism on Rosa's face.

"What are you doing for the day?" Rosa questioned now, wanting to get the timeline in order for the evening.

"I think I might go for a walk now to make room for the meal this evening. I don't want to be bursting out of my dress before we get to the coffee. I'll have to tidy the house as well and be organised before Barbara arrives."

"That'll be a godsend. What would we have done about our hair otherwise?"

Barbara Rohan, Cathy's younger sister, had agreed to call over to Lucy's at half four to do their hair for the evening. Shona, Gerry's girlfriend, was dropping over to have her hair straightened for the occasion, making the trip worthwhile for Barbara, who according to Cathy was delighted with the nixer after overspending madly on clothes in the run-up to Christmas.

"I know, it's great. There's no way I could get mine right doing it myself. What are you at for the morning?"

"I might call out to Mum and Dad and talk to them about the letter from Mother Bridget. I'll give you a ring when I'm back."

Rosa was like a whirlwind, Lucy grinned to herself after her friend had left with a breathless "*Ciao*, baby!".

Looking forward to having the day to herself to savour the anticipation of her first-ever dress dance, she headed upstairs to shower and change.

Passing the small hall table, Lucy noticed the thin film of dust that had accumulated and made a mental note to get some flowers for the hall later in the day after her big tidy-up. She scooped up, along with the litter of unsolicited flyers, the pile of late Christmas cards that had come to her parents' house and which her mother had dropped over the previous evening. She glanced through them now as she started to mount the stairs.

The familiar cold feeling came over her when she saw the cream envelope. She didn't have to turn it over to see the little intertwined D's that Doheny and Doheny stamped over the seal. Deflated, she sank down on the step of the stairs, her heart sinking to the bottom of her chest at the fact that Ned could still have the power to take the good out of her day.

The cream envelopes from Ned's solicitors had become an unwanted part of Lucy's life since her uncle had been killed. At first it had been deeds and land registry, later it had been administration fees and inheritance tax. The envelopes had dwindled in recent years but she recognised them with the same pang of dread no matter how infrequently they came.

Unable to imagine what Charles Doheny could want from her at this stage, she opened the envelope with a mixture of trepidation and defiance. Whatever it was, she wasn't going to let it ruin her night.

The headed paper was the usual embossed cream and there seemed to be a folded page of a different paper tucked in with it. Scanning quickly through the typed cover page, Lucy read that a person involved in the accident in which her uncle had died had requested that the enclosed letter be passed on to his next-of-kin. As she'd been the sole beneficiary of Mr Dalton's estate, Charles Doheny had deemed it prudent to forward the letter to Lucy.

Lucy knew that there had been another car involved on the night that Ned had been killed and was aware that the passenger in that car had died. She'd never really thought about the accident – the overwhelming feeling of relief that he was finally gone from her life had overshadowed any thoughts for the other people involved. She felt a pang of guilt at this suddenly.

Letting the envelope and cover letter drop to the floor, she slowly unfolded the enclosed paper, her eyes blurring with sudden tears as it occurred to her that Ned might be dead but there would always be reminders. Neat, rounded handwriting covered the single page and Lucy's eyes immediately flickered to the bottom to see the name of the person.

With a shock, she recognised the name of Kate Lewis. Her eyes darted to the top of the page – surely it couldn't be . . .? It was. The same address as her friend. Her heart hammered as she forced herself to calm down and read the letter properly. What could Kate have to do with her hateful uncle?

Five minutes later, Lucy was racing upstairs, anger surging through her like a current of electricity. Her shower could wait, she thought erratically as she pulled on a pair of jeans.

That Ned had ruined her own happiness for all these

years was one thing. But to think that such a burden of guilt had lain on Kate's shoulders for thirteen years was unbearable to Lucy and she was determined that her friend wouldn't suffer a moment longer.

Chapter 40

Kate stared balefully at the waistband of her skirt and realised that there was no way that the two sides of the zip would meet. Letting the dark green velvet fall to the floor, she stepped out of it and started to rummage through the wardrobe in a state of panic.

She'd often heard of people gaining weight when they fell in love but never so much that they couldn't fit into their clothes. Granted, Lorcan was a bit heavy-handed with things like avocados and coconut milk but this was ridiculous.

Petite Kate had always been blessed with a perfect Size 10 figure that never altered – even in the aftermath of the accident she hadn't lost so much as a pound. Or gained one from months of stodgy hospital food when she'd been immobilised in traction.

Vowing fleetingly to join Lucy and Rosa on their walks once the New Year kicked in, she put her mind to the immediate problem of finding something to wear. She loved the long skirt and fitted bodice that she'd only worn once and was disgusted that she now had to discard it.

She was holding up the russet taffeta skirt and wraparound top that she'd worn to her niece's wedding in November when the doorbell started to ring insistently. Uncharacteristically irritated that someone should call in the middle of her clothes crisis, she dashed to the window, praying that it wasn't Rosa checking up to see that she was definitely going. She knew it wasn't Lorcan because he'd left earlier that morning to check in on things at work and, besides, he had his own key now.

Seeing that it was Lucy who was ringing her bell repeatedly, she buzzed her in, wondering what the panic was about.

"Lucy, what's wrong? Sit down."

Lucy's hair was all over the place and she looked as if she'd just got out of bed. This mightn't have been a surprise to Kate a few months ago but she knew how seriously the younger girl took her grooming these days.

"Kate, did you write this?"

Shocked, Kate could see the letter that she'd written weeks ago being waved frantically in front of her face. Lucy looked furious and her face was set in angry lines that startled her. She was always so mild-mannered and here she was now practically shouting. It dawned on Kate that if the letter had come into Lucy's hands, then it must mean that the man had been a relative.

"Lucy, I'm sorry," she said quietly. "I said that in the letter. I didn't realise that the man I killed was related to you. I just needed to say properly how sorry I was – I never thought it would be you who'd get it."

"Sorry? For a start, I'm only sorry that it wasn't me

who got to kill him and secondly, you didn't kill him at all. He was full of drink, Kate. He'd been drinking all day at the races. It was all a cover-up because he knew a few people in the right places."

"Lucy, you don't have to try and make me feel better about this –"

"I'm not trying to make you feel better." Lucy was gripping Kate's shoulders now, almost shaking her in her need to let her know the true facts. "He was a horrible man. He was a – a paedophile," she spat out eventually. "I knew all along that he was drunk the night he was killed – loads of people mentioned it to my parents around the time of the funeral. It just never occurred to me that someone else might be taking the blame for what happened. I'm so sorry, Kate. He killed your husband and made you lose your baby." Lucy was crying now, all the anger gone out of her. She couldn't believe all the lives that her uncle had ruined with his drinking and his perverted ways.

"Lucy, I did have drink taken on the night."

"Kate, I have everything here. All the papers from the inquest and everything. I never read any of it until this morning. All the stuff about the cars being moved and the blood results going missing. *Your* blood results were there, with hardly any alcohol in the bloodstream. There were no results for Ned, of course," she finished bitterly.

Suddenly the room began to swim before Kate's eyes. Lucy let go of her, only now realising that she must have frightened her out of her wits, barging in and yelling all over the place. She was deathly pale. Looking worried,

Lucy eased her onto one of the sofas and pushed her head gently towards her lap.

Kate felt lights flashing behind her eyelids and realised that she was getting one of the flashbacks that had plagued her in the aftermath of the crash. For the first time in ages, she didn't try to stop it.

She let herself remember Timmy laughing about the bride's two spinster aunts fighting over the wedding bouquet, she felt the warmth of the car and the scent of the Paco Rabanne aftershave that had been Timmy's last birthday present, she watched the lights coming towards her and felt again the pain that had ripped through her right shoulder, the passenger window shattering as the car impacted with a tree. It was like watching a film clip, the way it stopped suddenly after that.

Kate had no memories of the following two weeks. Timmy had even been buried before she regained consciousness. She'd been so angry at that. It was like he'd just disappeared. His grave was an alien place that she couldn't identify with, almost as if she didn't believe that he was really there. For three years, she'd been in a wilderness, her life a shell with endless rounds of physiotherapy, callipers and exercise machines. Depression had flattened her, often immobilising her in bed for days at a time. Was it possible that she hadn't lost control of the car; that the oncoming car had hit *her*?

"Kate, are you okay? Here, take a sip of this," Lucy instructed, her face creased in concern when Kate opened her eyes.

A wave of dizziness hit her again and she sank back on

the sofa, accepting the glass of water that Lucy proffered.

"I'm grand – it all just hit me when I wasn't expecting it. I thought I'd never hear from the family that I wrote to. I just gave the letter to my solicitor to forward on to them."

"I'm sorry for shouting at you. It was just the thought of you worrying for years over somebody like him – it made me so angry."

"I did worry about it a lot, even though I never let myself think about what actually happened. I was in a desperate state afterwards, Lucy. And it wasn't just the injuries, though they were bad enough. I was in St James' for four months and then in the Rehab in Dún Laoghaire for another two. It was afterwards that it was really bad. I felt that I had nothing to live for, that it was all my own fault and that as well as killing my own husband and child, I'd taken someone else's life as well."

Lucy was shocked at the effect that Ned Dalton's death had had on her friend. She herself had been so relieved by it that she could hardly imagine anyone having a moment's guilt over him. But Kate had obviously thought that he was a decent man whose life had been cut short on account of her own recklessness.

"What happened on the night?"

"We were at a wedding in Kildare. I was driving home. I'd had most of a glass of wine earlier in the evening – mainly because I didn't want people at the table to cop on that I was pregnant. It sounds so stupid now but we hadn't told anyone at that stage. Timmy was laughing about something that had happened at the wedding. Then there were these lights coming towards us and I felt something hitting my right shoulder. The car skidded into the ditch, against a tree. That was what killed Timmy apparently."

"But, Kate, did it never occur to you that you had no memory of the car going out of control but that you do remember the lights and the impact when the other car hit you? Ned hit *you,* Kate, not the other way around. That's why his buddies moved the cars, even though it was supposedly because they were a danger where they were."

"I never actually tried to figure it out. I was on a ventilator for two weeks and when I woke up and found that Timmy was dead I just lost the plot. Then I was told that I'd lost the baby as well – I was bleeding by the time I arrived in the A&E, the nurses told me."

"This is so awful, Kate. I can't even imagine what you went through."

Kate grinned weakly at this. "I was a fright, Lucy. I was in bed all day after I got home. I couldn't face going back to work. I didn't even take a shower for days on end. My sisters were there all the time, trying to motivate me, but it was no good. Then I went on anti-depressants."

"Did that help?"

"A bit – even though I felt sort of muzzy on them. What did help was reflexology."

"You did it on yourself?"

"No, I didn't know anything about it then. Nancy, my younger sister, asked a friend of hers to call around one evening to give me a session. I'd say she thought I was mad. The house was in a state and I can't bear to think what I looked like. I actually fell asleep in the middle of the treatment which was amazing because I hadn't been able to sleep at all after leaving the Rehab."

"That *is* amazing."

"She came again a few days later and then started coming every week. I was able to talk to her as well. I think it was easier for me when I knew her attention wasn't focussed on me – she'd be preoccupied with the feet so it wasn't as intense as when I had counselling in the Rehab. It was just right for me, I suppose."

"Did you come to Cork after that?"

"It took me about three years to realise that I wanted to get away altogether. I didn't like my job any more and I'd started to get into the complementary therapies in a big way. I'd just finished the reflexology course when I saw the shop advertised in one of the Sunday newspapers."

"God, Kate, it must have been a huge move to leave your family and everything."

"I didn't mind really. I got a great price for the house so I was fairly independent. And I didn't mind not being near Timmy's grave because I never really believed he was there. I wasn't at his funeral so it never seemed real to me."

"Kate, I can't even begin to say how sorry I am that Ned took everything away from you." Lucy had tears in her eyes at the thought of Kate, so serene and elegant and poised, being driven almost to distraction by the loss of her whole life.

"Lucy, you're not responsible for what anyone else did, least of all him. I'm just glad I know a bit more about it now."

"I'm sorry I was so angry – it just seemed so unfair."

"Sometimes it's good to get angry. When you said he was a paedophile . . . did you mean that he'd . . ."

"Yes," Lucy said emphatically before Kate had even finished the question. "Of all days going, I don't want to talk about it – mainly because he took everything away from me and I'm determined to enjoy tonight. But someday soon, Kate, I'll call over and we can talk about it."

"Don't feel that you have to, Lucy. But I'm here if you *want* to."

"I will want to. The more you know about him, Kate, the less guilt you'll feel."

"Lucy, you've done so much for me today already. Thank you. It took a lot of courage."

"I actually feel better myself, to be honest – a bit whacked but better," Lucy admitted.

Cora Nolan had spoken to her about anger at a few of the sessions. It bothered Lucy that she'd always taken the blame for what her uncle did out on her parents, that she'd resented them and appreciated them so little. Now she could see what Cora meant about directing that anger to its rightful place. She'd been furious at Ned when she'd read Kate's letter and it felt good to have vented that, despite her regret at having frightened the life out of her friend.

"Here, I'll put the kettle on," said Kate. "I was actually having a crisis about what to wear tonight before you arrived so I probably need a Twix to get me back on track."

"I thought you had an outfit?" Lucy queried, following her through to the kitchen area.

"I had but I'm bursting out of it. Just as well I decided

to try it on this morning. Lorcan's a devil for putting cream in things. He calls tikka masala his signature dish," she giggled, although it wasn't a bit funny that she had to improvise for the evening out.

"I think you look brilliant," Lucy commented, taking in her creamy, almost translucent skin and glossy hair. "Have you anything else that you could wear instead?"

"I have a taffeta thing that I wore to a wedding lately. Bring the tea into the bedroom and I'll try it on. I had it out on the bed when you rang the bell."

"I thought I was bad on the chocolate bars in my day," Lucy teased as Kate followed her into the bedroom, bringing with her a blue and gold biscuit tin full to the brim of Penguins, Twixes and Time Outs.

"Lorcan keeps putting things into the shopping basket that I wouldn't buy in a million years – then I eat them just because they're sitting there. I'll have to put a stop to it when I move over to his place or I'll be huge in a matter of months."

"When will you move, do you think?"

"Soonish, I hope. I'm trying to get someone to rent this place first. I can always lock the door that opens into the shop and let them use the main door onto the street. Well, what do you think?"

"Kate, it's fabulous. You look brilliant in it."

"Are the shoes all right or should I wear sandals?"

"The shoes are great. What about jewellery?"

"I'm not sure. I'll need something decent – the neck's a bit bare."

"What about the pendant that Rosa's mother got me

in Italy – the Murano glass one? That'd go lovely with it. I'll go this way on my walk later and drop it in if you like."

"Lucy, that'd be gorgeous, if you're sure you don't mind."

Kate had admired the smooth russet and gold glass of the pendant a few times and knew that it would go well with her outfit. She couldn't believe that Lucy calling this morning would have made such a difference to her life but it had. It was as if the weight of thirteen years of guilt had been lifted from her and she felt almost buoyant. It was like she'd been given a new beginning, one that she could savour all the more now that she had Lorcan in her life.

She said as much to Lucy and thanked her for everything that she'd told her about Ned Dalton and also for the anger that she'd felt on Kate's behalf.

"I was livid, Kate," Lucy admitted. "I had no proper friendships when I was a teenager. Even sitting here watching you trying on your outfit – I missed out on all of that, things that teenagers do all the time. I know I'm able to put it behind me now and I think you should too."

"I can now, thanks to you," Kate said, hugging her, a gesture that brought tears to Lucy's eyes. "And thanks for vetting the outfit. Rosa would never forgive me if my zip gave out in the middle of the dinner."

Kate watched Lucy leave, her face relaxed after the trauma of receiving her letter. She sat on the end of the bed for ages after she'd departed, marvelling at the way that writing the letter had turned out. She wondered what Lorcan would make of it and whether it would rock the sense of peace that he'd found when he wrote a similar letter all those years ago. She thought not. Lorcan had been strong enough to let go of the past, even without the kind of absolution that she'd been given today.

Her musings continued until she glanced at the small carriage clock on her bedside table and realised that it was almost half twelve. She'd promised to be out at Lorcan's house for lunch at one. Startled into action, she jumped up but sank back onto the bed just as quickly when the same dizziness that she'd had earlier overcame her again.

She closed her eyes tightly, hoping that the scenes from the crash wouldn't replay for her again. They didn't, but something else did instead, a long-forgotten familiarity that floated at the edges of her consciousness. Gradually her head cleared and Kate sat bolt upright on the bed.

"Good God!"

With that she grabbed her car keys and handbag, praying fervently that one of the city's many pharmacies would have the good grace to be open on New Year's Eve.

Chapter 41

Agnes studied the embossed, gold-edged card that had been displayed on the mantelpiece for the past few weeks and decided that it was time to start getting ready. She had loads to do before the meal started but at the same time she didn't want to dress up too soon or she'd be crumpled by the time she sat down to the meal at eight.

Her first port of call as soon as she was dolled up would be The Friary so that she could show off her finery to Bea and the other residents. Then she needed to call to the Montgomerys, a couple she'd met at a few of the fund-raisers, to pick up a sculpture that their daughter, Emily, had donated for the auction.

Agnes had spent ages over the choosing of her outfit, wanting to look elegant and graceful, as if she'd been going to events like this all her life. She wasn't one hundred per cent sure about who'd be at her table, having missed the final meeting on Monday due to yet another appointment with Stephen Barrett at Barrett and Co.

Agnes knew that the other members of the St Angela's Ladies' Committee were amazed at her innovation and ability to engage all sorts of people in their fund-raising efforts, especially when she was so new to the whole thing. Little did they know that she'd spent years wheeling and dealing behind the scenes, simply to make ends meet.

Now that she'd have so much time on her hands, Agnes planned to channel as much of her time as possible into the hospital's voluntary work, especially now that she'd made such friends on the Ladies' Committee. A few years ago, she wouldn't have believed it possible that she'd be dealing with such illustrious people on a daily basis, yet now she was on first-name terms with the front-runners of Cork society.

Preparing for the charity ball had been the most exhilarating time of her life. The weeks had gone by in a whirl of activity that had somehow softened the blow of Beatrice's betrayal. She'd shopped for her outfit with a sense of pleasure that she could buy something that she liked for a change, rather than something that she could afford. The navy velvet dress had cost an arm and a leg but Agnes didn't care. It flowed full length to the floor and its beaded bodice was perfectly fitted with its scoop neck and dainty cap sleeves. Matching court shoes were an expensive but necessary accompaniment, as was the exquisite jewellery that she treated herself to in Keane's.

A worthwhile investment, she congratulated herself, as she admired her ensemble in the full-length mirror. She'd put rollers in her hair overnight and treated herself to some expensive make-up for the occasion. Spraying herself liberally with White Linen, she collected the little velvet purse that she'd bought to match her outfit and quietly let herself out of the house.

Beatrice was stunned at the glamour of her sister and immediately cast a canny eye over the softness of the velvet and the exquisite accessories, unable to help herself.

"That rig-out must have cost a pretty penny," she commented as she manoeuvred her new motorised wheelchair into the bedroom but smiled a little and added jokily, "I hope you're not going mad when I'm not there to keep an eye on the budget."

"To be honest, Bea," Agnes admitted, "I did go a bit mad on the outfit. I didn't want to make a show of myself with all the glamorous ladies from the Committee."

Strangely, now that she and Bea had called a truce, Agnes felt a little bit guilty about being so excited about the new life she had ahead of her, a life that wouldn't be possible if she were still tied to looking after her sister.

"The money won't last long if you keep buying outfits like that."

Since Stephen Barrett had visited The Friary and explained the full details of their finances, their relationship had improved immensely – to the point where they could discuss the money issues without their former angst.

"There's plenty. And I'll be getting my pension, don't forget. I'm thinking of changing the car in January. I could even get a wheelchair-accessible one if you like so that you'd be able to come out for drives in the summer."

Since Beatrice had been a resident of The Friary, she'd

been on several day trips with the other residents in the adapted minibus. Agnes had spent years trying to get her to go for a Sunday spin now and then, yet all of a sudden it was she telling Agnes that she should visit Fota Wildlife Park or the Jameson Heritage Centre in Midleton.

"That would be a good idea," Bea conceded in a tone that suggested that she was giving Agnes permission to buy the car rather than simply endorsing the idea. Agnes smiled to herself, knowing that old habits took a long time to die.

"I'd better go and get organised now, Bea," she said, anxious to get to the Montgomerys' house in Glanmire to collect the sculpture that would be one of the highlights of the auction.

"Well, I hope it's a great night and that the auction makes loads of money. You're to make sure and let Mrs Grainger know how much her grandson's things go for."

This, from Beatrice, was magnanimous in the extreme and Agnes knew that it was her way of saying sorry for all the covering-up of the inheritance and the life that she'd denied her sister in the past.

"I will, Bea, and I'll have loads of photos for you. Take care now." And she hugged her sister spontaneously for the first time in her life.

Rosa was ecstatic that everything was going so well. Lar had arrived as planned to escort her to Lucy's house and had complimented her profusely when she'd opened the door to him. She knew she looked well in her full-length, red dress and for once her hair seemed to be staying in place rather that escaping around her face in curls to make her look like a five-year-old. He'd offered her his arm for the short walk down the street, surprising Rosa with his quiet gallantry.

Martin was already installed in Lucy's house by the time she and Lar arrived, as were Gerry and Shona. The air of merriment was palpable. Martin was making cocktails with a silver shaker that he'd discovered in one of Lucy's cupboards.

"What'll it be, Rosa?" he'd called out as soon as she and Lar appeared. Lucy, she noticed, was giggling on one of the sofas with Shona, a sure sign that she'd already had something lethal from Martin's questionable repertoire.

"Surprise me," she challenged and was indeed surprised when she was landed with his version of a Whiskey Sour, a concoction of Jameson, orange juice and a hefty dose of pure lemon juice that he pulled out of Lucy's fridge and swizzed up with some crushed ice.

"Jesus, is he trying to poison me?" she spluttered, approaching Lucy and Shona to see what they'd got.

"I wanted one of those Long, Slow Screws but Martin says he doesn't do them. I got a Wham, Bam, Thank You, Mam instead," Shona told her dolefully, holding up a highball glass filled with a hazy purple mixture with a cherry at the bottom.

"Another Bombshell for you, Lucy?" Martin called over, brandishing a bottle of Malibu and the milk jug over the blender.

"I thought this was only supposed to happen when they were let loose with a barbecue," Lucy commented.

"At least the blender's safe enough. What about my poor fiancé and all those dangerous toothpicks?"

Lucy and Rosa giggled as they watched Gerry studiously spearing cherries and olives onto the thin wooden sticks on Martin's instructions.

An hour later, the taxi was beeping outside the door as the girls rushed up to Lucy's bedroom to top up their make-up and give a final spray of perfume. Martin's cocktails notwithstanding, they were in high good humour by the time they reached Hollygrove Manor.

Gravity returned momentarily when the straight-faced ushers arrived out of the five-star hotel to escort them from the car to the palatial front steps but once they were indoors amid the buzz of people their buoyant spirits returned.

When Kate and Lorcan arrived a few minutes later, the table was buzzing. Kate felt as if she were visibly glowing when she introduced Lorcan. Lucy and Rosa he knew already so Rosa proudly did the rounds of introducing Martin, Lar, Gerry and Shona.

Kate hated herself for lying when Martin started to take orders for a round of drinks.

"Orange juice?" he protested. "You can have orange juice tomorrow morning. What about a glass of champagne to celebrate the engagement?"

"Definitely orange juice. We didn't book our taxi in time so I had to drive."

"You got away very light, Lorcan," Lucy teased when Kate's partner ordered a Beamish.

"My defence is that I did all the driving over Christmas so it's payback time tonight. I can't have my wife-to-be on the booze all the time."

Thankfully, the moment passed and Kate was able to relax again. She squeezed Lorcan's hand under the table, grateful to him for deflecting the attention from her.

The afternoon had been a revelation in more ways than one for Kate. Hearing Lucy talk about the kind of man that her uncle had been and finding out that maybe the car crash hadn't been her fault had been amazing but it paled into insignificance in comparison to the realisation that maybe her clothes didn't fit her for a very good reason.

It had all come back to her in a flash – the memories of her first pregnancy that she'd buried along with all the other memories of her old life. The feeling of light-headedness every time she stood up suddenly, the constant craving for sweet things and the subsequent weight gain that had made the smiling midwife in Holles St remind her all those years ago that she wasn't eating for ten, only for one and a bit.

The race to find a pregnancy test had been an epic one and she'd ended up in Glanmire before she found an open pharmacy. The test, though, had been an academic exercise because Kate, once she calmed down and thought about it, was certain that she was pregnant.

Lorcan had been completely bowled over by the news, his face lighting up at the wonder of it. Like Kate, he could hardly believe his luck at meeting someone special to share his life with and now to hear that he was going to be a father was truly the icing on the cake! They'd spent the afternoon between crying and laughing and making love, both amazed that this wonderful thing had happened so quickly without them even having to try.

It was only when Kate realised that it was half two and she still hadn't had her lunch that she demanded that Lorcan get up and get her something to eat. Another hour passed as they sat up in bed eating their cheese and Ballymaloe relish sandwiches deliberating about how they were going to raise a child in Lorcan's little cottage.

"*Our* little cottage," he'd corrected, his hand caressing her tummy thoughtfully. "We could speed things up a bit and start looking for planning permission straightaway. I know the building would take a while but at least if we had it underway when the baby's born it'd be something."

"Imagine, we're actually talking about a baby. Even though it's early days yet. My period is only about a week late."

"I can't believe you were able to tell so quickly. Was it like that the last time?"

The crushing guilt that she'd felt since the car crash had always prevented Kate from talking about Timmy or the baby, her sense of blame so strong that she'd felt almost hypocritical about grieving fully for them. It was as if she didn't deserve the luxury of sympathy and support. Now though, since Lucy's visit, she was at last able to cry with someone else for her lost baby, something she'd only ever done alone before.

Lorcan had somehow understood the enormity of what she'd lost, marvelling at the fact that only a few hours before, he'd had no idea that they were going to have a baby yet now he knew with certainty that he couldn't bear to have it taken away from them.

The afternoon had gone by in a daze until they'd finally pulled themselves together enough to start getting organised for the charity ball. A night out in Hollygrove Manor seemed like a wonderful culmination to the almost surreal day that they'd had although Kate knew that it'd be hard to keep their secret to themselves.

Rosa broke in her thoughts suddenly, wanting to know if she'd spotted any of the footballers that Agnes had invited.

Baffled as to how Agnes would know any footballers, Kate looked askance at Lorcan who calmly announced that he thought he'd noticed Alasdair Grainger at a table down the back.

"Why didn't you say so?" Rosa, Lucy and Shona were outraged that he hadn't so much as mentioned it. "Who else did you see?" they demanded, trying to crane their necks unobtrusively.

"That Norman Logan fellow was there as well, I think. Are ye into the soccer, girls?" he enquired innocently.

"No," Rosa told him irritably, as if he should know that it was a purely social interest that was driving the inquisition. "But if Norman's here then maybe Jackie Morton will be as well. The one with all the handbags."

"Do you think we should go over and give Agnes a bit of support?" Lucy had spotted her near the stage where she seemed to be struggling with a large statue of some description. Maybe she might be able to wangle an introduction.

"Good idea. C'mon, Shona! And bring your handbag – it might get us chatting if we meet Jackie."

Shona collected her exquisite beaded handbag from its hiding place under the table and took off after the other two, eager to make the acquaintance of the WAGS, even if they couldn't get near the actual footballers.

"I can't believe they're gone off after that Norman Logan. He's supposed to be as thick as two short planks," Lar complained as he watched Rosa's slender figure sashaying across the floor.

"It's the money," Gerry told him philosophically, not minding a bit that his fiancée had taken off in search of another man.

"And I suppose it's our own fault for making them watch the premiership matches in the pub. All they're doing is ogling the players." This was Martin's contribution.

Kate, sitting next to him, laughed at his forlorn face.

"I don't think she'll actually take off with one of them, Martin. We women just like to make sure we're not missing out on anything."

"I know that, Kate." Martin was watching Lucy talking animatedly with Agnes and Rosa's mother in the middle of the auction items and thinking that she looked beautiful.

"Lucy looks fabulous tonight," Kate commented, following his gaze.

"Lucy looks fabulous all the time. Did she tell you about throwing a bottle of wine over me the first time we met?"

Kate laughed, having been filled in on the nightmare trip to the shop by Lucy and Rosa.

"I kept walking up and down past her house after that to see if I'd meet her. I'd say people were about to report me to *Crimeline*."

"Well, it was obviously worth it. I think Lucy's great – she's been really good to me and I've only known her since the start of the cookery course."

Kate couldn't believe the pride in Martin's smile when he heard her speak so highly of Lucy.

"Do you know, Kate, I'd never thought about getting married until I met Lucy. I was always into work and going out with the lads."

"Have you told Lucy this?" Kate enquired.

"I'm not sure if she's ready for all that yet. I was thinking of waiting a bit until she is."

"I think you're right, Martin. You've loads of time. Look at myself and Lorcan!"

The dinner bell rang at this point, causing a general flurry of activity as people made their way back to their own tables.

Agnes couldn't have asked for more. The place was buzzing with the fact that Alasdair Grainger, Norman Logan and Todd Stanley were in the building. Truthfully, she'd had no concept of what a big deal it was to have three Premiership footballers arriving at Hollygrove Manor.

And the skinny waif hanging onto Norman's sleeve seemed to be creating almost as much of a stir as the three young men. Lucy and Rosa had practically begged her to engineer an introduction to Jackie Morton, famous only for being Norman Logan's girlfriend and having a colossal amount of expensive handbags, as far as Agnes could make out.

The rest of the committee were bowled over, it seemed, by Agnes's contacts and her dedication to raising as much funding as possible for St. Angela's. It was inevitable, Marjorie Price-Canning kept saying, that the rich celebrities that Agnes had commandeered would raise the stakes at the auction. Thanks to her it would surely be a bumper evening for the coffers.

With the excitement of the celebrities arriving and the unprecedented arrival of the Cork press photographers, not to mention the task of arranging all the auction items to best advantage, Agnes had almost forgotten about the meal. It was only when the bell rang for dinner that she made her way to Table 1, hoping that whoever she was sitting beside wouldn't be too intimidating.

"Miss Cotter, I believe?"

The man who stood up to greet Agnes and pull out her chair was slightly smaller than her in her high heels but had, nonetheless, an air of importance about him.

"Indeed, but please call me Agnes," she murmured graciously, slipping into the seat as elegantly as she knew how.

"Now, I'm Nicholas Bryce," he announced in a voice that Agnes thought mightn't be out of place in the House of Lords, "and Marjorie there tells me that you're the best-connected lady in Cork. Knows everyone, she told me, and not afraid to pull out all the stops for the fund-raising effort."

Agnes was ecstatic, thinking briefly that heaven

couldn't possibly be better than this. To be sitting in Hollygrove Manor in her navy velvet ensemble and her expensive shoes with Professor Bryce, CEO of St Angela's, praising her to the nines was something that even her wildest fantasies couldn't have conjured up. If Bea could see her now, she'd collapse altogether.

"Really, she's too kind. After all, I've only joined the ranks very recently. Marjorie and the others have been working hard for years."

Agnes studied him surreptitiously as he continued to affirm what he'd been told by Marjorie Price-Canning. She imagined that he was around her own age, recalling that she'd heard some of the committee ladies talking about an upcoming retirement do. His sandy hair was thinning slightly at the crown but otherwise he looked younger than his years with the ruddy complexion of a man who liked the outdoors. Hunting or shooting, Agnes decided.

"Always a need for new people," he was saying. "And I hope you don't mind me mentioning it but Marjorie tells me that you've put in many years of good work before you joined us."

If she hadn't been so bamboozled by all the praise, it might have occurred to Agnes that Professor Bryce seemed to know quite a lot about her already. However, basking in the limelight for once in her life, she soaked it up and enjoyed the vision of herself as some kind of saint.

"I've been looking after my sister until recently but she's at The Friary now," Agnes told her companion. It felt good to have her years of hard work with Beatrice acknowledged.

"I understand perfectly. Cared for my wife for years

but she had to go to the hospice in the end. Wasn't what I wanted but I had to do what was best."

This was said matter-of-factly, but so sincerely that Agnes began to feel a pang of guilt that she was so relieved with her new-found freedom.

"I'm sorry to hear that. Was it long ago?" She hoped that she wasn't being too intrusive in asking but Nicholas Bryce had so far presented himself as forthright and quite outspoken.

"Fifteen years. My sons are living abroad now, one in Canada and one in Oxford."

He broke off as their first course, a delicate concoction of melon, Parma ham and a blue cheese sauce, was placed in front of them.

"Almost too good to touch," he commented, his plummy accent impressing Agnes no end.

She sipped her red wine delicately and was gratified to be able to respond appropriately when he commented on its quality, thanking providence that she'd paid attention the night that the wine expert had given the talk at The Gourmet Rooms.

As they slowly moved through the various courses, the evening went from strength to strength. The other gentleman near her was Maurice Mooney, with Bernadette beside him. He had heard all about Agnes from his beloved daughter and even thanked her for being so supportive of Rosa during the cookery course.

"She told us that it was her classmates being so helpful that got her through it. And how wonderful you all were when she was offered the job."

Maurice was beaming and again Agnes felt a surge of pleasure to be included in such praise.

"Well, Rosa was just marvellous to me too. Such a lovely pleasant girl," she told him, touched by how much he obviously adored Rosa. Both Maurice and Bernadette were smiling at her as if they'd already known that Rosa couldn't have been anything other than marvellous.

Marjorie Price-Canning, at the opposite side of the table, winked at her and raised her silver beaded purse delicately to indicate that she was going to the powder room.

Delighted to be an active part of such an illustrious gathering, Agnes accepted the invitation, excusing herself discreetly to her companions. She was more than impressed when Nicholas Bryce stood up as she left. Carefully picking her steps on the glossy parquet floor, she followed Marjorie to the ladies' room, wondering all the while if perhaps she'd persuaded her husband to give her a little jab of Botox for the night. She looked much younger than she had last week, Agnes noted.

"Well, didn't I do well with the place settings?"

Marjorie was perched on one of the gilt chairs studded around the large opulent room, her face a picture of coyness, making Agnes blush furiously at the idea that she'd been placed next to Nicholas Bryce on purpose. What if he found out and thought she was some sort of dubious man-hunter?

"Well, really, everyone is such good company," Agnes stammered, pretending that she didn't get Marjorie's drift.

"Honestly, Agnes, he's very taken with you. I can tell.

And he's very much a gentleman. In need of a bit of cultured company – very hard to find someone like-minded these days."

Impressed that Marjorie considered her to be 'like-minded' company for their dear friend Nicholas, Agnes took extra care repairing her make-up and thanked God that she'd found out about the inheritance in time to spend as much as she had on her outfit and accessories.

Rosa's heart had started to thump erratically as soon as Kate mentioned that she still hadn't found a renter for the flat above the shop. Now it seemed that she and Lorcan had decided to speed things up a bit and move in together straight away. The delicious looking sirloin atop its bed of peppered celeriac went untouched as the wheels of excitement began to whirr in her brain.

"What kind of rent would you be looking for or have you not decided that yet?"

Now that she'd started getting her weekly wage from The Gourmet Rooms paid into her bank account, a burgeoning sense of independence had started to flourish. It was time that she stood on her own two feet and now that she was finally earning her own money, she'd be able to.

She'd been to Kate's flat a few times and had adored the delicate blue and cream colour scheme that was carried throughout making it look much bigger than it actually was. Bramwell Court and Lucy would still only be a short walk away.

"It's only got one bedroom so it'll be cheap enough. I hadn't really thought about it, to be honest."

"Would you rent it to me?" For once, Rosa was timid as she asked this, fearing that Kate might think it was a bad idea and shatter her bid for independence.

"God, Rosa, I'd be delighted. It'd be great to know it was you looking after it. But what about your own house? Are you selling it or what?"

"Mum and Dad bought it as an investment a few years ago but I've been living there ever since. I think it's time I vacated it or it'll be the worst investment ever!"

"I'd be thrilled for you to have it, Rosa. And don't worry about the rent. We'll settle on something that suits us both. You could come over for lunch tomorrow and we'll talk about it properly."

"Brilliant!" Rosa squealed, kissing Kate in her excitement.

"Rosa's going to take the flat," Kate told Lorcan, detaching him from the other lads momentarily. They hadn't stopped their critical analysis of Alasdair, Todd and Norman yet.

"Are you, Rosa?" Lucy, overhearing, was thrilled for her friend. Having to manage her own affairs would be good for Rosa – it would give her more faith in herself, Lucy thought.

Lar immediately called a toast, looking proudly at Rosa as if she'd announced that she was going to the moon. Rosa smiled over at him, her face radiant with the thrill of being on her own steam for the first time in her life.

Table 12 was a riot – as Rosa found out when she made

her way over with the list for the auction. She'd purposely skirted around to the other tables first so as not to appear too eager to get to the one with the footballers.

"Hello, I'm Rosa Mooney and I'm here to tell you about the auction."

Where the table had been loud and raucous before, silence now fell and the nine men looked at her with interest. Jackie Morton, the celebrity girlfriend, looked at her svelte figure and perfect, angelic face with disgust.

She herself had made a rash decision about breast implants, hoping to surprise Norman for his birthday, but the whole thing had gone horribly wrong. Nothing that could be noticed, mind you, but enough to make her envy the small pert breasts of this girl in the red strapless dress.

Donnie, one of the newest of the St Angela's portering staff, was mesmerised. First they'd been told that they had to make up a full table of ten, which had been a nightmare seeing as none of the six night porters had wives or girlfriends. Then suddenly, having six at a table was okay because the Ladies' Committee had come up with a party of four who would be able to make up the table with them.

Donnie and the lads had nearly wet themselves when they'd seen Jackie Morton stalking towards their table in a miniscule gold lamé dress with Alasdair Grainger, Norman Logan and Todd Stanley bringing up the rear.

"Fucking hell!" This had come from Bill Rowley, the head porter, who spent half the night ogling Jackie in old copies of *OK* magazine that got left in the waiting-rooms.

Eventually, after a prolonged session of back-slapping

and shouts of "Go on, ya good thing!", the table had settled comfortably into a good night's drinking. Jackie, predictably, had flirted and preened, lapping up the attention of her newest subjects.

Now Rosa, a vision in red, was standing over them with an expectant look on her face and Donnie thought he'd died and gone to heaven.

"Now, this is the list of the various lots and the guide prices. Obviously," she smiled sweetly at the players, "St Angela's would like to thank you for your own contribution to the auction tonight."

"I'd like to make a contribution to you too, love," Norman Logan slurred drunkenly, jerking his hips in Rosa's direction. This earned him a sharp dig from Alasdair and a dirty look from Jackie.

Rosa looked suitably affronted but gave Alasdair a small smile to acknowledge the sharp poke he'd given Norman in her defence. After all, she'd been *asked* to go around to the tables outlining the auction items, having been advised by the shrewd committee ladies to draw particular attention to any items that might interest a particular patron. It wasn't as if she was some kind of groupie.

She'd already pointed out the football memorabilia and match tickets to the lads at her own table and now used the same tack with the porters, although she suspected that Martin might bid for them, being an Arsenal fan.

"Now, for the more discerning buyer," she began sweetly, giving the three wealthy celebrities her flirtiest wink, "something artistic, I think. We have two beautiful Goretti Macken watercolours here, not to mention a very beautiful and in fact startling 'Venus' by Emily Montgomery."

Goretti Macken was the wife of one of the cardiologists and her mother's best friend. Likewise, Emily Montgomery was the daughter of Leo Montgomery, one of the vascular consultants and had only recently graduated from the Crawford. Rosa had pronounced the names of the two amateur artists as if she were introducing Michelangelo, fully aware that none of the sports stars would have a clue who they were and would probably be afraid to ask. She was betting on them buying at least one of the pieces in the hope of looking cultured while flashing their money around.

She paused to study the effects of her pronouncement and was pleased to see that all three of them were looking at her in awe, pleased that she thought they were the type to be buying original art. Jackie was still spitting shards of steel at her.

"Well, I'll leave it with you," she concluded archly, "and remember, it's all for those little premature babies in the neonatal unit."

Now that the meal was over and she'd had a small brandy, compliments of Nicholas, Agnes was getting nervous. After all the fuss about the arrival of the footballers and the superb auction items that Alasdair Grainger had donated, she felt the onerous burden of too much responsibility. What if they didn't make the reserve or worse still, if there was no interest in them at all? Would it all wind up with her looking foolish in front of the other committee members and indeed Nicholas Bryce?

Nicholas had been more than attentive to her throughout the meal and after almost forty years of Silhouette Romances and television quiz shows, Agnes finally knew the meaning of stimulating conversation. They'd conversed on a variety of subjects including the benefits of organic produce, the dangers of genetic modification and the wonders of complementary therapies in conjunction with conventional medicine.

"Apparently they work very well together," Agnes commented knowledgably on the subject of complementary therapies. This was something that she'd read a great deal about in one of her typing assignments and had later discussed with Kate in detail.

"Quite right. I should pay more attention to the medical journals really. Don't have time these days."

"Well, perhaps when March comes you'll be able to get around to it."

He'd already mentioned his impending retirement with something like relief. Agnes had explained that with Beatrice's emergency admission to hospital she herself had effectively retired from a full-time job too.

"Difficult to adjust, I imagine. Do you play golf at all, Agnes?"

"I'm afraid I didn't have too much time on my hands during the day over the past few years. Although I imagine it's excellent exercise." Agnes could just visualise him stalking along the fairway with his distinguished companions.

"Marvellous, they tell me. I was thinking of taking a

few lessons myself in preparation for March. I don't suppose you'd care to join me?"

"Well, I – that'd be – well, marvellous. Although I'd need to be equipped," Agnes stammered, in seventh heaven. Wait until Bea got wind of this!

"Caddy Shack, I'm told, on Friar Street. Sort everything out apparently."

"Well, it's certainly worth a go."

"Capital," Nicholas declared as the gong struck to herald the start of the auction.

"Oh my God, this is it. Lucy, see the one at the front. What do you think, Kate? Will it match?"

Rosa was beside herself in her anxiety to buy the smaller of Goretti Macken's paintings now that she'd been given the all-clear to move into Kate's flat. The pale blue cornflowers would look super above the sofa on the back wall, she insisted.

"You're right, Rosa. It'd look great," Kate said, impressed. She'd never bothered much with paintings herself, preferring the small space to be as uncluttered as possible yet she could see that the delicate colour scheme and simple off-white frame wouldn't crowd the room at all.

"Shush. They're starting. I can't go more than three hundred on it so keep your fingers crossed."

Annoyed at herself that she'd done her damnedest to inveigle the three footballers into purchasing something arty, she was now praying that they were too drunk to catch on to her ploy. She'd only looked at the painting properly when she went up to the auction area to hand her mother the remainder of the auction lists and realised that it would be a way of putting her own personal touch to Kate's décor. She now positioned her chair a little out from the table in order to be visible to the auctioneer, Desmond Baldwin from Baldwin, Baldwin and Lacey.

"Now, first up we have 'Cornflower Sea', an exquisite watercolour by Goretti Macken. Starting the bidding at ? 100. Great, we have ? 100, ? 150 now to the gentleman at the front"?

Annoyed that there was someone bidding against her, Rosa glared at Conor Green from the neonatal unit and tipped her swizzle-stick defiantly. It was her painting.

"Marvellous − ? 200 to the lady in red. ? 250 from Dr Green. Excellent, madam, ? 300."

Rosa was nearly sick at this stage. Normally, if she really wanted something she'd just put it on her credit card and face the consequences later. Unfortunately, on foot of her new job at The Gourmet Rooms, she'd made a big production of telling her parents that she was intent on living independently and had cut up her credit card in front of them to prove her intent. Her upper limit would have to be ? 300.

"? 350 from Dr Green."

It only took a split second for Conor Green to raise his hand and shatter her dream of owning 'Cornflower Sea'. She felt like bursting into tears but instead tried to arrange her face to hide her bitter disappointment.

"Madam?" the auctioneer queried but Rosa bravely made a cut-off sign with her hand to let him know she was out of the bidding.

"Excellent – new bidder with ? 400," he continued, his eyes focussing on a spot behind Rosa's head. She turned sharply in time to see Lar's makeshift baton indicating his interest in the painting. She glared at him indignantly but he shushed her gently before turning his attention back to the business of the painting.

"We have ? 450 now for this beautiful painting by Goretti Macken. Do we have ? 500?"

Again Lar nodded, shocking Rosa with the fact that he hadn't expressed an interest in any of the paintings earlier in the evening.

"? 500 it is. Any advance on ? 500? Any advance on ? 500 for this lovely watercolour? Going once, going twice, gone to the gentleman at Table 8!"

The chandeliers almost shattered with the applause. The atmosphere was electric with this riveting start to the main business of the evening. Lar looked sheepish at all the attention and blushed to the roots of his hair when Rosa congratulated him shakily.

"It'll look great in the flat," he told her shyly. "I'll even come and hang it for you."

Rosa, for once, was speechless.

Alasdair Grainger sat up and took note as soon as the next Goretti Macken painting came under the hammer. He wasn't quite sure what the attraction was but the little one that looked like a sort of lavender blur had been in great demand and he wondered if his gran would like one for her bedroom in The Friary.

The slightly larger one was made up of a series of

coloured dots and blobs and the list said it was called 'Summer Meadow'. ?1000 should do it, he reasoned, seeing as the smaller one had gone for ?500.

Desmond Baldwin, however, had assimilated the general air of excitement in the room and swiftly upped the guide price ?400 to ?800, reckoning on the spending power of the illustrious audience.

Bidding took off swiftly, thanks to the precedent that Rosa, Lar and Conor Green had set earlier.

Cornelius Price-Canning and Professor Bryce had raised the stakes to ?1000 before Alasdair even got a look in. He now wished heartily that he hadn't consumed the last two pints of Murphy's and that he'd paid more attention to his mother and her daytime television auction shows. Pulling himself together he motioned with his rolled-up napkin as he had seen Lar do earlier, wondering muzzily how the auctioneer could tell how much he was raising the stakes by.

"Marvellous, ?1100 from Mr Grainger. Yes, ?1200 from the gentleman with the bow-tie."

Cornelius Price-Canning raised his fat unlit cigar again, followed by Alasdair who was now warming to the procedure.

"Do we have ?1500? Yes, sir, we do! Any advance on ?1500 for this terrific painting?"

Alasdair again raised his makeshift baton as Nicholas Bryce bowed out.

Cornelius Price-Canning, buoyed up by the three brandies that he'd consumed after his dinner, raised his cigar imperiously, only barely registering his wife's nudge in the ribs. It was only when Alasdair hit the ? 2000 mark that he came to his senses.

"Sold," declared Desmond Baldwin, "for ? 2000 to Mr Alasdair Grainger!

To the overwhelming joy of the Ladies' Committee, the auction went from strength to strength. Norman Logan, not to be outdone by a scut from Cork's northside, awoke from a drunken slumber in time to secure Emily Montgomery's enormous 'Venus' for ? 5000. Jackie, who'd remained sober in the hope that she might seduce Todd Stanley, kicked him under the table. Where on earth was she going to put an ugly, life-sized limestone Venus in her chrome and glass showhouse? And how, in the name of Jesus, were they going to transport it?

The makeover packages, fêted in Cork social circles since the successful makeover evening in the Price-Cannings' home earlier in the year, were a big hit with those of the audience who hadn't been lucky enough to be invited to the original event.

The football memorabilia, to Agnes's immense gratification, went down a bomb, with Martin securing the match tickers as Rosa had predicted. The night porters, not to be outshone by their heroes, blew their combined salaries on the signed jerseys and footballs.

To Rosa's intense excitement, the dinner-party packages from The Gourmet Rooms were snapped up, Alasdair Grainger leading the bidding. His parents, he confided to the night porters, never went anywhere so what better treat than a gourmet meal handed up to them in the comfort of their own home. Having raised the stakes yet again, the remainder of the dinner-party packages went away over the predicted guide prices.

Agnes, glowing with pleasure at the success of the evening, basked in the praise from the members of the Ladies' Committee. A force to be reckoned with, Bernadette Mooney affirmed. If Agnes was this innovative as a fledgling fund-raiser, she toasted, then the rest of them would be out of a job in a few years' time.

Lucy, Rosa and Shona took to the floor as soon as The Huckle Buccaneers struck the first note. Martin's eclectic cocktails, not to mention the copious amount of red wine that they'd consumed over dinner, had hit home and they were now in flying form. The Buccaneers – on yet another of their 'Back For One Night Only' post-retirement functions – were belting out the numbers that had made them one of the country's top show bands in their heyday.

Back at the table, Martin and Gerry were planning Lar's next strategic move. No amount of tutoring could have prepared him for his unprecedented declaration of intent at the auction but he was now at a loss as to how to proceed.

Martin was all for the straightforward notion of asking her to dance when the music slowed down a little. Lar wasn't so sure.

"I mean," he insisted earnestly, "I don't want her to feel that she has to be nice to me because of the painting."

"Talk to her then," Gerry advised emphatically with the wisdom of a man who'd experienced the highs and lows of a long-term relationship. "They love talking."

"What? Tell her I'm cracked about her? I think I'll go with the dancing," Lar concluded.

"Are you sure you're all right?"

"Don't be fretting. I was like this the last time as well. I even fell asleep in my boss's office one day at lunch-time and only woke up when I felt him trying to pull the file that my head was resting on."

Kate laughed at the memory, enjoying her ability to recall the feelings that she'd experienced in her first pregnancy without the overwhelming guilt that had hung over her for years.

"We can go home any time you like. Just say."

Kate leaned over to kiss him, touched by his concern. She'd been stifling yawns all evening, despite the long snooze that she'd had in Lorcan's bed earlier in the day.

Tiredness was the new morning sickness, she'd heard a woman say in the shop one day. Women hadn't time for morning sickness nowadays what with careers and housework and looking good. So they suffered from exhaustion instead, she'd pronounced. Kate had laughed with her at the time but now understood where she was coming from.

"Rosa would kill me if I abandoned ship at this stage. And there's no way I'm leaving until I see what Lar's next move will be."

"Well, he'd better make it fast or she'll be snapped up," Lorcan laughed, his eyes on the dance floor.

Sure enough, Rosa had been commandeered by an intoxicated Todd Stanley and was trying to maintain her balance in the face of a lively jive. Todd was all over the place and Norman Logan egging him on wasn't helping the situation. Lucy and Shona were looking on helplessly while simultaneously trying to make eye contact with their boyfriends in a bid to have Rosa rescued.

Alas, the three lads were in a huddle, comparing their Fantasy Football results. It was only when Todd made a particularly wide swing and knocked over a wineglass that was resting on a nearby table that they sat up and took note.

Lar spotted Rosa's horrified expression and sprang into action immediately, instinctively guessing that she'd hate a scene in front of her new boss and her parents' colleagues.

"Come on, lads, go up to those fellas and offer to buy them a drink. It'll distract them while I rescue Rosa," he instructed the other two.

Responding rapidly to the crisis, the two lads made their way onto the dance floor. Martin headed for Todd. Rosa by this time was being grasped in a sort of bear hug as her tormentor tried to maintain his balance. Gerry made a beeline for Norman.

"Todd Stanley," Martin exclaimed as he wedged himself partially between Todd and Rosa. "Mighty goal at the Emirates last weekend. Bloody super!" he said jovially, clapping him on the back and manoeuvring him away a little. "You must let me buy you a drink."

Todd, already full of drink, hardly knew where he was going.

"What'll it be, Todd? Another pint? Tell me, is the new stadium working out or what?"

Responding predictably to the adulation in his voice, Todd barely noticed his friend Norman, also being veered off in the direction of the bar by Gerry. Nor did he notice the object of his desire finishing 'Twist and Shout' with an exultant Lar.

"Jesus, Lucy, those lads are lunatics!" Martin said much later as they attempted a lively waltz to Dean Martin's 'That's Amore'.

After a further round of drinks, he and Gerry had assisted an embarrassed-looking Alasdair Grainger with cajoling Todd and Norman upstairs to their plush suites. Jackie Morton had been last seen shouting at the lady on the reception desk about getting her own suite now that she'd fallen out with Norman over his drunken flirting.

"Tell me about it! That Norman was looking for a foursome with us until Shona pointed out that it would be a fivesome if he included his girlfriend. Jackie overheard and went mental that he'd forgotten to include her in the action."

Martin laughed at the incredulity on her face and drew her a bit closer to him as the Buccaneers started a smoochy Dickie Rock number.

"You look gorgeous, Lucy," he told her, settling for the compliment rather than telling her straight out how much he loved her. He was terrified of frightening her off by coming on too strong, knowing that she wanted to take things slowly.

"Thanks," Lucy whispered into his ear, nibbling his earlobe and stroking the back of his neck with her nails.

Feeling mellow from the alcohol and exhilarated from the excitement of the evening, she settled herself a little closer into his arms, eliciting a low groan from him.

"God, Lucy, don't do that to me or I'll have to start shouting at the receptionist for a room as well."

"Well, if you can wait until we're back at my place . . ."

She smiled up at him and Martin could resist no longer.

"Lucy, I love you. I've wanted to tell you for ages and I know you don't want to rush things but –"

"Well, I love you too, Martin Kearney, so we're even."

Speechless, Martin held her tightly, thinking that it was the best night of his life.

Kate and Lorcan threw themselves down on the enormous bed and cracked up laughing.

"Thank God we got in before that virago let loose."

Kate had been shocked to hear the famous Jackie Morton yelling at the young receptionist as she and Lorcan filled out the booking slip for their room. It was Lorcan's idea to celebrate their wonderful news in style in the luxury of Hollygrove Manor.

As luck would have it, they'd secured the only vacant room – minutes before Jackie had arrived at the polished walnut desk, fresh from her row with Norman.

"What do you mean, no rooms?" she sniggered dismissively at the elegant and very refined receptionist.

"I'm afraid all our rooms are occupied tonight, madam."

"Well, that's not good enough! My boyfriend has paid

good money to charities here tonight," she announced in a high nasal twang. "The least you could do is see to it that I have a room."

"I'm afraid we don't have a free room at present," the receptionist explained patiently, "but perhaps I could contact Broomfield Lodge to see if they can help. It's quite near and there should be no difficulty with a taxi."

Silently, Lorcan had handed their booking slip to the receptionist whose pleasant smile was beginning to take on the grim exasperated look of one who knows there will be a long night ahead.

"I'd have to take a taxi? But all my stuff is here. I can't go off somewhere else with no clothes or make-up," she whined plaintively as if the whole fiasco was the fault of Hollygrove Manor.

"I'm sure that our night manager could accompany you upstairs to retrieve your luggage if that would be helpful."

"Oh, for God's sake, I may as well stay where I am at that rate!" Lorcan and Kate had heard as they made their way towards the lift, each of them casting a sympathetic glance at the ever-accommodating receptionist.

"So how far would you have gone?"

Rosa was still chuffed that Lar had got the painting for her and was insisting on paying him back the following month.

"Probably two or three grand. 'But you're worth it'," he laughed in a parody of the L'Oreal advert.

Rosa didn't know what to say to this. Lar hadn't

exactly said that he fancied her. He had offered to come over to the flat the following weekend and hang 'Cornflower Sea' for her, insisting that it was a gift, no strings attached.

He was normally so quiet and studious, his round glasses looking as if they'd grown on his face. Rosa actually thought studious men were quite sexy but he'd left the glasses off tonight and looked gorgeous in his dress suit with his black hair gelled into a very up-to-date style. He had nice dark blue eyes, she noticed too as she looked up at him now.

As the night had worn on, the Huckle Buccaneers had slowed down their tempo a little and Rosa was now suddenly very much aware of Lar's body where it touched against hers on the dance floor. When she'd first met him through Lucy and Martin, Lar had been very much in the background compared to his more outgoing friends. Lately, though, she'd started to notice that Martin and Gerry went to him for advice on everything from their pensions to their cars. He was that kind of person – sincere and dependable and a million miles away from the kind of men that she'd always gone for in the past. No wonder she'd had as many disasters in her love life as she'd had in her career path. It had always been glamorous Flash Harrys before, all slick gear and wafts of aftershave and no substance at all. She'd certainly never been with someone who'd have come to her rescue as gallantly as Lar had tonight. On *two* occasions, she realised, thinking of him saving the painting from Conor Green and saving her from that foul-mouthed Todd Stanley and his grubby hands.

Lucy reckoned that Lar was big into her and had even sussed out Martin, who seemed to think that his friend was merely afraid of being rejected. Rosa had been wondering all evening if *she* should make a move and was now adding up the plusses and minuses of this.

She had asked him to the night out in the first place and had paid for his ticket seeing as he was coming as her guest. At the time though, she'd made it clear that it was a platonic invitation to a night out with a group of friends. So far this evening, she reasoned, Lar had made most of the effort – buying the painting, offering to come and hang it and asking her out to dance. On balance, Rosa decided finally, her escort had done enough for one night.

"Lar? You know when you said that the painting was a gift, no strings attached?"

"Yeah, that's right."

"Well, I think I might like it better if there *were* strings attached."

Lar was looking at her as if he couldn't believe what he'd just heard. Rosa's heart was suddenly hammering – what if she'd put her foot in it, if she'd got it all wrong and he didn't fancy her at all?

Seeing the anxiety in her face, Lar leaned down and kissed her gently on the lips.

"Well, if strings are what you want, then strings are what you'll get."

Pamela Carter was taking advantage of her position on the dance floor to watch Rosa surreptitiously. Maurice Mooney was an excellent dancer, guiding Pamela confidently among the other couples like a professional, thus enabling her to observe her new assistant properly.

Rosa, as always, looked beautiful. She was dancing closely with a tall, thin, serious-looking fellow who was hanging on her every word. They looked very relaxed together, Pamela thought. She'd noticed her protégé's manner with the guests earlier in the evening when she'd been distributing the auction slips and had been impressed at the manner in which she was able to read the personality types at each table and focus in on the items that might be of particular interest to them. Needless to say, she was perfectly groomed and her poise was enviable in such a young woman. Pamela could tell that as soon as Rosa knew the ropes and was confident in her role, she would be able to take over much of the workload that was becoming so cumbersome of late.

Since Absolute Beginners at The Gourmet Rooms had been aired on national television she'd been inundated with calls from newspapers and magazines for interviews. In the past, she'd never even had to advertise. Word of mouth had been enough to keep all of her courses filled almost all of the time, usually with a waiting list. Now it seemed that everything had to be in the public domain, with people being considered celebrities whether they liked it or not.

From here on in, she decided, her assistant could take over that side of things. Rosa came across as warm and endearing with just the right mix of glamour and enthusiasm while Pamela was aware that she herself often appeared austere and unapproachable. It would be good for The Gourmet Rooms to have a new face at last.

Everything would be fine, she thought, if only this anxiety about whether she'd done the right thing in taking Rosa on in the first place would go away.

Chapter 42

Lucy woke in the slow, lazy way that she'd got used to of late and snuggled into Martin's back. Autumn sunlight was filtering in through the gap in the curtains, telling her that it was probably time to get up.

Another few minutes, she promised herself, her hand running over Martin's hip to stroke his thigh. She loved the feel of his skin against her own, her lips accustomed now to the fair, wiry hair along his back and the warmth of him next to her. Enjoying the sensation of her palm roving over his leg, she thought back to the first amazing night that they'd been together properly.

New Year's Eve had been the most liberating and exhilarating night of her life – the night that she'd finally put the past behind her. Sometimes it was as if she could only remember it in flashes. The excitement of dressing up for the evening out, the exquisite meal and dazzling surroundings, even the auction had taken on an almost surreal aura of glamour and anticipation. Martin holding her and telling her how much he loved her and the sense of certainty that he truly meant it had been magical. Nothing though could have prepared Lucy for the wonder of making love with him that first time. The sheer intensity, the way he whispered to her all the time, the wonder of how much she wanted to feel him inside her and the unbelievable feeling of giving herself up entirely to the pleasure of it were a cacophony of memories that would be imprinted in her mind forever.

"You'll be late for your first day if you start this carry-on."

Martin woke lazily and shifted around to face her, his lips searching out hers in the semi-darkness.

"I thought it might jizz me up a bit, get me in the right frame of mind maybe," Lucy told him cheekily as she felt his body responding. Rolling over to cover her body with his, Martin began to nibble his way along her throat and across her collarbone.

"I'm not sure that they study this kind of thing in UCC but I suppose I can't refuse you . . ."

"No, I don't suppose you can . . ."

Afterwards, Martin brought her breakfast in bed.

Facing into college for the first time was daunting to say the least. The campus was huge, she remembered, having cut through it once as a short cut from College Road to Western Road. Cathy had been with her that time – otherwise she'd have been too intimidated and would have taken the long way around rather than impose upon the hordes of confident-looking students who all looked as if they knew exactly where they were going in life.

She had to be at the Aula Maxima at ten for registration and God only knew what would happen after that. Not for the first time she wished that she'd gone straight from school to college. That way there would most likely be someone that she knew starting the same day. As it stood, she was nervous of not knowing anybody but Martin kept reassuring her that there would most likely be other mature students in the group.

Despite her nerves, Lucy was glad that she'd made the decision to go to college at last, even though it had been a wrench to leave The Friary. Her last year there had been better than the previous ten put together, something that she attributed to her new-found confidence in herself.

Her going-away night out, organised with military precision by Cathy and Una had been brilliant, with almost everyone who wasn't on duty arriving to wish her well. She'd even made a speech, albeit with a few glasses of wine on board. They'd met up with Martin and Rosa and Lar after the meal and the party had continued in Bramwell Court long after the Fiddler's Elbow had closed its doors on them.

Now, with all the partying over, the time had come for her first day in college and she was already a bit jittery. She was delighted now that Martin had taken the morning off so that he could go with her for moral support – and also because she had been fretting about whether she'd find her way around the sprawling campus despite getting a map with her prospectus and course details.

The outline of the four-year degree course had terrified her when she'd read it first. As well as the elements of biology and chemistry, the first year modules included mathematics, physics and even psychology. It had taken Martin and Rosa a full evening to convince her that she'd be well able for it, especially when she had honours in both biology and chemistry in her Leaving Cert.

"The psychology module might be interesting," Rosa had hinted darkly, trying to remind her friend that she really should talk to her boyfriend about her past.

To date, Lucy had kept the story of Ned to herself, not wanting it to place a shadow between herself and Martin. It wasn't that she didn't feel able to tell him, it was just that the right time hadn't come along yet.

Her heart was beating frantically by the time she and Martin had parked on O'Donovan's Road. What if she was the oldest in the class with nothing in common with anyone? She couldn't bear the thought of going through four years on her own. All the old feelings of insecurity started to flood back as they walked the short distance across the large grassy area that Martin said was called 'the quad'. Even his normally reassuring presence beside her wasn't doing its magic today.

"Here you go," he announced as they reached the imposing stone building that housed the registration office. The stone steps were dipping in the middle from years of the footfalls of students, reminding Lucy that she wasn't the first nervous fledgling to make her way up them.

Ah, feck this, she told herself firmly. I'm here to enjoy this and to make a new start – no point in pulling back at this stage. She tightened her grip on Martin's hand and took a deep breath.

"Excited?"

"Actually, I am. I'm very, very excited."

There. Now that she'd made up her mind to go forward, it didn't seem so daunting. Squaring her shoulders, she joined the tail end of the queue that had formed at the door of the registration office.

"Lucy Dalton? Is that you?"

Lucy turned, wide-eyed, to see who it was that could possibly know her.

"Kerrie? My God, I haven't seen you since school! How are you?"

"In bits," the girl behind her giggled nervously. "It's my first day and I haven't a clue where I'm going."

Lucy was casting her mind back to her school days and vaguely remembered that Kerrie Mulcahy had become pregnant before she'd even sat her Leaving Cert. At the time, the nuns had been furious that she'd thrown away her good education and her chance to go to university on a lad who was barely shaving. It had been the biggest uproar in the school that anyone could remember and the risk of Kerrie being a bad influence on the rest of the girls had been great enough for her to be advised to study at home for the remainder of the term. Lucy had a memory of her coming in to sit her exams, her eyes downcast.

"I'm the same," Lucy admitted. "What course are you doing?"

"Nutritional Science. I only hope I'm able for it."

"That's fantastic, Kerrie. I'm doing that too."

Lucy could see Martin grinning from ear to ear and introduced him to Kerrie as the queue shifted slowly in front of them.

"It's great to have someone with you. Fergus had to drop the kids to school this morning so I had to go solo."

"How many children do you have, Kerrie?"

Lucy vaguely recalled that the perpetrator of Kerrie's downfall had been one Fergus Donoghue. They'd obviously stayed together, despite the insistence of the nuns that Kerrie have the baby adopted in order that she could get on with her life.

"Two. Jody's ten now and Caroline is nearly six. They're in school now so I'm finally picking up where I left off."

Her proud grin told Lucy that putting her own future on hold for a while was something that Kerrie had accepted in order to keep her family together. Not for the first time, Lucy was aware that there were more people in the world besides herself whose path hadn't been too rosy.

"Well, girls, I'll leave ye to it," Martin said as the queue moved them nearer to the heavy wooden door. "I'm only glad I got all this out of the way years ago!"

"Thanks for the encouragement," Lucy accused good-naturedly, delighted to have Kerrie beside her. She kissed Martin quickly and relished the reassuring hug that he gave her before wishing them good luck. "I'll ring you later if I need to be rescued."

"Jesus, Lucy, you've no idea how good it is to see you,"

Kerrie said as soon as Martin had departed. "I was starting to get cold feet. I was even thinking that being a housewife wasn't such a bad career after all!"

"I've been in a state all morning as well," Lucy admitted. "I kept asking myself why I didn't go to college when everyone else was doing it."

"Well, at least we're here now. We might even be able to go for a coffee to calm our nerves when the registration is over."

"Good idea. Go on, she's calling – you go first."

Lucy looked around her in fascination while Kerrie presented herself at the registration desk. Now that she had a chance to study the people around her properly, she could see that they weren't all perky eighteen-year-olds.

The two lads directly behind her had Rasta hair and combat trousers and spoke with American accents. The girl who'd been in the queue before them was now sitting by the wall on a raggedy satchel going through her notes, her gypsy skirt spread out around her. She looked to be a bit older than Lucy with small round glasses and long hair tied back in a loose knot. Lucy started to see that she wouldn't actually look out of place here at all.

Soon it was her turn to register and she listened intently to all the details about student cards and the college's style for presenting written assignments. A bit overwhelmed by it all, she kept reassuring herself that everything she'd need to know was in her handbook and that Martin would be there to help her.

"Will we forget the coffee and go to the bar?" said Kerrie. "My head is bursting after that." Kerrie was looking as agitated as Lucy might have felt if she hadn't had Martin to talk her through everything the last few weeks.

"Good idea. I'm the same."

"I suppose we'll have to take it as it comes." Kerrie was consulting the small map in the college handbook to try and locate the pub.

Five minutes later, they were sitting back with two bottles of Budweiser, oblivious of the fact that it was still only eleven o'clock. Lucy couldn't believe that she had a friend in tow before she'd even attended her first class.

Kerrie told her about the struggle that she and Fergus had had in the early years of their relationship when there had been so much pressure on them to give up their first child.

"The nuns at school thought he should be adopted but to be fair to Mum and Dad and Fergus's parents, they never agreed. Mam wanted to keep it quiet at the beginning and pretend the baby was hers. He would've been reared as my younger brother but I didn't want that and neither did Fergus. When I think of the fights!"

"Fair play to you, Kerrie! It can't have been easy with Sister Carmel putting her oar in." Lucy recalled the disapproving demeanour of the school principal and admired Kerrie for the courage it must have taken to stand up to her.

"Tell me about it!" she giggled at the memory. "How come you decided to go to college now, Lucy? I thought you had a good job at The Friary?"

"You knew I worked in The Friary?" Lucy had

thought that nobody from school had noticed where she'd disappeared to.

"Fergus's granny used to be in the Alzheimer's Unit there eight or nine years ago. His mother often mentioned you. I saw you driving in the gates one day years ago and I remember being mad jealous."

"Jealous?" That someone could have been jealous of *her* had Lucy's mouth open in shock.

"There you were in your own car, all independent and working somewhere really posh and there I was pushing a buggy with not a penny to my name."

Lucy thought back to the little white Citroen AX that she'd bought with a Credit Union loan. She'd known about Ned's will at the time but it had taken a few years of legal administration before the money had started to arrive in her bank account. She now had a clear memory of how happy she'd been with her job and her second-hand car. Perhaps she might have been able to survive the memory of the abuse if the burden of the money and how to deal with it hadn't entered the picture.

"God, Kerrie, if only you knew! It was great at the beginning but after a few years I got into an awful rut. I was as big as a bus and I didn't care what I looked like. I was just sitting around watching the telly with nothing to do."

"But look at you now. What happened? Was it meeting your boyfriend?"

"No!" It was Lucy's turn to giggle now. "I decided to do a cookery course to get my mother off my back. I was really low starting off, Kerrie, but I got on great at the course and met loads of new people. I started walking to lose the weight and I started to take an interest in myself again. I only met Martin after that."

"Well, fair play to you too, Lucy!" Kerrie raised her bottle of Bud in a very student-like toast. "Here's to college life and new beginnings!"

"New beginnings!" Lucy echoed, clinking her bottle against Kerrie's. This, she thought with a surge of anticipation, is what life is all about.

Chapter 43

Around the same time that Lucy and Kerrie were toasting themselves in the bar in UCC, Kate and Lorcan were speeding towards St Angela's. It had been five that morning when she'd felt the first small twinge in her back but had dismissed it as one of the many pains and aches that she'd been having since she'd become really big. Twenty minutes later, she'd felt it again and had lain awake in the darkness wondering if the time had come. A slightly stronger twinge after another twenty minutes made her a little more convinced and by half seven she knew it was time to wake her husband. Lorcan immediately jumped out of bed, thinking the baby was coming at that particular minute and Kate, between contractions, had burst out laughing.

"Have a shower and check that we have everything ready," Kate had advised, feeling serene and in control. "Only make me some breakfast first. Everyone says I'll be starving for the day if I don't fill up before I go."

Kate's appetite, huge during her pregnancy, obviously wasn't going to fail her now in the face of a few contractions.

After breakfast, she'd had a long bath on the advice of a midwife in the Labour Ward at St Angela's that Lorcan had insisted on phoning for reassurance. The contractions were gradually getting stronger and she'd taken out the little TENS machine and attached the pads to her lower back, hoping that it'd keep the pains at bay for a while. It did until eleven when there had been a sudden ratcheting up in the tempo and Lorcan, terrified of things going too far and him not being able to cope with a home delivery, had insisted on heading for St Angela's.

Kate practised the meditation techniques that she'd learned in the alternative antenatal classes that she'd attended alongside the regular ones. During every contraction she focused on a good memory from her life. The day she'd met Lorcan in the vegetable market was one that lasted her through the first few pains, then she moved on to the night that they'd had dinner in Galligan's. The wonderful day that Lucy had eased her guilt about the accident and the moment when the second blue line had appeared on the pregnancy test followed, sustaining her through the gripping abdominal contractions.

By the time Lorcan was helping her into the car, she'd moved her meditation onto their wedding day last March.

Her bump had barely been showing then and she'd loved her ivory satin wedding dress. She'd had it made by a lady who came into the shop regularly and who knew about Kate's pregnancy. The final fitting had been done as late as possible to allow for an expanding waistline, something that took away any stress that Kate might have had about her dress not fitting. The clothes debacle the morning of the New Year's Eve Ball had been a lesson to her.

Ballymakeigh House had been a wonderful venue, the food exquisite and the service excellent. Both of their families had been delighted for them, with Lorcan's mother Vera crying throughout the Mass to see her son finding happiness at last.

Kate's engagement had been an enormous surprise to her own family, who'd become used to her almost reclusive life in Cork. As far as they were aware, she hadn't even gone on a date since Timmy's death. To see her surrounded by her friends with the handsome Lorcan by her side was amazing to them.

Lorcan had visited her parents' home in Leopardstown with her a few times in the run-up to the wedding and they were more than proud to have him as a son-in-law when he made their daughter so obviously happy. He'd been nervous telling them about the pregnancy but after all their daughter had been through, they were happy for them both.

The wedding had been a joyous affair for all of them and Kate had loved introducing her sisters to her Cork friends, as they called them.

Rosa and Lucy had been as glamorous as ever, arriving with Lar and Martin in tow. Lucy had generously offered to accommodate Kate's parents for the weekend and to drive them to the church on the morning of the wedding, an offer that had been gratefully accepted considering how little they knew Cork city. They'd been treated like royalty, they'd told Kate afterwards, with Lucy cooking them a huge breakfast and even driving Nora to the hair appointment that Kate had made for her.

Agnes had arrived accompanied by her new beau, Nicholas Bryce, who was a professor according to Rosa. Everyone was delighted for Agnes that she'd met someone special after all her years of caring for her sister and the scare she'd had when she thought she was about to lose her home.

Kate was focussing on all these positive people and events in her life as poor Lorcan negotiated the Kinsale Road roundabout on their way to St. Angela's. Traffic was a nightmare as usual and he cursed the fact that the long-awaited flyover was nowhere near finished. Kate gripped his thigh with each contraction, her eyes closed as she breathed deeply as the midwife at the antenatal classes had instructed.

Sweat broke out on his forehead as her nails dug into his leg during one particularly long contraction. The traffic began to move at last. They were on their way.

Chapter 44

Rosa was lounging around in a pair of silk pyjamas having her second cup of coffee when she heard the clatter of the letterbox downstairs. She knew it was childish but she loved getting post, even if it was only bills or junk mail. Propping open the door of the flat, she sped downstairs to see what had come.

Strangely, it was a plain cream envelope with no stamp, addressed in Pamela Carter's now familiar handwriting. More than curious, Rosa sank onto the bottom step and clutched the envelope to her chest, her heart sinking to a spot somewhere well below her navel.

In her heart, she'd known it was probably too good to be true. Only this morning she'd been congratulating herself on the fact that she was a career woman at last. She had her own small office at The Gourmet Rooms and the services of the highly efficient secretary, Fidelma, to help her through any difficulties. Although the past nine months had been a steep learning curve, she'd managed to carry it off without any major disasters. Or so she'd thought.

Rosa couldn't think of any reason other than firing her for Pamela to hand-deliver a letter to her. She was due into work at two to welcome the Intermediate group and hand out the curriculum and their starter packs. She'd had everything organised to perfection for the group of ten and now here she was getting a letter that could surely mean no good.

She remembered that it was Lucy's first day at college and thought of how ironic it was that her friend was just starting her new career when it looked as if Rosa's was combusting yet again. Deflated, she rose from the grainy sisal-carpeted stairs and made her way back upstairs.

Her coffee, she noticed, had a scum on it already so she made her way dolefully to the small kitchenette to make a fresh cup. All this will have to go, she realised in dismay, looking around the dainty blue and cream flat. And I'll have to ask Mum and Dad if I can move back into Bramwell Court when the lease is up for renewal. Another retrograde step in a series of many was all she could think as she sat down to study her employer's verdict.

These were the thoughts that flitted through Rosa's head just before she opened the letter. But if she thought that being dismissed from her job was the worst thing that could happen to her, Rosa realised that she'd been sorely mistaken as soon as she started to read.

Far from giving her personal assistant her P45, Pamela began the letter by assuring Rosa that what she would go on to reveal was not related to her work at The Gourmet

Rooms at all and that the past nine months had been the most privileged and wonderful of Pamela's career.

Her heart thumping erratically in her chest, Rosa read the news that she had been waiting for a whole lifetime. In the most painstaking of terms, Pamela Carter described the pain that she'd felt the day that she'd handed her beautiful baby over for adoption. Not a day had gone by that she didn't think of her, until the fateful evening that Rosa had appeared in The Gourmet Rooms. Other than the day that she'd given birth, seeing Rosa again had been the most wonderful moment of her life.

It had broken her heart, the letter went on, that she hadn't been able to disclose her true identity, having promised the Sisters at St Angela's all those years ago that she would never attempt to trace her child. She understood that this would have to come from Rosa.

To Rosa's shock, Pamela told of the way that she'd enquired every year on her birthday to see if there had been any request from her daughter for a reunion. It was only a week ago that she'd received a letter from an African mission base to say that Rosa was seeking her out.

Shellshocked, Rosa read the ending, tears of hurt and confusion wetting her face.

"It is with the utmost trepidation that I reveal myself now as your mother, although I know that precious title belongs to Bernadette. I hope you can forgive me, Rosa, for what you may see as my weakness in letting you go and for the deceit of almost a year.

To see the wonderful young woman that you have grown to be is the most overwhelming joy I could ever have imagined. Your presence in my home and in my life this past year has been both an honour and a privilege — you are everything that any mother could hope her child to be.

I pray, Rosa, that you may understand the agony I felt at parting with you and that there will somehow be a place for me in your life. For my part, your place here in my home is without question and your place in my heart is as constant as the day I first laid eyes on you.

The shock I have visited upon you today, Rosa, is unpardonable but I hope that I have at the very least opened the door into your past that you needed to find. I will be here, as always, in my home. Please come whenever you are ready.

With much love,

Pamela"

Dazed from the revelations, Rosa lay back against the squashy cushions of the sofa. Despite being almost light-headed with the mixture of emotions, one clear fact was emerging from the jumble of thoughts: I don't want Pamela to be my mother. I don't want Pamela to be my mother.

Rosa squeezed her eyes tightly shut and tried to make the mantra that was pounding in her head go away. It wasn't right. Her birth mother was supposed to be some anonymous, faceless person that she might or might not bond with. She'd spent months visualising what she might be like and could not now reconcile herself to the fact that she was not at all anonymous.

Rosa thought that she had visualised every possible scenario, from rushing into the arms of a woman who looked not unlike herself to coming face to face with someone who was from a different world altogether. Only two nights ago, she'd talked to Lar about what it might be like to find that her mother was academically inclined and how it might make her feel that she hadn't followed in either her adoptive parents' footsteps *or* those of her birth mother.

She'd even read an article in a magazine recently about a girl who traced her birth mother only to find herself disappointed that she couldn't relate to her at all, so different were their worlds. Having been raised in a wealthy and privileged environment, Rosa was very aware that she'd never been in a situation where she had to make ends meet. What if she were to find that her mother lived in a block of council flats in an underprivileged area? What if her step-siblings were drug addicts or were in and out of jail as the girl in the magazine had found?

All of these possible endings had been accounted for in Rosa's mind. Never had she accounted for the fact that she might actually *know* the person that she was looking for.

Yes, Pamela Carter was accounted for in Rosa's life but as her employer. She already occupied one place in Rosa's psyche – it was impossible to assimilate that she could ever take on this new role.

Scanning through the letter again, Rosa tried to focus on what exactly Pamela was trying to say. Bits and pieces of sentences jumped out at her and she found that she had to concentrate hard to take it all in. What struck her most was that Pamela Carter had known for almost a year – a year of duplicity and of scrutinising her daughter when Rosa herself was unaware of it.

She felt very exposed now at the thought of it. It was almost like knowing that she'd been spied on. She felt shaky and exhausted all of a sudden and didn't know what to do next.

For once in her life, she couldn't turn to Maurice and Bernadette. It wasn't that she couldn't trust them to listen to her and help her make sense of it all – but she felt too vulnerable to let them know how she was really feeling.

Lar, she thought now. Lar would help her to make sense of this. Purposefully, she made her way to the bedroom to retrieve the portable phone from her bedside locker. Shakily, she dialled Lar's work mobile, knowing without a doubt that he'd be beside her as soon as he could.

Around the same time that Rosa was dialling Lar's work number, Agnes was dialling her good friend Nicholas to impart the most exciting news of her life. It was beyond belief that she, Agnes Cotter, was finally entering the world of celebrity.

The ironic thing was that she'd actually stopped fantasising about an imaginary life of fame as soon as she'd started to fully participate in real life. Now here was celebrity chasing *her*.

The New Year's Eve Ball had been a pivotal point in Agnes's reinvention. Her friendship with Nicholas Bryce had opened up a kaleidoscope of new opportunities and, as well as their golf afternoons, they'd joined an orienteering group and purchased an annual ticket for the Opera House. Now that Agnes had her new car and enough money to dress in the manner that she'd always craved, she felt the equal of anyone and had made up her mind to enjoy herself thoroughly.

Her activities with the Ladies' Committee at St Angela's had intensified if anything and she was currently involved with fund-raising for a hospital in Calcutta that they'd 'twinned' with. The aim was to send a container-truck full of medical equipment that was considered obsolete in the developed world but that would be considered highly valuable to their under-resourced counterparts.

It had been Agnes's idea to contact the other health authorities in the south of the country to request any unused equipment that might be gathering dust. She'd roped Nicholas in to assist her in collecting the smaller donations such as baby-weighing scales, oxygen monitors and intravenous pumps, aware that many of the hospitals, despite the best of intentions, might not get around to having the equipment delivered to St Angela's on time.

The larger pieces, such as old hospital beds, incubators and ventilators, would be collected by the many local transport companies who gave freely of their services when a particular need arose.

The Calcutta hospital in question had a large paediatric and neonatal unit which Agnes planned to supply with as much as possible in the line of clothing for the premature infants. She'd mentioned her ideas to the Director of Nursing at The Friary one day and had been met with an overwhelming response from the residents when Una Riordan asked her to give a short talk on the subject.

The Occupational Therapy sessions had taken on a whole new meaning, with the participants producing a dizzying array of knitted bootees, cardigans and bonnets. Crocheted blankets in the softest of yarns were bound with pink and blue satin ribbons and folded carefully in the rapidly filling tea chest that Marjorie Price-Canning had resurrected from her attic.

The male residents too had contributed. Bill Buckley, a carpenter for years, had made twenty smooth wooden clipboards to hold the babies' case notes in the same way that the nursing notes were held together with hard plastic ones in The Friary.

"I haven't lost the use of my hands," Bill announced proudly when Agnes praised him for his efforts.

For many of the residents, leaving their own homes had meant losing a certain part of their individuality. Now Agnes had given them the chance to re-assert their usefulness, bringing a spark of enthusiasm back into their lives. Even Beatrice, who'd barely lifted a finger in all the years that Agnes had cared for her, was happily hemming soft flannelette cot sheets in a variety of pastel colours.

So enthused were the residents with the challenge of filling the tea chest that they were even urging their family members to contribute any unused baby clothes to the effort. Una Riordan had eventually set up a Calcutta Corner in the Day Room, providing another large box to supplement the ever-dwindling space in the tea chest.

The *coup de grâce* had come with the arrival one evening of Caroline Grimes, the granddaughter of Molly Grimes, an octogenarian who'd booked herself into The Friary for company following the death of her husband three years previously. Caroline, after many years of fertility treatment, was the proud mother of triplet girls, Casey, Laurie and Andie.

"I can assure you all, I won't be doing it again," she laughed, handing over three Moses baskets, three sterilisers, three baby-breathing monitors and a veritable mountain of pink baby clothes. Molly was beaming with pride at this generous donation from her granddaughter when Beatrice commenced a round of applause.

Now that her younger sister had become such a prominent figure in Cork's charitable elite, Bea had begun to appreciate her organisational skills and dedication and was vociferous in her praise of Agnes lest she be seen as ungrateful for all the years of care.

And now it seemed that Agnes's endeavours had not gone unnoticed in the right quarters. After all her years of toil, here was recognition at last. Her hands shook as she punched in the number of Nicholas' house, her heart fluttering with the excitement of the news that she'd just received.

"Nicholas? Yes, it's Agnes here. I have the most marvellous news!"

"Splendid. Let's have it then." Nicholas, as usual, was succinct.

"Oh, Nicholas, I've been nominated for a People of the Year Award. I'm to present myself at RTÉ on the first of December with nine guests. Imagine! I'll be on television! I'm going to be interviewed along with five other nominees."

"Absolutely marvellous. Mind you, I rather think you deserve it. Must go for a bite in Hollygrove to celebrate."

Chuffed at his response and his whole-hearted endorsement, Agnes delivered the *coup de grâce*.

"And, Nicholas, it's being presented by Irene Lucas of *Afternoon Tea*!"

Chapter 45

Lar's heart was thundering as he made his excuses to his boss, David Reilly, and left the building as quickly as he could.

A crisis, Rosa had said, one that she needed his help with. She needed him at her flat as soon as possible, she'd said, the sound of tears evident in her voice. Lar's heart had contracted painfully at the anguish in her voice and he'd immediately made his excuses to get away from the office.

He'd been in a meeting with David when the call had come through and he'd explained immediately that he had a family emergency and would have to leave. Considering that Lar had never been the type to invent much in the line of emergencies, David had told him to take the following day off as well.

Rosa had left the door open for him and he bounded up the stairs two at a time and rushed into the sitting-room. Sitting forlorn on the sofa with her head in her hands, her face blotchy from crying, was Rosa. Folding her tightly in his arms, Lar let her cry again, telling her over and over that he loved her and that everything would be fine.

Rosa, still unable to talk properly, kept going on about her mother. Lar, ever patient, told her that there was no rush – they could talk about whatever it was in their own time.

Calming down eventually, Rosa pulled a tissue out of a box she'd been clinging onto and handed her boyfriend a crumpled piece of paper that at first he thought was a used tissue.

"Do you want to read it?"

She sounded drained and miserable and Lar hugged her again, wondering where a letter came into the equation. Suddenly, it dawned on him that Rosa hadn't been talking about Bernadette.

Quickly he scanned the single page, trying to focus on the contents of the letter. No wonder Rosa had been so shocked. Her whole life had been upturned with its arrival.

"God, Rosa, I don't know what to say."

Lar was as stunned as she was. He'd met Pamela on several occasions but had been looking on her as his girlfriend's employer rather than as potential candidate for a long-lost birth mother. It was the fact that Rosa was nothing like Pamela at all that he couldn't get his head around. Where Rosa was lively and interesting with an air of innocence about her that endeared her to everyone she met, Pamela was calmly austere with a measured air about her.

"Well, if you don't know what to think, can you imagine how I feel?" She smiled weakly through the tears, feeling safer about it all now that Lar was here.

"I can't even begin to imagine. What's the worst thing about it, do you think?"

"You're beginning to sound like Dad!" Rosa warned him.

Lar grinned back at her and rolled his eyes, having heard this more than once over the past number of months.

"I think it's that I feel confused," said Rosa. "I thought I was ready for anything – you know – any sort of person. But it wasn't supposed to be someone that I've known for ages!"

"We never factored that in at all," Lar admitted, having been through the pros and cons of it with her on numerous occasions.

"I feel a bit like I've been taken advantage of as well. She knew all along who I was but I was going in and out of work every day completely in the dark. I keep thinking that this is what it must be like to have someone stalking you. The way she knew all about me and the way that every question she asked must have had a purpose."

"It looks like she had no choice until now. I think she was trying to respect the fact that you hadn't looked for her."

"But why didn't she just leave me alone altogether? Why did she have to give me a job at The Gourmet

Rooms? And that's another thing – I feel now that she only gave me a job because she knew I was her daughter. I feel like a fraud now as well." Rosa sniffed miserably at this, trying to stop herself from crying again.

"She had no need to give you that job at all if she didn't want to," Lar told her vehemently. "You're very good at it – you must know that by now. Pamela is a businesswoman at the end of the day and she'd be very slow to jeopardise the cookery school by bringing in someone who hadn't a clue, no matter how much she wanted to keep you around. So get that out of your head right now."

Rosa smiled at his loyalty and was glad that he was there beside her. Lar had a way of making sense of most things and despite the fact that she teased him about it mercilessly, he was very like Maurice in all the best ways.

"Thanks for that," she whispered gratefully, leaning over to kiss him. It dawned on her that she must look a fright with her hair all over the place and her face raw with crying but, for once, she didn't actually care.

"Well, it's true. What do you think about her giving you up in the first place?"

"I'm trying to get my head around that as well. I always wanted to think that maybe my mother was sixteen or seventeen and that she was forced to give me up. But Pamela must have been older than that. I wonder if her husband was my father?"

"She did say that she loved him very much," Lar reminded her softly, wanting her to remember what

Pamela had said about loving her from the moment she set eyes on her. "You weren't something that she regretted, Rosa. You have to remember that."

"Then why didn't she keep me?" Rosa retorted obstinately.

"We don't know what her circumstances were. Maybe they weren't able to marry for some reason. Maybe she was on her own."

"Why are you sticking up for her, Lar? She gave me away!"

"Because I can understand it when she said that she loved you from the moment she saw you. I know I did. And if I had to give you up, Rosa, I'd only do it if I thought it was better for you in some way."

"But *how* could it have been better? She's a wealthy woman with a huge house. It's not like she couldn't afford to keep me."

"We don't know that, Rosa."

"It's just that I can't picture her holding me as a baby. I'm so different to her – even to look at. She would have had dark hair in her day. And her eyes are a sort of grey. Who must I look like?"

"Is it that you feel you don't know who you belong to – is that it?"

"Something like that. I don't know. I can picture myself in the baby photos with Mum and she looks like a normal mother, smiling down at me and everything. I just *can't* see Pamela like that. I *can't*."

"Rosa, just remember – you don't have to do anything right now. You'll have to have time to absorb this. And you have all the time in the world to get used to it. Pamela's going nowhere."

"Well, that's true," she acknowledged, lying back against the cushions.

"Have you had your breakfast?" he asked now, concerned that Rosa would neglect herself in all this.

"Only coffee. I just can't believe it, Lar, that she'd do this to me. That she could work beside me day after day and pretend nothing. It just makes me feel that she could hide anything and I'd never know."

Lar was over in the kitchen refilling the kettle at this stage. "It's easy for us to see it that way but we have no idea what she went through." He knew that it was important for Rosa not to see her mother as a hateful figure who had dumped her readily rather than hang on to her against the odds. Rosa already had a big thing about being useless – it would only compound this if he was to agree that her mother hadn't cared much about her.

"God, I need this!" she said now, taking a sip of the coffee he'd placed in front of her.

Two slices of toast followed, with the butter and marmalade melting into it the way she liked it.

"It's a lot to take in, Rosa," Lar reminded her, settling into the sofa beside her with his arm around her shoulders. She was still in her pyjamas and looked young and vulnerable as she sat there with her legs tucked up under her.

"I just don't know what I'm expected to do. And I suppose I'll have to tell Mum and Dad. I think it might hurt them more that Pamela is in my life already. They probably thought it would be a stranger too."

"You don't have to tell anyone until you get your head around it a bit more. Although they would be great support."

"I know they'd do their best but it won't be as easy on them as they'll make out." Rosa was munching on her toast, calmer now that Lar had introduced something as ordinary as breakfast. It had put things in perspective, somehow.

"It's like a huge responsibility all of a sudden. All along, I'd only thought things out up as far as what my mother might be like. It was all about whether *she'd* want to meet *me* or whether she'd reject me maybe. I never really thought about what might happen if she was all about me and *I* didn't want *her*. Which is how it turns out now."

Lar was sipping his coffee thoughtfully. "Do you really not want to know her or is it that you're overwhelmed by it all and don't know how you're supposed to act?"

"That's exactly it, Lar. One minute she's Pamela and, to be fair, she's very good to me. But if I have to think about her as a mother, I just go blank."

"Would it be any good to go away for a few days? I'd book somewhere and come with you, if you wanted."

"Thanks, Lar. But I feel that I have to face it. I have my job to think about as well, you know."

"I'm sure that Pamela could put it on hold or something until you decide what you want. It's the least she can do." He knew that Rosa took her job seriously but surely Pamela Carter couldn't expect Rosa to carry on as normal under the present circumstances.

"But that's the thing, Lar. If I was in any other job, I'd

have to go in and put a brave face on it. I just couldn't drop everything and let people down at the last minute."

"You wouldn't be letting anyone down if you took a few days off," Lar reasoned.

"It's hard to know what to think." Rosa picked up the letter again and read bits of it. "She did *try* to contact me, though."

Glad that Rosa was coming around to seeing Pamela's point of view, Lar said quietly, "She must have loved you a lot not to want to let you go a second time."

Looking up at him sadly, Rosa acknowledged that what he said was true. "It's just that I didn't know it would be her. Now that I do know, it's hard to know what to think." Rosa knew that she was repeating herself but couldn't seem to get a grip on the practicalities of the situation.

"Would going to talk to Pamela help at all? Would you *like* to hear what happened? Or would it make it harder?"

"I'd just love to know why she couldn't keep me. And I feel bad saying that because it's like saying that I'd rather have been with her than Mum and Dad."

"You're not saying that at all, Rosa. Your mum and dad have been expecting this from the moment they got you. Your dad said that to me, you know, Rosa, about a month ago when we were there for Sunday lunch. That I should make sure you knew they'd be ready for whatever happened."

"I know that. I know that whatever I do, they'll try to understand."

"And you know I'll be here for you too. Whatever happens."

"I know, Lar. And I love you for that."

"Why don't you go and take a shower? We could go for a walk if you want to clear your head." He took Rosa by the hand and pulled her gently towards the bathroom.

"I'd love that," she said. "Then I might be able to make a decision on what to do next."

Taking her in his arms, Lar held her tightly and kissed the top of her head. "It'll be fine – I know it will. We'll just have to take it in small steps."

"I think you're right. After all, imagine how I would have felt if it had been someone who didn't want to know me at all!"

"That would have been bad all right," Lar acknowledged.

Twenty minutes later, the pair of them were striding briskly out the Carrigrohane Road, having parked the car outside the Kingsley Hotel. It was only an hour and a half since her life as she knew it had been shattered to bits but it felt as if she and Lar had been talking about it for a week.

"I'll crack up if I just leave it," Rosa said now, glad of the crisp morning breeze on her face. Her hair, still damp from the shower, would be a riot of curls when it dried fully and for once, her face was devoid of make-up.

"What are you thinking?" Lar, ever the accountant, was cautious.

"There's so much I need to know. I'd love if there was someone I could ask before going to Pamela but there's not. I'll just have to talk to her."

"Just take your time, Rosa. There might be things that it'll be hard to hear about."

"What about my father? I must look like him if I don't look like Pamela. Everyone always thinks about their mother but it's not just one person that's missing from my life – it's two. What if he's alive somewhere too?"

"It *could* have been Pamela's husband. Maybe they were able to marry later but couldn't get you back. What was his first name, do you know?"

"Thomas. She mentions him now and again. Actually there's a photo of him in her office. I never really looked at it properly but he had dark hair too. He was a serious-looking fellow with greased-back hair. I don't look a bit like him either."

"Rosa, a lot of people don't look all that much like their parents."

"But he looks so serious in the photo and Pamela is so reserved as well." Rosa knew that she was far from serious herself and felt like a bit of an alien at the thought that she belonged to Pamela and Thomas Carter. But then, maybe she didn't belong to both of them. "But if Thomas is not my father, then who is?" She couldn't visualise Pamela as the kind of silly girl who would have 'got herself in trouble' as it had been put years ago. She couldn't imagine her getting carried away and giving in to any great passion.

"You do need to talk to her," Lar conceded as they turned and made their way back towards the Kingsley. On a normal day if they went for a walk, they were in the habit of going into the four-star hotel for tea but today was far from normal.

"I know. I think I'll go to work after all. There will be a long gap between the time the Intermediates leave and the Beginners come so we can talk if Pamela wants to."

"You won't be able to work today, Rosa!"

"What am I going to do otherwise? Pick up the phone and tell her I won't be in? That would mean I'd have to talk to her anyway!"

"I could ring. I could tell her you'd be in touch in a few days."

"I have to be fair, Lar. I was the one who asked the nuns to find my mother for me. Now that she's there in front of me, I can't suddenly decide I don't want to see her. Imagine if it was Pamela who had sought me out and then changed her mind? How would I feel?"

"You always have such a generous way of looking at things." Lar stopped at the entrance of the Kingsley and took her in his arms. "I love you, Rosa. I think you're just great."

"Even if I called you home from work to melt your head?" she grinned. "Are you going to buy me tea and biscuits?"

"Are you up to it?"

"Of course, I'm up to it. When did I ever turn my nose up at a home-made biscuit?"

Together they made their way into the comfortable hotel foyer, immediately searching out the cosy armchairs at the back that overlooked the river.

"Do you really feel up to going to work?" Lar asked as soon as he'd ordered for both of them.

"I don't particularly feel like going to work as such but in a way I feel sorry for Pamela. I have you and Lucy and Mum and Dad to support me. I'm not sure who she has. Maybe she's never told anyone about me. I'd hate to think of her there waiting for me."

"You have to think about yourself, too, Rosa," Lar said, wanting to cover all the bases in case Rosa regretted rushing into it later.

"I am thinking about myself. I couldn't go to sleep tonight with all these questions. I have to see her today to find out how it all happened."

Lar could understand this. Rosa wasn't the type of person to stew on things interminably. The months of waiting had been torture to her already.

"I'll come with you then," he said eventually. "I don't have to come in. I'll just sit outside in the car in case you need me."

"And I might well need you if it doesn't work out the way I'd like. I'm not expecting it to be all hugs and things but I hope I don't get angry."

"You'd have every right if you did," Lar told her, loyal as ever. "She'll be expecting that, Rosa. She won't expect it to be all plain sailing."

"I know." Rosa was quiet now, thinking about the possibilities. "I've a few things to sort out at work anyway that I can't put off. I promised the girl from TV3 that I'd phone her after lunch to sort out when I'll be able to go on the *Morning Show*. That's something I can't just neglect."

"Well, come on then, if you're going to do it."

"Right then." Rosa smiled stoically as she finished the last of her tea. "Get me home fast. I need to get some make-up on for this."

"That's my girl!" Lar said proudly, taking her hand and leading her out into the clear morning air again.

Chapter 46

Kate's hair, normally in a sleek chestnut bob, hung around her face in rat's tails even though Lorcan kept trying to tie it back from her face between the contractions.

"Oh Jesus, Lorcan, I can't! I can't do it any more. Make it stop, please!"

Lorcan, terrified that he wouldn't be able to help his wife cope until the anaesthetist arrived, tried to reassure her that the damned man was on his way, all the while casting anxious glances at the midwife over the top of Kate's head.

"It's okay, Kate. He'll be here any minute," Lorcan soothed. "Slow down the breathing until the next pain comes."

Holding the glass to her chapped lips and tipping it up a little to allow her to take a sip of water, Lorcan prayed silently that the traffic on the Wilton roundabout wasn't too heavy, knowing that the anaesthetist could be delayed for ages if it was.

"Okay, Kate, ready again? There's another pain starting. Deep, deep breath now."

Lorcan marvelled at the power of the midwife to motivate Kate, despite the exhaustion of hours in labour. Maria had greeted them with a warm smile as soon as they'd arrived in the labour ward, easing Lorcan's mind immediately with her calm, authoritative manner. The responsibility of getting Kate safely to the hospital had been stressful, even though the midwife at the antenatal classes had assured them that it was very unlikely that a first baby would arrive unexpectedly on the way. Yet when Lorcan looked at some of the things that had happened in his own and Kate's lives, he wasn't so sure that they wouldn't be the exception to the rule.

Lorcan watched the pump that was now slowly infusing oxytocin into his wife's veins in the hope that it would speed the whole process up. Half an hour earlier, Maria had carried out yet another vaginal examination and had announced proudly that Kate's cervix was six centimetres dilated.

"Six only!" Kate had wailed. "I thought the baby would be ready to come out!"

Maria had tried to reassure her that cervical dilatation of one centimetre per hour was actually average and that she was well on the way but nothing could compensate Kate for the inability to have control over her own body. Disappointed, she'd looked at Lorcan with defeat in her eyes, finally making up her mind about the epidural that she'd hoped to avoid.

Now the minutes seemed like hours as they waited for

Dr Moloney to arrive and put an end to what Lorcan considered to be torture of the highest order. The dilatation of the cervix had slowed down a little earlier and Maria had suggested using the oxytocin drip as a means of speeding the labour up.

"Otherwise, you'll be here all night."

Kate and Lorcan had agreed that the oxytocin was the best thing, having been through such a scenario in the antenatal classes. She'd declined the offer of an epidural initially but now with the contractions coming hard and fast, she was willing to take anything.

Kate was the strongest person he'd ever met. If *she* thought that this was difficult then Lorcan could only wonder how he himself would cope under the same circumstances.

Paul, his brother-in-law, had described the whole thing as a tidal wave that you got caught up in and were powerless to do anything about. Lorcan, having attended the recommended antenatal classes with his wife every Thursday evening, had thought that he'd be well equipped to cope but nothing could have prepared him for the helplessness that he felt now.

"Great, Kate, you're doing brilliantly!" he encouraged now, wiping the beads of sweat off her forehead for the umpteenth time. The resting time between the contractions was getting shorter, giving her less and less time to recover and Lorcan wondered how much longer she'd be able to endure this.

"God, Lorcan, will he ever come? I feel like I'm going to die!" she moaned as the next contraction hit.

Maria talked her firmly through it, her voice calm and steady as her eyes scanned the bedside monitor that recorded the baby's heartbeat and the rise and fall of the contractions.

The door of the delivery room opened gently as the contraction receded and a distinguished-looking man peeked around it, his gaze meeting Kate's frantic one.

"I'm Michael Moloney. Do you still need me in here?"

"If you have any experience with epidurals, come right in!"

Lorcan, amazed at his wife's ability to remain her strong and very determined self in the face of the ordeal that she was in the midst of, kissed her tenderly on the forehead and helped her to sit forward on the edge of the bed as Maria instructed. The sooner the epidural was in place the better. Dr Moloney positioned himself on a small stool at Kate's back and prodded her spine thoughtfully. Lorcan supported her in position as Maria talked her through the next contraction, clamping the Entonox mask to her face to help her deal with the remainder of the pains.

"There you go, Mrs Reddy, all done. The next contraction should be a little easier. I hope that you'll be pain-free in the next five to ten minutes."

"Thanks so much," Kate groaned as the next contraction hit, clinging for dear life to the Entonox mask.

"God, that was definitely better," she exclaimed in surprise as the pain receded yet again.

"The miracle of modern science," the anaesthetist smiled from the corner as he scribbled in Kate's chart. He watched his patient's face as another wave of pain arrived. "Any better?"

"Any better? As soon as I'm released from here I'm going to start putting up billboards advising women to book their epidural as soon as they get a positive pregnancy test!" She grinned as she said this, grimacing almost immediately as a mild yet unmistakable contraction rippled through her abdomen. Suddenly she looked at Maria in horror. "If the contractions stop altogether, how will my cervix dilate?" In the throes of her earlier agony, she hadn't thought of this.

"They haven't actually stopped, Kate. It's just that you're numbed from the chest down. Look, put your hand here on your bump – you'll feel the abdomen getting tense with each contraction but you won't be aware of the pain. Actually, there's one there right now."

"You're joking." Kate's incredulous gaze swivelled in awe from the midwife to the anaesthetist to her husband.

"That's my job done then," Dr Moloney announced with a satisfied grin. "The very best of luck to both of you!"

After the anaesthetist had left the room, pulling the trolley of needles and empty packages with him, Maria once again sprang into action.

"Your next examination's almost due, Kate, so how about if we do that and help you to freshen up a bit. Then we can turn down the lights a little and let you rest before the main event."

Lorcan resurrected the small sponge bag that they'd been advised to bring to the delivery room and started to unpack the wet-wipes and deodorant while Maria set up a trolley for the examination. Again he thanked God for the practicality of the antenatal classes. Otherwise he'd have felt like a right spare part. He felt completely comfortable in Maria's presence and was happy to follow her gentle orders as the evening progressed.

"Back in a minute. I'll just pop out for more gloves."

The swing door settled into place after her and husband and wife were alone for the first time since their arrival in the labour ward.

"Are you all right, love?" Kate asked.

"Jesus, Kate, I can't believe you just asked me if *I'm* all right. You're the one in labour. I can't believe how great you were for all that." Lorcan took her in his arms as he said this, smelling the dampness of her hair through the scent of her perfume.

"Lorcan, I couldn't do this without you here. You're brilliant! But I hope I'm all right for the pushing bit," she said anxiously.

"We'll worry about the pushing when we get to it," Maria soothed confidently as she arrived back with the packs of sterile gloves and pushed the trolley towards the bed. "Now let's see if things have progressed at all."

Silence descended as she skilfully examined Kate, her task made somewhat easier by the fact that her patient was now relaxed and cooperative.

"Nine centimetres," she announced eventually, "not long to go. We'll examine again in an hour. Let's get sorted and let you have some rest before the really hard work starts."

She smiled as she said this, causing Kate to riposte, "I though you said the hard bit was over!"

The midwife grinned back at her as Lorcan started to help Kate to freshen up and change her nightdress, damp from the exertion of the past few hours.

"That feels like heaven," she groaned in appreciation as he sprayed her face with Evian water.

Kate's hands were still hampered by the drip so Lorcan had to help her slide the cotton nightie over her head. Maria and he changed the sheet and pillowcases together as Kate moved slowly from left to right to assist them.

"I might draw the blinds and turn down the lights for a little while. I'll still be able to see the monitor to keep an eye on the heartbeat and the contractions. Doze off to sleep if you're able and Lorcan and I will be as quiet as we can."

Lorcan liked this about Maria, the way she was able to instruct him on what was best to do without treating him like an imbecile. A strong bond had developed between the three of them from the moment that Maria had directed them into Room 3 and now after so many hours marooned together in their sterile, insulated world it felt as if they were the only three people left on earth. It was only another ordinary day for the rest of the world while for Lorcan and Kate it was the most special and frightening day of their lives.

The constant throb of the baby's heartbeat ticked away on the monitor, reassuring him that all was well. *Our baby.* Maria watched the tracings on the screen with a practised eye, jotting down the readings at intervals. Lorcan felt a peace descend on him, a feeling that he never failed to appreciate these days. He watched Kate as she slept, her face serene in the aftermath of the pain that she'd endured. Please God, let the delivery go well. Let Kate or the baby not be in any danger.

He came out of his reverie when he realised that something in the room had changed. Maria was shaking Kate gently, simultaneously clicking on the light switch at the back of the bed.

"I think it's time, Kate."

Kate sat up as best she could, looking around her as if she couldn't believe that she had actually fallen asleep.

"Over onto your left side for a moment, Kate," Maria instructed, already assisting her patient into the lateral position. Lorcan detected a slight urgency in her voice and Maria, as if she sensed his question, explained calmly that the baby's heartbeat was 'dipping' a little. "Lying on the left side will ease the pressure on the major blood vessels and allow it to recover. We'll need to examine again, Kate, and see if you're fully dilated."

This time the examination was swift, with Maria announcing almost immediately that the baby was well on its way and that the change in the heartbeat, now recovered fully, was as a result of the increasing strength of the contractions.

"As I explained earlier, I'll need to ask a second midwife to assist. So, Lorcan, you can position yourself at the top of the bed to encourage Kate. Do you feel any sensation at all yet, Kate?"

"Only a little – nothing painful."

"Good. I'll just call Monica."

Monica Lane had stepped in earlier in the day when Maria had taken her breaks so she was already a familiar figure to Kate and Lorcan. They were delighted that she'd be assisting in the delivery, rather than somebody that they hadn't met before.

"Hello again, Kate," Monica greeted her. "Maria tells me that the head is very well down so I'm expecting a young Reddy before the end of my shift."

"Please tell me that you're on an eight-hour shift to say nothing of a twelve-hour one!"

"We have forty-five minutes left to go," she said with a smile, "so let's not waste a minute of it."

The promise of a specific timescale galvanised Kate, exactly as the midwife had intended. She pulled herself bolt upright in the bed and declared staunchly that she'd be damned if either of the midwives were leaving the hospital until they'd presided over the delivery of her baby.

"Okay, then, let's get moving!"

Clearly and concisely, Maria explained the procedure for the second stage of labour, how instead of breathing steadily during each contraction, she'd now be asked to bear down in order to push her baby into the world. She also indicated a raised unit in the corner of the room that Monica was preparing efficiently.

"As soon as the baby is delivered, we may have to bring him or her over to the resuscitation area for extra heat and a little oxygen. It's quite common so don't be overly alarmed if it happens. You'll be able to see the baby at all times and we'll explain everything as it happens."

Although it might have made many a person anxious, somehow the resus area only instilled a greater sense of security in Kate. If anything did go wrong, at least everything was at the ready.

"All ready then? Even if you can't feel each contraction fully, I'll be able to tell you when it's on the way."

Twenty minutes later, Kate's hair was wet with perspiration as Maria told her urgently that the baby's head would be delivered with the next push.

"Listen to me, Kate. With the next push, you're going to feel enormous pressure. I'll be telling you to stop pushing and to just pant instead. It's really important that you pant, to avoid getting a bad tear. Lorcan will do it with you once he hears me telling you. Okay, Lorcan?"

"Oh, God, I can feel it coming again." Kate thought she'd never get through it and locked her eyes onto Lorcan's for strength as she tried to concentrate on Maria's voice, urging her to push even harder.

"Okay, Kate, this is it. Stop pushing! Pant, just pant, that's it, Kate, Baby's head is nearly here. Here we go – look down, Kate. Look here. Lorcan. That's your baby – look at that little face!"

Tears coursed down Lorcan's face as he held Kate and tried to focus on the dark head and wizened face that had appeared.

"Oh, God, Kate, look! Look, Kate!"

"Jesus, Lorcan, another contraction!"

She automatically took another deep breath, determined that this would be her last contraction. This baby was coming out.

"Okay, Kate, same again now. Pushing first – then panting."

This time she was fully in control, straining to see her baby as it slithered from her in a whoosh of amniotic fluid.

Suddenly, Monica was there, a green towel in her hands, rubbing the baby briskly.

"A little lady," she exclaimed in wonder, just as the tiny form spluttered and emitted a loud shriek, all four limbs unfurling at the indignity of being so vigorously stimulated by Monica Lane.

"Here you go, darling. Have a cuddle with your mum and dad."

With that she placed the baby in Kate's arms, her little head instinctively settling against her chest.

"Lorcan, a little girl, imagine!" Kate sobbed, hardly able to get the words out.

"Aisling," Lorcan said softly. "*Little dream*."

"Aisling Ellen," Kate whispered in wonder, unable to believe that this day had come at last.

Chapter 47

Martin was putting the finishing touches to the lunch when he heard Lucy's car pull up in the drive. He'd done a lamb korma, not from scratch the way his girlfriend would but by using a bag of pre-mixed spices that he'd got in the English Market. It smelled great, as did the scented rice that was bubbling gently on the cooker.

He was dying to know how her day had progressed after he'd left her in the registration office. Meeting Kerrie, another mature student, was a major bonus especially when Lucy had been terrified about being the only 'oldie' in the class.

Martin planned to wait until later to tell Lucy about John Leyland's offer. He wasn't sure what it would mean to them as a couple but he did know that it would require a lot of thought on his own part before he'd decide whether to take him up on it or not.

The previous day, Martin's boss had asked if he could speak to him when the final patient had departed. It seemed that John had been diagnosed with angina due to blocked blood vessels in his heart and would need a triple bypass in the very near future. Martin had been shocked to hear this although he'd known for a while that the older man was being treated for mild chest pains that he'd been putting down to indigestion.

"Not half as shocked as I was," John had smiled grimly. "Carmel insisted on me having an angiogram as a precaution. Just as well that I gave in."

"When will you have the bypass? Should you be working at all?"

Martin got on well with John and was concerned that he'd already carried out a few particularly difficult procedures in the past week.

"That's the thing. I've been advised to take some time off but, being honest, I've had enough. I'm hoping to take early retirement."

"That's a big step, John. Are you sure you're ready for that? We could get in a locum for a while and I could take over a few of your cases. It'd give you time to think."

"Thanks Martin for being supportive. But I've done plenty of thinking over the past few weeks. I'm fifty-eight anyway. There's no point in pushing myself. It's time to have more of a life with Carmel and the kids."

"You're right, John, when you put it like that. When do you think you'll finish up?"

"That depends on you, Martin, and whether you'd like to take over here. I know it's a bit sudden but it's a thriving business and I'd like you to have it."

"I'd have to look at the finances of it first, John. But I'm definitely interested."

The two men had talked for almost an hour about how much capital Martin would need if he were to take over the practice. He'd been disappointed when he'd been gazumped last year on the house in Bishopstown. The house had been in an ideal location and boasted a small granny flat that he'd envisaged converting into a surgery when he was ready to start a practice himself. He'd continued to look but nothing in the same line had presented itself since. Now as it stood, he had nothing to hold him back from going to the bank in order to acquire the dental surgery that he knew like the back of his hand and where he'd already built up his own sizeable client base.

"Can you give me a few days to think about it, John?" he'd said finally, anxious to be by himself to think on this sudden development. Lar, he knew, would have the inside track on what he should do next. He'd talk to him over the next few days and get his advice on the financial side of things.

It was Lucy, though, that he needed to talk to first. But he didn't know quite what to say and so had put it off until now.

She bounded into the kitchen now, full of excitement after her first day at college.

"That smells fabulous. What's in it?"

Martin laughed. "I have no idea. It said Korma on the sachet – that's all I know. I fried up the lamb and threw in the spices and a carton of yogurt. Easy."

"Cheat."

"I suppose you'll refuse to eat it now!" Martin was

already serving up the mouth-watering dish accompanied by a few of Lucy's favourite garlic naans and the rice.

"I don't think," Lucy said, scooping up some of the sauce with a piece of bread. "Gorgeous!"

"So, how did it go?" he asked.

"Brilliant." Lucy spent the next twenty minutes telling him all about the various subjects and tutors and the timetable that she'd be following for the college year. She also told him about Kerrie and the struggle that she'd had to keep her first baby in the face of enormous disapproval.

Lucy thought she was amazing. She and Fergus had stayed together despite everything, living with their respective parents until they could afford to get a house together. Fergus had taken up an apprenticeship with his uncle, a plumber, and now ran his own business, with Kerrie working part-time in Tesco as soon as both of the children were in school. It was only when Fergus's business had taken off with the Celtic Tiger that Kerrie had been in a position to go to college as a mature student.

"So how did your morning go after you left me?" Lucy asked him eventually, having exhausted all of her own news and answered all of Martin's queries.

"Not much happened – but yesterday was eventful," Martin said, dying to tell her all about it but nervous as well, knowing that the conversation he was about to have wasn't going to be at all as he'd planned it in his mind weeks ago.

"Go on," Lucy encouraged, her mouth relishing another spoonful of Darina Allen's chocolate ice cream.

"John wanted to talk to me before we finished up. He has to have a heart bypass so he's planning to retire soon."

"That's terrible. Should he be working at all?" Lucy had liked John and his wife Carmel a lot the few times they'd been out together. It still amazed her that she now enjoyed going out socially instead of being completely intimidated as she might have been even a year ago. As well as going out for a meal in Galligan's with them at Christmas, Lucy and Martin had attended the Dental Institute's annual dinner with John and Carmel in June.

"That's what I asked him as well. He's on medication at the moment until his surgery so it's okay for him to work. But he's taking early retirement as soon as he can sell the practice. He wants me to take it on, Lucy."

"That's fantastic, Martin! You would have done it over the next few years anyway."

They'd talked about this on and off and Lucy knew how much he wanted to get exactly the right premises before taking the plunge. Now he had a ready-made practice with a very solid clientele.

"It *is* good, isn't it?" Martin was glad of his girlfriend's enthusiasm but wondered if she was concerned at all about how it'd affect their future.

"You don't sound so sure, Martin. I thought it would be ideal." Lucy was perplexed. It wasn't like Martin to dither over things.

"I'm delighted about the idea of taking over the practice. It's just the timing . . ."

Lucy was looking at him, waiting for him to continue.

"I was going to talk to you about this soon, Lucy – not the business, I mean, about us."

"What about us?" Lucy had been ecstatically happy

since they'd met. Shocked, she realised that she'd taken it for granted that Martin felt the same.

"I didn't plan it like this, Lucy. I was going to take you off to Paris when you got your midterm break and ask you then."

"Ask what?" Lucy's voice came out in a hoarse whisper.

"Ask you to marry me. But now with all this – if I buy into the practice now I'll have huge overheads for the first few years. I'd have to take on another dentist – there'd be salaries for the dental nurses as well. How would we manage, Lucy? We have your mortgage to think about and four years in college."

Finally, Lucy could see what Martin was getting at. At the present time, his salary was enough to cover both of them for the next few years. Martin presumed that she had a mortgage and she realised with a pang that she'd allowed him to believe this. Just as she'd been vague when he asked her how she'd manage when she gave up her job at The Friary and allowed him to believe that she had savings to tide her over for a while.

Now, Martin was getting in a state because he thought they wouldn't be able to manage as a married couple if he took on a huge debt. Martin had been planning to support her financially if that was what she needed to get through college. Martin had been planning to ask her to marry him.

"Martin, I have to tell you something."

Now it was Martin's turn to be shocked. He'd blurted out about wanting to propose to her and Lucy had just stared at him. He'd worried about it being too soon but he'd booked the flights to Paris and the hotel anyway. He'd even bought an engagement ring to present to her, a ring that was now resting in his trousers pocket with the weight of a bag of stones.

"Lucy, I know this is all wrong – I wanted to ask you properly . . ."

"It's not that. It's about, well . . . there's something I wanted to tell you about. Something big. It was just never the right time."

She was white in the face at this stage and shaking. She stood and walked into the sitting room. Martin followed and sat beside her on the sofa.

"Jesus, Lucy, what is it?" Concern was written all over his face. Whatever it was, he'd started it with all his talk about the practice and getting married.

"I know I should have talked about it before. It wasn't that I didn't trust you. Don't think that. I just didn't want it to spoil everything for me – for us."

"Tell me, Lucy."

Slowly, almost in a whisper, Lucy told him about the events of years ago and the effect that it'd had on her life. About the early years where she'd felt so guilty and how she'd hated herself for so long. Tears came when she told him about the first time she'd spoken of the abuse to Rosa and how much the counselling had helped her to make sense of it all.

Martin let her talk, his arm around her shoulders as she got through her story. Sometimes he kissed the top of her head and when she'd finished she looked at him and saw tears in his eyes.

Unable to speak, he pulled her closer and wrapped his arms around her protectively. Lucy curled up in the circle of his arms and suddenly felt tired, as if an enormous weight had been lifted from her and she could rest at last.

"I'm so glad he's gone," Martin said eventually. "I can't imagine how anyone could hurt you like that. I just wish I could have been there for you before now."

"But you have been. That's why I didn't want to let him in."

She knew it sounded mad but for whatever irrational reason, she hadn't wanted Ned to be any part of her special life with Martin. Now that she'd finally been able to talk about it though, she felt that it had come in its own time and was glad.

"Lucy, nothing can come between us that we don't want. I know you mightn't want to get married yet but . . ."

"I'd love to get married!"

"But I thought, I mean . . . you didn't say anything when I talked about it just now!"

Lucy laughed, with relief more than anything. "I was so wound up with wanting to tell you everything that I sort of bypassed the bit about the proposal. Are we really going to Paris?"

"If you'd like to, then yes, we're going to Paris."

Lucy was beaming. Despite the whole roundabout way that it had happened, it seemed that she and Martin had just become engaged. Martin too was grinning widely.

"Actually, seeing as we seem to be deciding on getting engaged, I guess we'd better do it properly."

Lucy was stunned when he resurrected the tiny box from the depths of his pocket.

"Martin!"

"I'd love it if you agreed to marry me. Will you?"

"Oh, my God, yes, definitely yes."

Lucy's breath almost left her when she opened the box and revealed the most exquisite diamond solitaire. She'd never seen anything so beautiful. Slowly, carefully, she lifted it from its luxurious velvet bed and slipped it on her finger.

"It's beautiful. It's just gorgeous. And it fits perfectly."

"You didn't miss the ring with the blue stone a few weeks ago?" Martin was laughing at the expression on his fiancée's face.

"You used that to get the size?"

"I'm so smart, aren't I?"

"You are that. And you've great taste in women."

"Haven't I just? And even if we're broke for a while, so what? It'll only be for a few years."

"Actually, that's the other thing I forgot to tell you. We're not actually broke at all . . ."

Chapter 48

Pamela sat at the window of her home in Sunday's Well and waited. The chaise longue was beginning to feel hard and uncomfortable but she barely cared. She'd sat there since she'd come back from dropping the letter to Rosa earlier that morning, hoping against hope that she'd come.

She still wasn't sure if she'd done the right thing by writing to her but it had seemed fairer than telling her face to face, thus denying her the chance to react in whatever way she chose. It was bad enough that Rosa had to cope with finding out that her employer was in fact her birth mother. It was quite another to have to hear it in her working environment with no privacy to think it over or assimilate the news.

Pamela could understand the shock that her letter would have given Rosa. It was a full year ago since Bernadette Mooney had phoned her and asked if there was any possibility that her daughter could be given a place on the Absolute Beginners course. They were acquainted with each other through their work for St Angela's but Pamela hadn't been aware of whether Bernadette had any children or not.

Reluctant to upset her well-organised schedule, she'd been in the midst of apologising for having to refuse when Bernadette had said how disappointed Rosa would be but that maybe she could book for the next available class. As it had done on many occasions since Pamela had last seen her baby, her heart had started to hammer furiously at the mention of the name 'Rosa'.

"What age group would your daughter fit into?" she asked in as business-like a voice as she could manage. "It's just that we like to keep a fairly mixed profile in the classes."

"She's twenty-eight. Do you think there might be a place in the near future?"

"Definitely in the next ten-week course there would be. There may even be a late cancellation for this one – I'll certainly phone you immediately if anything comes up."

Pamela had been shaking like a leaf when she'd finally said goodbye to Bernadette Mooney. In the twenty-eight years since she'd walked out of the Mother and Baby Home, her mind had never relinquished the possibility that she and her daughter might be reunited. And even though she knew in her head that her precious Rosa could be anywhere in the country, she'd always held out the hope that maybe she was as near in reality as she was in her imagination. She also knew that the adoptive parents may well not have retained the name she had given the baby.

She'd followed up so many spurious leads in the past to no avail – a First Communion picture that she'd seen in The *Examiner* of a child called Rosa, a child with blonde curls that she'd spotted in a park years ago, even an advert in the paper a decade ago from a young girl trying to trace her mother. She knew that this could be another rainbow that would disappear but she couldn't take a chance on her daughter slipping away from her again.

In the most unprofessional action that she ever taken since she'd opened her home for the business of cooking, Pamela had picked up the phone and told an earnest young man from Waterford that he'd inadvertently been double-booked for the Absolute Beginners class but that she'd be happy to place him on an upcoming course at half-price. A place was suddenly available for Rosa Mooney.

Seeing Rosa bound up the steps and into her house that first night had been like taking a step back in time. It was almost as if Robert himself were there in person. The same blonde curls and excited smile, the same liveliness that had made Pamela fall in love with him the moment she'd met him.

She'd known straight away that Rosa was her daughter and the effort of restraining herself from starting to cry at the beauty of her almost choked her. That first class, she'd spent every free moment examining her daughter's face, her voice and her mannerisms. Over the ten weeks, she'd been unable to stop herself asking the small questions that would give her some insight into the kind of life that her daughter had now, whether she was loved and if she was happy. She knew that she could never approach her directly to tell her the truth, having given up her rights as a mother when her baby was only weeks old.

Rosa had never tried to locate her – Pamela knew this from the enquiry that she made to Sister Ignatius every year on Rosa's birthday. Therefore it wasn't Pamela's place to inflict a burden on the daughter that she'd never sought out. Rosa might not even know that she'd been adopted.

As the ten weeks had neared their end, she'd become aware of the fact that she couldn't just let Rosa go. She needed an assistant and Rosa's vivacious personality, she knew, would bring a new image to The Gourmet Rooms. She'd seen the way that Lucy Dalton had blossomed under her influence and had noticed how engaging she was, even with the often-frazzled Agnes.

As Pamela had predicted, Rosa had risen to the challenge of her new job immediately. Her energy was boundless and it was a relief to have her take over so much of the public work that she herself found so trying. Watching her on New Year's Eve as she charmed her way around Hollygrove Manor had been mesmerising for Pamela, although she'd still had pangs of guilt and anxiety about the duplicitous manner in which she was keeping her daughter within her range of contact.

It had been an enormous shock to Pamela to open the letter with the African postmark and find that her daughter actually *had* been looking for her. Even though the postmark said it had been posted months earlier, it was there in black and white, something that she'd almost given up hope of ever happening. What scant records did exist were known only to Mother Bridget. In all the years that she'd enquired, Sister Ignatius had been unaware of who the Mooneys' daughter really belonged to.

It had taken an anguished week for Pamela to choose the right course of action, a week that had unfurled a raft of pain and memories that she'd kept under wraps for years. Memories of Robert mostly and the wonder of the precious few weeks that they'd had together.

She'd heard about him of course – the eldest of the Donnellys who was away working in England. As soon as she'd set eyes on him at Noreen Keely's wedding, Pamela had been smitten. He was home from England for good, with a job lined up in Austin's Hardware. On her Christmas holidays from the Domestic Science course at the Commercial College in Cork, Pamela had spent every waking moment with Robert.

Nowhere was too far to drive to for a dance and it seemed like only yesterday that they'd whizzed off to Blarney or Midleton on a Saturday night in the shiny black Morris Minor. Soon, he'd told her as he held her in his arms with the car pulled in under the beech trees outside her parents' house, the farm at home would be his and they'd be able to marry.

It had been Larry Baily, the postman, who'd stood at the garden gate and told Pamela and her mother that the high jinks had finally caught up with Robert Donnelly. His parents were heartbroken, Larry said, but at least there had been nobody else in the car when it went over a ditch near the Viaduct.

For Pamela, it had been unbearable. Her whole future was gone in the blink of an eye. Nobody had known about the plans that they'd made together. Heartbroken, she'd gone back to the college in Cork, her mind a million miles away.

It was only when she could hide her secret no longer that Pamela had faced the wrath of her parents. The parish priest had been involved immediately and a sum of money requested which the Hynes had been happy to muster.

The months that followed at St Angela's Mother and Baby Home had been almost peaceful, the obligatory Commercial Course a welcome distraction. She'd hammered away at her typewriter, practised her shorthand and learned how to organise a filing system, never allowing herself to think about what would happen at the end of that precious time.

After a day and a night of torture, Rosa had come into the world. Tiny and beautiful with small whorls of almost white hair stuck to her head, Pamela had fallen in love with her immediately, causing the midwife to warn her against getting too attached.

"It won't do you any good," she'd cautioned kindly. "Only God knows it won't do the child any harm."

Pamela had had no reservations about loving her baby. It was easy to wash her perfect little body with a soft flannel and rub her with handfuls of Perfect baby powder from the large communal tin in the nursery. It was easy to pour the powdered milk into the newly boiled glass bottles and watch the little rosebud mouth sucking away industriously. It was easy once she didn't think about what the next step would be.

The reality had been harsh. Two weeks had passed, lulling Pamela into a false sense of security. There had been no discussion and no warning, just the call to Mother Bridget's rooms on a Friday evening and the order to pack her things. A position had been found for her, a good position thanks to her training with the Sisters, and one for which she ought to be grateful. The sooner she could get started the better. Sister Aquinas, the young nun in charge of the nursery, had looked at her pitifully when she'd asked whether there would be a cot for Rosa.

"The baby will be staying," Mother Bridget had snapped, as if Pamela were an imbecile. "You'll be collected after tea so be sure to be well turned out."

Sister Aquinas had quickly escorted her from the room lest she break down and appear ungracious in the face of the assistance that Mother had given her.

"That's why you came here," Sister Aquinas had reminded her gently and Pamela had understood.

She would have no home to go to with a small baby and no employment to maintain them. Her parents certainly wouldn't countenance a child born out of wedlock, especially when they'd gone to such expense to conceal the fact in the first place. There was nowhere to turn, not when Sister Aquinas asked her if she wanted the little girl to be an outcast. It would be the best thing for her to be reared in a good home with the best of everything, instead of being an object of pity in an unforgiving world. And, of course, it would be the best thing for Pamela as well.

Even though it had been 1978, Ireland still hadn't caught up with the rest of the world when it came to the dreaded word, illegitimate. Her new job in the office at Carter's Grain Store would be a fresh start for her. If she played her cards right, she might in time meet someone who'd be willing to marry her despite her past.

Or even because of it, Sister Aquinas had suggested. Maybe some nice widower with a few children or an older man who'd missed the boat. The thought of such a contrived bargain sickened Pamela but she'd just nodded repeatedly for the nun's benefit, all the while wondering who would feed Rosa when she woke from her nap.

"You'll have no need to concern yourself with that any more," the nun had told her firmly when she voiced her worry timidly. "Your priority now is to prove yourself at Carter's and make sure that the trial period that Mother Bridget has organised for you will be continued."

"But, Sister, it's just that —"

"It's up to yourself now," Sister Aquinas had interrupted her. "Your parents have laid out a lot of money to get you settled. You'll have to make the most of it."

This guilt over the financial cost to their parents had been drummed into all of the girls and it was this that made Pamela determined to prove to her mother and father that it had been worth it to deprive her brothers of the education that had been planned for them.

Their money had been well spent, as it transpired.

That same Friday evening, Sister Aquinas had introduced Pamela to Mona McCoy, her landlady in the boarding house that would be her new home.

"This, Mrs McCoy, is Pamela Hynes," she'd announced in the tone of a Garda presenting a criminal to a judge.

Pamela had stared mutely at the large lady with the enormous bust and noticed immediately that there was no sign of the disapproving sniff that even the nicer of the nuns displayed as a matter of course. Her face was as round as the rest of her and red from the exertion of rushing to the door in response to Sister Aquinas's sharp stab at the doorbell. Pamela could see the outline of rollers under the headscarf that was tied tightly around her perspiring forehead and secured at the back in a series of knots.

"You're welcome, girl. Now come on in out of the cold. Benny has the tea on."

Sister Aquinas, Pamela noticed, was dispensed with almost immediately by Mona McCoy.

"That's grand now, Sister. I'll take over from here," she said firmly as soon as the nun started to reiterate her advice on Pamela working hard and not letting Mother Bridget down.

Pamela thanked the nun feebly for all her help and followed Mrs McCoy through a narrow hall towards the back of the house, all the while wondering if her baby would be handed over on a doorstep like this, perhaps somewhere a little more distant than North Main Street. The departure of Sister Aquinas was almost a wrench, severing what was to Pamela her last link with Rosa.

"Here, give that to me. Benny will carry it up for you after tea and you can unpack in peace and get a bit of rest before the big day."

Pamela relinquished her suitcase gratefully and Mrs McCoy placed it carefully in one of the rooms off the hallway before leading her into a tiny kitchen that was made smaller by the fact that it was crammed to the rafters with all kinds of everything.

The pine dresser held enough dishes to feed a wedding party and the shelves were covered with pots and pans of all shapes and sizes. Every available bit of wall space was covered with pictures and ornaments, as was the sideboard. Noticing Pamela's enthralled assessment of her kitchen, her hostess commented that she was waiting for Benny to give it a good going-over.

Benny, she soon found out, was Mrs McCoy's husband. A slight man in his mid-sixties, he was as thin and pale as his wife was large and florid. Despite the fact that it was his wife who was wearing an apron, Benny was standing over the cooker ministering to a large pan of rashers and sausages. The table had been set for three, something that made Pamela feel more welcome than she'd felt in all her months at St Angela's.

"Now, love," he greeted her, wiping his hands in the tea towel that was tucked into the waistband of his trousers, "sit in to the table and we'll have a right chat over the supper."

"Is the tea made yet?" his wife queried, settling herself in at the table next to Pamela, having first taken her coat from her and hung it on the back of the kitchen door.

"Give me a minute and we'll be right," Benny promised, placing two loaded plates in front of the women. Scurrying back to the cooker, he rinsed the teapot and filled it from a shiny brass kettle that was almost hopping with the heat.

Pamela, overwhelmed with the suddenness of her transfer from the tranquillity of the convent to this bustling new environment, uttered her thanks to both of them.

"Isn't it great to be out of there all the same?" said Mrs McCoy. "The nuns are grand but it's no harm to be back out in the world."

"It's lovely to be here, Mrs McCoy." Pamela knew she sounded dull and dutiful but all she could think of was Rosa waking up and making strange with whoever was allocated to feed and change her. She knew what the procedure would be as she herself had looked after other babies often enough when their mothers had to leave the convent.

"Don't mind your 'Mrs McCoy'. I'm called Mona and that's what you'll call me too. I know well you've no appetite but don't force yourself."

Pamela was only picking at the delicious meal Benny had served up. "I'm sorry —"

"That's all right, love," Benny reassured her. "You'll be thinking about the small one for a while. What did you call her?"

Relieved that it was permissible to actually mention

the fact that she'd left her baby behind, Pamela told them about Rosa and her worries about how she was going to be cared for.

"All the girls who come here are like that for a while. I'm not saying you'll forget about her," Mona said sagely, "but after a few days hopefully she'll be with the new people and you'll have to start letting go a bit."

Pamela then realised that she wasn't the first girl from St Angela's to be placed with the McCoys in the transition from St Angela's to a new life. Sister Aquinas had told her very little – just that she'd be lodging with a respectable couple in North Main Street and starting her job as a junior secretary in Carter's Grain Store the following Monday. Her first week's rent would be paid until she started to earn her own money.

It would be up to herself whether she made a success of herself or not, the nun had told her. Pamela knew that she had no choice now but to make the most of it and decided to focus on her new job instead of the heart-breaking thought of Rosa alone in the convent.

"Is the Grain Store far from here?" she asked, more out of politeness and an effort to acknowledge the kindness of Mona and Benny than any real interest.

"Only down the street. One of us will walk down that far with you on Monday. Sister said you'd have to buy some suitable clothes so we can do that tomorrow if you like."

Mona sounded enthusiastic at the idea of going shopping whereas it was the farthest thing from Pamela's mind. Although she had to admit that she had very little in the line of office wear after months of smocks and oversized sweaters.

"What kind of things do you think I'll need?"

Sister Aquinas had mentioned getting a few respectable rig-outs on the way over in the car but she hadn't expanded on the exact requirements for the job.

"A few skirts below the knee and a nice blouse or two. And a pair of good shoes. You'll be able to see what the other girls are wearing once you get started."

Mona seemed to know it all and Pamela was more than happy to let her take control of the situation. All she wanted now was to escape to her room and cry her heart out.

Pamela remembered her first day at Carter's as if it had happened only a week ago. A light rain drizzled her face as she walked down to Cornmarket Street with Mona in the new tan leather court shoes and the brown tweed skirt that stopped, as Mona had advised, well below the knee. A light wool twinset completed the outfit and gave her the confidence she needed to face this next trial in her already tumultuous life.

"Come home at lunch-time if you like and Benny will have something ready for you. It'll take a while to get to know people."

Mona referring to her house in North Main Street as 'home' wasn't lost on Pamela. Her parents hadn't even phoned to wish her luck and the thought of returning home to Mallow brought her out in a cold sweat. The few times that they'd visited her in the convent they'd been nervous and stilted, bowing and scraping gratefully to Mother Bridget as if she'd saved their lives times over. They'd never set eyes on their grandchild, preferring to ignore the result of their daughter's 'trouble', a word that covered everything from the scandal of the pregnancy to the concealment of it.

"I'll be fine, Mona," she said stoutly, looking in awe at the enormous brick building in front of her. To the left of it was a smaller building with two windows either side of a frosted glass door. Pamela could see people bustling back and forth behind a long counter, obviously attending to the queue of farmers waiting patiently in a haphazard line. A small white sign with the word '*Office*' painted on it pointed her in the direction of the door.

Bidding Mona goodbye, she took a deep breath and stepped through the door, frantically rehearsing her words of introduction. The air inside was damp and permeated with the odour of wet overcoats. Thankfully the row of customers parted and allowed her to approach the counter, manned by a girl of about her own age with frizzy red hair and a startling amount of make-up.

"My name is Pamela Hynes and I was told to report to Mr Carter," she began, conscious of the fact that she could be overheard by the line of farmers behind her.

"Oh, you're the new girl." The redhead sounded delighted, her green eyes twinkling as she announced to all and sundry that it was about time she had some help.

"I'm Queenie and I'm supposed to show you the ropes. Mr Carter is away today. Put your bag over there in the drawer and we'll tackle these fellows together."

Obediently, Pamela did as she was told, her face reddening as she heard one of the men waiting riposting that he wouldn't mind at all being tackled by such a pair of good-looking girls.

"Mind yourself now," Queenie warned him as Pamela joined her behind the counter, "or there'll be no cheques for any of you!"

The rest of the men laughed good-naturedly and Queenie gave a wink and a smart "Next please!", very obviously in control of the situation. Pamela could take the names and relieve each customer of his docket, she instructed. She herself would make out the cheque to the appropriate amount and hand it over while Pamela would get the person to sign on receiving it. Pamela soon got the hang of it, spearing the green dockets onto the spikes and pointing out the space in the ledger for the customer to sign.

If it hadn't been for Queenie that first week, Pamela doubted that she could have managed at all. The training that she'd been given at the convent had covered everything that she needed to know – it was just the fact that she couldn't seem to concentrate on anything that was holding her back. That and the pain that she felt in her chest from the moment she woke to the moment she fell asleep at night, aided by the hot milk and nutmeg that Mona insisted on her drinking before she went up to her room.

It was the following Monday that she met Thomas Carter. She'd become used to the routine of the office and had almost forgotten that there was a boss at all. Back from a trip to England where he'd been looking at new machinery, he was already ensconced in the small office to the right of the counter when Pamela arrived for work on the Monday.

"Go on," Queenie had instructed. "He'll have forgotten you're here at all. You'd better make yourself known."

Nervously smoothing the new black skirt that she'd bought with her first wage packet the previous Saturday, she knocked quietly on the door.

"Oh, hello. You must be Miss Hynes."

Startled, Pamela took in the thin young man in front of her. She'd been expecting someone at least middle-aged but this Mr Carter was only barely older than herself. He had jet-black hair, parted severely and a pale anxious face that made him look worried, even as he smiled at her and invited her to sit down.

"Thank you for giving me the opportunity to work here," Pamela began, conscious that she had very little in the line of options if her job in Carter's didn't continue. She couldn't imagine her parents paying for her to continue the Domestic Science course that she'd abandoned so suddenly.

"I hope Queenie is looking after you and showing you the ropes? And if there's anything that I can help you with, don't hesitate to ask."

"Thank you," she'd murmured gratefully. "Queenie's been marvellous and I hope I'm doing things properly."

"I'm sure you are. Mother Bridget recommended you highly. You were at St Angela's for a while, I understand?"

Pamela had been totally unprepared for a reference to her recent past and faltered as she acknowledged that she had indeed spent six months there. He didn't sound disapproving at all, something that she found strange after the web of shame that some of the nuns and indeed her own parents had placed over the girls at the convent.

"I hope that you're, well – recovered now," he said kindly.

"Thank you," Pamela said again, standing to leave, glad that her past was out in the open.

"I was expecting an old fellow. I can't believe he's so young and in charge of all this," she whispered to Queenie as they started on the pile of typing that seemed to appear relentlessly as soon as they'd cleared it.

"You should have seen his father! He'd drink the Lee dry and had all the signs of it. He was always finding an excuse to squeeze in behind me at the counter, the old pervert! And a desperate man for the horses."

"Where is he now?" Pamela was curious as to how the young Mr Carter seemed to be in charge at such a young age.

"Drank himself senseless after the Listowel Races a few years ago. He was found unconscious in the hotel and couldn't be revived. Just as well or we'd all be out of a job the way he was going on."

Queenie seemed to have the inside track on absolutely everything and Pamela was fascinated.

"What do you mean, Queenie? This place must be making a fortune."

"It's starting to pick up again since the young man took it over. The old fellow left a lot of debt, so Malachy tells me."

Malachy was Queenie's boyfriend and was well tuned in to the financial state of Carter's due to his job as the accounts assistant for the past number of years.

"No wonder he's so thin and bothered-looking," Pamela commented.

Queenie was full of admiration for their boss and over the following months, Pamela came to see him as earnest and hardworking but always with time for a word with the staff and an open door for any problems that arose.

Occasionally, he asked Pamela how she was getting on and if she was over her time at the convent. She'd been reticent with her answers, of course, heeding the warnings of Mother Bridget but wondered nonetheless what he really thought of her and her past. When the time came that they did talk about it, she was surprised to hear that he thought it was all so unnecessary. Why couldn't she have had her job at the Grain Store *and* her baby?

Pamela had explained to him in the cynical voice that she seemed to have developed since she'd left Rosa behind that her parents, like many other parents in their position, had hopes that their daughter would eventually marry once she'd put her scandalous past behind her.

"Is that what you want?"

He had a natural curiosity that was never offensive or intrusive so Pamela was able to answer him honestly.

"No. But if it meant I could get Rosa back, I would."

In her heart, she'd known that this would be impossible. She knew Rosa had already been placed with a suitable family and would never know that Pamela was out there, wanting her back.

Months later, when she finally became aware of his feelings for her, Thomas had promised her faithfully that they would have their own children someday.

"If you'll marry me, that is," he'd added hopefully, his eyes anxiously awaiting her answer across the table in the Imperial Hotel.

It was enough for her that Thomas loved her, even if her own heart was still too broken to love him properly in return.

Pamela remembered her wedding day as if it was a dream. Queenie had been there beside her, resplendent in an emerald green two-piece with her frizzy hair tamed into a sedate bun. Her parents were there, of course, proud that they'd made the right decision for their daughter and marvelling at how well it had all worked out. Her brothers, in awe of the grandeur of Hollygrove Manor, had been timid and well-behaved in their new suits.

Hanora Carter, whom Pamela had met on only a handful of occasions, welcomed the new bride grudgingly into her home. While grateful that her only son was to marry at last and carry on the family name, she was nonetheless terrified that the reserved young girl with the serious eyes would disclose her past and shame the family.

Meredith, Thomas's older sister, arrived the evening

before with her husband James Shaw who would serve as best man for the occasion.

Moving to the house in Sunday's Well from her cosy room at Mona and Benny's house had been easier than Pamela had expected, mainly because she'd been able to continue to work at the Grain Store. Hanora, of course, hadn't approved of this but had had to relent when Thomas reminded her of the state of his father's affairs on his death. Pamela's skills were a necessity if the family were to recoup some of the losses that had been incurred at the racetrack. When and if circumstances changed, her position would have to be reconsidered.

As it happened, her circumstances did change but not in the way that she might have expected. She'd gone to the bank to lodge the wad of cheques that had been received that morning. It was Queenie who came running to fetch her back, her face red with the exertion of running all the way from Cornmarket Street to Patrick's Bridge in high heels.

"One of the belts snapped as soon as they started it up!" she panted breathlessly.

Pamela took it that her friend was talking about one of the new machines that had arrived a week ago. She left the queue and followed Queenie back out onto Patrick Street.

"Is Thomas hurt? Is that what you're saying, Queenie?" She felt weak and was glad of the fresh air on her face.

"He was standing next to Paudge McCarthy when it went. They're taking the two of them to the South Infirmary."

"I heard the ambulances. I have to see him before he goes," Pamela cried frantically, lifting the hem of her narrow skirt a little so that she could keep up with Queenie who'd already started off in the direction of Cornmarket Street.

By the time they reached the Grain Store the ambulances had already departed. The place was in chaos with everyone running around in circles. Paudge McCarthy's wife had been telephoned with the news. Leaving Queenie to organise the office, Pamela made the short trip to Sunday's Well in Thomas's car to collect Hanora for the journey to the hospital.

She knew straight away that he was gone when the Day Sister on duty guided them into a small waiting room.

Her face sombre, the Sister told them quietly, "I'm afraid Mr Carter had lost too much blood."

Pamela had crumbled in the aftermath of Thomas's death. Later, she knew that it was the loss of Robert and Rosa that she was grieving, as well as the loss of her husband of three months. Hanora had been patient with her, understanding her need to hide from the world.

It was Queenie who finally brought her back to reality with the news that, despite Thomas's best efforts, the Grain Store was perilously close to collapse. The warning was timely and prepared Pamela for the bank manager's disclosure that unless a significant sum of money appeared immediately, there would be no option but to foreclose on the outstanding loans.

"Let them take it," was Hanora's summing up of the situation when Pamela advised her of her interview at the bank. "Surely there will be something left for us to live on."

As it transpired, Thomas Senior's capacity to gamble had been far greater than anyone could have imagined. Even the house had been mortgaged.

"Whatever happens, we'll hold on to the house," Pamela had promised her mother-in-law, her tenuous hold on the situation getting stronger every day.

"I'm afraid that there will be very little left for you, young lady," Mr Foley had told her soberly. "We have secured a buyer for the business premises. The offer would cover all loans and mortgages, including that on the house. There will be a small amount of cash remaining but nothing significant, I regret to tell you."

Pamela, grateful that they at least had a roof over their heads, had applied for work in various offices around the city immediately, preferring to start earning before the money ran out altogether. Her first interview had been for a position at the Cork Commercial College, the vocational training school where she'd studied Domestic Science almost two years previously.

"Your application form says that you left the Domestic Science course and went on to attend a secretarial course at St Angela's." Mrs Morris had been the principal of the Commercial College for ten years and recognised Pamela as a once promising student.

"Yes, indeed. I've since held a secretarial position at

Carter's Grain Store," Pamela told her, anxious to get away from the subject of St Angela's.

"So I see."

Pamela could almost see the wheels of her mind filling in the blanks.

"Would you be able to start immediately?"

"Of course," said Pamela eagerly.

"Are you aware, Pamela, that the Domestic Science Diploma is now being run as an evening course? Perhaps you might be interested in completing the final year after work in the evenings?"

"I'll certainly consider it."

Pamela's priority was to get home to Hanora to tell her the good news. Although only in her sixties, Hanora had been dependent on her husband all her married life and had never had to earn her own money. She was terrified of being destitute and losing her home and her pride.

Eventually it had been Hanora who'd suggested investing a small amount of the remaining money in the completion of Pamela's diploma.

"You might even be able to teach at the college then."

Pamela saw the wisdom in it and agreed. The teachers' salaries were much greater than her own, as she knew from sorting out the wages every week. When the time came, Mrs Morris had done all in her power to support Pamela's application to the board of management.

The first time she'd stood in front of a class of eager faces, she'd been terrified. Soon, she was reeling off the curriculum without even thinking about it.

The loss of Hanora in the winter of 1981 had been heartbreaking. Alone in the enormous old house, Pamela contemplated her life and its many losses. First Robert, then Rosa followed closely by Thomas and now Hanora. And for all that they visited now and again, Pamela had considered her parents lost since the day that they'd left her in St Angela's to fend for herself.

Her 'future' – something that she'd been terrified to contemplate too closely – had come about quite by accident when she'd noticed the number of calls every week to the Commercial College with enquiries about the evening course in Domestic Science. It occurred to her that there was a market for evening classes in cookery and domestic skills that could be filled if she were to open her home to the public in small numbers.

Her first class was made up of a mere two pupils but soon word of mouth took over and The Gourmet Rooms had been born.

Now, more than twenty-five years later, she wondered if it had all been worth it. She'd thought of Rosa every single day, hoping that someday she'd be proud of her mother's achievements. She'd never expected it to be like this. In her imagination, she'd had visions of her daughter making contact through the Sisters at St Angela's. An emotional meeting would follow in which Pamela would get to tell her daughter how much she'd thought of her over the years and how much she'd always loved her.

Instead, she'd jumped the gun and placed both of them

in an impossible position. Rosa thought of her only as an employer, a stern cookery instructor. Would she ever be able to forgive her for her duplicity and see her as something more than that?

Chapter 49

Lar held Rosa in his arms in the security of the car and told her again that she didn't have to do anything yet.

"I have to, Lar," she told him vehemently. "I have to know what happened or I'll crack up before the day is out. My head is bursting with all the questions."

"But, Rosa, nobody could expect this of you. Pamela won't expect you to go into work after dropping a bombshell like this."

"It's my job."

"You don't have to prove yourself to anyone, Rosa. If Pamela really is your mother – and it looks like she is – then she'll have accepted you already. She's known you for almost a year now."

"Well, I've known her for the same length of time," Rosa said obstinately, not sure exactly what her point was.

"Will you be able to get through a whole class?" Although she had applied her make-up carefully, Lar could still see the puffiness of her eyes that she'd tried to conceal. She hadn't even phoned her parents, something that Lar had suggested a few times in the course of the morning.

"I'll wait and see what happens today. I have to stand on my own two feet and sort this out properly."

"I'll sit here until you come out again, Rosa. It doesn't matter whether it's ten minutes or all day. And if you need me, just phone and I'll come in."

Lar had parked at the far end of the leafy road where he knew the car couldn't be seen if Pamela was looking out for Rosa.

"Thanks, Lar. You've been brilliant about all this. I know you think it doesn't make sense to go in for the class but it's something I have to do. I think it'll be easier to talk to her here."

"You have no idea how proud I am of you, Rosa. And whatever happens, I'll still be proud of you. And I love you, remember that."

"I will. Now here goes." A quick kiss and she was out of the car, striding down the footpath more purposeful than he'd ever seen her. It was five to two and a few cars were starting to pull up in the street.

Rosa's heart started hammering as soon as she left the safety of the car and she hoped that she'd be as strong as she'd led Lar to believe. The front door opened as she reached it and suddenly Pamela was standing before her. The woman who'd given birth to her.

"Rosa . . ." Her voice was almost a whisper.

"Hello, Pamela." Rosa had planned to sound normal but her voice too came out hoarsely in a choked whisper.

"Rosa, I'm so sorry for everything . . . the letter . . . I didn't expect you to come for the class . . ."

Her face, Rosa could see, was pale and creased with anxiety. Her own face softened when she realised just what a big moment this was in Pamela's life. This woman had said in her letter that she had loved Rosa and hadn't wanted to give her away.

"I know that, Pamela. But we have to talk, you know."

"Only when you want to, Rosa. I know what a shock it must have been. I just didn't know how else to go about it."

"I know that now. It's just a pity that . . . I don't know . . . that it didn't all happen sooner." Rosa sighed, the feeling that Pamela knew all about her coming back again.

"You have a lovely life, Rosa. I wouldn't have interfered with that for anything. Until I heard from Mother Bridget, of course."

"It's a lot to take in. And I have a lot to ask you."

"Ask me anything and I'll tell you."

The first two members of the Intermediate class were making their way towards the steps now and automatically both Rosa and Pamela turned to greet them. It occurred to Rosa then that maybe they were a little more alike than she'd imagined.

Smiling a little at the thought, she turned to Pamela again.

"We have a job to do now, Pamela," Rosa said softly, "but maybe we can talk when the bell rings?"

Pamela's face broke into a small, relieved smile at that. Although there was no actual bell at The Gourmet

Rooms, she always used the phrase when she was speaking about the end of a class. Rosa had teased her about it from the beginning and had even threatened to get a bell the next time she saw one.

Glad that she'd made the decision to come to work, Rosa smiled back as a few more class members mounted the steps. Again, they greeted them together, each aware of how incongruous the situation was.

For Rosa, it was momentous that she was here in The Gourmet Rooms the same as she had been every day for the past nine months, almost as if nothing had happened. But something *had* happened and, strangely, she was beginning to feel glad that it had.

Seeing the look of wonderment on Pamela's face, Rosa knew that she had done the right thing.

"Come on," she said softly to Pamela as the last of their pupils passed through the door. "We have work to do. And then you can tell me everything – starting right from the beginning."

"Everything, Rosa. I promise." Pamela's eyes misted over as she said this, her gratitude immense at being given a second chance.

Rosa smiled at her then as they stood together at the door of The Gourmet Rooms, with a new day about to begin.

The End

Direct to your home!

If you enjoyed this book why not
visit our website:

www.poolbeg.com

and get another book delivered straight
to your home or to a friend's home!

www.poolbeg.com

All orders are despatched within 24 hours.

Also published by Poolbeg.com

Pebble Cove

MAIREAD O'DRISCOLL

Welcome to Pebble Cove, an exclusive housing development with even more exclusive residents . . .

Linda Colton seems to have been born lucky, with a successful business, a beautiful new house and a talented boyfriend. But when Charlie is less than enthusiastic about Linda's plans for an ambitious new health spa, cracks begin to show in her perfect life.

Meanwhile, Deirdre and Marcus Fleming's lives are turned upside down with the premature birth of their first child, Alex. Can these ordinary people find resources within themselves to cope with this extraordinary situation?

Next door, Shay Deegan is living life in the fast lane – working hard and partying harder. But when tragedy strikes, the young accountant is forced to re-evaluate his life and draw strength from some unlikely sources.

And neonatal nurse Amy Harkin is working hard at her stressful but rewarding job. It seems to be paying off until sadness unexpectedly enters her life. Can Amy muster the determination to get through?

Through good times and bad, the people of Mairead O'Driscoll's *Pebble Cove* will stay with you long after the tide has turned.

ISBN 978-1-84223-267-5